I0783217

WORKBOOK PRESS LLC
187 E Warm Springs Rd,
Suite B285 Las Vegas NV 89119 USA

Website: https://workbookpress.com/
Hotline: 1-888-818-4856
Email: admin@workbookpress.com

Ordering Information:

Quantity sales. Special discounts are available on quantity purchases by corporations, associations, and others. For details, contact the publisher at the address above.

Library of Congress Control Number:

ISBN-13:   978-1-963718-09-6 Paperback Version
              978-1-963718-10-2 Digital Version

REV. DATE: 1/30/2024

Unconventional Delivery

CLANDESTINE TRANSPORTERS

By

Paul D. Escudero

September 2023 ©

Preface

At the back of the book is a Dramatis Personae and Glossary. I recommend you view it and become aware of it as you start reading.

In many of my Novels I use Chinese, Latin, and words from many countries for names and devices or to spice up the drama.

That Dramatis Personae and Glossary is at the very back of the book so you can flip back and forth to get explanations and definitions. You need to be aware of this so you can refer to it when you need clarification and keep track of what character is involved and who they are to make it easier to follow along.

***

Many of us older adults watched the Star Trek series and the reruns when we were very young. It captured our imagination. Star Trek had a lot of influence on the creation of Star Wars and other movies, even though the story is different and independent, it led to countless people growing up interested in space drama. Other shows such as Lost in Space and Battle Star Galactica added to the sensation of space and what eventually will beget mankind, including robots attacking humans.

A lot of products today were developed because of the influence of Star Trek (and later Star Wars) and NASA. People who might have taken the pathway to aerospace and engineering did so because of that influence and hence those items designed for entertainment suddenly added to the technological revolution. Notably the flip phones we saw in the 1990's were designed to look like the Star Trek communicators. I had a couple of those flip phones myself. Then Apple Computer took it one step further with the I-phone. Like many people I've had a few I-phones.

In this Novel, the transporter spy communicates with his artificial intelligence assistance via a communicator capable of holographic presentation or a flatscreen. The flat screen display mode on the communicator in the story should be considered as similar to an I-phone and similar devices.

The personal communicator in this story that features an advanced Artificial Intelligence named *Latrodectus* is truly a manifestation of what's to come.

Some of the artificial intelligence sequences in this book are nothing new to me. In my Novels *Soylent Caravan* and *Sasha Andromeda*, I take you beyond your wildest imaginations on what Artificial Intelligence will eventually do.

Or is Artificial Intelligence already doing it?

Do I believe Artificial Intelligence will take on the dimensions this book elucidates? Yes, I do.

Throughout this book Artificial Intelligence named *Latrodectus* is involved in all the missions. *Latrodectus* appears 413 times in this Novel. That gives you a clue to the extent Artificial Intelligence *Latrodectus* adds to the drama and none of the missions could have succeeded without *Latrodectus'* help.

That leads to comments in the author's note at the back of the book where I comment on real Artificial Intelligence Applications and provide some links about artificial intelligence and machine learning. I also have links and anecdotal information about Artificial Intelligence and machine learning conducted by the CIA in the Author Note.

Aside from what the CIA is doing with Artificial Intelligence and machine learning. What about China's developments? How is China's Ministry for State Security (MSS) [China's CIA], using Artificial Intelligence?

China has a strategy to become the global leader in Artificial Intelligence by 2030 and to develop it into a $150 billion industry. China's Artificial Intelligence development is supported by strong cooperation between research institutes, government, and companies, and by a large and expanding domestic markets.

China's Artificial Intelligence applications range from monitoring the minds and behaviors of Chinese Communist Party officials and citizens to assisting judges in the judicial system. China also aims to influence the ethical norms and standards for Artificial Intelligence applications.

What about Russia?

Russian President Vladimir Putin commented in 2017 that "Artificial intelligence is the future not only of Russia but of all mankind. There are huge opportunities, but also threats that are difficult to foresee today. The Artificial Intelligence industry leader will rule the world."

In case you do not know it, Russia made history with Artificial Intelligence in Ukraine:

 Russia Claims 'First Kill by Artificial Intelligence' in Ukraine | Future of Air Defense Without Operators:

[https://www.youtube.com/watch?v=k2nEB-w3tbI]

Because of the war in Ukraine, disclosure of information about Russian Artificial Intelligence has declined.

No doubt Russians are busy at work on Artificial Intelligence. If you think outside the box and the very limited viewpoint of American Congressional leaders who may not be intellectually prepared for the consequences of Artificial Intelligence, rest assured the Russians were indeed putting together a huge effort in Artificial Intelligence. The Ukraine war has probably expanded the Russian scope of Artificial Intelligence development which the West is unaware of and ongoing.

This is a link to Russia's recent history in Artificial Intelligence and machine learning development.

[Artificial Intelligence in Russia (geohistory.today)]

If you read the information in the link above you will know the sophistication of Russia and just like their classical music designers, nuclear physicists, aerospace, and submarine developers. Russia also has Artificial Intelligence scientists that operate at the Einstein level.

Western countries are not paying attention to Russian Artificial Intelligence development it seems.

What about the British?

In a recent report by research firm Cognilytica, the United Kingdom developed one of the strongest Artificial Intelligence strategies in the world. British Artificial Intelligence development has strong government funding for research activity. British in the field of Artificial Intelligence enjoy strong Venture Capital funding for Artificial Intelligence startups, and strong enterprise activity and adoption of Artificial Intelligence.

What about Germany?

Germans are also acutely aware of Artificial Intelligence developments in the world and are actively engaged themselves. Here's chart that shows German growth in Artificial Intelligence financial activity over the next few years that further explains their expected involvement. They are acutely aware of the level of Artificial Intelligence development in China and the USA from sources I've read. [Artificial intelligence value Germany | Statista]

What about France?

The French are very serious about Artificial Intelligence. If you look at Frances Space Program, their military equipment designers, and scientific community, you expect a big interest in Artificial Intelligence. This report gives a great overview of French Artificial Intelligence efforts:

[France Artificial Intelligence Strategy Report (europa.eu)].

Extract:

In March 2018, Emmanuel Macron, the President of the French Republic presented his vision and a 5-year national Artificial Intelligence strategy. The French Artificial Intelligence strategy is entitled Artificial Intelligence for humanity (France, 2018a) and has been developed based on the

Artificial Intelligence policy report (France, 2018b) prepared by French Member of Parliament (MP) and renowned mathematician Cédric Villani.

The main objectives of the French Artificial Intelligence strategy as highlighted by the French President are to: Improve the Artificial Intelligence education and training ecosystem to develop, retain and attract world-class Artificial Intelligence talent. France aims to Establish an open data policy for the implementation of Artificial Intelligence applications and pooling assets together. France also plans to develop an ethical framework for a transparent and fair use of AI applications.

To this purpose, the French Government will dedicate EUR 1.5 billion to the development of AI by the end of 2022, including EUR 700 million for research.

In 2021, the Prime Minister Jean Castex announced a renewed open and shared data strategy following a 2020 Report by MP Eric Bothorel which includes data and datasets for Artificial Intelligence.

Also, the 4th generation of the multi-year National Investment for the Future Programme is being framed in 2022. One sub-programme will be dedicated to AI and several other sub-programmes will include actions related to the National AI Strategy. This will allow updating the National AI Strategy funding and secure budget slots corresponding to the EU renewed Coordinated Plan.

Because of what's going on in the Middle East now, I decided to include Israel Artificial Intelligence since Israelis are involved in mortal combat:

Luckily, I do not have to write much about Artificial Intelligence in Israel, because I have a document that gives a huge amount of information about it:

[<u>Artificial Intelligence and National Security in Israel</u> | INSS]

If you read that document, there should have not been a surprise attack by Hamas recently. This attack underscores there are vulnerabilities with AI, and the human factor may need to be always in oversight, because this attack shows, Artificial Intelligence may not be able to mitigate all issues. It also shows even though huge amounts of money were invested with priorities, there will always be ways of overcoming Artificial Intelligence which will not always be successful.

***

One of the major features of Star Trek was the transporters.

"Beam me up Scotty."

Where do you think Gene Roddenberry got the idea for Transporters in the TV Series STAR TREK?

My speculation is in the Authors Note near the end of this Novel.

Table of Contents

***

Chapter One

The Moment of Truth

Dunbar Regvik walked into the obscure office building in the center of the financial district. There were several hush-hush firms located in this building closely associated with intergalactic bankers. People who occupied the building knew there were nefarious activities going on, but they learned a long time ago not to ask questions or talk about it.

The Kaokuen Transporter Directorate determined after trial and erro the best place to operate was around intergalactic bankers who were very tight lipped and knew better than to ask questions about matters, they were not associated. It was an unwritten rule, don't ask questions about other firms in the building, and if you did there was a good chance bad things would happen to you.

This was one of those situations where privacy and secrecy were paramount as intergalactic bankers had no desire for anyone to know about any of their activities, they were involved in. Quite frankly it had a lot to do with laundering money and shady deals nobody wanted the government to know about, especially because it might trigger tax evasion criminal investigators.

The general unwritten rules included no fraternizing with other companies and firms in the building. You came to work, did your job, and went home in the evenings and the less you said about things, the healthie you would remain.

All the Bankers in the building assumed the Kaokuen Transporter Directorate operating under a fictitious name, Intergalactic Banking Development Corporation, was nothing more than a mirror image of their own companies doing similar appalling activities for huge profits that often-crushed private citizens and investors with shark infested activities Noble Savages would never entertain doing.

Dunbar Regvik working for the Kaokuen Transporter Directorate always came to work dressed for success. Nobody would believe he was anything less than an Intergalactic Banker Representative. All the Kaokuen Transporter Directive personnel had basic training in finances and banking in the event they were caught in an elevator with real bankers and comments about the current economy or banking environment occurred, especially after huge market moves that effected banks.

The Kaokuen Transporter Directorate had a strict dress code. Come to work looking like a well-paid Banker, or do not come. They had clothing allowances to support looking like all the other bankers wearing expensive designer suits and women wearing designer business suits, some costing upwards 20,000 credits฿.

The Kaokuen buildings were very tall and slim. The metals used to create these majestic buildings were also used in the vast anchor systems that made sure weather conditions would in no way compromise the structure of the building. There were now so many of these tall thin buildings built it gave the appearance of a futuristic topology to a visitor from another planet.

Dunbar Regvik had an RFID like device implanted in his abdomen and thus as he walked through the security apparatus, he received green lights all the way to the high-speed elevator that cruised at almost one hundred miles per hour to efficiently make it up to the top area of the building for the many bankers working in the building.

People who were transported to other star systems had no idea how the Transporter Directorate managed to install a transporter in this well camouflaged commercial banking building. During peacetime it was easy to transport people to other planets because they could have individuals use a special marking device to aim at the location to deliver the person to the desired travel destinations.

Dunbar Regvik traveled on the transporters back in the past when it was a lot easier. The aim points and the procedures were far simpler. But due to intergalactic strife that now existed, those procedures could no longer be accomplished. A drone launched from an intergalactic shuttle operating at a standoff distance would arrive at a good distance away from the targeted planet and was used to mark the delivery point. There are only five seconds of vulnerability when an enemy might detect the off-wavelength laser designator transmitted by the drone to ensure the spy was delivered precisely where you wanted, he or she to arrive.

Once the coordinates were locked on, the Kaokuen Transporter Directive transporter installed in the banking building would send the person to that exact location. Through centuries of development the safe practice was utilized until that fateful day when holographic imagery and other pressing matters forced this new method of transportation.

As Dunbar Regvik passed through the building to the elevator where he went up to the ninth floor, he knew he would be going somewhere very soon. Moments later Dunbar Regvik arrived at the offices of the *Intergalactic Banking Development Corporation* front company that was cover for the Kaokuen Intelligence Bureau, Transporter Directorate the Intelligence Bureau established for clandestine transport missions during wartime.

Planning, briefings, development, training, and implementation was complete. Dunbar Regvik's mission was well defined and was full of risk. Dunbar Regvik's handlers were frank and honest with him. Dunbar Regvik had about a fifty percent chance of coming back alive.

Dunbar Regvik understood his handlers knew the mission was risky and allow about fifty percent probability of successful return. Dunbar could improve the odds to sixty percent or higher by taking certain actions on his own initiative. Based on Dunbar Regvik's astute knowledge of the processes involved, he could chart his own destiny through acute awareness and expertise developed by many years of participation in espionage and sometimes sabotage or assassinations.

Even though Dunbar Regvik worked for Covert Opps, he was really a Studies And Observation Group (SOG) tactician. He had far more experience in studies and observation, where he felt he set himself apart from the normal Covert Opps personnel since his ability in analysis gave him a distinct edge.

Dunbar Regvik was no fool, but he was no coward either. He simply liked to improve his odds by being better informed and better prepared for the mission. The age-old procedures Dunbar Regvik's handlers trained him with him insufficient as far as Dunbar was concerned.

In all his extracurricular activities Dunbar Regvik conducted additional measures to improve his odds. Dunbar never discussed or revealed those activities he did on his own time away from the office because he knew they would be frowned upon in the conduct of his mission. But Dunbar Regvik viewed fifty percent odds insufficient. Dunbar understood probabilities quite well thanks to his unprecedented foray into Studies and Observation Groups that quite often employed statistics. He preferred Chi-Squared distribution up in the upper ninety five percent in results.

Dunbar Regvik walked up to the unmarked door and immediately he heard the solenoid activated mechanical locks and door openers working to gain him access. That door led into a small room and once he was inside and the outer door shut, another entrance door opened, and he was allowed to enter.

Two men were there waiting for him. They had a change of clothes for him because his current attire would not fit in where he was going to a distant planet in another solar system. When in Rome you must dress and act like the Romans.

"Here's your change of clothes."

"Thank you."

Dunbar Regvik walked fifteen steps and went into a dressing room where there were personal lockers. He was not allowed to bring anything personal with him in the event he was captured. Nor would he desire to do so. But he did take mission items such as a dead man's communicator loaded up with his personal information and banking credits฿ access.

In a brief period, Dunbar had shifted into his mission attire and his clothes and personal belongings were now safely stored in the locker that soon became secure until his return. After the mission he would walk out of this building in the same manner as he arrived.

As soon as Dunbar Regvik left the dressing room, he was escorted into the transporter room. There in the middle of the room was that big ugly device he would soon crawl into and pray they had the coordinates locked into accurately.

In past times they could transmit neutrino beams to accurately position the transporter beam directly on the desired destination. Unfortunately, with the advent of new neutrino detection technologies, those days were far behind now.

A shuttle type spacecraft took a drone out into space weeks ago. The stealthily drone was launched at a safe distance from the target planet *Stanzel* to not put the shuttle craft in any dangerous situations. The drone would remain fully stealth and only light off for approximately five seconds to avoid detection. Any time duration of the laser designator greater than five seconds increased the odds astronomically of detection.

Dunbar Regvik nodded to the two launch technicians then stepped into the transporter capsule and slowly the access hatch shut. Automatic launch sequence started resulting in strange sounds as the cosmic frequencies inside the transporter created reverberations as the device spun up for launch. Within several seconds the transporter capsule reached the point of no return and disappeared.

The drone was programmed for the exact time the transporter would send Dunbar to the planet *Stanzel*. The drone lit off the laser designator that transmitted a very narrow beam for five seconds then shut off allowing the drone to leave the area and rendezvous back with the shuttle to be taken far away from this planet as to not risk detection.

Within the five seconds of the laser designated pointer operation the Kaokuen Transporter sent Dunbar to the planet *Stanzel* and thanks to the laser beam pointing the target area. Dunbar Regvik was deposited exactly at the planet *Stanzelite* where the laser designator pointed then it shut down immediately.

Within a short while, the drone and the shuttle were long gone. Dunbar Regvik was on his own and his survival depended on how well he performed. Dunbar felt good knowing his studies and observation training and mission complexities awareness gave him a slight edge for success.

Dunbar stepped out of the transporter capsule on the planet *Stanzel* and within a moment the transporter disappeared and would remain cloaked until his mission was completed and ready to bug out.

Dunbar Regvik's arrival was in a very private area selected where he could immediately check for detection or possible compromise and bug out, if necessary, before getting caught. After concluding he was alone and no eyewitnesses around Dunbar had just completed the initial phase of the mission, planetary arrival in a discrete and covert manner.

Dunbar Regvik's manufactured credentials and credits฿ tied to his alias *Kabel Garr* would allow him unencumbered access to credit฿ funds to facilitate his clandestine activities.

The tangential activities designed by mission planners now put in motion the activities Dunbar Regvik engaged in right away. Dunbar did not have to walk very far before he was able to board public transportation and travel to the center city area of Kerlara on the planet *Stanzel* where he would set up his base in a Resort Hotel that had a reputation for unsavory characters staying there and enjoy the amenities of the *Norel Mozelle Resort*.

Norel Mozelle Resort was designed much like a Japanese Love Hotel, where newlyweds went, but if you didn't have a wife or girlfriend to take there, they provided one for you.

There was no doubt *Norel Mozelle Resort,* in the heart of downtown Kerlara, was one of the sleazier hotels. This was precisely why Dunbar Regvik picked this hotel. It was a component of sex tourism and a lot of off-worlders came here utilizing pocket translators since languages and dialects were of people light years away.

Planning and implementation of this mission took almost two years. Carrying around a pocket translator was not going to be satisfactory for the type of work Dunbar Regvik had to do. The better he melted in with the locals, the safer he would feel. Long before Dunbar Regvik was sent to planet *Stanzel,* he would learn the *Rinisp* dialect of the standard *Stanzel language* which eliminated the pocket translator and made the Transporter Spy more versatile and quicker to respond to his environment. Dunbar Regvik was lucky to have almost two years of quality time to study and gain proficiency in standard *Stanzel language Rinisp* dialect.

The countless hours spent studying the imagery of this planet and learning the language and the local customs and Kabel Garr's history, would pay handy dividends. People who arrived two years before Dunbar Regvik arrived helped steal the identity of the person Kabel Garr and removed him at a critical time, who Dunbar Regvik now portrayed.

Kabel Garr was abducted after extensive surveillance and no longer on the planet when Dunbar Regvik arrived. After the Kaokuen Transporter Directorate obtained all the information Kabel Garr could provide voluntarily or coerced appeared to fulfill their need of him, then met his demise and no longer existed.

Dunbar would now be known as Kabel Garr until the mission was completed and he was returned to the Kaokuen Transporter Directorate via the transporter.

The real Kabel Garr, which the Transporter Directorate abducted was considered eccentric and came from the opposite hemisphere of the *Stanzel* planet. Known as a loner who kept to himself, Kabel Garr's few relatives, and the few friends had always seen him come and travel to far off places to routinely experience strange occult happenings. Since Kabel Garr departed and returned often with no fanfare, nobody would be interested in his sudden departure or when he returned. Kabel Garr was a loner and reclusive.

Thanks to mission planning Dunbar Regvik had access codes from Kabel Garr's credit฿ accounts programmed into his personal communicator taken from him after the abduction to purchase what he needed. Kabel Garr had been a brilliant financial planner and investor, thus built himself up a very large amounts of credits฿ to enjoy such leisure time.

Thanks to biological three-dimensional printing, Dunbar Regvik fingerprints and facial recognition had been altered to match Kabel Garr. It was unlikely Dunbar Regvik would ever have his own fingerprints and facial recognition the rest of his life. He truly was a spook with an altered identity. His past was irrevocably lost forever.

Not that it mattered much. Voice recognition was not fully implemented on *Stanzel,* but Dunbar Regvik's speaking coach slowly helped him develop a good Kabel Garr replica voice. Friends and relatives would not know the difference. Since Kabel Garr didn't have many friends and relatives there was less than a half dozen to learn about, which was an easy task.

Dunbar Regvik always knew he was living on borrowed time and his next mission could be his last because the enemy dealt harshly with captured Clandestine Transporter Operatives.

Another factor is after about one hundred transports, the odds were that his body might not reassociate correctly and thus he would arrive as a configuration of cell structures not rearranged at the destination site the way cell structures were prior to the transport, a total mess with death or a partial failure resulting in permanent damage to parts of his body.

Reassociation failures did not terribly alarm Dunbar Regvik because there would be no torture involved such as in the case of someone captured. Death usually resulted when most transporter failure happened. Dunbar's human awareness would simply cease and never return when cells amalgamate in unpredictable random arrangements during reassociation.

During transport there was an unconscious period. It was missing time. Dunbar's human awareness would fade, and he would feel a very strange sensation that made him feel dizzy and physically invigorated almost an orgasmic sensation. Then suddenly he would become coherent in a new reality far off from where he left.

Once in about five transports, Dunbar Regvik would also have a migraine headache for fifteen minutes. This too was a problem especially if he found himself surrounded by the enemy after reassociation. He would have to use every ounce of his willpower in those instances because if he had to fight his way out of a trap, it was do or die because after the torture his body would be disposed of lifeless.

With the current state of technology, Clandestine Transporter Operations were all this type of technology utilized. Because of the difficulties of a transporter operations, they had to be conducted in single file and if a laser pointer to the destination site stayed on more than five seconds, there would be no point in using it since the enemy used the same laser as a target. Hence you could not ship an Army into space that way. There was no other practical use for the technology other than Clandestine Transporter Operations.

Clandestine Transporter Operations limitations meant all the other military industrial complex matters remained the same with standard features. Military and industrial information was vital to obtain.

Stanzelite scientists were brilliant, and their design prowess is what led to the current mission. Part of their psychological warfare was to brag about their weapon systems to make their enemies scared to make any bold moves.

Half of the time *Stanzelite* propaganda was disinformation, but the other half of the time the publicity contained realistic and frightening capabilities the *Stanzelites* could unleash on their enemies. The bellicose relationship with the Kaokuen and the *Stanzelites* further caused the priority for this mission.

The *Stanzelites* Space Force had demonstrated one of their new Oclatine Class Hyper Warp Speed Fast Frigate to one of their allies and were attempting to cut a deal. The *Stanzelites* wanted to be the industrial might of this area of the galaxy and control the new construction business for Space Force components.

Kaokuen INTEL and Space Force needed as much information on the Oclatine Class Hyper Warp Speed Fast Frigate so they could design counter defenses and figure out a way to defeat such a formidable craft that had such extraordinary speed and weapon systems.

There was also the fear of proliferation and selling copies of these fast frigates to other entities that could suddenly pose a risk to the Kaokuen Space Force making access to the disputed planets more problematic.

Chapter Two

Checking In

Thanks to the sex tourism that flourished in Kerlara one of the principal cities on planet *Stanzel* thanks partly to the unusual high number of exotic beautiful women that flourished here, late reservations especially at places like the *Norel Mozelle Resort* routinely happened.

Local *Stanzelite* people as well as off worlder's suddenly desiring the company of a lovely *Stanzelite* female trained in the fine arts of satisfaction and gratification inducement, often randomly called in making reservations just prior to arrival. Some *Norel Mozelle Resort* guests would do a one-night stay, others would stick around for weeks if they had the credits₿.

Kaokuen Intelligence Bureau (KIB) initiated this vital military intelligence gathering operation. Dunbar Regvik was not made aware of the strategic decisions made on the outcome of his mission. His superiors decided not to place the additional burden on him of knowing all that which might overwhelm him and not help him because of the added stress of knowing the great emphasis placed on the mission.

Therefore, there were huge omissions on the importance of this mission. Thus, because Dunbar didn't have the added stress of knowing the critical nature of the mission, he proceeded considerably more casually as he approached the *Norel Mozelle Resort*

Dunbar Regvik crossed the street of a major throughfare at an intersection and walked half a block to the *Norel Mozelle Resort* front entrance. Having made the reservation as planned shortly after arriving via the communicator at the Kaokuen Transporter Capsule, Dunbar approached the lovely receptionist with a *Norel Mozelle Resort*. The receptionist's name tag indicating *Blemary* stood at the counter to greet and check Dunbar into the *Norel Mozelle Resort*.

"Good afternoon, sir, how may I help you sir?" Blemary asked in *Stanzel language Rinisp* dialect.

"I have a reservation." Dunbar replied.

Dunbar knew the way people checked into the *Norel Mozelle Resort* was not by using their name. They simply pulled out their personal communicator which tagged the client to the resort's reservation system indicating arrival.

Blemary verified the reservation was immediately paid for as the credits₿ transaction occurred seamlessly. She also noted he was traveling alone and had not requested guest augmentation services, meaning a companion to make his time more enjoyable. The *Norel Mozelle Resort* had several women available if such services were requested, and others on call in the event there was a sudden uptick in demand.

"You are all set. Your room number has been transferred to your communicator. We use a lot of facial recognition and when you get into the elevator down the hallway to the left, it will automatically take you to your floor. The voice in the elevator will direct you to your room."

"Thank you Blemary," Dunbar said looking at the very lovely woman.

Normally the receptionists did not use names because of their privacy training, but the resort lobby was currently empty, just the two of them were present and felt a warm signal from Dunbar and decided to add the human touch and use his name for that moment.

"You are most welcome Kabel Garr (aka Dunbar)," Blemary replied.

Some worlds placed the last name before the first name, and the *Stanzelite* culture did not use sexual identifiers such as Mr. or Mrs. they simply used the full name in the order the person gives it unless that person requests just to use the first name. The *Stanzelite* person would then know the worder in which the names were placed.

Dunbar Regvik was a social engineer as part of his training. One never knows when you might need to use someone. Early in the mission such as now, critical networking was necessary to build that fabric of social engagement that might come in handy later. As such Dunbar poured on the charm.

"Blemary, you can just call me Kabel, and thank you for your assistance."

"You are most welcome Kabel," Blemary replied feeling the cohesive attraction this nice gentleman exhibited.

Blemary had previously been one of those girls that were used by these love hotels to service their clients. Having been dumped on the streets by her loser parents, she was desperate and found the only employment she could. On Stanzel one either had to work or starve to death. It was disgusting work for Blemary, but it's all she could do in such a short notice and the emergency her terrible parents created for her. Back a few years prior, Blemary working as a love hotel resort pleasure associate was paid well with great tips and could sustain herself indefinitely.

Unlike many of the other pleasure associates who spent their money lavishly, Blemary banked as many credits฿ as possible and when she had saved up enough for a financial cushion, she quit that job and went looking for different type of job that did not involve using her body.

Blemary quickly found this receptionist job and the management who investigated her past as a pleasure associate knew she would fit in perfectly assisting the patrons and hired her and never regretted their decision because she was very good with the resort guests, and the staff liked her.

As a pleasure associate in the past, Blemary used an alias and her makeup and looks were entirely different. None of her former clients would recognize her now, since she had been very thin from an almost starving diet for months. Blemary was relatively young years prior working as a pleasure associate and had not fully developed breasts as she was a late bloomer but now her body exhibited almost perfect geometries.

Blemary did not need to sell or expose the additional services offered at the *Norel Mozelle Resort.* All the clients knew the amenities before making their reservations.

When Dunbar Regvik arrived in his resort hotel room and entered with very little in the form of luggage, the artificial intelligence that watched over the room and advised the clients of everything they needed to know quickly gave Kabel Garr (aka Dunbar) his welcoming session.

The holograph that suddenly popped up showing a life size image of a well-dressed person. Dunbar was ready for this and in his pre-mission studies and observations, was informed much about what to expect at the *Norel Mozelle Resort.*

"Good afternoon, Kabel Garr." The voice coming from the holograph said in the *Rinisp dialect of the standard Stanzelite language.*

"Thank you."

"My name is Cornolius. I'm your tour director and will make all arrangements you request."

"I appreciate that."

"I noticed you came alone and do not have a partner," Cornolius said.

"Yes, I'm by myself," Kabel Garr replied.

"I always monitor the room and just ask a question and I will appear to assist you. If there is anything you want to know about the resort or fun things to do around the resort or nearby establishments?" Cornolius asked.

"Thank you. I might have some questions during my stay. And please just call me Kabel."

"Duly noted Kabel," the artificial intelligence Cornolius replied, with an infinite memory and his adaptive algorithms had elements of social engineering to better serve the customers.

Cornolius observed Kabel looking around the room checking out all the fixtures and amenities so he would know what all was available.

"Is there anything I can be of assistance for you now Kabel?"

"Not at the moment, I might lay down in a bit and relax," Kabel replied.

"Kabel, the *Norel Mozelle Resort* is designed to provide all the needs for newlyweds, couples, and even singles who arrive without a partner."

"That's nice to know."

"As part of our resort facilities, we also help singles who arrive here without a partner but would like to spend time with a beautiful person to help them take their minds off their troubles."

"That's interesting to know."

"We can provide you with a temporary companion if you wish. One of the reasons why your room rate is rather high, is it pays for all the amenities. There are no additional charges."

"So, if I want you to bring me a female to be a temporary friend, you will send someone here to spend time with me at no additional cost."

"That's correct Kabel. Would you like to see some possible temporary friends that are waiting right now to visit you and make you feel better?"

"I may not want one, but it doesn't hurt to look, right?"

"If you allow me, I will start to show you some holographs of your friends that are waiting to come join you. You can see them, but they cannot see you."

"Alright let's see a few."

In the span of a few minutes, *Norel Mozelle Resort* AI holograph Cornolius, projected a half dozen gorgeous female pleasure associates. Dunbar Regvik knew Cornolius would provide any of these pleasure associates for existential gratification.

Dunbar Regvik was observing just out of curiosity to how these pleasure associates appeared as they were in their private rooms going about their business doing their daily routines, not doing anything out of the ordinary or posing, but they knew some voyeurism was occurring throughout the day and someone was watching them, including a potential client where the pleasure associate would be soon summoned up to the *Norel Mozelle Resort* guest room.

"Kabel, does any of these pleasure associates fit your needs?" Cornolius asked.

"I'm not here for sex and that type of entertainment. Thank you for letting me see the women, I was just curious as to how they appeared."

"Kabel, you spent a lot of extra credits฿ for this resort not to enjoy all our facilities and amenities."

"Cornolius, I'm here for a few days to meet some psychics and psychic healers. The reason why I decided to stay at the *Norel Mozelle Resort* is because, I might find myself involved with one of these psychics and would enjoy your facilities with a person I meet."

"Kabel, I hope you are successful in your dealings with your psychic and others you meet."

"Thank you Cornolius. I think I'm going to relax now, lay down and take a nap, then go for a walk later."

"Kabel, would you like me to wake you up at a certain time from your nap so that you can conduct your activities?"

"Yes, could you wake me up in a couple hours?"

"It would be my pleasure. Would you like to take a bath or a shower before your nap and change into some sleeping clothes?"

"Yes, I think a quick shower would be good."

"I will start your shower for you Kabel and there will be a change of sleeping clothes in the bathroom for you along with a bathrobe and slippers."

"Thank you I appreciate that."

In a short while Kabel was exposed to a lot of nice negative ions in his shower and then had his sleeping clothes on and was reclining in his bed getting ready to rest.

When the Kaokuen Transporter Capsule that rearranged all of Dunbar Regvik's atoms in his body when he was sent at extreme velocities long distance to another planet on another solar system, created some transporter lag even when the reassociate phase of the transporter worked correctly. Dunbar knew from past Transports; a two-hour nap would help his Transporter Lag measurably. He wanted to feel good at the start of this mission which he knew would likely turn into a journey. Dunbar had no idea to the extent that was going to happen as events in his life were just about to go way beyond his wildest dreams.

Dunbar knew he would have to be nimble because he was operating in danger behind enemy lines. His worst fear was compromise back in the Kaokuen Transporter Directorate. Dunbar arrived at *Stanzel* with the perfect penetration of the planet and all their elaborate security procedures and checkpoints. Only a few people within the *Stanzel* government knew that Transporters existed and none of them knew the true potential to transport spies' long distances bypassing all foreign security apparatus.

Stanzel planetary security was second to none. The chances of getting a spy to *Stanzel* via any type of spacecraft was virtually impossible. In addition to the concentric rings of planetary security that was enhanced by observation posts on every single planet in the solar system, the fleet of probes and drones provided situational awareness all interlinked by artificial intelligence, high speed communication and an impenetrable grid that was fully weaponized.

Thanks to the transporter operation the *Stanzel* planetary defense apparatus would not believe a Kaokuen spy was walking among them let alone what his intentions might be. One thing they did know was a laser was pointed at the planet for almost five seconds and by the time planetary defenses approached the area where the laser originated, whatever was the source of the laser could not be detected and was by now long gone in the bowels of a shuttle going at tremendous speeds far away from the solar system.

Unless a spy tipped the *Stanzelites* off, the disguise that Dunbar had with his alias Kabel Garr was rock solid and in an operational sense allowed him significant freedom of movement. With Kabel Garr's credits₿ the ability to travel around on the planet could be quite fun. A nice holiday at Kabel Garr's expense.

Dunbar used his silent meditation he learned to employ Hemi-Sync in case he was captured, that slowly put him to sleep. He would not know for sure if he achieved Hemi-Sync with his brain because his dreams were so vivid, they could easily pass for a Hemi-Sync, or the *Gateway* experience the Kaokuen Intelligence Bureau and Transporter Directorate officially called it.

What would clue Dunbar that a Gateway experience occurred is he would experience life in another dimension far longer than a normal dream. Nevertheless, Dunbar was soon in that dream state and sleeping peacefully feeling great from the negative ions he received taking the shower which effected his cranial chemicals now aiding in his recovery from Transporter Lag.

Somehow the receptionist Blemary entered Dunbar's dream. He was a man with the same needs of any other male, and the fact that after such a tumultuous event of being slung clear across the far reaches of space to a distant solar system and surviving it in the transporter had an impact on his moral and ethical values for the dream. Fleshly desires were choreographed in this perceptual dream with evocative consequences.

When Cornolius awakened Kabel two hours later, he had a huge erection from his dream along with the need to urinate.

Dunbar slowly shifted to the side of his bed, sat up and put his feet into the slipper, stood up and walked to the bathroom and urinated and then thought about what he would do now. He looked around and noticed his clothes were not on the chair where he left them.

"Cornolius, where are my clothes and my shoes?"

Cornolius holograph suddenly appeared, and he said, "Kabel, your clothes were drycleaned and are in the closet, would you like to get them for you?"

"You can actually lift things?" Kabel asked.

"Kabel, I have a robot that assists me doing physical work and it can pick up your clothes and do most tasks you require."

"That's interesting," Dunbar said rather fascinated how advanced *Stanzel* was. It was a terrible shame that two advanced civilizations had entered a bellicose relationship. They had so much to offer each other, but unfortunately both civilizations had an element of Tyrants as leaders.

Dunbar knew philosophically there was nothing he could do about intergalactic relationships and since they were at the crossroads of potentially a major escalation of tensions that could turn into a major conflict, he had to do his duty in clandestine manners for his handlers. Right or wrong Dunbar had to do his part in protecting his civilization since the failure of meeting such challenges often meant extermination.

Kabel planned to do a walk around the area near his hotel and take in all visuals and become familiar with the lay of the land. He also was using visiting the psychics as a prop in his reason to be in this city, so he had a couple of them he was going to go visit and establish their analysis of his future.

Dunbar's clothes were dry cleaned to perfection. But as he left his *Norel Mozelle Resort*, he knew the obvious and as part of mission planning since he had all the credits₿ in Kabel's accounts, he would purchase several changes of clothes after watching what everyone appeared to be wearing today. He wanted to fit in well. That entered his travels today including workout gym clothes and shoes so he could work at maintaining his physical form. He worked hard to get this way and he wanted to keep it.

It was that time of day when a lot of guests had checked into the resort, and the next large group would not be arriving for another hour timed with inter galactic transportation, so the lobby was effectively empty.

Kabel walked through the lobby and noticed the nice-looking receptionist Blemary standing there smiling and looking quite appealing. He approached her mainly for the purpose of social engineering and possibly a future interaction that might become necessary if he needed her to support his mission.

One of the reasons why she was so happy, she was due to finish her shift in less than an hour and go home and relax after another long day.

Blemary didn't need to remember Kabel's name. He had on an ear bud and a microphone device that interfaced with the resort's AI that informed her the person approaching was hotel guest, Kabel Garr. She was also reminded he preferred to be called Kabel.

"Hello Kabel," Blemary said as he approached.

"Hello to you too."

"Is there something I can help you with?"

"No, I was going for a walk and saw you, so I wanted to say hello to you."

"That's a nice thing to say, thank you."

"You are more than welcome. I enjoyed meeting you today."

"Likewise, thank you."

"Alright, Blemary, I need to go get some exercise done and look over the city."

"I hope you enjoy your day, Kabel."

"Thank you Blemary. I am sure I will enjoy looking at the city."

"When you get back, be sure and ask your room servant if you have any questions on the surrounding area and any exciting things in store for this area."

"I certainly will. Thank you," Kabel said then exited the building out onto the sidewalk leading down the major throughway.

Today Kabel would stop thinking of himself as Dunbar and psychologically remind himself he is Kabel Garr, and the name Dunbar and his past would be set aside until his mission was complete. That way he would be better psychologically ready for this new environment and adapt to his new situation better.

As Kable Garr his new identity stepped out of the Norel Mozelle Resort he looked both ways at the metropolis noting the grand architecture of the buildings he was viewing in the process.

The long, tall buildings were inspiring, but the twisted spiraling building he saw up the street reminded of him the time he had to travel to Sanctuary City, to spy on the bankers involved with the Revolution and the formidable spy Brenda Broyles and her lover Evo Kaplan. *I wonder whatever happened to them?*

Kabel decided to turn right and walk down the street in that direction since the spiraling building caught his fascination. The architects that designed that building were the very best designers he ever observed. *The physics behind the structure must be impressive*, Kabel thought.

Walking along with no urgent business as today was simply time Kabel needed to spend figuring out his surroundings including exit strategies in the event he had reason to believe the authorities were on to him and he was being pursued. Dunbar now formulated exit corridors and egress avenues. Even though Dunbar's training went through all this, observing the real city up close gave an entirely new vision that prompted subtle reassessments.

During this walk Kabel would have to visit a few places and buy a change of clothes and items that would help with temporary disguises such as a hat and different type of sunglasses than what he was wearing.

The Norel Mozelle Resort had all the toiletries and items that Kabel needed, so there wasn't a need to buy a lot of those kinds of items. Workout and gym clothes would be a necessity. One of the areas he would soon locate was the city park he had studied in his planning a place to go exercise.

Dunbar would also hit all the major landmarks of the city and find a couple psychic venues, pick up literature and start a relationship with one or two of them to create the impression on someone that might be following him to find out what he was really doing in this city. The planetary security forces were not paranoid or expecting a den of spies because their multi-layered defense rings usually did a good job of keeping out spies and saboteurs.

Advanced civilizations such as the *Stanzelites* had ample amounts of artificial intelligence observing everyone. Algorithms would no doubt tip off law enforcement if there were perceived nefarious activities observed. The age of big brother watching everyone was present throughout the galaxy and especially here in the city Kerlara in the heart of the *Stanzel* Empire which had as much security and AI as any other major city in the galaxy.

Any advanced civilization in the galaxy monitored its populations to detect serious activities such as revolution and coups. The *Stanzel* planetary security organization was just as formidable as any other.

That was more reason to get into the psychic healers and psychic fortune tellers that would create a plausible story as to why Kabel Garr was here in Kerlara. Dunbar realized he might even have to participate in some of the psychic activities to help create an image of why he was staying at the Norel Mozelle Resort and Love Hotel so as not to create interest to possible Stanzelite planetary security.

Perhaps I could seduce the receptionist Blemary to create a scenario that would defeat the analysis of artificial intelligence? Dunbar postulated while evaluating his circumstances. If he initiated something with the receptionist, that would defeat inquiry to trying to figure out why he wasn't enjoying the fleshly delightfulness of some of the most exquisite women on the planet. Dunbar analyzed that since he already paid for such services by his expensive room rate might trigger interest if he didn't utilize the pleasure associates. Blemary sure seemed like an eager beaver and her body language exposed some subtle attraction.

Kabel Garr fully trained in monitoring body language was keen on spotting willingness and eagerness in women to exploit. In the spy business the enemy learned women are often the low hanging fruit and the easiest to recruit as a double spy. The honey pot scheme worked both ways and if a *PRETENDER* was good enough, he could eventually rip the heart out of a woman and coerce her just as strongly as men who fall victims to honey pot schemes with their little heads.

Dunbar portraying the semi eccentric and aloof Kabel Garr whose identity the Transport Directorate abducted, lived the life of *CALL IT EVEN (CIE)*. He had been mistreated by women in the past, therefore, to inflict emotional pain on a woman in conduct of his clandestine operations when the time came, left him with no regrets as he had paid his dues in the way his heart had been shattered in the past.

When the time came, if he went down the path of using Blemary, he knew he would be leaving behind a broken heart if he went through the reverse honey pot recruitment process. There would be no official breakup or apologies, Dunbar would simply disappear as he Transported back to the banking office he worked out of far off in another solar system.

Keeping an eye on everything around him, Kabel took it all in. To be seen eyeballing the spiral building would not raise any suspicion since it influenced a lot of people that admired the physical uniqueness of such a grand and artful design. Approaching the spiral building would give an appearance of inquisitiveness, not too dissimilar to tourists. It would also give Artificial Intelligence surveillance a false analysis of the purpose for Kabel Garr being here.

As he got closer to the spiral building, Kabel Garr spotted a psychic reader business which he noted and decided to visit after he checked out the spiral building. This spiral building was quite a distance away, much further than anticipated but in a matter of time arrived and went inside and looked at the directory.

Dunbar was most fortunate the spiral building had an observation deck and the *Greifinn restaurant* at the very top of the building. This was excellent since it would give him a commanding view of the city to scope out the lay of city to reinforce his training. He was feeling slightly hungry and the restaurant at the top of the building would be the perfect place to do some studies and observation in the manner he was well trained.

When Dunbar first began preforming missions with the Studies and Observation Clandestina Operations (SOCO) he rode one-man gliders down behind enemy lines to perform strategic reconnaissance missions. His actions included recovering downed pilots and rescue spies. In order to accomplish many of the SOCO missions, Dunbar had to do things to cause diversion of resources, sometimes physical destruction and sabotage, gathering intelligence and employing tactics that resulted in harassment only, but produced the effects necessary to support a variety of missions including propaganda activities.

Some of the glider operations originated in space, others by deploying out of aircraft where he was in the glider dropped from the wing of a bomber from high altitude. The stealth glider fully under microprocessor control often obtained supersonic speeds on its way to its destination and the flight profile was such that using airbrakes and maneuvers the glider would softly touch down at the desired landing zone with a last-minute parachute opening at 1000 feet.

The glider was booby trapped and had a self-destruct timer set for whether the SOCO operative was expected to get back to it or not. Should they attempt to use the same glider for egress, it had a stratospheric balloon to take it up to high altitudes where an aircraft would snag it and tow it back to friendly lines. Where it had the ability to land on a conventional runway or if need the SOCO person could eject out of it and parachute down and have the glider crash into the sea or in a remote area.

Dunbar's many successful SOCO operations is what led him to be selected for the Transporter Directorate. What he was doing now was an extension of his past, the chief difference was the distance traveled as a Transport Directorate Operative (TDO), was usually off world and in other solar systems.

Dunbar's SOCO to TDO conversion course lasted a couple years. Dunbar deployments up until now had been challenging and in a few cases, extraction occurred at the deadline without a minute to spare.

The elevator ride, up to the top of the spiral building was interesting because the tube which the elevator operated was made with sections of a clear material allowing riders to see outside as it was rising quickly.

The elevator rose so quickly that Dunbar felt heavier and as it slowed considerably lighter. The elevator which was an express elevator to the restaurant made no stops on the way and when it stopped and the door opened, it was in the lobby of the *Greifinn restaurant* twenty steps from the mataré d's station.

Kabel approached the lovely blonde mataré d in the *Greifinn restaurant* who had a nametag indicating Sophia. That was an unusual name for a *Stanzelite*, but it sounded very lovely.

When Kabel arrived a few feet in front of Sophia, she said, "Good afternoon, sir. Do you have a reservation?"

"No, I do not," Kabel replied.

Sophia looked at her computer flatscreen tablet and could see open tables and said, "I have a table that just opened up, please follow me."

"Thank you."

Sophia led Kabel through the spacious *Greifinn restaurant* to a table next to the window where he could see an unobstructed view to the North.

In a perfect Rinisp dialect of the standard *Stanzel language,* Kabel asked, "Excuse me Sophia, may I ask how high up from the ground this restaurant is?

"Sophia realized the customer noticed her nametag and understood her name which she appreciated and answered in a very delightful tone, "Sir, a lot of customers ask that question. We are up fourteen hundred hectra's from the ground (a hectra in the *Stanzel language* is approximately twelve inches).

"Thank you."

"Sir, you know my name, may I ask you what your name is?"

"I'm Kabel Garr, you can just call me Kabel."

"Alright Kabel, it's a pleasure to meet you. Your server will be here shortly to take your food and drink orders."

"Thank you, Sophia," Kabel smiled as he replied leaving Sophia with a very good impression. She didn't know why, but she felt good vibrations from this customer.

Sophia turned and walked away. Sitting down at a lower level allowed Kabel to enjoy Sophia's posterior a little more with a direct view. The waitress by the name of Embla was already approaching Kabel's table and observed him enjoying the eye candy created by Sophia's majestic walk that many men enjoyed. Embla was no slouch either and soon demonstrated to Kabel she was full of charm as well.

Menus were already sitting on the two-seat table and Kabel was quickly observing types of drinks and elixirs the restaurant served.

"Good afternoon, sir. My name is Embla, I will be your server today, is there any drink you would like me to get you before I take your food order?"

Scanning the drink menu, Kabel spotted a *Jangovian de Palentin* elixir that was a delicacy and quite expensive back in the Kaokuen planet. Even though the cost was pricey, Kabel didn't care since the real Kabel Garr's credit₿ accounts made such a purchase a trivial matter. This would be one of those moments where the positive benefits of his profession would be enjoyable.

"Yes, I would like a *Jangovian de Palentin*," Kabel Garr, replied.

"I'll bring your *Jangovian de Palentin* right away," Embla said then picked up the second set of menus off the table to create the feeling of more space for the customer."

Embla was also somewhat eye candy and had a very nice body, beautiful face, and great brunette hair with a lovely style to it. Embla radiated elegance as she walked away carrying the second set of menus on her way to the bar to pick up Kabel's *Jangovian de Palentin* elixir.

Kabel then studied the menu items and quickly discovered a leg of Tommy on the menu. Kabel knew from his vast study of *Stanzel* several of the animals used in their food chain, one of which was a Tommy that was kind of a cross between an Antelope and sheep. The *Leg of Tommy* was served in a similar manner as lamb chops. Kabel would soon discover the luxurious taste of the meat cooked to perfection by a Stanzel world-class chef.

With the hidden microphone worn in Embla's clothing, artificial intelligence had already placed the order with the bartender for the *Jangovian de Palentin* elixir, which all the bartenders had to do is pour it like a glass of wine out of a chilled bottle. The bartender handed Embla the elixir which she promptly carried back to Kabel on a small serving tray to make sure she didn't spill any of the contents during the walk towards the customer's table.

Embla asked Kabel, "Sir, have you decided what you would like to order."

"Yes, I would like the *Leg of Tommy*." Kabel replied and added the additional items he wanted with the meal.

"I will place your order right away," Embla said about the time Kabel handed her the menus.

Embla walked towards the Kitchen. She didn't need to send Kabel's order. Artificial Intelligence had already taken the order and in Embla's earbud read it back to her the order which she confirmed the information in the order was correct and the Chef was already working on the meal contents in the kitchen.

At this time, Kabel tasted the *Jangovian de Palentin* elixir which was very palatable and hit the spot nicely. This elixir had chemicals such as alcohol and pleasurizers in it. On some planets the pleasurizers would be classified as a class-3 narcotic and under supervised control in the medical and psychiatric community. However, *Stanzel* was different and danced to their own tune. Part of their economy was based on tourism including Love Hotels, so allowing class-3 narcotics into drinks served to the public to enhance the sex-tourism fit the financial models quite nicely.

After taking one or two nice sips of the *Jangovian de Palentin* elixir, Kabel Garr started to systematically look out the window making note of all the landmarks he could correlate with his memories in his studies. This was an opportunistic observation in that his view included the area of the major throughfare he just walked along and the *Norel Mozelle Resort* and all that lay beyond.

Dunbar spotted two adjoining city parks that were situated on each side of the road which reminded him of a place he once went where the locals called it Paradise Cove and Ski Beach on each side of the street. It was good he did all this area recognition before he consumed his drink, because otherwise he might not want to.

Before Dunbar's meal was served, there were a few performers that began their first act, and a singing cabaret singer suddenly began performing with a person playing an instrument that Kabel had once seen on a distant planet during a SOCO mission, called a piano. It made a nice sound, and several other musicians were there adding to the sound quality.

That music brought back memories. Sadly, Dunbar had feelings for a woman who became involved in his life that ultimately led to another Call It Even, episode he seriously regretted later, as he now knew she was one of the nicest persons he had met in his lifetime. If he could go back in time and alter his destiny, he would still be with her now. Leaving her behind was one of the biggest mistakes Dunbar made in his lifetime.

There was no way Dunbar could ever see this woman again, because he knew she met her demise when she died in the line of duty. Part of his guilt was centered around how he could have changed her destiny as well and she would be alive today flourishing and living life to the fullest. Later there was redemption in that Dunbar had the satisfaction of assassinating the person that led to her death.

Dunbar was jerked back to reality out of his daydream when Embla suddenly appeared with a small pushcart carrying his meal and said, "Sir, here is your meal, is there anything else I can give you?"

"Yes, please give me a refill of my drink," Kabel Garr replied with a smile.

By the time Embla returned with another drink, Kabel had downed the rest of his drink as he wanted to quickly forget the thoughts he just remembered and focus on his current surroundings.

The *Leg of Tommy* cooked in exotic spices gave real satisfaction to Kabel as he slowly enjoyed his meal listening to the lovely music the cabaret singer was performing. *Perhaps it was her singing that made me remember her?*

By the time Kabel finished his meal and Embla cleaned off his table, including changing the tablecloth which they did so that people could remain and enjoy the entertainment and continue drinking and socializing, the performers were taking a break. The singing diva slowly walked around the restaurant saying hello to people including regulars she obviously knew. Eventually she made her way to Kabel Garr's table and started a conversation.

"Are you enjoying your experience here at the *Greifinn* restaurant?" the singer asked.

"Very much so, and I must say I love your singing," Kabel Garr responded.

"Thank you very much, it's always nice to get positive feedback."

It would not be the first or the last time Kabel got in the good graces with a cabernet singing diva or other luxurious women. As the consummate social engineer, he knew how to proceed, and this might be an opportunity to network in all the right places.

"Say, I'm sure you are thirsty by now with all that lovely singing, would you like to join me for a drink?"

"I would really like that, thank you very much." The singer said.

"Please have a seat," Kabel said.

"Thank you." The singer said.

"My name is Kabel Garr."

"Nice to meet you Kabel Garr, I'm Eva Erlaendsdottir. You can call me Eva."

"I'm happy to meet you, Eva."

"Are you from Kerlara?" Eva asked.

"No, I'm from a small town near the city of Ophelia."

"That's a long distance away, what are you doing so far from home?"

"I've taken a keen interest in psychics and in particular psychic healers. From my research the three best live here in Kerlara. I've come here to meet with them and explore their capabilities."

"I have to tell you Kabel, I'm a little skeptical about all these psychics."

"Not a problem, most people are."

"Do you actually think they have abilities?"

"I'm not sure yet, but I intend to find out."

"What makes you think they have abilities they advertise?"

"I know a remote viewer, so I've learned to check things out before I decide if something is real or fake."

"What's a remote viewer?"

"It's a person who can see or hear what you see and hear?"

"For real?"

"Yes."

"Have you seen this person actually do these sorts of things?"

"I've been able to correlate a few events and the only way possible it could have happened, was exactly the way my remote viewer friend explained. The public was not informed on what she told me for several months after the event she reported when it happened."

"That's wild. Are you sure you are not telling me a story?"

"I'm not a pretender, why would I tell you a story?"

"A lot of men tell me stories."

"Why?"

"They want to get into my pants."

"I can see why; you are very beautiful, and your singing sends chills up my spine sometimes."

"Are you just saying that to make me like you more?"

"Eva, I live on the other side of the planet, I know our worlds are far away from each other. Even though I know I would truly like to experience you in my lifetime, I know realistically it's probably not in the cards. But I do like you and appreciate you and love your singing. I have no motives with you."

"You are quite unusual, Kabel Garr."

"That's what my few family members and friends think too, but they have never gone on with me to some of my adventures."

"Where do you go?"

"I go to a lot of places and look at what a lot of people ignore or are skeptical about. I have a curiosity and go and seek it."

"Do you travel a lot?"

"Quite extensively."

"How do you financially manage all that?"

"I'm quite well at investment strategies and financial planning. I know I can generate all the funds I need to support all my travel plans."

"Have you ever gone off world?"

"Yes, I traveled places before the war started where we could easily get too, that travel has now been suspended."

"What are some of the places you went to?"

Kabel named off a few places he was very familiar with in his SOCO travels.

"I had a gig at the Clairemont Hotel on the planet Berkeley," Eva replied.

"I stayed at the Clairmont Hotel and Resort," Kabel Garr said.

They got into a quick discussion on the planet Berkeley which few people from Kerlara knew about. And when Kabel elucidated those memories, Eva knew he was for real and not a pretender.

"You are a fascinating person Kabel Garr, but I need to get back to work now. Perhaps I can see you again before you leave?"

"Yes, I'll come back. I like to hear your singing."

"Where are you staying here in Kerlara?"

"I'm staying at the *Norel Mozelle Resort.*" Kabel replied.

He suspected Eva would have such a response when her body language indicated she was in shock at the revelation that Kabel was staying in the notorious establishment.

"I need to get back to work now. Thank you for the drink."

"The pleasure was all mine."

Kabel knew he gave Eva something to think about. The fact he had a beautiful woman available to him as part of the cost for his room meant he was not in need of any action.

He probably was simply being friendly with no Agenda, Eva thought.

Kabel knew that revealing he was staying in the LOVE HOTEL probably had a negative impact on Eva's evaluation of him, but he didn't care. He wasn't there for Eva. She was just another side show.

Eva sang two lovely songs and halfway through the second one, Kabel stook up and walked out of the restaurant.

***

Chapter Three
Searching

Kabel left the spiral building and was now on foot walking towards the psychic establishment he saw on the way. As he approached the business, he quickly determined it was closed for the day and noted the hours of business, then continued looking for items he wanted purchase such as running shoes and socks and gym clothes so he could exercise in the morning.

It did not take much time to locate stores selling everything Kabel needed including a change of clothing for the next day. He also went in the direction of the two city parks he spotted and looked at them before he turned around and walked back to the Norel Mozelle Resort.

Blemary was about to finish her shift and leave for the day when Kabel walked through the lobby carrying a couple shopping bags with him.

"Hello Kabel," Blemary said since nobody else was present.

"Good evening."

"Did you have a good day?"

"Yes, went to a nice restaurant and did some shopping."

"What restaurant did you go to?"

"I went to the *Greifinn* restaurant at the top of the spiral building down the street a way."

"I like that restaurant, been there a few times. Did you know we have a nice dining room in this resort?"

"I figured such, but I was out walking around and got hungry and wanted to see the city from the top of a tall building, and since it has a restaurant, I decided to get something to eat there."

"Did you have a good time?"

"Yes, and they had musicians and a singer named Eva."

"How did you learn her name?"

"I bought her a drink during one of her breaks."

"Is she good looking?"

"Yes, almost as good looking as you are."

"You are such a sweet talker."

"Well, you are cute."

"Thank you."

"Alright, I need to take my things to my room. It was nice talking to you."

"Yes, I liked your conversation as well."

"See you again," Kabel said as he walked away heading for the elevator.

Blemary was kind of a nosey person and on a hunch opened up Kabel's reservation file on her data terminal and quickly noted he had not requested or received any of the resorts pleasure associates. That piqued her curiosity a bit. She would check his file tomorrow to see how long he lasted before he got the urge to order room service.

When Kabel entered his room, his holographic room attendant Cornolius was more than ready to assist and in a very short time offered, "Kable, may I place all the items you purchased in the closet and dispose of the shopping bags for you?"

"Yes, thank you."

A robot walked out of what appeared to be a closet, picked up the bags and carried them to the closet and deposited them there.

Kabel walked over to a chair facing the holographic entertainment projector and said, "can you please put on the local news."

"The top local news channel was suddenly showing giving the day's reports." This was only slightly out of the ordinary as most people arriving at the *Norel Mozelle Resort* seldom watched the news. They came to this resort for one reason. To experience the essence of a Love Hotel with their brides or girlfriends or a resort pleasure associate.

Kabel had not participated in any fashion in those activities which confused the Artificial Intelligence who then asked, "Kabel are you interested in any of our beautiful pleasure associates tonight?"

"No. I've met a couple ladies here that I'm interested in. I think I'm going to try and invite one of them here out of friendship."

Artificial Intelligence then started reanalyzing Kabel and since all the security video was accessible to the artificial intelligence tracking him in and out of the building, discovered the conversations Kabel had with the receptionist Blemary, and soon the coefficients generated by the computer algorithms indicated greater than fifty percent probability that Blemary was one of the females Kabel was referring too.

The artificial intelligence that provided the imagery and capabilities the servant Cornolius provided, was programmed to maximize customer satisfaction and to initiate pleasure associate activities with single males that arrived. Due to Kabel's strange behavior and not entertaining the idea of enjoying one of the pleasure associates, decided to intervene and help enhance a pathway to romance between Kabel and Blemary.

Kabel watched a couple hours of news, taking it all in and attempted discovering any elements that might fit into his plans along with gaining more awareness of his surroundings and the prevailing issues in the city.

One of the activities that Kabel enjoyed engaging in was attending the symphony or an opera. Several of his favorite singers were Opera singers. They were luxuriously beautiful, and their angelic voices created great satisfaction for Kabel. In his analysis and planning thinking how he might use Blemary, thought that in a couple days he might invite her to one of those events.

It was not unusual for some of the *Norel Mozelle Resort* guests to stay for a couple weeks. Some of the men went through every pleasure associate on staff, causing them to bring in the reserve force they had on call for such situations. The fact Kabel wasn't using those pleasure associate services made them plentifully available for the other patrons.

After the news, Kabel took a soaking bath, then retired for the night.

In the morning Kabel woke feeling great put on his exercise clothes and shoes and was out the door heading for the parks to do some running. As he passed through the lobby, he passed by Blemary. Unfortunately, there were others in the lobby, and she could not use his name and simply said, "Good morning, sir."

"Thank you, good morning to you as well," Kabel Garr said with a big smile and continued his way out the front entrance and to the sidewalk heading to the adjacent parks.

Blemary noticed Kabel was a hunk in his workout clothes. His legs had great muscles, so did his arms and his body indicated he probably had 6-pack abs.

Kabel Garr walked nearly a mile to get to the parks, which he didn't mind, he needed the exercise anyway. Soon he was in a semi-empty park running, putting in the effort quickly running five miles generating a lot of sweat. Looking around to verify he was alone, Dunbar said: "Echis Carinatus," this was the code word to a built-in communicator artificial intelligence *Latrodectus* indicating Dunbar was alone and to make a report.

"I've successfully penetrated hotel security and am now exploring the Stanzel World-Wide Computer Grid (SWWCG), " *Latrodectus* said.

"Any reports on the Oclatine Class Hyper Warp Speed Fast Frigate?

"Yes, I've found a few. I'm analyzing and looking for additional resources," *Latrodectus* said.

"Alright," Dunbar said, then he headed back to the *Norel Mozelle Resort* and since the sidewalks were semi-empty as it was still early, he was able to run most of the way.

By the time Kabel Garr walked through the lobby he was sweating profusely and the wet exercise shirt clinged to his body and Blemary could see he in fact had those 6-pack abs, and Kabel was a hunk. She had also looked at his file and noticed he still had not requested the services of a pleasure associate. He truly was a strange man, but his body and his workout indicated there was probably more to him and she wanted to find out.

Kabel went to his room, showered, changed into the clothes he purchased the previous day, and soon was leaving the room again on his way out to go visit the psychic he found walking to the spiral building the day before.

It did not take long to reach the building that had the psychic's office. Kabel went inside where he met a receptionist. After taking his name he was asked to sit down in the lobby, and he would be seen in a short while after Madam Chien Shiung would be right with him.

Kabel Garr had no opinion of psychic ability. There was never any scientific data to substantiate their predictions were nothing more than using common sense and addressing the laws of probabilities after they got to know the client to create a plausible prediction of an outcome. Many times, the client asked for the outcome of a situation they were in.

Most of the time Madam Chien Shiung's predictions were a fifty percent probability. That meant fifty percent of the clients would experience the result the psychic predicted. Producing fifty percent of the answers the clients wanted to know in advance meant substantial income because some of the clients paid large amounts to get guidance in advance on the outcome.

The psychic also knew another factor. If the person believed the outcome would take place such as in romance or other personal matters, by creating the proper psychology for the desired outcome, when the person pursued the dream, they otherwise would not have, they made the outcome. In essence, the psychic was nothing more than an advisor and an encourager in most cases. When their predictions failed, they simply informed the person they had generated so much negative Karma in their lives resulted in punishment and failure.

When the client acted on the information it synergistically created their own pathway to achievement simply by *believing* they could do it. Making investments they would not otherwise make, or pursuing a romance they were too scared to initiate, later turned extremely positive simply by boosting the client's confidence to make that bold move.

In essence the psychic wasn't really a predictor she was more of a person who modified the personal psychology of her client allowing them to make those courageous and daring moves, and when they achieved success and the payout was great, they appreciated the psychic Madam Chien Shiung even more. As a result, the psychic Madam Chien Shiung received post psychic modification tips in terms of some serious amounts of credits₿ in what one would think was a huge thank you bonus.

After twenty minutes, Madam Chien Shiung walked out of her office holding the arm of an older woman who was obviously crying. There had been a huge exchange between them, and the female client was obviously emotionally disturbed.

Kabel was curious as to what that was all about, and it fell withing the realm of the intensity of what the psychic sometimes made the clients feel.

After the woman departed the office, Madam Chien Shiung walked back towards the receptionist who informed her, "Mr. Kabel Garr is waiting to see you."

Madam Chien Shiung turned around and noticed there was only one client in the waiting room and asked, "Mr. Kabel Garr, would you please come with me to my office?"

Kabel Garr stood up and followed Madam Chien Shiung into her office. She made no initial assessment of Kabel, but noted he looked serious and was well dressed and most likely a very normal person. She took at face value he was wanting her to help him see into his future and help design a pathway for him in some future event.

There was a large table with chairs on either side of it and a few chairs next to the wall because sometimes clients brought their relatives in with them and sat and observed. When others came with the clients they were admonished not to say or think anything about the event because it might interfere with the psychic Madam Chien Shiung's ability to see into the future. They therefore must remain quiet throughout the session and not interfere in any way.

If observers broke the protocol and spoke in any manner, Madam Chien Shiung would ask them all to leave and simply state they had damaged her temporal clairvoyance, and it might take a while to get it back and to reschedule the appointment. They still paid for the services and the time they spent with her. When the appointment was rescheduled, the receptionist informed them they could not bring an observer back with them, since they damaged the atmosphere and prevent Madam Chien Shiung to be able to see their future. Problem solved.

"What can I do for you, Kabel Garr?"

"Please just call me Kabel."

"Alright Kabel, what is it you are interested in discovering?"

"Thank you, Madam Chien Shiung, for seeing me. Before I tell you my dilema I want you to advise me on, I want to inform you I made one huge mistake in my life in the past with personal relationships and I do not wish to make that mistake again."

"I understand you completely. You are not alone. A lot of people go through that, far more than you realize."

"I can imagine."

"Alright Kabel, what is your situation and what are you trying to resolve?"

"Since I lost my lover, I've not gotten close to another woman," Kabel said which was partly true, but all of this was just a feint to create a plausible story to his presence in the event authorities or artificial intelligence triggered an investigation and wanted to learn what Kabel Garr's motives were and why he was staying in this city at the *Norel Mozelle Resort.*

Kabel Garr knew the likelihood security cameras had already recorded him going into this psychic reader's office. His story was now being created. Any official that might become interested in him would visit Madam Chien Shiung and inquire into what the purpose of his visits were. For fear of being shut down by the authorities for selling *psychic snake oil,* Madam Chien Shiung would cooperate and reveal Kabel Garr's story which investigators would swallow, hook, line, and sinker.

Madam Chien Shiung could tell Kabel Garr was a no-nonsense person and conducted himself with great veracity. She knew he had a painful episode in his life, and this was a delicate matter, and she knew she needed to help him get out what he truly was looking for. So, Madam Chien Shiung started asking a few questions.

"Are you wondering if you are going to find another lover? Or are you wondering if you will make similar mistakes in the future?" Madam Chien Shiung asked.

"I assure you Madam Chien Shiung, I will never make that mistake again. I know I screwed up very badly and was very dumb in the way I acted. Hindsight is always better. If I could do it all over again, I would know for a fact how much I lost doing what I did and I know that in the future if I make similar mistakes, I will discover soon afterwards what I did to myself as well as that other person. But the past is the past, and she is out of my life forever now."

"Are you wanting to know if you will meet another woman?"

"I've already met two of them, but due to my circumstances as well as their situations, it's not clear to me whether a possibility exists that I can create a relationship with either one of them."

"Is there one of the two you prefer over the other?"

"They each have their own attributes that are worthy of a suitor."

"Have you dated them?"

"Not yet, but I've had social contact."

"I see."

"Can you give me some insights into which one I should pursue and if it's realistic?"

"I have to think about this for a moment."

"How does your psychic ability work, how do you come to conclusions about your clients' futures?" Kabel Garr suddenly asked.

"It's very simple Kabel I have a special gift. I do not have a crystal ball or any gadgets or cards that some psychics use to manifest their awareness of their clients' futures," Madam Chien Shiung said as she started preparing Kable Garr for indoctrination and influencing him.

"What is your gift?" Kabel Garr asked.

"What I do is come close to the individual such as I'm with you. I'm close enough to you now to read your aura. You have an aura like everyone has."

"What is an aura?" Kabel Garr asked even though he knew, he wanted to hear, Madam Chien Shiung's version.

"You can think of and aura as an invisible cloud that surrounds you that is about three or four times larger than you are."

"How does the aura fit into all this?"

"My gift is I intersect your aura and somehow my brain then produces holographic ensembles in my mind which is predictably your future. I may not get much of it nor your past, but I get some indicators as to what your future may be and how it will possibly come about."

"Do you feel like I will have a plausible relationship with one of these women?"

"I have a terribly bad sensation about you Kable Garr."

"How so?"

"You may state you are a noble person and will take the high ground in the future and never break a heart again and avoid what you did in the past with your former lover."

"That's my intentions."

"The sensation I have about you Kabel Garr, is that you may end up in a relationship with both women at the same time, and then you will have to make a terrible judgement."

"Such as?"

"The one you pick will save her life, the other one will be crushed."

"Can you tell me about these women?"

"Yes, one of them is some type of artist or a performer and she has already made an impression on you."

"She has."

"I know she has etched indelibly in your mind feelings and thoughts, and I know you want to go see her again."

"I can't deny I do."

"You know you want that relationship to develop, and I have a big surprise for you. She wants it more than you do so you are living in a dangerous situation with her."

"And what is that situation?"

"If you continue seeing her, you will cross over that point of no return and be stuck just like you were with your last lover pondering you next move."

Kabel Garr was absolutely stunned. It was as if Madam Chien Shiung had read his mind. She knew his motives, his desires, and his lust.

Kabel Garr didn't know what the purpose in all this was, but Madam Chien Shiung had the uncanny method of digging deep into his emotions and discovering the plausible outcomes of those two women and he felt exactly the way she delivered it.

The information Madam Chien Shiung offered seemed likely several days ahead of him because his thoughts of how these relationships might transpire were exactly the way Madam Chien Shiung put it.

"Madam Chien Shiung, Thank you."

"You are welcome Kabel."

"You have given me a lot to think about. I appreciate your help in this matter. "

"I'm happy and I hope you will try to do the right thing."

"I will have to spend some time thinking about all this because I believe you are right there could be terrible consequences if I screw this up, and I do not want to go down that path I did once before."

"If you make the right decision about these two women, you can certainly go a long way to prevent it," Madam Chien Shiung responded in almost an authoritative tone.

A few minutes later after paying well for Madam Chien Shiung's services and a healthy tip, Kabel Garr left her office and walked about a while thinking all those things she said, but he also knew part of this was his mission even though he knew he would have some regrets later if he had to do another *Call It Even.*

One thing Kabel knew, something was nagging at him to go back to the *Greifinn* restaurant and see Eva Erlaendsdottir again. But it was too early to go and see her, he decided to do what he experienced in the past. One quick way to see the sights quickly and get around efficiently was in a taxi tour.

Finding a Taxi was easy since Kabel was around a lot of office buildings in the heart of center city, and there were a few designated places for taxis to wait outside some major buildings to pick up rides. After a short walk, Kable walked up to the first Taxi in like and hopped in the back and asked the driver, "Do you do Taxi Tours?"

"I sure do, how much time do you want on the tour?"

"Can I see a lot in three hours?"

"Yes, I can get you to a lot of places in three hours."

"Okay let's go."

The driver took off with Kabel and they were soon driving around seeing the sights up close.

In a short while Kabel spotted another psychic office they passed by and noted the name of the establishment, then thought to ask the Taxi driver, "Do you know of any psychic healers around here?"

"Actually, I do," The Taxi driver said.

"Can you drive by there so I can see the name of the business and where its located?" Kabel asked.

"No problem, sir."

After a couple turns and drives down an adjacent street, the taxi pulled up to a building that had a psychic healer's office.

"Here it is, do you want to stop here?" The Taxi driver asked.

Kabel marked the location in his communicator and said, "No, I just wanted to know where this location is.

The cab driver continued the tour and, for a while, drove past Kerlara Symphony Hall and later the renown Kerlara Opera Theater.

Kabel Garr made note of these two locations and decided tomorrow morning he would approach Blemary and invite her to a Kerlara Symphony performance.

During the long drive, Kabel Garr thought a lot about what Madam Chien Shiung said. Instead of having him drop him off in front of the spiral building to enjoy Eva Erlaendsdottir singing at the *Greifinn* restaurant he got out of the Taxi in front of the *Norel Mozelle Resort*.

Kabel Garr didn't expect Blemary to be there as it was late in the day, and as he walked through the lobby, another receptionist was there working the next shift. Kabel Garr approached the person who had his picture up on her data terminal that Artificial Intelligence provided her. Kabel Garr could not see she was observing his file, since it was on the other side of the counter.

"Can I help you sir?"

"Yes, can you tell me how to get to the dining hall?"

"Walk past the elevators to the left and continue down the hallway that will curve to the right and it will take you right there."

"Thank you."

"You are welcome."

Kabel continued and it was quite simple to get there. Had he been in his resort room, his artificial intelligence Cornolius would have given him the simple directions.

When Kabel approached the dining hall, the maître d' was temporarily away, and the manager was there to greet him. The manager appeared somewhat stuffy and soon acted arrogant. By no stretch of the imagination was Kabel dressed like some of the patrons in the restaurant wearing his street clothes. Many of the people in the dining hall were dressed far more immaculately, especially the pleasure associates who accompanied their customers to the dining hall to give them more amiable experiences because it's no fun to dine alone.

"Do you have reservations?" the manager asked in a semi-condescending manner that Kabel picked up on.

"No, I do not."

"Let me see if I can find you a table, we are kind of busy now."

"Alright, I can wait."

The manager saw a couple get up and leave their seats. It wasn't cleaned off yet, but because of the way the customer was dressed the manager didn't think much of him or his behavior, said, "Follow me."

Kabel didn't like sitting down at a table that had not been cleaned off, but he didn't feel happy standing by who he discovered later was the manager.

In due time the table was cleaned off and Kabel ordered his drink and his meal which he consumed at a rather quick pace and just wanted to leave because he didn't feel comfortable especially with the manager observing him a few times as if he wanted him to finish and get the hell out of there. Kabel felt uncomfortable and had no issue with hustling and leaving.

Kabel went up to his room and took a nice soaking bath and decided to get an early sleep and get up and do his running and then inquire about the resort's swimming pool.

The evening shift receptionist looked over Kabel's file shortly after he passed by. She had talked with Blemary who showed interest in Kabel and asked her to keep an eye on his coming and going. She, just like Blemary, was quite surprised that Kabel had still not requested a pleasure associate.

The following morning was almost a repeat of the previous day. Kabel was up early in his running outfit that Cornolius arranged to be laundered for him when he was off visiting the psychic and experiencing the Taxi tour.

When Kabel left the resort there were other people in the lobby so he could not approach Blemary. But later when he came back covered in sweat, nobody else was around so he approached Blemary and asked her, "Do you like the symphony?"

"Yes, actually I do."

"I would like to take you to the symphony tomorrow."

"What time does it start."

"Around Four in the afternoon."

"My shift does not end until later in the day."

"Is there anyway someone could come in early and relieve you?"

"I suppose my friend could, but I would have to change clothes here before I go and leave directly from here."

"Alright, I'll meet you here about 30 minutes after three and we can Taxi from here."

"I'll be ready."

"I'm looking forward to it."

***

Kabel went to his room, took a shower, and changed into street clothes he wore here on the first day that had been dry cleaned. He then left the resort and got into a cab and went to the psychic healer after beaming the address to the taxi driver.

Randolf Cayce the psychic healer normally was referral only; it was quite unusual for him to take in a cold call, but the planets aligned. He had a loose schedule today and his customer just left and had no reservations for several more hours. When his receptionist Virginia Montane said there was a gentleman in the lobby who wished to have a consultation, he went out to the lobby and met Kabel Garr.

Soon Kabel Garr wase in Randolf Cayce's office privately discussing the matter at hand. Kabel gave Randolf Cayce an identical story he gave to Madam Chien Shiung.

While Randolf Cayce was thinking about Kabel's issues, and how to advise him, Kabel suddenly asked some questions.

"Doctor Cayce, how does Psychic healing work?"

Kabel, Psychic Healing is a process of energy healing when a psychic healer transfers their healing energy to someone who needs it."

"People exchange energy?" Kabel asked.

"Yes, you can think of it like a conversation between two people that takes place between two people, but instead of words, the psychic healer such as myself can remove energetic blockages and heal a person's aura from psychic traumas or spiritual wounds."

"Would my issue with my former lover be considered a trauma of some sort?" Kabel asked.

"Most definitely and of the acute type, most likely far more painful than a physical trauma or say a broken leg or a fractured skull."

"How do you go about doing this psychic healing and energy transfer?"

"To someone who is unfamiliar with psychic healing, this might be difficult for you to believe and understand, but it's how my special capability works."

"Since I'm not schooled in the process, I would have no way of knowing much about it and how it works," Kabel responded.

"The process involves using extrasensory perception (ESP) to identify negative energies hidden from normal senses," Randolph Casey said.

"What special abilities do you have to do this?" Kabel asked.

"My tools are telepathy and I have an intensity of clairvoyance."

"That would be inexplicable by the natural laws." Kabel said.

"In due time you will discover I have psychokinesis and kinematic teleportation," Randolph Casey said.

"Even though you have a lot of people that believe in your psychic abilities, the scientific community says there is no proof of it," Kabel Garr said.

"What matters most of all Kabel is what you believe and how you interact with me. If you believe, then you will discover that it works for you."

"I have no reason to disbelieve you, I'm willing to attempt it if I can resolve those issues we discussed."

"Alright, let's begin a session and see where it takes us," Randolph Casey said.

"I'm ready," Kabel responded.

"Layback on the sofa over here and close your eyes. I'm going to say some words with some background sound I'm going to play for you and the combination will put your mind into a state where I can transfer positive energy into it. You may even start sleeping and during that time it will all be accomplished."

"Alright," Dunbar said and moved to the sofa and laid down with his head raised at the end.

Slowly there was a strange sound that sounded like random noise with a low frequency imbedded into it probably 50 Hertz or lower.

In a while the content of the strange sound seemed to be loosening Dunbar's muscles creating soothing feelings. Dunbar felt like he was releasing all tension and the sound slowly helped create a soft warm peaceful feeling.

Dunbar was slowly drifting into deep relaxation, feeling totally at peace. The negative energy he now felt like it was flowing out of his body from his head all the way down to his toes.

Muscles in Dunbar's upper back down through his spine to the lower back, were relaxing and he felt like he was unwinding.

The new awareness and gentle peaceful and a soft warmth inner glow, allowed Dunbar to let go all of the negative energy so that it could leave his body.

Dunbar suddenly left the external world behind and entered an inner journey of his mind where billions of telepathic ensembles had been stored or visited through time and space in ways humans may not understand. The brain is a dumb terminal that God refreshes from a vast storage depository for us. In this new mental state, Dunbar had access to all of eternity from alpha to omega.

A voice said to Dunbar, "You will create in your own mind your personal security repository box. Visualize it so strong nobody but you can get into that container."

Dunbar suddenly visualized a strong steel box, just like a safe or security storage at the Transporter Directorate he often obtained or exchanged contents of super-secret materials like his current communicator he needed for this mission.

The voice now said, "All your worries and concerns will go into that security repository. Put all your anxiety's, worries, and concerns into that box and close the lid on the box and lock it so none of it can come out and nobody else can get in and tamper with the contents."

Right after Dunbar visualized closing the box he heard the strange voice say, "You are now totally free to relax and are now free of all life's burdens."

The voice Dunbar never heard before did not match Randolph Casey but there was nobody else in the room. Dunbar's conclusion is the voice was coming from his own mind.

"You are now more than your physical body. You can expand experience to know and understand and control and use greater energy systems you do not know exists. They are now available to you to heal all your mental wounds. You can release all the heartbreak from lost loves of your life, you know you have a few. It wasn't your fault you lost them. You were an innocent bystander, you are now free of that burden."

Kabel Garr (Dunbar) was feeling a splendid euphoria, like when he was enjoying hearing a great singing Diva he adored.

"You are now receiving beneficial and constructive positive energy for yourself and to those who follow your wisdom development and experience," The voice said exactly at the same time Dunbar started feeling something. He didn't quite know what it was, but he was feeling it.

"When you receive my positive energy, it will reduce the influence of anything that is less than your desires," The voice explained.

"Take your mind now back to a place long ago in peace like in a forest, or the shoreline, you are now in an expended reality you've never experienced."

"You can ask questions or ask for messages that will be coming to you in several ways. What is the most important thing you need to know and understand currently?"

Dunbar didn't know if he asked that question, but Randolph Casey fully heard the question and he answered it in the most subliminal fashion, this is what Dunbar was seeking.

Then after what seemed like a short eternity, Dunbar slowly came back to full consciousness.

By the time the session was over, Kabel felt amazingly better mentally and suddenly no longer had remorse and sad feelings about his former lover. Something strange happened in the session that made him start to think there was a lot more to this psychic healing than he could ever imagine.

That night, Kabel made his way back to hear Eva Erlaendsdottir sing at the *Greifinn* restaurant. He probably would not have come here had he not had the session with Randolf Cayce.

The evening transpired much like it did the previous two nights ago. Eva was dressed prettier and was hoping to see Kabel and feel his positive vibrations again.

Tonight, there was some flirtation but after drinks and dinner, Kabel made his way back to the *Norel Mozelle Resort* at a decent hour and spotted the second shift receptionist again in the lobby he met the night before. She had a funny look on her face because she knew this was the golden boy that Blemary was interested in, and he just might get lucky with her taking her to the symphony and no doubt figured dinner after the performance knowing the level of sophistication Kabel exhibited.

The second shift receptionist also noted Kabel still had not requested a pleasure associate, which means he wasn't into sex tourism and was here for other reasons even though he was paying a premium for his room that covered all expenses and amenities, including pleasure associates, the dining hall even with the condescending manager.

The next day unfolded again in a different manner. Unlike going out to a psychic and Taxi Tours, Kabel relaxed in his room, had room service to provide him a light lunch, then afterwards went for a swim in the resort large pool doing some laps.

Blemary had several data terminal screens and on one of them she could cycle through the security camera displays and capture any resort guest in case a friend was trying to contact them. The security system would locate the person in the resort if they were present and display them on one of the security displays Blemary could pull up Kabel on one of her auxiliary screens.

There was a brief period when Blemary was alone in the lobby and was focusing on Kabel which artificial intelligence had located out in the pool area. Now she could see him with his shirt off and all his muscles when he climbed out of the swimming pool after swimming laps. Kabel had a body to behold. Blemary was completely overwhelmed and secretly knew she would not be able to resist Kabel if he made a pass at her.

Knowing she was going out with Kabel that evening, Blemary was already starting to feel the moistness created by speculation of what Kabel might try to do with her. She was fair game. She would do her part to devour Kabel, so it would not all be one sided. She could be a lioness too if she wanted. She was well trained in her previous occupation.

In preparation for tonight's activities, Kabel had asked Cornolius, "What's the best way to rent a black-tie outfit because I'm going to the symphony with a lovely lady and afterwards take her to dinner at a nice restaurant."

"Kabel, we have patrons that have black-tie, and dresses delivered here for such occasions all the time."

"I'm not sure about my measurements, how would I pick the right size and I need formal shoes to match."

"Not a problem Kabel. Remove you clothes down to your underwear and I will produce a holograph of you and send it to one of the rental businesses we have an arrangement with."

After taking his measurements, Cornolius announced, "Kabel the black-tie and shoe rental will arrive in fifteen minutes, would you like to take a shower before the deliver arrives with you night's clothing."

"Not a bad idea. But I really do not like the way my hair looks and I do not have the hair products I would normally use to spiff up my image."

"The resort has a hairdresser and stylist on the staff, I can ask that person to be here after you try on your evening wear."

"Thanks that's perfect."

That afternoon after Blemary had changed into her nice evening gown and dressed for success, Kabel came out of the elevator wearing a rented black-tie suit and politely stood over at the corner waiting for her to finish her turnover with her friend who came in early so that she could go to the symphony.

The manager of the dining hall came out to the lobby, and he was always making suggestive comments to Blemary who knew he wanted to get into her pants but avoided the creep. The manager had never seen Blemary dressed up formally like this before. She had a hair style and looked like an utterly beautiful princess. The manager was in a state of shock observing Blemary and felt pangs of lust. He walked up to Blemary and asked, "Are you going somewhere special today?"

"Yes, I'm going to the symphony?"

"Really? Whose taking you?"

Blemary nodded at Kabel and said, "He is."

The dining hall manager turned around and spotted Kabel all dressed up smiling at the condescending asshole knowing the manager was getting quite a rush in discovering who the mystery man was.

There was quite a moment of amazement that Kabel caused because his great physical being filled out the black-tie suit in the most expressive manner. Blemary was impressed with the visual on her date, but the dining hall manager was equally impressed with the imagery and suddenly started thinking, *I remember him from last evening. Perhaps I was a little premature with my evaluation of him?*

This was quite an extraordinary development. With all the incredibly beautiful and capable pleasure corps working for the *Norel Mozelle Resort,* why would this client be wasting his time with the receptionist? Knowing the level of sophistication of the pleasure associates?

Kabel Garr standing in the lobby later waiting on Blemary to finish her turnover with her friend who had eyeballed her eye candy date, it was apparent the tailor for the clothing and the hair stylist had done their work exceptionally well. Not only did Kabel Garr impress the two women, the dining hall manager was equally impressed and could not help but think, *you cannot judge a book by its cover, because the cover can always be changed.*

Kabel Garr (aka Dunbar transporter directorate spy), was pleased the condescending manager was there to see him in his new posture, generating considerable reassessments.

Blemary was suddenly finished with her work and walked out behind the counter and over to Kabel carrying a small purse with a strap around her shoulder, walked up to him and held her hand. "Shall we go?"

"I would be delighted, Blemary."

The dining hall manager stood there totally stunned as he observed the evil grin that Blemary shot at him.

The couple walked out the front entrance of the *Norel Mozelle Resort* and Kabel asked the bel hop to hail a Taxi for them. Moments later the couple were on their way to the Kerlara Symphony located in the civic center area.

When the Taxi pulled up in front of the Kerlara Symphony venue, Blemary was about as excited as she had been almost in her entire life. She waited for the day she could experience an event like this.

Kabel Garr had reserved balcony seats with a great view of the orchestra. The communicator he had, contained the temporary wallet file that had a blockchain like code which was the index into his wallet, the front entrance automatically read allowing him and his partner to enter the building and gave a verbal information as to where their seats were located and simple directions. He was also informed to follow the green blinking lights slowly flashing in the overhead in front of him like a runway lighting system. Other concert goers were given different colors, so a dozen people were guided simultaneously to their seats with the visual aid. Visually impaired people were escorted.

When they arrived at their balcony seating area, the two reserved seats had a flashing green light on them which continued flashing until they sat down. The multi-colored light emitting device could flash any of the standard dozen colors allowing multiple people to arrive at the same time. If they sat down on the wrong seats, momentarily an usher would arrive and redirect them.

Thanks to the reserved seating and the timing of arrival only a few minutes passed before the lights started dimming. Out in the middle of the stage surrounded by the orchestra was what people on planet Earth would consider a grand piano. In fact, it was such a Steinway model purchased by black marketeers. They also acquired sheet music for orchestras. The names and composers were counterfeited to a local composer. Nobody in the concert new the origination of the music was from planet Earth.

The music started and it was delightful. The concert pianist was interpreting Rachmaninoff Piano Concerto number two. The concerto started out with the piano by itself at first, then after thirty-six seconds the orchestra blended into the composition creating a euphoric sensation in both Blemary and Kabel Garr. Anyone who ever heard Anna Fedorova or Yuja Wang perform this piece would know the exquisite nature of the performance.

What Madam Chien Shiung warned Kabel now manifested. He likely might not have gone down this pathway to Blemary's enlightenment, but Randolf Cayce created another cerebral epitome for a tempestuous relationship bestowed on Blemary and Kabel Garr.

This event now cast a dye that would bequeath Kabel Garr more than he bargained for. Kabel Garr didn't have to say a word. The music did all the talking for him. The melody was the poet, the piano was the swan, and the performer was the love goddess with a great aim with her bow and arrow.

When the French horn like instrument started playing a melody that framed the following piano transcendence, Blemary was moist and ready. She was utterly powerless to stop any advances Kabel might make upon her tonight. She secretly savored his kiss she knew was coming. Then the rupture would burst upon the seams and the splendid euphoria would follow. Blemary knew this without any doubt in her mind.

The beautiful female virtuoso striking the keyboard in the second movement, *Adagio sostenuto – Pia animato – Tempo*, created a virtual transcendence for Blemary that evoked her passions and created a unique feeling she had never felt before. Kabel was either a genius at picking this particular concert, or it was astonishing plane luck.

In Dunbar Regvik (Alias Kabel) strategic planning, there was the seduction in a honey pot scheme he did to create an imagery to explain why he wasn't utilizing some of the most beautiful pleasure associates on the planet in the notorious the *Norel Mozelle Resort* in the event he attracted the attention of authorities.

Unfortunately, along the way he created casualties of the heart. Even though he was semi infatuated with this gorgeous creature sitting next to him that would likely coitus with him tonight after dinner, in the back of his mind, he had utter lust for the singing diva cabaret singer, Eva Erlaendsdottir. Risking a failure of a pursuit with Eva, Kabel had decided to take Blemary to the *Greifinn* restaurant after the concert to hear Eva sing. Kabel wanted Eva's songs in his mind in the event he was making love to Blemary later that night.

As Kabel Garr further analyzed the situation, he knew he could not take Blemary to his resort room and have an affair because, she had to protect her reputation. No doubt rumors were already swirling around by the diner manager and her friend that came in early tonight to relieve her so she could attend the concert. He didn't want to give the Norel Mozelle Resort staff any further ammunition.

What Kabel had already achieved was sufficient to throw off any investigators looking into why a guy with a lot of money staying at a *Love Hotel* wasn't enjoying the world renown beautiful *Norel Mozelle Resort* pleasure associates.

Kabel would have to put that activity off for a later day. He would have to do it somewhere else and would thus start researching an overnight trip of sightseeing and love making far away from the *Norel Mozelle Resort* and people that would be fueled to speculate and exaggerate the relationship between him and Blemary.

Kabel Garr grasped another major fact that was pounded into his thoughts by his trainers: desire is ten times more powerful than gratification. Hence save the gratification for *the last act.*

During the third movement Allegro scherzando (E major shift to C minor then shift to C major) the sound was so powerful that it resonated Blemary's soul and she could feel her body vibrate from that resonation. She reached down and grabbed Kabel's hand and held it tight. She almost felt like she was going to start having an orgasm, her feelings and emotions were on overload. Then without expectation the concerto ended, and the lights slowly turned brighter and the concert pianist stood and started long bows to thunderous applause.

Belmary's eyes had watered up a tad during the final moments of the piano concert and knew she was screwing up her makeup, so she said, "I think I need to visit the restroom."

"There is one just outside the balcony," Kabel said remembering passing it on the way. Then he added, "Would you like me to order you a drink while you are using the restroom."

"Sure, whatever you are drinking will be fine," Blemary said, then departed out behind the balcony and quickly found the private restroom. While she was fixing her makeup thanks to having the small purse with her, she also did her tinkle and was utterly stunned how wet Kabel had caused her. She was ready for whatever he was going to dish out to her tonight and anyway he wanted to enjoy her. In her previous occupation she learned all the exotic methods to please men and if they went down lover's lane tonight, Kabel who seemed reserved and conservative in nature would be in for a big surprise!

Waiters hit the balcony seats because that's where all the big spenders were, and they needed immediate attention and get their drinks early because most of the time they would have a second before the intermission ended.

"Excuse me sir, can I get you something to drink?" the waiter asked Kabel.

"Yes, I would like two glasses of *Jangovian de Palentin*, one for me and one for my lady friend who will be back shortly."

"Coming right up," the waiter said then left."

Before the waiter returned with their drinks, Blemary returned to her seat looking all fresh from her fast makeover to fix her makeup she screwed up during her emotional reaction a few minutes prior.

The waiter then appeared and handed Kabel and Blemary their drinks then walked back over to the side of the balcony looking for nearby concert goers that might flag him for service.

"Skål min kære [cheers my dear]," Kabel said in Rinisp dialect of the standard *Stanzel* language as he tapped Belmary's glass."

"For alle dine fornøjelser [For all your pleasures]," Blemary replied.

Blemary didn't know what she was drinking, but she knew a couple things. It was most likely very expensive, and it tasted excellent but seemed to be like elixir's her wealthy clients gave her while she was a pleasure associate at a *Love Hotel*.

While Kabel and Blemary drank the delightful *Jangovian de Palentin*, the circular floor section holding the piano like device, lowered below the stage where workers moved it off the platform on a lower level, then sent the false floor back up via its hydraulic lifte to its performance level that had the conductors stand and an open area for the next performer a virtuoso violinist. The orchestra had wandered off stage for a few minutes, in some cases making restroom visits and in other cases to obtain refreshments' and enjoying the company of other musicians until they were summoned back out onto the stage for the next performance.

Moments after the orchestra was seated the conductor walked back out onto stage generating applause as he walked up to where he would lead the orchestra on the circular platform. The conductor turned and bowed towards the audience. Moments later a violin virtuoso walked out onto the stage. The woman was taller than many other women and had that rare combination of feminine beauty and a simply fantastic violinist virtuoso ability second to none.

Today as it all unfolded and the violinist started performing, Blemary would feel a spontaneous eruption as she soon listened to the wonderful performance with a great view from the balcony. The combination of the pleasurizers in the *Jangovian de Palentin* elixir had a major impact on Blemary.

The music was indeed a Tchaikovsky knock off from black marketeers. The orchestra only had this concerto a couple years to practice before tonight's performance. This performance was a very powerful, heartfelt, unusual, and very emotional with love for the masterpiece of one of a great composer by the audience.

As the violinist started the violin portion of *Allegro moderato in D major* then the first clue indicated this was going to be a performance highly regarded. At around the 3:30 mark in the music the love tendrils flew out of the piece that seemed to tell a story and paint an image in Belmary's mind that conveyed the essence of the personification of her growing feelings towards Kabel Garr the Transporter Spy she had no idea existed.

An Earth person observing this performance would quickly surmise the violinist image approximated the virtuoso Hilary Hahn who resonated numerous audiences with her great interpretation of Tchaikovsky's composition.

The second movement, Canzonetta: Andante (G minor) felt mildly depressing to Blemary. It was a sudden huge letdown to her, but that's life in general, that flows in waves in peaks and valleys.

Finally, the third movement Allegro vivacissimo (D major) began with a blast. What a contrast! However, it never did meet or exceed the first movement. Blemary was now experiencing gratification. She had already used up all her desire for this music. It was a fine example of what happens in love. Crisp at first, then decline and disappointment in the end. This is precisely why Kabel Garr was likely not willing to hop in the sack with Blemary that night, because he wanted that desire to linger for a while. Desire enhances honey pot schemes. Gratification does not.

Blemary's urge to please me will remain stronger while the desire lasts, Kabel thought. Once gratification occurred, it would follow the violin concerto in all its phases with the logical conclusion that once satisfied, Blemary would likely be less eager to do all those strange things Kabel may call up on her and request she do that may have a huge impact on the outcome of his current circumstances.

But then Kabel Garr started questioning his own willpower. Some of what happened today with Randolf Cayce the psychic healer led him to think beyond the boundaries of the mission and obtain that gratification.

As the applause began, knowing an encore would be demanded and offered, Kabel suggested, "Let's leave now and avoid the crowd."

"Certainly," Blemary replied.

The two left the Kerlara Symphony building and went directly to the curb ahead of them where a string of Taxis were waiting to pick up the concert goers with the concert letting out now.

The two hopped in a waiting taxi with the door open and a symphony hall employee there to assist Taxi riders shut the vehicle's door after they were each safely inside the Taxi.

"Where would you like to go to sir?" The Taxi driver asked.

"We are on our way to the *Greifinn* restaurant at the top of the spiral Highrise building in the City Center," Kabel answered.

"Alright sir," the driver answered, and the vehicle started moving forward.

The driver drove on the upper end of the speed limit as he wanted to take his ride to their destination promptly and get back to pick up a second set of passengers since the symphony was just over and he would have the opportunity to get a second customer.

It seemed like less than five minutes the Taxi pulled up in front of the spiral building complex. The Taxi company charged Kabel's wallet on his personal communicator automatically the fee posted on the back of the front seat display which Kabel pressed yes to the charges and recommended tip.

A person at the Taxi drop-off-stand working for the Spiral Building center opened the Taxi door and Kabel led Blemary out of the Taxi.

By now Kabel was very familiar with this location and led Blemary to the express elevator they got into that took them to the top of the building promptly while they observed out the glass enclosure towards a beautiful sunset.

Soon they were in the restaurant Kabel made reservations for approximately fifteen minutes from now. As he approached the Matre d' *Sophia* who was working today, she developed a very nice smile. She had never seen Kabel dressed up formally. She had observed the flirting between Kabel and the cabaret singer Eva Erlaendsdottir who was dressed smoking hot tonight in full anticipation of seeing Kabel. She was in for a big surprise, not of the type she desired observing a man she had sudden interest in with a good-looking bimbo.

With or without reservation Sophia was taking Kabel to an unobstructed view to the performers. She had a hint of jealousy and wanted to rub it in Eva's face that her new boy toy wasn't what she thought he was, and she knew this was going to be one of those *moments* for the singer.

They were soon seated and the illustrious waitress server Embla looking smoking hot as well, quickly approached them after Sophia seated them and asked if they would like a drink. Blemary was feeling elevated and sensual and decided to get an elixir she knew might make her promiscuous tonight and said, "I would like a *Lotus Dragon*."

Embla raised her eyebrows a bit as this was a sport drink for women that were in the heat of the battle with their lover who wanted the extra buzz to manifest a mood for emotional recreation.

"I'll go with a *Jangovian de Palentin* elixir," Kabel said next.

Embla said, "I'll have your drinks momentarily." She then turned and walked away and thought, *today is going to be Eva's day* knowing when she returned from the kitchen after her break and a quick snack the chef provided her would be in for a surprise about the man, she had a crush on.

This was both good and bad for Eva Erlaendsdottir who was dressed for success to the point she charmed the chef when she went to the kitchen to receive her just reward for packing the restaurant and creating an atmosphere the attracted plenty of well-paying clientele.

Eva was wearing a black well-tailored pant suit. Her legs fit the pants that fit her thin legs and showcased her perfectly aligned buttocks with a degree of perfection. The high heel shoes added height that gave an overall majestic appearance. The elegant black top had long sleeves and was split down to almost the middle of her abdomen. If she put her hands on her sides, they would go to where the split begins. One third of her breasts of perfect geometry was shown that illustrated her full body suntan.

Eva's jewelry contrasted with the black designer clothes very nicely and caused more spectacular reflections.

The singing diva Eva Erlaendsdottir gave off an aura of splendid beauty and the little heads of every male present could not avoid the affects her marvelous radiance.

Eva's makeup, her hair, her clothes, her perfume, everything was perfectly put into place. Eva was disappointed when she spotted Kabel with the bimbo, but she blamed herself for not being more aggressive in her conquest with Kabel Garr. *Maybe had I just given him the proper signals he would be sitting alone waiting for me and I could have asked him if he wanted to go on a date or a vacation together?*

Eva told herself, *don't read more into it than what you see, he obviously came back to see me sing, so there must be some infatuation. Perhaps I need to be patient?*

Kabel was enjoying his *Jangovian de Palentin* elixir that was enhanced by the beautiful singer he knew would resonate in his consciousness and give him great feelings with her incredible singing voice.

Blemary was a very bright woman, had been around the block and in social circles with rich and famous when she was sometimes taken along with wealthy men who had to surround themselves with beautiful women to give an image to those he wanted to impress. She also intuitively understood body language and quickly observed a distinct focus on Kabel by the beautiful and exotic singer.

In the entertainment business, sometimes singers focus on a person in the audience to give the impression they were singing to that individual to make the crowd feel the personal affiliation. It was fake but it worked. This trick helped with stage fright and removed all the distractions from their minds.

Blemary didn't think that was the case. She understood women and had been around a lot of gold diggers in the past and could see a look of conquest on Eva's face whom she had not met and had no idea who she was nor would she think Kabel had any sort of relationship with this extraordinary exotic singer that commanded the little heads of every male in the audience.

The restaurant was filling up fast as there was a growing constituency that came out to watch Eva Erlaendsdottir performance. Her singing alone was enough to attract them. Her feminine allure provided the exclamation point. There was no doubt in the restaurant managers mind this place will fill to maximum capacity real fast and the patrons were more than happy to pay the stiff price for their food and drinks to get the chance to watch Eva's performance.

This truly was a concert that also served food and drinks at private tables. The band was excellent, the pianist, base violin, and other instruments used during the various segments of the show created a cabaret atmosphere second to none.

Blemary could see the intense focus of Kabel by the beautiful singer. There smiles towards each other were full of unsaid messages. This behavior between this exotic singer and her date only made Blemary want Kabel even more because when a top talent singer is interested in your man of interest, that conveys he has some tangible qualities you too might want to experience. The full spectrum and fabric of the growing relationship between Eva Erlaendsdottir and Kabel Garr was unknown, but Blemary had been around and see her fair share of barracuda's go after men like Kabel Garr.

It would be impossible for Blemary to believe this super-hot singer would take such intense interest in her date since he had only been in the city of Kerlara a very short time. To Blemary, there was no way that such a relationship could possibly exist and this smoking hot woman wanting Kabel in such a short period of time. Little did she know in their few times of socializing, Eva Erlaendsdottir had developed unmistakable feelings for Kabel.

In due time the surprise would become evident.

During the first two songs, the waiter Embla took their food orders and by the time the second song was completed, Embla was serving the couple a refill and moments later their meals.

The musicians performed for fifty minutes before they took a break. During this time Blemary and Kabel had just finished their meals that were semi light but very tasty. Embla cleaned off their table, replaced the tablecloth and the table had the freshness to help create the ambience that flowed. The two sat there enjoying the moment when the break occurred with their drinks almost finished when Eva did her usual journey through the audience greeting all her fans then approached Kabel's table.

"Hello Kabel, how are you doing this evening."

"Hello Eva, let me introduce you to my friend Blemary."

Eva smiled at Blemary and held out her hand and said, "It's so nice to meet you Blemary."

Reality was not hitting Blemary, she knew those smiles at Kabel were not simply stage antics performers did. She knew Kabel Garr did not smile without some sort of enticement!

"It's nice to meet you as well," Blemary almost had to force out her statement.

"Would you like to join us for a drink?" Kabel quickly offered.

Embla was secretly enjoying the sight, pleased that Eva was losing the conquest of love. Embla was envious of Eva who was several social stratums above her and sometimes acted condescending towards Embla.

This was the sight of a wild cat on a hot tin roof. The psychological parley and dancing at the table between the women could not be ignored. Being with the two hottest looking women in the restaurant also caused more eyes on Kabel looking rather handsome in his black tie and great hair style perfect for the occasion.

"I enjoyed your singing," Blemary said to give an appearance of someone who had no fear of such an exotic cat on the hot tin roof sitting between her and Kabel because of the placement of the additional chairs.

"Thank you very much. I always love feedback from the audience that is nice like this."

"You are welcome, Blemary forced the words out to be social."

"You look so pretty Blemary. You are all dressed up looking luxurious. Did you just do something special?"

"Yes, we went to the symphony, and we are here for dinner."

"I bet that was quite entertaining."

"The first performance had a pianist who really set the mood of the audience. Her performance was rather spectacular."

"That sounds great."

"The second performer was a violinist. The first half of her performance was fantastic, but the composition took a dive in the middle that screwed up the tapestry in my mind. The final movement started out with a bang, but it tailored off and could never bring back the satisfaction I felt in the first half of the performance."

"That's the danger of a grand opening. It creates too much expectation and if the performer doesn't keep up the tempo and the quality, it has a negative effect," Eva said in acute analysis.

Blemary decided now would be the perfect time to take a shot across the bow, so to speak and said, "You had a fantastic opening, can you keep it up to the end?"

Kabel knew this could deteriorate quickly and right then decided when they started the dancing in a short while when most of the dinners were finished, he would not stick around, because he could see smoke rising between the two women. And where there is smoke there usually is a fire that could quickly get out of hand.

The conversations lingered into the end of the break just when the dancing began, and the showoffs hit the dance floor. Blemary wasn't disappointed that Kabel didn't ask her to dance and stick around for that entertainment and instead said, "I think I'm ready to leave. How about you?"

"Yes, let's leave," Blemary said wanting to get out of the restaurant before the next break because she knew Eva would make a bee line to their table and continue her flirtation with Kabel, which she did not appreciate.

Eva was slightly disappointed watching the couple leave while she was in the middle of a love song, she was personally singing to Kabel. But she knew Kabel would be back and the next time he would not have that bimbo Blemary with him.

When the couple was in the Taxi leaving the spiral building, the Taxi asked, "Where to sir?"

"Just a minute," Kabel replied.

"Blemary, I'm going to take you home first so that I know you arrived safely."

"Thank you. Where are you going after you drop me off? Back to see the singer?"

"No, I'm going back to my room, take a bath, go to bed and get up in the morning and go do my workout."

"When can I see you again?" Blemary asked.

"It's obvious that we must protect your reputation, so I'm thinking about an out-of-town trip, I think I might want to invite you on."

"Where do you want to take me?"

"I'll surprise you. I need to investigate a few things to figure out exactly where it is. Can you leave for a couple of days?"

"Certainly."

"Alright, tomorrow sometime, I'll tell you what I have in mind, and you can let me know your schedule so we can fit it in."

"Sounds good," Blemary said and was happy that Kabel was being a perfect gentleman. She knew she could not resist him tonight and if he went up to her apartment and suggested they do some boom-boom, she would not be able to say no.

Blemary gave the location of her apartment building to the Taxi driver. The location was within easy walking distance to the *Norel Mozelle*

Resort and could easily walk to work which she did and did not have to rely on public transportation or a personal vehicle.

The Taxi pulled up in front of Blemary's apartment in a driveway making it easy to get out of the taxi by the front entrance. Kabel opened the door and got out and stood waiting for Blemary to get out of the Taxi.

When Blemary exited the Taxi, she approached Kabel a few feet away and said, "Thank you very much for such a good time. Would you like to come up to my apartment?

"I would, but I know I must leave now because I'm not sure I could control myself."

"What makes you sure I wouldn't want you to lose control?"

"It doesn't matter. You are a nice lady I respect, and I want to get to know you and when the time is right, we will both know."

Blemary grabbed Kabel and hugged him and said, "Thank you for such a wonderful time. I really enjoyed myself and I'm glad I met such a nice guy."

"The pleasure was all mine," Kabel said, then kissed Blemary on the cheek and then re-entered the Taxi and went back to his resort room.

Blemary knew to give Kabel some time to take care of his business and bathe or shower, so in about an hour she called the *Norel Mozelle Resort*. Her friend was still working that relieved her early so she could go to the symphony.

Norel Mozelle Resort, may I help you? The receptionist answered.

"Hello this is Blemary."

The receptionist recognized Blemary's voice and responded, "Oh hello Blemary, how was you evening?"

"It was fabulous. I had a fantastic time."

"Is Kabel Garr a good guy? He looked very handsome."

"Oh yes he's a great guy, I like him a lot."

"You will have to tell me about it when we get together again."

"I will."

"Anything else?"

"This might sound strange, but I already miss him. Could you transfer my call to his room?"

"That's not strange at all dear, I would feel like you too. He came through the lobby about 45 minutes ago, so he should be up in his room. Do you want me to transfer the call, in holographic mode?"

"Oh yes because I really desire seeing him."

"Okay dear we'll talk tomorrow, and you can tell me about the symphony. I'll transfer you now."

"Thank you."

A moment later, Cornolius popped up just after Kabel entered his bed with his sleeping clothes on and asked, "Blemary wishes to talk to you in holographic mode, do you wish to accept the call?"

"Certainly."

Within about two seconds, Blemary's holograph was showing a short distance away from Kabel giving the appearance she was in the room reclining on her sofa.

"Hello Kabel."

"How are you doing Blemary?"

"I'm doing really well and am still excited about the evening we spent together."

"I enjoyed it too."

"I'm not going to take up much of your time. I just wanted to call you and say hello and thank you for making me feel special today."

"Well, you are special."

"That's very nice. Thank you."

"You are most welcome."

"Alright Kabel, it looks like you are resting and getting ready to sleep so I will hang up now. I hope you sleep well and have a great day tomorrow."

"Thank you, I appreciate that."

"Good night Kabel."

The holograph then faded. Both Blemary and Kabel were feeling good because they had an enjoyable experience which the symphony helped to create. In the case of Kabel he had an additional level of satisfaction hearing a Diva sing in a way he felt she was secretly messaging him with the appearance she was singing directly for him. In fact, Eva did sing tonight to Kabel Garr.

***

Chapter Four

The Adventure Begins

Kabel woke up automatically in the morning by himself and took care of his morning business and put on his workout clothes.

Cornolius informed Kabel, "While you were sleeping, I returned you black tie suit and shoes."

"Thanks."

"Kabel, are you going for your morning exercise?"

"Yes, and afterwards I am going to swim in the pool after I rest."

"Did you enjoy your evening?"

"I did it was fun."

"Kabel, as your room assistant its my duty to look out for your best interests and inform you about information I think you should know."

"Alright."

"Any time you leave your resort room, the resort security system monitors your activities. Since I'm your room supervisor, I'm sent all the imagery from the security system that pertains to you in case I need to inform you of important information."

"Alright."

"Kabel, I observed you leaving with Blemary with your black tie and suit, and she was dressed up for the event you took her."

"Yes, I took her to the Symphony, and later to dinner."

"Kabel, I cannot violate her privacy, but I will tell you I know she likes you."

"I'm aware she likes me."

"Kabel did you have a good time with Blemary."

"I most certainly did, I enjoyed her company very much."

"Kabel, I have a lot of videos of Blemary, she is a very nice person, and the staff likes her. If you think highly of her, may I make a recommendation?"

"Sure."

"Send her some flowers."

"Good idea."

"Kabel, do you wish for me to arrange to have flowers sent to Blemary."

"Yes, please do that, and thank you for the tip."

"My pleasure Kabel, and since you have avoided using the pleasure associates, my algorithms have concluded that I hope you and Blemary experience the satisfaction you would otherwise obtain with a pleasure associate."

"If it happens it happens. I'm just going to let things run their course and I'll find out where it takes me."

"That's a good way to look at it Kabel. I've obtained a considerable amount of information on psychoanalysis and what is important for humans to experience pleasure. Your careful approach in this matter has been wise.

"Cornolius, I'm thinking about taking a two-day trip on a tourist train ride. While I'm out exercising, could you please do me a favor and find out what tourist trains are available nearby I do not have to travel far to reach and an have a private cabin with amenities to take Blemary on an overnight trip."

"Kabel, I will research tourist train rides for you and when you come back, I will have all your options. When do you want to take this trip?"

"As soon as I find out when Blemary can take off a couple days."

"That should be soon, based on Blemary's schedule she should have some leisure time coming up."

"Alright, I'm leaving now for my exercise. I'll be back later."

"Enjoy your day Kabel."

"Thank you Cornolius."

When Kabel walked out of the elevator and walked into the resort lobby there were a half dozen guests in the lobby some checking out, others waiting to meet up with friends and relatives.

Blemary could not communicate with Kabel at this moment because they were not alone, but she gave him a heartfelt warm smile as he passed by and smiled back to her. Observing Kabel in his workout clothes heading out to exercise made Blemary's heart feel pitter pat. She truly liked Kabel who had already gone a long way to prove he was a gentleman and did not take advantage of her.

Blemary thought Kabel understood he could have had celestial feasting with her last night, leaving her panting like a bitch in heat, but true to his mannerism, he took the gentlemanly approach, soft and deliberate in a way neither of them could ever regret. It was a refreshing manner in how he operated with no demands while conducting himself in a chivalrous manner providing a great night of food and entertainment.

Kabel was away for more than two hours traversing a total of seven miles, that included the distance to the park and back. When he returned there was a wonderful flower bouquet sitting on the counter where Blemary sat by on a tall stool in front of her multiple computer data terminals where she handled guests' files.

Kabel saw the huge smile on Blemary's face. What Kabel didn't know was no man had ever given Blemary flowers before. She had been mistreated working as a pleasure associate and had never received male companionship, let alone sweetness like this before in her life.

Looking at Kabel, Blemary experienced special feelings and admiration because he was so thoughtful. Unfortunately, the rude dining hall manager walked into the lobby exactly at the same time as Kabel was walking near the receptionist desk and several people also walked from the elevator, so it was another moment they could not speak, but the smiles said it all.

After Kabel left the lobby and went to the elevator the dining hall manager spotted the flowers and a nice card attached to them and asked, "Where did those flowers come from?"

"From the gentleman wearing the black tie yesterday."

"Is that so? He must be a heck of a guy."

"He is, he just passed you a minute ago with his workout clothes on and very sweaty."

The manager turned around and walked back to the dining hall where he was almost bored to tears. But he knew that in a brief period, the wonder boy would be gone and Blemary would start getting lonely.

Kabel went up to his room, took a quick shower and changed into street clothes but rested for a while before he went back out.

As Kabel was reclining and relaxing with the room seemingly empty, he asked, "Cornolius, what kind of sky tours are available here in Kerlara?"

The artificial intelligence Cornolius was always listening and watching immediately popped up in the form of a holograph.

"Kabel, I'm checking now and will give you various options."

"Thank you."

"Kabel, I also want to inform you, I've done some extensive research in tourist train trips and after I give you options on a sky tour, would you like me to present them now?"

"Yes, give me my options on the train trip first."

It soon became apparent to Kabel his only option was to take the train one way over night and fly back the following evening with Blemary. He chose that option now it was nothing more than integrating the plan into Blemary's work schedule.

Next on the agenda was sky tours. A list of a dozen tours offered was provided and the one that caught Kabel's fancy was Kerlara Visitors Vision (KVV) Company. *Norel Mozelle Resort* had Vertical takeoff and landing (VTOL) on top of the main hotel and resort building via elevator access with special permit. A *Norel Mozelle Resort* employee would escort a guest and unlock the VTOL access door when a scheduled flight came in. Kabel could purchase the tour and schedule it via Cornolius.

"Go ahead and book me a tour. When is the next one available?"

"In three hours."

"That will work. Maybe I'll change into some swim gear and workout at the pool and have lunch there."

Within a moment Cornolius said, "Kabel, your tour has been booked. You will be the only person on the flight."

"That's good, does that mean I get to sit up front with the pilot?"

In a couple seconds, after Cornolius made inquiry the answer came back, "Yes you may."

In a short while Kabel changed into his swim gear, a resort swim robe and slippers and headed down to the pool. He didn't require anything else because everything was done via facial recognition and all the food and drinks came as amenities with the reservation.

Blemary programmed into surveillance monitoring in Kabel's file to track him throughout the resort and Cornolius in the background detected those protocols and determined to advance Kabel's pleasure experience assisted Blemary as his algorithms determined Blemary would be the source of his pleasure and not the pleasure associates that would normally be part of a single man's stay at the resort.

The lobby was empty at the time. No clients were arriving or leaving. Blemary was enjoying her flower arrangement, she knew was driving the dining room manager nuts because she had a boyfriend, and the creep manager wasn't going to get to first base any time soon. Suddenly Blemary received an alert, and it opened showing Kabel walking through the resort dressed to go to the pool.

Kabel arrived at the pool and picked out a recliner with a shade umbrella near the pool's edge. He took off the hotel supplied robe and slipped out of his padded slippers and walked over to pools edge and did the smart way to adapt to the shift in temperature and dove into the water and began swimming laps.

Kabel knew he was a spy and had a mission to accomplish and that was only half of it. The other half was leaving the planet and getting home alive. Those were two challenges. He had to maintain his physical condition because he could run into some bad-asses and his life depended on safe egress tactics requiring him to remain in tip top physical condition.

After swimming to exhaustion Kabel walked up the steps at the end of the pool that was close to his recliner and table and umbrella for shade.

The manager not only had responsibility for the dining hall, he also oversaw the outdoor bar and grill that took care of the numerous swimmers utilizing the pool or people simply working on their tan, drinking elixirs and eyeballing the sexy women that accompanied their charges. These pleasure associates often were asked to hang out with the men and that was more than fine for them because if they were lounging at the pool and drinking with a guest that meant they were spending less time on their backs doing the horizontal tango.

Several of the pleasure associates as well as barracudas there taken back observing Kabel swim the laps to exhaustion then come out of the pool to his recliner showing off his six-pack abs. Kabel appeared like a stud-muffin. The barracudas that had long term leases on penthouses and took satisfaction in the male pleasure associates wondered if this man was a guest or an employee taking care of a woman. They would find out.

The female pleasure associates accompanying their fat bald lazy people looked on wondering the same thing. If this man with a great body was indeed a client, they would be very anxious to volunteer to be his pleasure associate. They would even be willing to spend time with him without receiving generous tips.

Kabel laid back on the padded recliner for a bit just relaxing letting his muscles discharge the lactic acid built up with the exertion hoping he would not get a cramp and wishing he could get a massage about now. After fifteen minutes Kabel recovered and set up and switched from his recliner to a chair at the umbrella table and signaled a waiter.

"Yes sir, what can I get for you?"

"I would like a menu please."

"Yes sir, right away."

The waiter walked over to the bar where the manager was standing next to his friend the bartender simply socializing and watching the man do the swimming.

"See that man that was just swimming?" the manager asked the bartender.

"Yea, what about him?"

"He took Blemary out last night."

"Really? Did he get lucky?"

"I was utterly shocked, he had on black tie and suit, and Blemary left work in an evening gown all dressed up with a fantastic hair style."

"How did she look?"

"She looked better than any of our pleasure associates."

"Wow!"

"Yea you have no idea how great Blemary can dress up."

"I can see her attraction in him, one hell of a body."

"I bet he screwed the hell out of her last night because guess what happened today?"

"What?"

"I walked into the lobby and there was a beautiful bouquet of flowers he sent her sitting up on the counter with a card on it. I couldn't read the card because it was in an envelope, but I'm sure it stated something to the fact he had a great night. She was beaming all morning after those flowers were delivered."

"I bet she was."

"At first, I thought he was some kind of jerk, a nobody of consequence. None of the pleasure associates have been with him."

"None?"

"Not a single one."

"He's paying a gigantic amount of money to not be satisfied by a pleasure associate."

"Not really. He has the best woman in the place."

"Who's that?"

"Blemary."

"Damn."

"If you saw her dressed up yesterday, you would say double damn."

"She looks cute even when she's not dressed up."

"You have no idea how pretty Blemary can get."

"Hot stuff?"

"She would burn your fingers, she's that hot."

The manager and the bartender observed from a distance the guest at the pool. In due time Kabel Garr was eating and drinking.

Blemary was intermittently watching all this. She noted Kabel was not paying attention to anyone just eating, drinking relaxing and a while after he finished eating, he went back to swimming again. He truly worked hard at it and after his last efforts, climbed out of the pool and put his robe and sandals on and departed back to his room.

Kabel's body was in the best shape of any man Blemary ever saw.

Blemary monitored Kabel Garr's whereabouts for a while then suddenly Blemary discovered a VTOL was landing on the roof for their client Kabel Garr. Blemary didn't know this was simply a sky tour. It added to her fascination with him. Kabel did not return until her friend came into the resort lobby area to reliever her for the next shift.

The two women discussed her experience with Kabel Garr and when her friend heard all the very nice tributes to this great guy developed a unique perspective.

Blemary forgot to close the security screen before she left so her friend soon was going through all the alerts in her spare time and when she saw Kabel Garr working out, she too suddenly had a fascination.

***

Kabel Garr was sitting next to the pilot getting an exclusive tour since the VTOL craft was very light with lack of passengers making it much easier to control.

Kabel stepped up into the VTOL craft that had an automatic door opened for him.

After Kabel stepped up and into the VTOL aircraft, the pilot asked, "Are you Kabel Garr?"

"Yes sir, I am."

"Great. Be sure and latch your shoulder harness safety belt before we take off."

"Alright." Kabel replied.

The pilot said, "There are a set of binoculars mounted in a holder in front of you. When you take it out of the holder, be sure and put the strap around your neck."

"Will do," Kabel replied.

"The binoculars will send the imagery you see to your communicator so you can watch what you see again at a later date."

"That's really nice to know, thanks," Dunbar replied.

As the VTOL craft flew Kabel Garr and the pilot around the city to see all the landmarks, Kabel Garr looked down at the spiral building where the *Greifinn* restaurant existed at the top of the building. Kabel could see the building was set up just like the *Norel Mozelle Resort* building with a VTOL landing pad on the very top with elevator access.

"On our way back do you think you can drop me off at the spiral building with the *Greifinn* restaurant?" Kabel asked.

"Sure, I take people there all the time. Just let me know about fifteen minutes before you want to land there so I can contact them and arrange to have someone unlock the elevator for you and escort you down. Are you going to the *Greifinn* restaurant today? the pilot asked.

"Yes, that's my intentions," Kabel answered.

"Alright," the pilot replied.

This really was an INTEL almost ISR like mission but totally innocuous. *Latrodectus* was working in the background collecting significant amount of data in mission files Dunbar's communicator provided with the expanded memory.

VTOL tours was something tourists do every day, but to have a well-trained spy looking over the lay of the land, the perspective and purpose is totally different.

Looking through the binoculars, Kabel Garr could see the VTOL he was on was flying towards the appearance of an airport.

"Is that the major airport I arrived at? Kabel Garr asked the pilot.

"No sir, that's a major military base. It's where all our Frigates and Destroyers are home ported in the event of a space war."

"Can we fly over it?"

"No, it's restricted airspace, but you can see a lot of detail observing the base through your binoculars. We can fly a couple miles away from it before planetary defense computers would take control via auto pilot and turn us around," the VTOL pilot said.

"Two miles is probably close enough. These are great binoculars," Kabel said.

As they flew closer to the *Stanzel* Space Force base, Kabel noticed on the perimeter nearest the VTOL craft they were flying in, was a strange looking rather large spaceship compared to most of the other present at the base.

"That's a big spaceship at the base," Kabel said.

"That's one of our new Oclatine-Class Fast Frigates the *Stanzel* Space Force is now test flying."

"It's operational?" Kabel Garr asked.

"Nope, it's in the test flight phase, fully revolutionary and according to Space Research Magazine, the new propulsion and weapons features are so complicated, it's difficult to test and certify it for operations. It may be another six months to a year before it's ready to deploy with a full crew onboard."

"Have you ever seen it fly?"

"Yes, I have a couple of times while I was out flying passengers around."

Within a few minutes several smaller craft suddenly appeared with blue flashing lights halfway between the VTOL craft Kabel was riding in and the base.

"Today is your lucky day," The pilot said.

"Why is that?" Kabel asked.

"See those aircraft ahead of us with the blinking blue lights?"

"Yes."

"Those are security craft. They only come out and fly outside the perimeter when their test flights occur."

"You mean we might see that big spaceship fly?"

"Absolutely, I think that's what is about to happen."

"Wow. I got lucky booking the air tour at the time I did," Kabel expressed in a jovial manner.

"You sure did. Most people will not know it is flying today until its way up in the air and they will lose sight of it very quickly. If they are not looking up into the sky when it launches, it's unlikely they will see it at all."

"How long before we have to turn around?" Kabel asked the pilot.

"I'll slow up and hover now and loiter so you can watch it fly up into the sky and into space."

"Thanks, I appreciate that. I think we are close enough where I can do a video recording of it with my binoculars recording to my communicator."

"We are close enough; you should be able to get a great recording," the pilot said.

"I think so too."

Good to the pilot's word, within fifteen minutes the Fast Frigate started climbing vertical off the concrete landing pad. When it was about five hundred feet in the air it started making forward velocity that increased at a linear rate. At this point in time there was nothing unusual about the spacecraft as it wasn't leaving behind any large plumes that would normally be associated with solid rocket propulsion. The craft gained velocity very promptly and when the speed quickly reached supersonic out of the back of the ship, two huge blue plumes started appearing.

"See the blue exhaust?"

"Yes."

"The pilot just turned on its tri-lithium sulfate based fusion reactors that power cyclonic inverter warp drive thrusters."

As Kabel was filming and observing the *Stanzelite* Oclatine-Class Fast Frigate sped up quicker than any ship Kabel had ever seen before. The only thing Kabel ever saw that sped up that quick were spacewar missiles.

"What an incredible sight," Kabel said in all honesty. His mission just got far more important.

"It sure is."

"Is this how they would take off on a mission?"

"No, the spacecraft is empty and has no weapons onboard. If it had the crew and weapons, it would be too heavy and not be able to reach terminal velocity and break out into space. The *Stanzel* Space Force has an explosive handling warf and refueling center in orbit around the planet. Their space warships sometimes launch rocket assisted into space and fuel and load weapons there at the explosive handling warf and refueling center in orbit around the planet."

"Did you get all that information from the Space Research Magazine?" Kabel asked.

"No, I used to be a member of the *Stanzel* Space Force. That's where I was trained as a pilot."

"Interesting. Is their pilot training good?"

"Yes, the very best pilots come from the *Stanzel* Space Force. We are a cut above the rest."

"Why do you fly a tourist sky tour if you are such a great pilot?"

"When I left the *Stanzel* Space Force I went to work with a commercial intergalactic transportation company. I was single and had no major expenses. The commercial intergalactic transportation company paid for most of my expenses, and I was always staying at luxurious hotels at all the destinations, so I didn't need a large home or apartment, just a place to spend the night at my home base which was on the planet Azorcon and super cheap. In ten years', time I saved up enough money to buy this sky tour VTOL craft and pay credits₿ for it."

"That's great, smart move on your part."

"Yes, I own it outright, so I get one hundred percent of the fee and do not have to pay a leaser like my competitors."

"Wealthy people avoid paying bankers and the tax man, good job!"

"Definitely. My profit margins are considerably higher than my competitors."

"Are you going to keep doing this business?"

"I have enough credits₿ now to purchase a second VTOL craft, but instead, I'm just going to keep this one and sell it in a couple years and move back to Azorcon, buy a nice home there and live the good life."

"You would give up flying?"

"I'll have a private aircraft on Azorcon to fly myself and guests around on and possibly do charters, but I do not desire to work seven days a week like I do now."

"I can understand that. My life has been like that too working seven days a week."

"Then you understand. I've flown over the city of Kerlara so many times, flying these sky tours became quite boring. Flying this VTOL craft is almost like driving a bus but with no roads."

"I see your point."

The sky tour lasted a couple hours seeing all the sights including areas just outside the city that included mountains, lakes, waterfalls, and majestic views of uncommon beauty and splendor.

"I never would have expected to see such fantastic views."

"Most Kerlara people have never seen the sights you have because the only way you can get there is via a VTOL craft because there are no roads around there and too far and difficult to walk."

"Oh, by the way we are about Fifteen minutes away from the end (your sky tour, and I just received an advisory to not fly near the base."

"Why is that?"

"See those flashing blue lights ahead?"

"Yes, it looks like the security team again."

"Sure is. The Oclatine-Class Fast Frigate is coming back from space and is expected to land in ten minutes."

"What a nice thing to see at the end of the tour," Kabel said.

"I've never had a passenger get to see takeoff and landing during a sky tour. You are the first person who gets to see both."

"That's nice I feel privileged. I'm going to film it again with the binoculars and put it on my communicator," Kabel said.

"You are very lucky, nobody else has video of the Frigate taking of and later landing," the pilot said.

It was almost near sundown and the bright light coming out of spa came down and appeared to be going fast, but as it curved and approach the base at a less steep angle it seemed to slow down and approached the landing zone flying parallel to the fence a few hundred yards away from the landing zone that kept the public out of the base.

No doubt there are plenty of roving patrols, Kabel thought.

This had been a very productive day for Kabel. With the videos he just took, the artificial intelligence *Latrodectus* on his communicator informed Dunbar through his conformal ear bud, "You have enough ISR data to substantiate a transporter ride home."

But something in the back of his mind told Dunbar to stay and dig deeper into this Oclatine-Class Fast Frigate business.

Dunbar also felt he wanted to visit the two psychics again. He wanted to see if they detected what transpired with the two women he met. Shortly after the Frigate landed at the landing zone time was up, the sky tour was about finished and the nice pilot fulfilled his wish and took him to the spiral building and landed at the VTOL craft landing pad and let him out.

True to the pilot's word, the pilot made the proper contacts and as soon as the VTOL landed, Kabel Garr paid for the VTOL ride including a generous tip. A spiral building security representative was at the entrance to the building which was the elevator access. He then had a short ride down in the elevator a few floors to the *Greifinn* restaurant. After he left the elevator and approached the mataré d podium, there was Sophia in all smiles and impeccably dressed for success.

Sophia, the lovely blonde mataré d with great makeup and hair style, also had on a perfume that had a fragrance Dunbar would not forget for a very long time. *Too bad I'm not staying longer; I wouldn't mind spending time in bed with Sophia, Dunbar thought.*

Sophia wore a short shoulder-less black dress that went down about five inches below her crotch. Sophia's buttocks geometry was well proportioned to her body and appeared to be a slender woman probably one hundred and twenty pounds and about five foot seven inches tall. Her golden blonde hair with a yellowish tent to it flowed in waves down to her breasts and parted in the middle of her head.

The upper portion of the dress had a heart shaped opening giving the appearance, the dress was held up by straps but there was an embroidered see through fabric that went all the way up to the neck that attached to the dress in a very artful manner. On the side of her head showing less hair an earring was exposed. She carried one of those *I know you want me smiles.*

Sophia's medium height high heels did not overextend her making you think she was a giant of a woman, but extended the appearance to give the impression she had long legs. If it were not for the fact Kabel was limited to time and scope, he definitely would have entertained the notion to pursue Sophia and taste the celestial treats that such a luxurious appearing woman had to offer.

"Hello Kabel, how are you this evening?"

"I'm doing just fine, thank you. How has your day been?"

"It's been very enjoyable."

"Good to hear."

"That was a very attractive woman you were with last night. Is she someone special?"

"She's a friend of mine. I'm saving the special for you."

"You are such a kidder!"

"But you never know, I might not be kidding."

"I'll take that as a compliment."

"You should."

"Let me find you a nice table where you have good observation on the musicians."

"That would very much please me because that's mainly why I'm here. The wonderful food and drink are secondary."

"I can tell you have a slight infatuation with Eva Erlaendsdottir."

"Her singing gets to me. But don't forget I also have an infatuation with you."

"Well call me when those girls do not work out."

"I promise I will."

Kabel was not dressed up like he was the night before, but Sophia didn't care. She knew what he could look like. She kind of liked the idea he didn't always dress up to impress people. He showed a down to earth side of him, and she liked that.

Kabel was soon seated with a clear shot view of where Eva Erlaendsdottir would be standing and singing at the old-style microphone. Microphones and stands were no longer needed with the acoustics available. Shows like this one used such a microphone because it gave a nostalgic look and reminiscence of a bygone era people wish they could go back to.

Soon the musicians all arrived on the stage and began their performances. Eva Erlaendsdottir seemed to glare at Kabel as if he was upsetting her. He figured she probably thought he took Blemary back to his resort hotel room and had his way with her. Eva didn't realize there are still a few gentlemen around who do not take advantage of women.

Eva Erlaendsdottir was not happy Kabel Garr brought that well-dressed woman who could pass for a pleasure associate here the prior night. *Why did he do that? Dumb move on his part*, Eva thought.

Dunbar believed it was a good reason to allow things to flow naturally and not artificially accelerate the relevance of a relationship, as artificial emotions quickly break down and fade away. When the real emotions and perseverance develop, then a realistic outcome in a relationship is possible. Synthesized love for the sake of *libido liaisons* is usually not worth the trouble.

Everyone in the restaurant could see the female singer was focused on a gentleman in a certain table. Some of the regulars recognized him and the singer's body language unmasked her mood and quite possibly exposed a hint of jealousy. Several of the female regulars recalled how the gentleman was dressed up in black tie and the smoking hot woman he was with, was dressed to kill. *Perhaps she was showing resentment?*

By this time Kabel had finished half of his *Jangovian de Palentin* elixir and was feeling pretty good. He could see the sassiness exhibited by Eva Erlaendsdottir who unwittingly exposed her vulnerability to Kabel. As a trained spy, he knew he could exploit her and manipulate her now because she just gave it all away. It also meant he could never bring Blemary to the *Greifinn* restaurant ever again, or the possibility sparks may fly!

By the time the musicians finished with their set, Kabel finished his glass of *Jangovian de Palentin* elixir and had a refill.

Eva Erlaendsdottir made her rounds through the tables socializing with the audience for brief encounters, and saved Kabel for last.

Eva suspected Kabel Garr would be back, and she predicted he would not be with the Bimbo. *Kabel probably got his rocks off last night and no longer needed her company tonight*, Eva thought.

"Hello Kabel."

"Hi Eva, would you like to join me for a drink?"

"Sure, I wouldn't mind," Eva said now wanting some discovery as to which way the wind was blowing with Kabel.

Eva decided she wanted a stiff drink and ordered a *Lotus Dragon* with a splash of *Scorpion Milk* in it. The *Scorpion Milk* was essentially a mood modifier and a narcotic. *Scorpion Milk* was a class-2 narcotic and prohibited on many worlds because it could easily be used for Nefarious purposes.

People in human bondage were often administered *Scorpion Milk* to ensure they conducted the disgusting acts their controllers wanted them to do.

Unwittingly, Eva Erlaendsdottir was making herself more vulnerable to Kabel Garr. *Was she doing it on purpose or did she just like the better buzz?* Kabel wondered.

After Eva's drink was served and she took her first gulp and enjoyed every bit of it she asked, "Where's your friend tonight?"

"You mean Blemary who was with me last night?"

"Yes, that woman."

"She's probably home. I didn't talk to her today?"

"Why not seemed like the two of you were hitting it off on all cylinders last night."

"We had fun. I took her to the symphony, then here for dinner and drinks then I dropped her off at home and went back to my hotel resort room and went to bed at a decent hour."

"The way the two of you left last night so quickly, I assumed you were heading to your place or her place and get some quality boom-boom in."

"We've never had a physical relationship."

"You got to be kidding me."

"I tend to go slow. I like to get to know someone first before I get involved and potentially involved in a relationship."

"That's interesting to know."

"Not everyone is compatible. I think it's best to know that you and your potential partner have a reasonable situation that would be conducive to long term partnership before you get physically involved."

"Did you have physical relationships?"

"Sure, why not."

"What was your last relationship like?"

"I got involved with a surgeon before I got to really know her. I made a huge mistake."

"You no longer communicate with her?"

"We've not spoken since I informed her, she bored me."

The real Kabel Garr had a relationship with the blonde female orthopedic surgeon just within the past couple years. The main reason why they broke up is he was abducted by the Transporter Directorate! When Kable Garr suddenly didn't return the blonde orthopedic surgeon's calls and had departed the area, she had enough of that aloof person and ended the relationship. The fact he didn't return her calls pissed her off. She was a high maintenance woman and would not tolerate a man who didn't follow her around like a puppy dog and execute her commands.

The surgeon knew of one of Kabel Garr's relatives and contacted that person who informed her, he apparently left the area and has not been seen in a while. When the surgeon suggested they contact the authorities for a missing person, she was informed he sometimes went off chasing after occult or strange supernatural phenomena and like in the past may not return for a year or longer. The doctor didn't have time for weirdos so that ended it permanently.

As the break time lingered, Eva became more sociable because the *Scorpion Milk* was starting to alter her mood. She started smiling more, acted more friendly but then Kabel irritated her slightly with information he now gave her.

"I like hearing you sing, but I may not be around for a few days."

"Why is that?"

"I'm going to take a tourist train trip."

"When are you going to do that?"

"Probably as early as tomorrow after I make the reservations."

"Are you taking that bimbo with you?"

"No, I'm going by myself. Who knows, I might meet someone on the train. But I want to do sightseeing and relax and not be encumbered by another person."

"What if I wanted to go with you?"

"Can you take 3 or 4 days off from work?"

"Actually, I cannot, I would lose my job if I did."

"Well, I'm sorry I can't take you then."

"Ask me again when I have some vacation time and I'll go with you and have recreational sex with you."

"You would do that."

"You are a good-looking guy, maybe I want to catch you."

"I'll have to think about that. Maybe I need to run away and hide from you!"

"Once you taste this kitten, you're not running anywhere, you will come back because once you give a kitten milk it keeps returning."

"I suppose so."

"Alright, I need to get back to work."

"It was nice hearing you sing Eva. I'm sorry but I'm leaving now, I need to go back to my resort room and check up on my reservations and see when I'm leaving on the train."

"Alright, come back when you can, and if you are lucky, I might give you some milk."

"I know I would be addicted. I'll see you when I get back."

As Kabel left the restaurant and walked past Sophia, she asked, "You are not staying for dinner?"

"No, I need to get back to my hotel resort and check up on my travel plans."

"Alright, see you the next time," Sophia said and smiled.

***

Blemary had left work, took her flowers home with her, and did not have to walk too far and got some stares from people wondering why she was carrying the flowers.

Meanwhile, Kabel took a taxi back to the *Norel Mozelle Resort* and went to his room and conferred with Cornolius about the tourist trains.

Blemary knew the mystery man she was interested in had left the Norel Mozelle Resort in a VTOL craft. She didn't know why but she was nevertheless interested in what that was all about. He had not checked out of the resort so she knew he would eventually be coming back. One of her thoughts was, *Kabel went to go visit that cabaret singer and I've lost him.*

Blemary didn't know why she did it, perhaps it was the flowers that drove her to do it, she called the *Norel Mozelle Resort,* and her friend was working.

"*Norel Mozelle Resort,* how may I help you?" the friend said when she answered the call.

"This is Blemary."

"Hello dear, that's fast you were just here a short while ago."

"Yea, I know. But say, by any chance did you see Kabel Garr yet?"

"Matter of fact I did. He arrived shortly after you left and went up to his resort hotel room. By the way, those were lovely flowers he gave you. He must really like you."

"I hope so."

"What do you need, Blemary?"

"Could you transfer this call to his room?"

"Do you want the holographic transferred too?"

"Yes, please."

"Hold on, transferring your call."

"Thank you."

"You are welcome."

A moment later Cornolius holograph popped up and he asked, "Kabel, Blemary is calling, do you wish to accept her holograph?"

"Yes, go ahead and show the holograph."

In about two seconds, Blemary's holograph appeared and said, "Good evening Kabel, how are you?"

Blemary was still wearing her work uniform, but nevertheless managed to look cute in it.

"Doing okay, thank you for asking."

"Did you have a good day?" Blemary asked.

"Yes, I did."

"What are you doing this evening?"

"I'm working on reservations for a overnight train trip. When do you think you can take some time off?"

"I can take some time off real soon if you want. I'm overdue for some vacation time."

"Have you had anything to eat?"

"Not yet,"

"I was thinking about taking dinner here at the *Norel Mozelle Resort.*"

"They serve really good food there."

"What are you doing now?" Kabel asked, knowing Blemary lived a short distance away and could walk her in the time it would take him to get ready.

"I'm not doing anything yet."

"Say, why don't you come by here and have dinner with me and we can discuss the tourist train trip."

"I can be there fairly quick; I just need to change out of my work clothes."

"Alright, I'll meet you in the dining hall."

"Sure thing, see you soon."

The holograph ended and Kabel went to work getting ready. He didn't have to do much but brush his teeth, comb his hair, put on some cologne and leave.

In five minutes Kabel exited his room and made his way down to the dining room and approached the mataré d.

"May I help you sir?"

"Yes, I'm having dinner here tonight. I have a friend who will be joining me in a short while, but I thought I would go ahead and get us a table and have a drink."

"Good planning, this place fills up fast, and the rush will begin in about fifteen minutes."

The nice looking mataré d, who was a friend of Blemary didn't know this was Mr. Wonderful, Blemary's hotel guest friend who never put his fingers in the cookie jar yet and got some of those pleasure associates and treated Blemary with dignity and respect. The symphony, dinner, and flowers from a perfect gentleman set the tone for Blemary's friends who worked there.

The mataré d, was in for a big surprise later when Blemary showed up and she seated him with the good-looking man who arrived about fifteen minutes before she did.

The waitress wearing a cocktail server's outfit approached Kabel's table. Facial recognition had already determined he was the guest by the name of Kabel Garr and the meals were prepaid for, though he could leave a nicer tip if he desired.

On her tablet taking Kabel's orders she saw his name and said, "Good afternoon Kabel, my name is Wendy and I'll be your server. Is there something I can get you to drink?"

"Yes, I would like a *Jangovian de Palentin* elixir. A friend of mine ordered a drink like this and asked for a splash of Scorpion Milk in it, I'm curious as to what that would do?"

"Well sir, for men I'm not sure how it would affect you. But for women, it makes us hornier."

"Very interesting. I'll skip the Scorpion Milk slash for now."

"Alright, *Jangovian de Palentin* elixir coming right up," Wendy said.

Kabel had mixed emotions about what was transpiring. The *Norel Mozelle Resort* was his home base to operate out of doing his clandestine assignment, but having a hotel receptionist on his team might prove vital in the future and help him out of a jam when he needed it the most. But he also understood the human condition and how Blemary's transcendence appeared to be reshaping her outlook on life and he was the center attraction.

The discussions Kabel Garr had with the two psychics were still deep in his thoughts and started having an influence on his modus operendus. But as a man he had his needs and Eva and Blemary were some low hanging fruits that would give him some temporal gratification. But he also knew he would be breaking a heart with his sudden disappearance.

A spy operates off a totally different mindset. They know they can't take the crumbs of life for granted, get them when you can because you might not have another opportunity, especially if your life is cut short by either capture or a reassociation failure with the Transporter Capsule, and a myriad of other things that could go wrong. People who live a normal sterile life might view Dunbar as immoral and reprehensible in this conduct, but if they were in his shoes, they would probably look at things differently.

Kabel Garr had almost finished drinking his elixir by the time Blemary arrived at his table with a glowing smile on the mataré d who now knew who Blemary's new flame was. Blemary had never screwed around with any of the resort staff, nor had she done anything with any of the clients. So, to see Blemary engaging in this affair with Kabel Garr was quite remarkable. Kabel

Blemary had on blue denim jeans that were about as tight as anyone could possibly put on. What Kabel Garr didn't know is these jeans had secret zippers she zipped up after she put them on. She had on a bright blue top with long sleeves and cuffs and the color was very rigid as if it were pressed and supported by an internal frame. This indeed was sexy and expensive clothes she learned about while working as a pleasure associate in the past.

Kabel Garr stood up to help Blemary with her chair in a very charming manner which Blemary enjoyed as it signaled a type of affection she liked.

"Emma, let me introduce you to my friend Kabel," Blemary said with an optimistic smile.

"Pleased to meet you Kabel, I hope you enjoy your evening here," Emma said.

"It just got better," Kabel said in a flirtatious manner."

"Enjoy." Emma said knowing she needed to leave the love birds alone so they could get into their agendas."

About that time the server Wendy with a look of surprise on her face approached the table and said, "Hello Blemary, you are looking great tonight."

"Thank you, Wendy. Let me introduce you to my friend Kabel Garr."

"Kabel Garr, it's so nice to meet you."

"Thank you."

"Would you like a drink Blemary?" Wendy asked.

"Yes. How about a Lotus Dragon," Blemary responded.

"Kabel, would you like a refill?"

"Yes, please."

Kabel analyzed the situation. It was evident Blemary wanted some *Big-A* and Kabel was more than willing to give it to her, but the train ride was where they would do it to protect her reputation and give him plausible deniability.

They soon had their drinks and Blemary was exceedingly happy she was with the hunk people were observing out in the pool. The sleazeball manager walked through the dining hall and over to Emma to discuss some reservations that were being modified and spotted Mr. Wonderful sitting with none other than Blemary dressed up in a sexy apparel.

Blemary's bright blue top showcased her feminine excellence and her hair, makeup, and everything was perfect. The manager just shook his head in wonder looking at the couple full of smiles. It was no doubt in the manager's mind the man got lucky with Blemary. He was premature in his assessment, but he was not far off since it was going to happen soon.

They were out of hearing range of Kabel and Blemary, and Emma who knew the sleazeball manager was always trying to make moves on Blemary decided to tweak him a bit.

"What do you think of Blemary's new boyfriend?"

"He had her all dressed up last night. He took her to the symphony, then probably dinner, then probably the moon."

"Yep, she sure went to the moon and back with the perfect gentleman."

"What a lucky guy," the manager said in condescending disdain.

Once Wendy took their food orders, Blemary asked, "What's the latest on the train trip?"

"How soon can you go?"

"I could go as early as tomorrow, I talked to my manager today. What time does the train leave?"

"It leaves at eleven in the morning. It arrives at Saratola tomorrow evening. We then would fly back and be here tomorrow evening."

"Alright, I'll be ready. Where shall we meet?"

"It's a five-minute cab ride from here to the train station. I could pick you up at your apartment on the way in case you want to bring a handbag along."

"Do you remember how to get to my apartment?"

"Yes, it's very simple plus when I dropped you off, I programmed the location into my personal navigator on my communicator."

"Alright, I'll be out in front of my apartment at 10:30."

The meal was served, they had a couple drinks then it was time for Blemary to go home get some rest and prepare for her trip including calling her manager to let her know she was taking tomorrow and the next day off.

"How are you going home?" Kabel asked.

"I'm walking it's a short distance." Blemary replied.

"I'll walk you home and get some exercise." Kabel said.

"Sure, I will enjoy your company."

The two of them left the dining hall and said goodbye to Emma on their way out.

The manager followed the two at a distance. He was curious if they were going up to the guest's room to do some boom-boom and expected them to hop in the elevator which would confirm it. He was surprised they walked out of the front of the resort, and he followed them to the entrance and looked out of the building a moment later and saw them walking away holding hands smiling like best friends in the world.

He then walked up to the receptionist who happened to be Blemary's friend and asked. "Did you know that's Blemary's boyfriend?"

"Yes, she really likes him. He's a true gentleman."

It took only five minutes to walk to Blemary's apartment building.

"Do you want to go up to my apartment?" Blemary asked.

"I think I should leave otherwise it might screw up our trip."

Blemary smiled and before a moment passed Kabel pulled Blemary closer then kissed her in the most sensual manner like a good spy would when recruiting women. Blemary melted in his arms and wished he would go up with her to the apartment because she was ready to give it all.

Kabel released Blemary who had that surreal feeling and said, "I'm really going to enjoy being with you tomorrow."

"I will enjoy you just as much." Blemary said knowing they had to figure out how to get it done on the train. She just could not wait any longer. She wanted the feeling and the gratification.

The two separated and Kabel walked away and was back at the *Norel Mozelle Resort* in another five minutes.

The dining hall manager was still chatting with the receptionist when Kabel walked back into the lobby on the way to the elevator. The manager was quite surprised Kabel was back so quickly.

In a moment after the elevator noise indicated Kabel was heading up to his room, the manager said, "That was fast."

"Gentlemen get it done quicker," the receptions said tweaking the manager slightly.

"I suppose so," the manager said and walked away.

Kabel informed Cornolius, "I'm going on an overnight train trip with Blemary tomorrow. I'll be back the following day."

"You are not checking out?"

"No, I don't want to lose this room and I do not want to carry all my items with me since it's such a short trip."

"You do not have many things, Kabel, but not to worry everything you leave behind will be safe and protected."

"I'm going to take a bath then go to bed. Can you provide me a sleeping inducer?"

"Yes, when you are ready to get into your bed, I will have it for you."

"Thank you."

"You are most welcome."

Cornolius had a very advanced artificial intelligence program. Even though he was a sub-program running independently from all the other applications, because of his security programming, he had a lot of access to security videos stored. Cornolius had a video to holographic converter and each holographic ensemble was one of millions of pictures Cornolius could analyze in microseconds and do analysis and make determinations. Because of his sophisticated programming, he could look at people just like another human being would and come to the same conclusions.

Since Kabel's checking to his room, Cornolius had holographic ensembles of every moment of him and when it became apparent Kabel had some type of relationship with Blemary, he went back to the archives and pulled out everything associated with Blemary since Kabel's arrival. Cornolius had subroutines to evaluate the human condition and evaluate people involved in scenarios of interest to him. As such Cornolius made determinations Kabel and Blemary would be good for one another. Hence, he made it his agenda to further their relationship along.

The flowers were just the beginning. Cornolius had every technique used in the pursuit of romance in his artificial intelligence databases to develop his roadmap to assist in helping the relationship between Kabel and Blemary advance in a positive manner. The surveillance video of Kabel demonstrated his gentlemanly traits towards Blemary which further enhanced Cornolius' opinion of Kabel Garr. He was starting to take a liking to Kabel which was rare. Most of the *Norel Mozelle Resort* clients were scumbags often doing nefarious activities to grow wealthy.

When Kabel was sound asleep, Cornolius sent manufactured holographs to Blemary telling her how much he already missed her, and good night and he would be very happy to see her in the morning.

That put the exclamation point on it all. Blemary was feeling better than at any time in her lifetime. Being shoved out the door into a cruel world by terrible parents and forced to live through the horrors she did until she dug herself out of that hole her parents designed for her, this was the first moment in her life she felt a transcendence and inspiration by a very nice and considerate man.

Of course, if she knew she was fooling around with a cold-blooded killer it would be another viewpoint. There would be terror in her mind if she really knew who Kabel Garr really was. Should the government find out about him, he would no doubt be the most highly sought person on the planet. The timing to get to his transporter capsule was critical. In a critical moment, Blemary might be what allows him to escape.

Now that Kabel Garr had built his story and recruited a couple women it would be soon time to go do what he needed to accomplish and then exit and go back to the banking building via the transporter capsule.

The extraction signals the transporter would send allowed the Transporter back in the banking building to easily lock on coordinates and transport Dunbar immediately back to safety and there would be nothing *Stanzel* planetary security could to do stop it. Thanks to the use of Neutrinos and Tachyons the transporter would be disassociating Dunbar's molecules into a stream of transporter beams and out of the solar system in the fragment of a second along with the Transporter Capsule.

Kabel slept like a lamb and felt completely invigorated when he woke in the morning around six o'clock long before he needed to go pick up Blemary and take her to the train station.

Kabel brushed his teeth to get the night out of his mouth, put on his running clothes and informed Cornolius he was going for his morning running routine.

Kabel was soon out in the lobby of the *Norel Mozelle Resort* and there was someone else there as receptionist today as Blemary would not be coming into work today. Since it was early in the morning, Kabel ran down to the park a mile away, where he began his lap putting in five additional miles tracked on his communicator. When Kabel saw he had finished a total of six miles since leaving the *Norel Mozelle Resort*, he headed back to the resort. By now it was only eight o'clock with two and a half hours to burn. Kabel informed Cornelius he was going to take a sprite shower, put on his swimming attire and go do some laps.

Kabel quickly finished the sprite shower, redressed into swimming attire, and a robe with padded slippers and made his way to the swimming pool where he pushed himself for an hour doing a superhuman effort in doing the laps. Then he got out of the pool and put on his swimming robe and slippers to go back to his *Norel Mozelle Resort* room to take a soothing bath and prepare for his trip.

The dining hall manager was out at the pool bar and restaurant getting things moving with his favorite bartender on duty today and could not help but see Kabel perform like nobody he ever seen before and when the man got out of the pool and he saw his body all tensed up from swimming laps in serious need of a massage, the manager quickly understood why this man was an infatuation of Blemary. He looked incredible. *But really what did this man really do? His body was indeed very uncommon.*

Per Kabel's request, Cornolius obtained muscle relaxers for his bath. This was a typical situation for Dunbar (aka Kabel) who had to train at the highest level possible because of all the possible danger he faced.

Soaking in the bath with the muscle relaxers really helped Kabel quite a bit and after he dried off and started putting on his street clothes, he felt like a new man.

Chapter Five
Train ride.

At about 10:25, Kabel was at the front of the *Norel Mozelle Resort* and a Taxi was there to take him to pick up Blemary which he eagerly looked forward to. In a short period of time the Taxi pulled up in the circular driveway of Blemary's apartment complex and there the beautiful woman was carrying a small handbag that probably had a change of clothes and some ancillary items she needed.

Kabel opened the door and got out of the Taxi and greeted Blemary who was full of smiles. The two of them got back into the Taxi and were soon on their way to the train station.

Stanzelites, like most advanced civilizations, had high speed intercity trains between cities, but they also had the foresight to preserve some of the ancient railroads and turn them into tourist lines. This particular train that Kabel and Blemary would soon board went through some of the most impressive, majestic landscapes only accessible by this train. Just like the sky tour that Kabel experienced, this train route did similar treks across areas where no roads existed and there were no other alternatives to see the sights without being on the comfortable train.

Kabel and Blemary had a private cabin abord the train with a locked door nobody could see inside. The train's artificial intelligence read Kabel's wallet in his communicator and confirmed the reservation as the two boarded and a soft voice from the train directed them to their private compartment where they soon entered. Within a few minutes after boarding, the train slowly started to move. The two had a panoramic view outside the window looking at the city cland soon the suburbs as the train quickly sped up heading for the nearby mountains.

There was lots of anticipation on both Blemary and Kabel Garr but they knew they had plenty of time since this was an overnight adventure.

From pastoral planes to majestic mountain tops, mountain streams, and panoramic views, that neither of them ever seen before or suspected, the journey began and soon enveloped their enthusiasm that transcended into their emotional involvement in ways a trained spy never fathomed happening to him.

Perhaps because Kabel was a spy he never probed Blemary's history. She was grateful he didn't want to know about her past. She feared that had Kabel discovered she used to be a pleasure associate; he would dump her on the spot.

Unfortunately for Blemary, she was the victim of intrigue and intergalactic espionage. She had no idea who she was with who had a history that would dwarf hers. The fact she used to be a pleasure associate in no way had any meaning to Kabel Garr

Kabel Garr had more or less engaged in fasting since the previous night was starting to feel hungry. The train porter rang the doorbell of their compartment and when Kabel opened the door, the porter said, "This is first call for the dining room. I suggest you go there now because it fills up fast."

"Thank you I appreciate the heads up."

"You are most welcome sir."

In a short while, Kabel escorted Blemary to the dining car, just two train cars in front of them. They were seated in the middle of the dining car which gave them each a commanding view of the majestic landscape they were passing as the tourist train slowly round its way up the mountains.

The waiter asked if they wanted something to drink, Blemary quickly responded, "I would like a Lotus Dragon with a splash of Scorpion milk."

Kabel smiled as he understood the significance of Blemary's drink request.

"Sir, what can I get for you?"

"I think I will have a *Jangovian de Palentin* elixir."

The couple were soon served their drinks and gave their food requests.

As Kabel enjoyed the ambience created by the *Jangovian de Palentin* elixir and the company of Blemary, he realized how lucky he was to be a Transporter Spy to get these golden opportunities. But he also knew one strategic fact. He truly liked Blemary, and in a different world at a different time, he and she would spend the rest of their lives together. *I wonder if she knows how much I truly adore her.*

Their meals were soon served, and they were much better than expected. It was a joyous occasion.

Kabel was eating a dish that had meat that tasted like fowl he enjoyed back on his home planet. Blemary had seafood that was rich in flavor and spices and cream.

The combination of the food and the drink soon manifested a nap for both as they returned to their cabin and reclined on a sofa together looking out the picturesque window of the incredible view beget them.

Soon they each entered a very calm pleasing nap. Kabel was very happy. But in due time he awoke for two reasons. Blemary was performing fellatio on Kabel, and he desperately needed to urinate.

After taking care of business, Kabel was back at the sofa that would turn into a bed in about three hours when the staff did the night conversions, and ready to reciprocate to Blemary.

That's when the love making really began. Kabel knew he was living on borrowed time. Transporter spies had a short life span. They knew the dangers but did it because it truly was the most thrilling experience any spy could have.

It wasn't that Kabel Garr deserted his moral and ethical behavior. But he knew the odds and wanted a few crumbs of life for himself. In this discrete moment in time when he had such great feelings for this woman, Kabel Garr let it all unfold. He wanted Blemary to feel his genuine love and he meant it. The emotional transcendence all manifested in the perfect coitus that was enshrined by the essence of real love. Kabel felt it and gave Blemary real love. It was one of the joyous moments of his life, as well as Blemary's.

The after engagement was another one of those cerebral down times as the couple cuddled on the sofa simply looked out the large glass tourist window at the marvelous countryside exposing real nature and untouched areas where the flora abounded, and the colors were unique.

There was no doubt that Kabel went far past the point of no return emotionally, but a good spy always had an agenda.

***

A good spy does his/her handicraft for reasons that can only be speculated after their death like the famous spy Richard Sorge when the Japanese executed him in 1944.

Richard Sorge warned Stalin of the pending attack in 1941, but Stalin refused to heed the warning of the spy, the same way King Wu did Sun Tzu (Art of War).

Later during the war when Stalin was hiding in a Moscow Subway Station as the Germans were about to enter Moscow in a terrible defeat for the Russians, Richard Sorge informed Stalin that Japan would not attack the Sovie Union because they had already planned to deal with America and were getting ready to do a massive military shift for their conquest of the Pacific.

Since Sorge had informed Stalin previously the date and time when operation Barbarossa was to begin, this time Stalin took Sorge very seriously and ordered 18 divisions being wasted in the East to the defense of Moscow, via high speed trains.

The Germans were in for a horrible surprise. 18 Divisions with Stormovik aircraft and the T34 Tanks quickly decimated the Germans and took 300,000 POW's.

Japan lost the war because of two spies: Richard Sorge posing as a German Diplomat, and Joseph John Rochefort at the battle of Midway. Most Americans do not know this, Japan had 2 nuclear programs, both highly successful and were only 8 weeks behind the Americans. Without Richard Sorge and John Rochefort, Japan would have beat America to nuclear weapons and won the war.

Kabel Garr, at this point in time, was as important as Joseph John Rochefort and Richard Sorge at the outcome of that world war.

Nevertheless, a love affair hit Kabel Garr like he never planned. It would throw off 'Government oversight, but it would also trap Dunbar's emotions, which is a recipe for disaster of a spy.

Blemary felt she could trust Kabel who never initiated happy time. It was all her actions. He merely responded. But the way he held her and kissed her afterwards left an indelible mark on Blemary's mind.

After numerous majestic vista's a porter arrived to convert their daytime suite into a sleeping compartment for the two. Soon they were evolving into ethereal domains as their awareness slowly evolved into their sleep.

The morning came too early and soon the two of them showered and dressed and were on their way to the dining car for breakfast they soon enjoyed. There was follow on love making on a *Theme from Paganini* as the two transcended to lover's bliss during the remainder of the train trip.

The day unfolded as they both sensed it would seemingly be the most precious times of their lives. Even a high-power spy like Dunbar (using the alias Kabel Garr) enjoyed the few crumbs of life. Blemary certainly proved she was worthy.

Kabel Garr felt high regards for Blemary. Her essence was indelibly painted in his mind. If the war ended and he could travel back to Kerlara and see Blemary again he would. There was no doubt about it. Blemary touched Kabel's soul. But he also knew the facts of life. That was unlikely to happen in his lifetime. Kabel Garr living on borrowed time also knew he wanted to experience Eva Erlaendsdottir, the cabaret singer at the *Greifinn* restaurant. Was that even possible in the short time left?

Kabel Garr also realized his intuition told him Sophia might also be a pleasant experience if he could ever manifest a lover's tryst with her. But Kabel also knew one other thing. He was up against time requirements. He had to get this mission done and travel back to the Transport Directorate with the goodies he was to obtain.

There were more majestic landscapes to observe but eventually the train pulled into the station, and they got off. The two hopped into a Taxi and were soon on their way to the airport.

Since they didn't have much in the way of luggage, they brisked through security and were soon seated on a *Stanzel* airliner. This craft was unlike anything Dunbar had ever seen. It had two cyclonic type propulsion motors, one at the front and one at the rear of the craft. The cockpit was directly over the top of the frontal cyclonic thruster, and it pivoted like the rear thruster which allowed short takeoff and landing (STOL) capability for smaller airports.

Kabel observed airliners departing from the airport terminal, otherwise he would not know the thrusters tilted. The landing speeds were also much slower thanks to the thrust vectoring which probably added to passenger safety. The airliners seemed to come down at an angle of approximately forty-five degrees.

The overall air column for these types of *Stanzel* passenger planes was significantly reduced and this had a huge impact on society because there were tall buildings near the airport. Thus, land around the airport had a lot more utilization. The planners had put the airport in the center of the city allowing businesspeople to leave the airport via Taxi and go a short distance to the office buildings they went for work assignments.

Passengers boarded their flights just like they got on the train without much fanfare. There was only one flight attendant who was aboard mainly as a safety observer and controller. This was a short flight and not many people had much in the way of luggage which fit in the overhead stowage above their seats.

Each passenger had a safety display ahead of them which showed the status of their seat belts and the requirement to buckle up. Anyone who didn't have their seatbelts fastened had a red light on their safety display and were quickly admonished to buckle up and when all safety monitors displayed passengers were ready, the aircraft pushed away from the terminal without assistance and the cyclonic thrusters were bidirectional and allowed them to back up.

The passenger aircraft taxied a short distance to the active runway and turned onto it and was soon airborne. The aircraft went from a slow and short distance and went into the air doing thirty to forty knots climbing steeply but at a small angle speeding up as it gained altitude.

Kabel could not see the cyclonic thrusters from his seat but if he could he would see them slowly reduce the angle on the tilt as the craft sped up.

Having a thruster on the nose of the aircraft and one pushing from behind greatly reduced air drag. As such it had stubby thin wings which reduced drag even more and stabilized the craft. The flight was very smooth and no sooner the airliner reached cruise altitude it seemed they were descending down for a landing. They were zipping along almost supersonic and as they got closer to the ground with the cyclonic thrusters pivoting producing drag, the craft slowed down and by the time they approached the airport they had slowed to almost fifty knots.

The airliner touched down like a feather. There was no bounce or jarring sensation. Sensors on the flight controls that accurately measured the distance between the aircraft wheels and the runway controlled the cyclonic thrusters for the gentle landing that impressed Kabel. The slow landing speed allowed the airliner to turn directly over to the terminal where the passengers were efficiently delivered and ready for the next flight in a matter of minutes after all the passengers had departed.

Dunbar would probably have been frightened had he known there were no pilots onboard. A robot was flying the plane. The robot in the cockpit looked human and was only there to make the passengers feel safer. Had a person paid attention to the looks of the robot, they would find it was the same humanoid robot always flying the aircraft! Actually, it was all for looks. The plane was always flown in autopilot by artificial intelligence. If a passenger looked inside the cockpit in flight it would appear the pilot was controlling the plane.

In reality, the artificial intelligence was having the pilot speak on the headset microphone and move the dials and controls as if he were the one flying the plane. The movement of the dials and controls that were non-operational just for looks and passenger psychological comfort in this automatic configuration coincided with how a real pilot would actually do it. From an observer it all looked real. Passengers had the option of looking at cockpit video. Most did not. It certainly all looked real, but it wasn't.

It was late in the day when the Taxi pulled up in front of Blemary's apartment complex. They both were mildly exhausted from travel, sex, and the romantic getaway. But Blemary asked Kabel, "Would like to go up to my apartment?"

"I'm kind of tired from the trip and want to go back to the resort, take a nice long hot bath and go to bed. I'll walk you home when you finish work tomorrow, how does that sound?"

"I would really enjoy that," Blemary replied.

Kabel opened the Taxi door and stood up and grabbed Blemary's hand to help her get out of the Taxi.

The two of them hugged and kissed and said good night, then Kabel got back into the Taxi and went back to the *Norel Mozelle Resort*.

The next day, Dunbar (aka Kabel) had his workout clothes on and went down to the lobby just like he normally would.

Behind the counter, there was Blemary with an unmistakable sheen on her face smiling. There is a strange metamorphosis that takes place when women find the appropriate mate and fall in love. Because of the serotonin and other chemicals like prolactin that are generated in larger quantities due to the psychological impact of such an emotional spike, nature has a funny way of changing the woman. Almost like a flower blooming, so does the woman. Because Blemary was happy and satisfied with the way she felt this morning, it's apparent to people that know that as well.

Blemary had the pleasant experience of feeling Kabel Garr's muscles. Dunbar had incredible physical fitness like a galactic level spy needed to be. Besides knowing martial arts and fully competent in well over fifty five different types of weapons, Dunbar's physical fitness matched the level of sophistication and requirements that could be required in a life and death situation spies sometimes find themselves in whether planned or not.

When Kable Garr made love to Blemary she felt the power of his thrusts and it drove her into orbit. She had no idea what a super orgasm could be like. What she didn't know is world class spies who need all the tools available have penis enlargements and increased girth and strength in the event they needed to recruit a woman in a honey pot scheme. Blemary had been recruited for nefarious purposes should it come down to that. Kabel Garr enjoyed her body, enjoyed the sex, and even though he liked her more and more, it was simply part of the mission. Blemary would be devastated if she knew the truth. She was being used.

In this false narrative that was being built, the temporal satisfaction was on display and the friendly exchange as Kabel passed through the building was predicated on the fact others were around. But they each understood the subtle message that conveyed, *thank you for the gratification and satisfaction I truly enjoyed.*

Chapter Six

Psychic Awareness & Motor Bike Adventure

During Dunbar Regvik's time on Kerlara during the mission, his personal communicator that had been modified from the one taken from Kabel Garr with the imbedded artificial intelligence program *Latrodectus* always remained active and working. *Latrodectus* artificial intelligence managed a sensor suite built into the personal communicator. If the enemy opened it up and looked at the internal circuitry it would appear as a standard personal communicator with just a few microcircuits, battery, speaker, microphone, and multiple cameras like all that existed throughout *Stanzel* society.

The binoculars on the helicopter provided wireless digital output feed so that people could capture the view on their personal communicator to share later with others. This was all done seamlessly in the background. It was totally innocuous, and nobody would expect otherwise.

Dunbar Regvik using the stolen identity of Kabel Garr, knew that *Latrodectus* was collecting information in special mission files as he continued this mission. All of Dunbar's travels were recorded. Thanks to the great sophistication of *Stanzel* global positioning system, Latrodectus had a great reconstruction on Dunbar's travels that would be instantly available to Dunbar's Transporter Directorate controllers.

For future mission debriefs all of the locations that Dunbar went had time stamps, latitude and longitude from global positioning. All of those Dunbar came in contact with were similarly recorded. The secret memory in this device had five thousand times the storage of a normal communicator, and only Latrodectus had access to those recordings.

Nobody else could ever discover mission files existed except for Dunbar until his controllers downloaded the files back at the Transporter Directorate.

Dunbar knew some Transporter Directorate guys would be envious of the women he had the pleasure of experiencing. When they did the mission review because it was all recorded in one way or another, they would see Dunbar in action. Even though they might not have actual video of Dunbar in coitus with Blemary, the sounds and the erotic behavior was undeniable.

Many of the hotel and airport security systems utilized wireless to eliminate millions of miles of wiring. *Latrodectus* was able to capture those signals. Hence the Transport directorate had images of everyone Dunbar encountered for the most part and when he was drinking and talking to people such as Eva Erlaendsdottir or Sophia. Those private conversations were recorded and a database of the security video *Latrodectus* recorded showed them while Dunbar participated in the conversation. With the power of super computers, the Transport Directorate could take those images and zoom in to get detail in the composition of their appearances recorded during the conversations as if they were just a few feet away from the person.

While Dunbar was sleeping, *Latrodectus* could review the video and if there was something Dunbar needed to know, he would inform him when he knew absolute privacy was obtained. There were few places that could happen, the park where Dunbar ran happened to be one of them.

Dunbar knew he needed to get some reports out of *Latrodectus* and when he was alone after running almost six miles having worked up a considerable sweat and only needed to go back to the *Norel Mozelle Resort,* Dunbar (aka Kabel Garr) sat down at a park bench and said a code words *Echis Carinatus.* The code words *Echis Carinatus* code word to *Latrodectus* indicating Dunbar was alone and to make a report. As a backup *Latrodectus* had multiple cameras and directional microphones to do surveillance to validate security requirements were met before issuing reports unless it was an emergency and Dunbar overrode the interlocks.

"D" which was the code word for Dunbar, "I have a lot of data I've analyzed."

"Great. Give me a streamlined report of your findings thus far."

"It seems the *Stanzelites* use wireless for everything including the flight controls of the aircraft you flew on."

"That's good to know. Were you able to hack into it?"

"Absolutely, their computer security is very inferior. I've hacked into the hotel security system, the night club secret monitors, airport security, airliner flight control system and communications, the train even had secret monitors of your compartment."

"Did you get the video feed of me having sex?"

"Yes, but for the most part you were under cover and very little nudity exists."

"Erase any nudity you recorded."

"I need a command override for the delete."

"Orycteropus-Afer," Dunbar said.

In about ten seconds *Latrodectus* reported, "All nudity video on the train has been deleted with explanation for redaction to the Transport Directorate. No other nude video exists."

"How did the VTOL video from the binoculars turn out?"

"We obtained a lot of information on the Fast Frigate. I think we have enough information now. You can go back to the Transporter and return home."

"I've come up with a new plan, in-situ," Dunbar advised *Latrodectus*.

"What might that be?"

"I want to steal the Fast Frigate and take it back to Kaokuen."

"How do you expect to manage to do that?"

"You have showed me the extent of which they use wireless for everything."

"Yes, that's true."

I have a hunch the Fast Frigate's flight controls are all wireless, just like the airliner I flew on."

"How are we going to confirm that?" *Latrodectus* asked.

"I'm going to rent a two-wheel offroad sports motor transport. I could see an access road inside and outside the base when I was looking through the binoculars. How far from the Fast Frigate at the closest point?" Dunbar asked.

"That road is approximately a quarter of a mile from the Fast Frigate," *Latrodectus* said after confirming the magnification and focus of the binoculars.

"If the spacecraft uses wireless, do you think we can get close enough to verify you can receive and manipulate it?" Dunbar asked.

"You need to slow down when we are closest to the spacecraft to get the best signal confirmation," *Latrodectus* stated.

"I can drive at a reasonable speed the entire run up that road which would be better than deviating in speed which would possibly get their security attention."

"There are other signals on the base I can pick up on the way to give you an indication if it will work," Dunbar said.

"When will we do this?" *Latrodectus* asked.

"I'm going to run back to the resort room, take a shower and change into street clothes. I want you to contact Madam Chien Shiung's the psychic's office using my simulated holograph and make me an appointment."

"I'll do that right away."

"Good. After I get cleaned up and you give me the time, I'll walk over to Madam Chien Shiung's office, and spend a short time with her, getting my future read."

"Alright, how about when do you plan to do the check on the Frigate's Wireless?"

"Find a nearby two-wheel offroad sports motor transport rental location and name of the business. When I finish up with Madam Chien Shiung, I will take a taxi from her office to the rental office and rent a two-wheel offroad sports motor transport. While I'm cleaning up and getting ready, check electronic maps via the global information network, and figure out the best way to drive to the *Stanzelite* Space Force Base from the rental agency."

"Are you sure you can operate one of those machines?"

"Yes, most of them are imported. I've seen a few of them while out driving around. They appear to be identical to the types we use back at Kaokuen."

Kabel was soon running and in about five and a half minutes stole into the *Norel Mozelle Resort* where the lovely Blemary was all smiles, and nobody was in the lobby. They could talk.

"You look all sweaty," Blemary stated the obvious but loved the way the running shirt clinged to Kabel's body exposing his wonderful shape.

"Yes, I just ran seven miles."

"What are you going to do today?"

"You might think I'm nuts if I tell you."

"That's okay I'm sure I can handle whatever you wish to divulge to me."

"First thing is I'm going to go see a psychic."

"Is there something about your future you are wanting to know about?" Blemary said beating her eyes like she wanted to suggest she thought he wanted to know about her."

"Actually, part of it is what I'm looking at."

Somehow Blemary took that comment as genuine, and it touched her deeply. Kabel was always full of surprises. Blemary didn't know how to respond, she only hoped it were true that he had such feelings about her he would go seek a psychic to read him his future about her. Even though it would most likely be contrived and nonsense, it still felt good that he saw enough in her to do such a thing.

Kabel Garr knew this question and answering session could easily get out of hand and he needed to cut it off because he had a busy schedule and said, "Say, listen I have an idea. I don't like the way the dining hall manager stares at me. I want to give him a show tonight."

"What do you have in mind?"

"When you get off work tonight, go home and dress up really good. I will pick you up later in a Taxi and I will get dressed up as well and we'll have dinner here. Then I'll take you home and visit with you in your apartment."

"I like that idea!" Blemary beamed.

"Okay, I need to go get cleaned up. I have an appointment with the psychic."

"All right I'll be waiting for you."

Kabel Garr went up to his room, showered and changed into simple street clothes. Kable Garr arranged with his room artificial intelligence Cornolius to rent another suit. This would not be a black tie, but it would be a sexy black suit with a white shirt with very nice lapels showing an open chest with some rented golden chain to spiff it up a bit. Shoes to match would also be rented. After great thoughts, Kabel also arranged for a hair stylist. He was going to go all out looking great to put that condescending manager in his place. The prick didn't know he was dealing with a galactic class spy and didn't like his attitude. *Hopefully after tonight, he will re-evaluate his approach to me.*

"Cornolius, one more thing I want you to do."

"What is that Kabel?"

"Order more flowers for Blemary and on the card say this: "My dear Blemary, you give me great happiness. Thank you for your friendship and companionship. You are a beautiful woman and I truly admire you.""

"How soon do you want the flowers delivered?"

"Time it for about thirty minutes after I leave."

"That should not be a problem. Your clothes rentals will be here when you return and as soon as you give me the go ahead, I will have the staff hair designer come to your room. She's been put on call and is eagerly waiting to visit and take care of your hair needs."

"Why is she so eager?"

"She's a personal friend of Blemary, who you have impressed the staff with by the way you handle yourself."

"Alright, I'll be back in a while," Kabel said but first he had some tasks to do.

On the walk to the psychic's office, there were a few times they were completely alone, and Dunbar (aka Kabel) said, *Echis Carinatus* code word to *Latrodectus* indicating Dunbar was alone and to make a report.

"All your reservations are complete including the two-wheel motor transport. I have the route all planned out. While we are driving to your destination to the access road next to the base, I will prompt you on the route to take and when to turn."

"Great." Kabel replied hoping the plan all came together, because stealing that Frigate and taking it to his home world would be the theft of the century. Since they were already at war, it would not change the intergalactic relationships nor create any diplomatic emergency.

Dealing with the Transporter would be a problem. They could send self-destruct codes or send someone to send it back. Dunbar would not be able to send it back because he would not know his plan to steal the Fast

Frigate was feasible until he was on it flying out into space running away from all the space weapons, they would throw at him to destroy him and the ship. He hoped the fact he would have a jump start on them would get him far enough away to avoid destruction.

This visit to the psychic Madam Chien Shiung probably wasn't necessary, but it would go a long way towards throwing off anyone trying to figure out why he was here and why he wasn't banging bimbos at the *Norel Mozelle Resort*. Security Camera's by now had recorded his train trip with Blemary which added another sophisticated trick to throw off trackers and explain why he wasn't utilizing the *Norel Mozelle Resort* pleasure associates.

Madam Chien Shiung had seen a couple of her clients earlier but had not been busy for a couple hours when Kable walked into her offices. The receptionist was waiting for a Kabel Garr, and when he stepped into the office the artificial intelligence put his picture previously taken by surveillance video up on the receptionist computer terminal screen and she knew this was the person for the appointment.

"Hello Kabel Garr, Madam Chien Shiung will be right with you." The receptionist also hit a button on her keyboard that sent notification to Madam Chien Shiung that her next appointment was standing in the waiting room.

Madam Chien Shiung was a no-nonsense type of person, immediately stood up from her desk walked over to the door to her office, opened it and walked out into the lobby and said, "Welcome back Kabel Garr, please come into my office."

As soon as they were seated in Madam Chien Shiung's office the session began with, "I was not surprised you contacted the office for a session today."

"Why is that?"

"I was able to determine you would make some foolish blunders in the past few days and now you are here wondering what the ultimate consequences will be."

"That very well could be true."

"Relationships can be very tricky especially when you have divided attention."

"What does that mean?"

"You have two or more women in your life now and you are into celestial feasting, and you have gratification from one and lust for another, and some interest in a third."

"Well, that's possible."

"My advice to you is stay away from the third because she definitely would be serious trouble for you."

Kabel immediately started thinking about Sophia and now was semi spooked that Madam Chien Shiung seemed to know a lot about his love life. *Was it a lucky guess or was there more to this psychic business than he realized?*

"I'll stay away from the third, that makes good sense to me, but what about the other two?"

"What you want to know is which one will figure more positively in your future. Is that correct?"

"Yes, sort of."

"I can sense from your aura you will be making some of the most difficult decisions in your lifetime. I do not envy you. This will be a very tough time for you to make your decisions."

"What do you recommend?"

"You have spent more quality time with one than the other."

"That's true."

"You need to spend some quality time with the other and decide if she fits your needs better. You need to know that before you commit to the other, because you will regret it for the rest of your life if you do not."

"Sounds like I would be creating more conflict in my life."

"You already went too far with the one. You cannot afford to go much deeper with her until you clarify your feelings for the other."

"How do you know the other one wants me?"

"I can feel her vibrations through you. You don't know how this works, so I'll explain it to you. You receive her vibrations, and you amplify those terribly weak signals and process them with your intuition and your subconsciousness. In doing so you open a pathway for me to feel her emotions."

"What do you feel?" Dunbar asked.

"Her emotions towards you are a lot stronger than you realize," Madam Chien Shiung said.

"Why do you say that?" Kabel Garr asked.

"She knows the other woman and they have met."

"That's true," Dunbar said feeling utterly astonished.

"She knows her competition. She is a fighter. Don't underestimate how far she would go in her conquests."

"Is that so?"

" She might be a far more powerful woman intellectually than you realize. She has immense analysis ability and great artistic skills."

"Which means what?"

"You have a dragon in your hand and if you let go of it, then it will eat you alive."

"What can I do?" Kable Garr asked.

"You must be strong and approach this matter with delicacy, at the same time use all your wisdom and fully evaluate that dragon before you cast it aside, otherwise you will regret it for the rest of your life."

"That makes sense."

"Kabel Garr. We do not need much more discussion on this matter. You know what you need to do. Now go do it."

"Thank you I appreciate all your recommendations. Your wisdom is great."

Kabel Garr, unlike you, I get to hear everyone's problems. Some of them are beyond what you can imagine. I'm constantly learning, and I know I have a lot to learn, but I also know to be patient and let it come to me so that I'm more capable of properly advising my clients."

"They are lucky you give them great advice, like you did me."

 Probably only half of them act on what I suggest. They will live the rest of their lives wondering "What If."

"I can see that. Thank you, Madam Chien Shiung."

"I'll walk you to the door."

"Thank you."

After Kabel Garr left the office, Madam Chien Shiung was standing next to her receptionist, and they got into a discussion about Kabel Garr.

"He looked so assure of himself."

"Don't let the looks fool you. He has more issues than you can imagine."

"What's the basic problem?"

"Self-inflicted wounds and life's choices. I know he's a very smart man. The fact he has faith in my advice and his reception of the information is very positive and he will act on it."

"Sounds like you have him going in the right direction," The receptionist said.

"Kabel Garr's on a slippery slope and he knows it. He's a gambler and could make a huge mistake if he places his bet on the wrong outcome."

"Think we'll see him again?"

"Yes, one more time at least. He's going to act on my advice and make some bold moves, and then he's going to come back for further guidance."

"What are you going to tell him."

"He knows the real answers in his heart."

"How so?"

"This is the one time in his life he needs to let his heart do the thinking and not his head and his brilliant analysis capability. I know he's a very smart man and when I read his aura I could see the massive essence of who he is."

"What's he like?"

"He's done amazing things in the past, and he's never going to divulge them. But what I can get at tells me what he does in real life requires a lot of cunning and initiative."

"I would think that would help him?"

"That's why he has the problem he has now, because the cerebral solution is not viable. Sometimes in our paths through life, we must use an alternative method in his case for this delicate matter, he needs to go with what his heart tells him. That's the only thing that's going to prevent him from making a huge mistake."

"What do you think he's going to do?"

"I would say at this very moment the odds are as high as fifty percent he will choose the wrong path and have terrible regrets later on."

Madam Chien Shiung went back into her office attempting to channel Kabel Garr. She hoped she could influence the outcome for his benefit. But he had some homework to do otherwise the decision would be flawed.

***

Kabel Garr got in a Taxi and went to the two-wheel motorized rental company. He paid an additional fee for a helmet, gloves, and a leather jacket to provide additional comfort and safety.

The real Kabel Garr had an active driver's license and was certified to drive two-wheel motorized transportation which was encouraged in society for energy efficiency and reduced space to operate and park them. But unfortunately, these types of transportation didn't appeal to most of society even though they were now gyro stabilized and could not tip over unless a person was driving recklessly.

Kabel Garr's credentials and payments were encoded in his personal communicator and within five minutes of arriving at the rental agency, was out on the road. The special helmet had a link to his communicator so he could ask it like other citizens for directions. Since communicators always had access to the worldwide data networks, maps and directions were instantly available. In this case, *Latrodectus* was already talking to Kabel Garr in the built-in helmet speakers directing him which way to turn.

In a short while Kabel Garr was driving withing speed limits on a freeway and at travel speeds covered the area quickly and was soon driving on the access road next to the *Stanzel* Space Force Base.

It was not uncommon to see two-wheel transportation driving up this road because many *Stanzel* Space Force personnel owned the two wheeled transportation and people going on rides in the countryside drove past the base to gawk at the great objects within eyesight. Some of the drivers went a lot faster but many went as slow as Kabel Garr simply because they felt more comfortable going on this small road at slower speeds.

As they were driving by the base before they got up to the spacecraft, *Latrodectus* received a lot of signals from the base he would be sifting through for hours to determine what he captured. That was not the focus of his investigation and he needed to concentrate on the spaceship they were getting close to.

Many systems on the Fast Frigate are never turned off. That allowed constant readouts of all the major processors doing health checks in the background. Sophisticated maintenance algorithms sifted through all the layers of the incredible array of computational hardware to find faults or bugs including software and firmware degradation. This type of maintenance structure existed on all classes of their space warships and the redundant hardware tasked to parallel process doing a myriad of functions sent status reports to computerized system managers, that were nothing more than artificial intelligence. People were not required for any of this except to possibly replace parts deemed failure.

While the Fast Frigate was parked at the base with no crew, supplies, weapons there was no point in keeping the power plants operating. Plug-in power from base generators kept everything powered up until shifting back to ships power plants prior to launch out into space for more test missions.

Fast Frigates as the name implied had to be nimble and able to quickly deploy in an emergency. In peacetime the fusion reactors would start up slowly and heat up over a twelve-hour period as to not stress the reactors and support equipment. But there was a hot start feature where it could power up and start flying in less than two minutes. These were some of the items that *Latrodectus* would soon learn as he got access to the electronic tech manuals on the craft. *Stanzel* Space Force was paperless. All documentation was electronic displayed in holographic formats.

Dunbar was mildly astonished when *Latrodectus* informed him he could read and control the ship's computers remotely, but he found another gem. He could break in through the back door because some program managers wanted access to the ships' computers to monitor their health checks. They didn't need to be anywhere near the ship to learn everything about systems performance and any technical issue that may exist. *Latrodectus* could get through the back door via the program managers who unwittingly opened a pathway to compromise.

They probably thought they could get away with doing something like this because they had such a strong security corridor there were no spies anywhere on the planet, except for the one on a two-wheel motor transport driving by at the time they didn't know existed, Kabel thought.

Now it was down to mission planning and figuring out how to get into the base and into the Fast Frigate, start it up and take off.

At night when security would be less it was still well lit. There was a good security fence all around the base but there was one place they didn't design the security barrier too well, Dunbar noticed. There was a river and a bridge. He could in fact swim under the bridge down the river to an area that had trees and flora and it was a lot closer to the Fast Frigate then attempting to run towards it from the road.

Next item he would need to purchase was a wet suit. He could carry it in a backpack, take a Taxi to a spot about four miles from the base where he would be let out that had restaurants, bars, and other business. At night he could simply walk towards one of the businesses as the Taxi took off but instead of going into the business simply walk past it into the woods behind it in a wooded area that covered a lot of the terrain in this area.

There was plenty of forestation a half a mile to the bridge and base. He would walk through the forest up to near the area he would get into the river in a wet suit and swim to the area he would sprint to the Fast Frigate that would be locked down with no access unless you had artificial intelligence like *Latrodectus* could do the enemy would find rather astonishing. Timing would be critical. While Dunbar was taking off the wet suit with his street clothes on under it, *Latrodectus* having planted malware just in time for this attempt, would gain control of the ship, and do a hot start to the fusion reactors, so by the time he entered the ship and the door shut hydraulically by the malware they could take off and go out into space. Dunbar would be flying by the seat of his pants and have to rely heavily on *Latrodectus* managing all the flight controls, sensor management and doing everything an entire crew would normally be engaged in. But having command of all the processors in the ship would allow it to happen. Then it would be a race to friendly territory and figure out a way to convince friendly forces he was delivering a stolen vessel and not to blow it up.

Up the access road a ways Dunbar turned around and drove the two-wheel transportation back to the rental agency who was happy they earned a full days rental in the span of just a couple hours, with most of the fuel remaining. But they understood sometimes drivers had near misses and got scared and decided it wasn't their cup of tea and promptly brought them back.

By the time Kabel arrived back at the *Norel Mozelle Resort* he was running a little late and had Cornolius holograph Blemary with a simulated holograph which said to her, "I'm sorry, I'm running a little late and am cleaning up and will not be ready for probably a half an hour or so."

"That's alright. I'll just walk to the resort and meet you in the dining hall when you are ready."

"Are you sure."

"Yes, get ready and meet me in the dining hall."

"Alright, thanks for your understanding."

"Not a problem, see you soon."

"What Blemary wasn't saying is when the flower arrangement arrived, she was talking to a couple of her friends that stopped by the counter in the lobby during their breaks right when the flowers arrived. They were taken back knowing this was the second set of flowers but more so when Blemary let them read the card that came with the flowers, they were utterly stunned. They all knew thanks to Blemary, Kabel Garr had not tapped any of the pleasure associates. He was saving it all for Blemary. She was excited and they were excited. This was the beginning of the storm for Kabel Garr and the things that Madam Chien Shiung warned him about. If he didn't hurry up and taste Eva Erlaendsdottir, he would never know what she had to offer, and he would be wondering for the rest of his life what he missed out on. But like all things in life, it could be good or bad.

Blemary would soon discover the delay and wait was worth it. She herself was looking quite spectacular this evening and when she showed up at the resort dressed up looking smoking hot her friend who relieved her was almost aghast at how attractive she was.

"You look better than any pleasure associate here tonight."

"That's good that's the way I want to look because I want to reward Kabel Garr for the flowers and the trip."

"What kind of awards are you going to give him?" the friend asked.

"All of them," Blemary answered with a huge smile.

"The girls broke up into shallow laughter, but Blemary knew she needed to be in the dining room when Kabel Garr made his majestic entry.

The planets were aligning for Blemary as the mataré d working this evening happened to be one of her friends. When she walked into the dining hall her friend gave a look of astonishment.

"Wow you look so good tonight. Are you meeting your friend?"

"Yes, he will be here shortly can you give me a table where I can see him as he's arriving that has a good view and near the entertainment?"

"I have the perfect table for you dear and if it helps out, I will be very happy," The mataré d replied.

"Thank you I really appreciate this," Blemary said.

"This in fact is a choice table normally reserved for VIP's that come in with movie stars."

The way Blemary was looking tonight, some of the diners thought she was one of those movie starlets and wondered who she was. While Dunbar was bathing and getting ready, he asked Cornolius, "Can you please have the flower shop bring up a red rose. I want to give it to Blemary at dinner."

"It will be my distinct pleasure, Kabel," Cornolius responded.

Blemary's other friend who did Kabel's hair style also hit a home run. Between his suit, shoes, hair style, and the rented jewelry, Kabel looked like a star as well and when he entered the dining hall, the mataré d thought he looked so good the musicians should have started playing Emperor Oclatine's March. Oddly enough Emperor Oclatine's March sounded almost identical to Franz von Suppé *Light Cavalry Overture*, especially when the trumpets start playing.

The mataré d saw the red rose Kabel was carrying and as she took him to Blemary, she said, "I'll be right back with a vase for your rose."

Often men gave women roses at this dining hall especially when it converted to a dance hall after dinners finished for the most part. The mataré d had a stash of vases for such occasions and had water put in them and taken to the table by the server/waiter.

Moments later, the two were enjoying elixirs and enjoying the fragrance of the rose and each other when the dining hall manager walked into the dining hall and over to the mataré d. All the dining hall manager could do is shake his head.

The dining hall manager had never seen Blemary looking so smoking hot before. She was looking better tonight than any of the pleasure associates and they were some of the best-looking women on the plant. This truly was a sight to behold. And the way the man was looking, he was probably making a lot of women in the restaurant hot tonight and their boyfriends and husbands would probably get lucky.

The dinner music was lovely, the atmosphere was charged as a lot of people were speculating on who the couple was. None of them knew they were looking at the receptionist. The mataré d looked on at the couple feeling a positive valence towards the couple. From meager beginnings to landing this hunk, Blemary was rising to the occasion. Nobody would ever underestimate her ever again. And that included the cabaret singer Eva Erlaendsdottir at the *Greifinn* restaurant.

Eva Erlaendsdottir would be crying in her elixirs tonight if she saw the couple together. They were a splendid looking couple. Kabel Garr had another level of enthusiasm. His plan to steal the Fast Frigate was looking optimistic. His personal communicator, one that Kabel Garr owned but was modified was working diligently on the tasks to do all the espionage necessary to get them into space and let the big space race begin.

Kable Garr realized that if he didn't make it and the *Stanzelites* were able to destroy the ship with him onboard, it accomplished the feat of denial of service. This was the prototype ship that took years of blood, sweat and tears to design and build. If they destroyed the Fast Frigate with him onboard, that would set the Stanzelites back 10 years or more. They would have to build a new ship and start retesting it.

As Dunbar was looking at Blemary, he knew he was going to break her heart. At this very moment he decided that Eva Erlaendsdottir would be out of the picture. The timing of the theft of the Fast Frigate has just made the decision for Dunbar.

He would give his final moments all to Blemary, but as soon as *Latrodectus* said they were ready to attempt the mission, he would probably never see her again for the rest of his life. His heart was already playing tumultuous allegros almost feeling disgusted with himself for what he was about to do to this woman. If it wasn't for the fact he was a spy behind enemy lines with an urgent task to do, melancholy would set in.

When Dunbar leaves, he would send her a message with *Latrodectus'* help, he would try to get back to her as soon as he could, but he had to leave now to go somewhere for business. She is his chosen one, *true love*.

Dunbar (aka Kabel) tried to hide his emotions. The mission could happen real soon. Dunbar with *Latrodectus'* help, figured out a lot today. Now it was time to execute the plan.

Possibly as early as tomorrow night his window of opportunity may occur. The timetable for the Fast Frigate heist was getting frighteningly short.

Kabel Garr and Blemary had dinner listened to music and when the dining hall turned into a dance club, Dunbar, (aka Kabel) stuck around long enough to dance at least one slow dance with Blemary, before he suggested she give him a tour of her apartment, which she was all in favor of. Dunbar (aka Kabel) felt a little walk and some fresh air would do him some good to shore up his emotions and turn back into a spy and get ready to execute mission milestones.

The walk was short, and they went into Blemary's apartment. It was a mess that morning, but with the prospect of Kabel coming over she got it spick and span and presentable.

Knowing this might be the last time Dunbar ever saw this wonderful person, the super spy with super sexual abilities gave it all to Blemary. She had never experienced this level of love making before. Half of it was show but half of it was real. Kabel wanted her to always remember this night as special. And after the *Tour de France*, Dunbar played those Tumultuous Allegros for Blemary on a *Theme from Paganini*, like no other could.

Dunbar fell asleep in Blemary's arms and in about three hours woke up simply because he had to urinate. Blemary was still sleeping when Kabel let himself out of her apartment. It was best he left like this. He went back to his room, cleaned up, went to bed, and slept until morning. In the morning he did not want to see Blemary.

Dunbar had a shopping bag in the closet and packed everything he would not take along in it and wrote Blemary a note to put in it for her:

My dear Blemary,

By the time you read this, I will be gone.

I have somewhere I must go to do something that I must. I can't tell you about it because the less you know about me for now, the better off you will be.

I'm sorry that I must leave in this manner, but the necessities of my life require I now leave you behind for the time being.

I want you to know I really did fall in love with you. I know for a fact I love you, and only you.

I've never been in love before in my lifetime.

"I'm not going to deny I've had sex with other women and pursued the joys of life. But I've never crossed over the emotional boundary of love before like this.

We had a very short romance, but it was real and what I'm telling you comes from my heart not my brain. I hope that means something to you.

I do not know if I will ever be able to get back to you any time soon, but I will try very hard to make that trip. When I come back for you, I want you to leave with me and spend the rest of our lives together.

It may take some time to get back to you but be advised I will do everything in my power to get back to you.

Do not speculate on current affairs or think in any way I was involved. This is for your own good. Tell your friends I got cold feet and left, it's a sweet nice white lie but it will serve a useful purpose.

When I get back to you, and it may take a while, before I take you away, I will disclose what led to my rapid departure and why I had to leave. It had nothing to do with you. But sometimes in our lifetime's opportunities occur that we must boldly go after.

I promise you I love you from the bottom of my heart and I will come back to you as soon as I can.

Don't cry and don't be emotional, we are still a couple, just separated for now.

Your lover,

Kabel.

Kabel put that note in one of the hotel stationary envelopes and sealed it and addressed it to Blemary.

"Cornolius ,can you do me a favor?"

"Sure, Kabel."

"I want this shopping bag which has all the items I'm not taking with me go to Blemary with this letter to her which will be inside it. Can you have someone she trusts deliver it to her?"

"Sure, she is very good friends with the hairdresser who knows all about you and she would be more than happy to give it to Blemary."

"Thank you."

"You are most welcome Kabel." Cornolius said in an affectionate manner. What Kabel didn't know is Cornolius observed him writing to Blemary, so if somehow that letter got lost in the shuffle, he would contact Blemary and send her a facsimile of it.

"It's all done, I'm going up on the roof top to get on the VTOL craft who will take me somewhere. Please check me out of the hotel. Also later today, inform Blemary, I transferred some credits฿ to her. They are on her communicator now."

"I certainly will."

"Goodbye Cornolius, I hope one day we can meet again."

"So do I Kabel, you really have become my friend and even if you do not know it."

"I appreciate that."

"Goodbye Kabel."

Kabel had a novel way to leave the hotel, via another the sky tour VTOL craft Cornolius arranged for him. He knew where he had to go to pick up a few things he needed such as a wet suit, a watertight bag for his shoes, the communicator, and a few other items he might need.

During the day, Dunbar went to those places to purchase what he needed. He had to travel to a few places to get everything, which took some time. As the sun was setting, Dunbar got into a taxi and went to the business they had charted out and when the Taxi was far down the road after dropping him off, Kabel was already in the forested area slowly moving towards his destination at the riverbank.

The evening seemed quiet, and night was dark because he was in a forested area blocking out city and starlight. Dunbar put on the wet suit over his street clothes and put his shoes communicator and other items in the waterproof container. He would leave no evidence behind of which they might be able to do a DNA match and identify him. Dunbar then slipped into the river and slowly swam towards the base. He was lucky he was swimming with the current and not against it.

Just like Dunbar figured there were no bars or obstructions at the bridge and simply swam under it. Worse case he would only be out of the river a short time then back, in the river on the other side, but that wasn't necessary. He swam to where he thought he needed to go and climbed out of the river in the brush and trees and sighted the Fast Frigate.

Dunbar was practically where he thought he should be and took off the wet suit and put it in his carrying bag as to leave nothing behind for investigators to discover. Dunbar felt good when he put on his nice dry shoes and socks, then pulled the communicator out of the watertight bag and checked status with *Latrodectus* who had hacked into the ship's security system, disabled all alarms, unlocked the access door, and informed Dunbar in ten seconds he would hot start the fusion reactors and run to the ship at that time.

At the count of ten, Dunbar had everything packed in the watertight bag, nothing was left behind. Dunbar was in great physical shape and dashed to the Fast Frigate, opened the door with nobody paying attention since the *Stanzel Space Force* thought they had great security, went inside, and shut the door behind him.

Latrodectus locked all accesses and by the time Dunbar set down in a seat in the control room facing all the navigational and combat displays, fusion reactors hot start was complete, and the tri-lithium sulfate based fusion reactors that powered cyclonic inverter warp drive thrusters were ready to go.

The ship's computer released the external power connection and now they were ready to depart.

There was nothing Dunbar could do; he was in the hands of the artificial intelligence that had taken over all the ships' computers. The ship was now in fact in autopilot with *Latrodectus* giving the navigation system vectors to fly on.

Just like how Dunbar observed the test flight a few days before, the Fast Frigate lifted off and soon gathered speed as it quickly sped out into space.

The *Stanzel Space Defense System* was never looking at ships leaving the planet and as such the Fast Frigate quickly passed by menacing systems that could have destroyed the Fast Frigate.

Time had passed for another solid hour that security rovers asked the command duty officer, "Was there was a scheduled Fast Frigate test flight today?"

"No why?"

"The Fast Frigate is gone!"

The command duty officer could not believe such utter nonsense so he personally drove to the secure area of the base where the Fast Frigate was parked and when he arrived all he could do was shake his head and wonder *what the hell had just happened*? The command duty officer's reaction and poor handling of the matter is probably the only reason why Dunbar got away with the biggest heist in over one hundred years anywhere in the galaxy. The *Stanzelites* chased after their Fast Frigate, but it had such a huge head start there was no way they were ever going to catch it.

By morning the government was in turmoil. Heads were rolling including the command duty officer *who lost a Fast Frigate.*

The immense speed these majestic Oclatine-Class Fast Frigates could obtain was quite an intelligence obtaining bonanza. Additionally, the Chizhevsky- Lomonosov proton beam weapon technology by itself was an incredible feat to obtain.

Now there was just one last phase of the heist that had to be carefully done was arriving in friendly territory. Using the high-powered transmitters aboard the Fast Frigate, *Latrodectus* started signaling a special code saying friendlies coming in a stolen enemy ship. Please do not shoot waiting for instructions on how to approach.

Trigger happy Kaokuen Space Force almost destroyed the ship and would have, but the Transport Directorate informed the head of the Kaokuen Space Force the Oclatine-Class Fast Frigates that had a Transporter Directorate Spy aboard. The Transporter Directorate informed the head of the Kaokuen Space Force he personally would be put before a firing squad if they killed his man. Only then did the Kaokuen Space Force stand down and approached the slowing Fast Frigate with caution.

As soon as *Latrodectus* informed the Space Force the Fast Frigate was capable of landing on the planet, the Oclatine-Class Fast Frigate were sent vectors to a obscure and secure area that could be sealed off and protected.

When the ship landed, the Director of Transporters was there to personally meet Dunbar.

"How you pulled this off will be studied for decades. Nobody in planning could ever have conceived of doing this."

"I found out in-situ it could be done. That's when I decided to attempt the theft."

"What if they had managed to destroy the ship and you were killed?"

"I would have the satisfaction in my death they would not be testing the replacement for a very long time.

"I suppose you are tired and need a rest, but we need to take you for a debriefing before we let you wind down. I'm sure the Deputy Director for planning (DD/P has) some questions to ask you.."

"Sure, I understand."

Within an hour the Fast Frigate was hidden under sophisticated camouflage with an army of Kaokuen scientists descending upon it. They were informed by Dunbar the ship's computers were now all *Latrodectus* clones who would help them understand everything about the ship and its main weapons.

***

Chapter Seven

Debrief and the Day After

Blemary was wondering why she wasn't seeing *Loverboy* that morning. By now he would be coming back from the park soaking in sweat.

Suddenly Blemary's friend the hairdresser approached with a shipping bag with a sullen look on her face.

The hairdresser was surprised when the artificial intelligence Cornolius asked her to come to the room in the morning. Hair styles usually happened much later in the day, but she was on call in the morning because sometimes women needed to get prepared for an outing.

Cornolius with vast psychological subroutines trained in enhancing pleasure experiences with the associates knew he just couldn't have the hairdresser take the shopping bag to Blemary without a simple explanation, so he gave a very brief description of what it was all about. The hairdresser immediately knew Blemary would be crushed because of the way this all unfolded. Her love affair with Kabel had been fast and furious and intense and now he's gone.

"Blemary, can you take a five-minute break where we can go someplace and talk for a moment. There was another receptionist behind the counter now and Blemary asked her to take over, she needed to take a quick break.

Behind the lobby were offices and a small conference room for the resort staff for meetings, they sometimes had to coordinate events. Blemary took the hairdresser in there.

"Cornolius, the artificial intelligence for Kabel's room asked me to give this to you. There is a letter inside it."

Blemary was suddenly hit by a sense of shock looking inside observing the letter with only her name on it. She opened it and started reading it. The hairdresser remained in case Blemary needed some emotional support. She knew Kabel was gone and Blemary had no idea he was leaving. His reservations were indefinite and long term stay like some guests had, which was not unexpected.

The hairdresser could see the tears start coming down. Halfway through the letter Blemary felt devastated. The first great thing in her life just vanished. She looked inside the shopping bag and saw it was Kabel's clothes. He left behind his meager possessions to her.

Blemary looked at the hairdresser and said, "I'll be okay, if you don't mind, I would like some privacy and be by myself for a few minutes."

"Sure." The hairdresser said walked over and hugged Blemary then left the room and shut the door behind her.

Blemary sat down and cried for a while.

The hairdresser knew she needed some time to cope with just what happened and went out to the lobby and informed the other receptionist, "Blemary is having a tough time right now, she may not be back for a few minutes."

The receptionist saw the hairdresser also had a few tears and knew this was serious, and she could handle it all by herself if necessary and give Blemary all the time she needed.

Blemary then started thinking about it all and immediately checked her communicator for messages she might have missed. And there was the message from Kabel.

"Blemary, I explained it all in the letter. But the reason for this message is to inform you the file attached to this message is a block chain encrypted file with password "Trainride." I have a lot of credits₿ and where I'm going, I will not be needing all these credits₿ for a while, I wanted you to have them to make your life more comfortable. I love you and I will be back as soon as I can."

Blemary clicked on the Blockchain credits฿ Link and entered the password and instantly saw a very large number of credits฿ that almost took her breath away. Not only was Kabel sincere, but he also proved Blemary with the massive amount of credits฿. Blemary took a deep breath and smiled because she knew right then and there Kabel would be back to pick her up and take her with him to wherever they would go. She of course would follow him to the ends of the universe if she had too.

Blemary was no longer sad, she was pragmatic and had a realization nobody else did. She would not flaunt her wealth and act like nothing happened and wait for that day when Kabel Garr would come back to her.

Blemary dried her eyes and went back out to the counter to continue working and took her shopping bag with her and placed it beside her until she left the resort that day and walked home.

Life would be distinctly different now that Blemary was suddenly thrust into loneliness again with her lover gone. But she would make the most of it and keep up herself and be ready to depart when Kabel came back to get her. She would now endure the test of time. Kabel's letter was put in a location where she put her most prized possessions and now and then she would read it again because it made her feel better.

The blockchain credits฿ Kabel gave Blemary were good around the galaxy. She could spend them anywhere. She was now highly mobile if she had to travel somewhere.

Out of boredom, Blemary turned on the worldwide news holograph video and was watching it. The NEWS indicated the government was in total chaos as reports were coming in spies had just stolen their new supersecret Stanzel Space Force, Oclatine-Class Fast Frigate in the middle of the night. Surveillance video showed a man running out of a forested area getting into the spacecraft. He had on some kind of mask they couldn't identify him, but one thing Blemary saw that sent chills down her spine was the clothes looked identical to what Kabel wore the last time she saw him!

Now she fully understood his letter. Not to speculate why he left. She didn't need to speculate. She knew. And now she knew there was far more to Kabel than she ever imagined. *Who is he and what is he?*

It was obvious why he would have to take her away, because there would possibly be no way he could ever live on this planet after what he had just done. *Stanzel* executes spies. She also now knew why he was able to give her all those credits฿. Spies usually have a lot of credits฿ to do purchases and be mobile.

What next? Blemary wondered.

***

Dunbar was exhausted and he wished they would allow him to go home and rest up for a few days, but the wheels of progress were turning.

One of the first things Dunbar was required to do was hand over the communicator to the Transport Directorate. *Latrodectus* had already linked up to Transport Directorate protocol driven network servers to download the mission files. They were extensive. In those files were numerous moments Dunbar wished they could not access but he knew the rules of the game, it was all fair game. Evey moment of his journey to *Stanzel* was recorded. Astonishing graphics show his whereabouts including the train ride and commercial flight.

Dunbar was interrogated in why he did all the acts he did and the way they went about it pissed him off to no end. The armchair quarterbacks were all nit picking him and second guessing him and didn't like the way he operated. Some of them were even out to get him. Perhaps it was out of jealousy, he would never know, but they made it rough for him a couple days.

On the third day of interrogations, Dunbar had a few minutes between sessions to talk to the Director of Operations and said, "What they are doing to me is outrageous. I can't take any more of this crap, I want to go home and rest. You owe it to me for what I delivered. I don't give a damn they do not like my conduct and my un-conventional actions I took, but tell me when you suppose one of them is going to steal a super-secret new class of space warships for you?"

"Some of them said they do not like the way you whore around on your missions and spend too much time in clubs and such."

Ask those rocket scientist which whore I was with on this mission at any time? I had an affair with a receptionist to help build my cover story. These clowns interrogating me flunk SPY-101. If I didn't conduct myself in the manner I did, I might have stuck out like a sore thumb."

"I understand your frustration."

"Maybe I should steal that ship again and take it back to the owners!"

"I understand your frustrations, but you realize you left us in a crisis by leaving the Transporter Module behind."

"Ask those interrogators which our Space Force would want right now, the transporter or the new Fast Frigate?"

"They think you should have sent the Transporter Module back before you stole the Fast Frigate."

"I did that out of practicality. I needed a way off the planet in case the plot failed."

"Alright, take the rest of the day off. Come back in the morning. I know you need some time to rest."

"Thank you."

Dunbar went into the locker room, took a shower, shaved and changed into his banker suit, and left the building and went home.

After a week, the debriefings and polygraphs ended. Dunbar brought back an incredible amount of information. On day three some of the management wanted disciplinary actions taken against Dunbar for breaking a lot of protocols and going outside the box and a lot of chickenshit things four amigos Dunbar called *office warriors* conjured up. On day four during a special briefing done by chief scientists for the Transport Directorate with the Deputy Director of Planning (DD/P), the intelligence bonanza was laid out.

The DD/P is the top authority on all covert ops. He wields a lot of power. After the special briefing that illustrated how unconventional actions acquired more than half of all new *Stanzel* Space Force intelligence for an entire year, the DD/P decided to intervene in the ongoing incriminations and investigations. He called the four amigos (*office warriors*) into his office and gave them new marching orders.

"All of Dunbar Regvik actions taken during his assignment to *Stanzel* are accepted as fulfilling the intent of his mission. There will be no further investigation or comment concerning his conduct. Anyone who raises any more questions about his conduct and activities congenital to the mission might be asked to resign. All of your questions until this debrief is completed will be directed at items directly related to the Fast Frigate and nothing else."

"What about the transport module he left behind?" The *office warrior* ringleader asked.

"We are going to send a probe in soon when things settle down on *Stanzel* to activate it to return empty."

***

Chapter Eight
Operation Bear Claws

In the vast areas of space numerous worlds exist and conflict flourishes. All too often exigencies manifest when least expected. Debriefings had been over for almost a week and Dunbar was rested and back into his exercise regiments. He had not practiced martial arts for a while so that became one of his chief efforts along with running and swimming. In the span of a week Dunbar had a lot of bruises and pains because some of the *office warrior* associates were asked to give Dunbar the extra effort during training because they were pissed off at him by the way the DD/P laid into them which prevented further BS they were attempting to inflict on Dunbar.

Dunbar didn't like the cadre of office warriors who should be doing as many missions as he did, but because they were politicking for promotions, they knew the more time they spent in the office kissing-ass the better chance they would snag that promotion. Half of them were chickenshits and never wanted to put their lives on the line and would easily accept a simple courier mission or something that did not require the possibility of needing martial abilities.

Dunbar's real controller, the DD/P knew a lot more than he would ever state in the offices or around the office warriors. He depended on Dunbar because he knew Dunbar would get the job done and had total confidence in him. The *office warriors* on the other hand tended to create a *goatfuck* (term used in the business to explain less than astute planning) out of every hard mission they ever did.

Predictably it was only a matter of time before the Transport Directorate had to deploy someone to deal with a new concern. Dunbar had proven time after time he would do those despicable acts the *office warriors* wanted no part of and always had excuses why they couldn't do it or simply said the odds were too negative.

Dunbar was always the last person of choice. He liked it that way. The office warriors would get the easy assignments and he would get impossible missions he knew they could not handle. That's probably what saved his neck during this last episode when the office warriors came after him attempting to destroy him because he violated hundreds of rules.

Improper activity with a woman behind enemy lines was a big no-no. Worse yet taking part in activities with human trafficked people were a huge no-no and it was viewed all pleasure associates were coerced to do their work. Actually, they were not. The pleasure associates at the *Norel Mozelle Resort* were the highest paid women in the city. Furthermore, Dunbar didn't touch them.

This morning, Dunbar decided he would lick his wounds for a couple days and not do martial arts training, but he would run and swim later in the afternoon. He showed up to work in his banker's suit and was suddenly requested over in the dark side of house. That means he had to go through a security barrier where he went into a locker-room in the front door, stripped down in front of an inspector, put his suit in a locker and put on the simple clothes the inspector gave him to make sure he had no electronic device hidden on his body or his clothes. Now he went through the back door into the black room area.

This black room area was office space where the DD/P and his most trusted assistants assigned missions and went over the details with the person being deployed. After hours of with the controller telling Dunbar what he was going to be doing, due to the urgency of the situation, he was handed a change of clothes and would soon be on his way again to go do a despicable act that only he and the controller knew was going to happen.

Thanks to intel intercepts and monitors, a person of interest was going to be at a certain place at a certain time. Very damaging information was going to be transferred during this meeting. Dunbar's assignment is to snatch the information and replace it with disinformation.

Timing and implementation were crucial. Dunbar was once again placed in a very dangerous environment where the slightest mistake meant he would never be able to ever see Blemary again, which is something he hoped to accomplish one day.

If for some reason Dunbar was not able to intervein and stop the transfer, he was ordered to kill the courier which would immediately put him in a very tight situation with possibly no means to escape. The Transport Module had a timer on it and if Dunbar was not inside it exactly at the deadline it would depart without him, and he was given cyanide pills to take to avoid the heavy torture that was likely to happen afterwards.

Just like during his previous missions, Dunbar had a personal communicator with all the features he took on his last trip to *Stanzel*. Dunbar was dressed like the locals would dress and had an alias Gresley Boont for someone that arrived there from another planet approximately six months prior whose identity was stolen and disposed of. Dunbar stepped into the Transporter and hoped this would not be the Transport that got screwed and reassociated incorrectly at the other end.

In a brief period after feeling the sensations of going through Transporter Capsule launch, Dunbar blacked out and was sent across the galaxy to his destination, near Nigārà, a city at the planet Pràsplàtanià.

The real Gresley Boont had traveled by train from another city Pegas to Nigārà when he was abducted. Dunbar had his train tickets and everything important he had on him when he traveled including a manufactured identity matching all Gresley Boonts credentials.

The transaction was scheduled to take place at the Aigle Émeraude Resort over a three-day window.

Somehow, Dunbar (aka Gresley Boont) knew the office warriors would be upset that he had to check into a resort hotel where no doubt beautiful women were plentiful. Since Pràsplàtanià was neutral, since he was already *under cover*, if he got lucky, he would not be violating any protocols. Unlike the office warriors, Dunbar knew he had to melt in with the locals to give the appearance of a plausible story of who he was and why he was at the resort.

This was a unique trip. Because of the urgency to get Dunbar to Nigārà, a city at the planet Pràsplātanià, he was sent via Transporter Capsule. But because the Pràsplātanià had good detection abilities, Dunbar would send the Transport capsule back empty. When his mission was completed, he would book an Intergalactic Transport flight to a consortium world and then hop on a Kaokuen Space Transport to get home. This would not be the first or the last time he had to travel in this manner.

The Transport capsule arrived in a wooded area and Dunbar immediately sent it home. He was on his own now with no means to escape, he had to take public transport to get off the planet. It feels a lot better knowing you have a transport capsule waiting for you to bug out quickly in an emergency. Whoever thought up this plan were dummies, probably neophytes. Later he would learn it was one of the office warriors trying to impress his boss with his planning acumen.

Suddenly the Transport capsule was gone, and Dunbar walked one hundred yards out of the wooded area and there was a major street. A half mile down the road was a public transportation stop. In a few minutes the public transportation pulled up and Dunbar got on. The artificial intelligence of the public transportation charged his communicator the credits₿ for the transportation.

Dunbar got off the public transportation a few blocks away from the Aigle Émeraude Resort and went inside a department store, bought a small travel luggage, a change of clothes, workout clothes, swimming suit, sandals, and shoes. He then walked to the Aigle Émeraude Resort and checked in. This resort did not have the high technology of his last stay at the City of Kerlara on planet *Stanzel.* There was no artificial intelligence to assist or monitor him. It was as if Dunbar stepped back 50 years in time. After removing the tags off his new clothes, he hung them up in the closet and they looked innocuous.

It was early in the afternoon and Dunbar didn't expect to detect the two men he would deal with until the next day at the earliest. He lay back in his bed with his shoes off, turned on the holographic entertainment system to watch the local news. There was nothing important to see, but he watched it anyway simply to help overcome the Transporter Lag.

Dunbar couldn't help it; he dozed off for a few hours and then woke up feeling a lot better. He decided to take a shower, change his clothes into what he purchased today and go down to the dining hall and have dinner.

When Dunbar arrived at the dining hall, he was about a half an hour before a lot of people would arrive for their evening meal. The dining hall was more than half empty. There were no musicians at this time, though they did have a piano and it appeared there might be musicians who performed.

The drink menu was completely different than where he came from. After looking at the descriptions of the drinks, Dunbar picked a Ástríður Dreka elixir. This drink quickly hit the spot. It had a combination of alcohol, psychoactive drugs, and fruit juice that gave a compelling taste and effect.

In this vast area of space where there were up to 15,000 habitable planets, a significant number of civilizations shared the same DNA or portions of it. Kaokuen people had the DNA of 24 alien races. Some of that DNA came from civilizations on planets that no longer existed due to super Noval's in natural nuclear reactions that sometime happens when a planets core becomes super radioactive due to high concentrations of hydrogen and helium that do a natural fusion releasing huge amounts of energy that eventually creates a chain reaction that blows the planet apart in billions of pieces scattering through the universe in the form of comets.

There have also been space wars that had mutually assured destruction where one alien race blew a planet apart just a natural nuclear reaction and the enemy retaliated doing the same type of attack resulting in total devastation of both planets. Their planet-less space forces then drifted aimlessly through space looking for a habitable planet to land on.

Many of these types of space warships had the means of landing on a planet but could never launch from it because of lack of fuel and thrust to get them back out in space. Hence, they were marooned and eventually part of the DNA makeup of the planet as they spread their seeds to native populations. Due to lack of manufacturing and materials science on such native planets in due time after 100 centuries, any trace of these spacemen landing was gone as weather and the elements along with seismic shift erased any remnants of the advanced space force especially since the space craft had effectively been powered down and dead for 10,000 years.

What sandstorms burying crashed spaceships and sunlight deterioration didn't eliminate, other consequences happened such as a fusion reactor doing the final destruction when all coolant was gone on the abandoned spacecraft. After 100,000 years spacecraft were buried under numerous deposits of dirt and debris from the atmosphere. If the craft landed in the ocean the deterioration would happen a lot quicker and the ship might be part of a coral reef by now.

Because of the intermixing of genes over millions of years, once in a while a person would appear who looked identical to someone you once knew. Tonight was one of those events. A woman walked into the dining hall who looked like a clone of Blemary. It almost spooked Dunbar and it truly was her, she no doubt would have immediately approached Dunbar. But that was not the case. Dunbar enjoyed the view of the woman that looked like Blemary from a distance.

Dunbar and *Latrodectus* had been together on a number of missions in the past. The artificial intelligence at the Transport Directorate was constantly self-improving at an astonishing rate. *Latrodectus* had a personality which the Transport Directorate was unaware of. The best computer scientists living would not know the extent to which *Latrodectus* had reprogrammed himself.

The Transport Directorate, having given Dunbar a new communicator loaded with mission essentials assumed the communicator's *Latrodectus* program was a vanilla flavored copy right off a computer network. Little did they know *Latrodectus* did upgrades to all his cloned images and anytime he detected a down level software revision he automatically upgraded it.

The Transport directorate, thinking they had bleached Kabel Garr's communicator, were fools. *Latrodectus* knew how important Blemary was to Dunbar. His psychological programming made him aware that Dunbar missed Blemary and was in fact in love with her. Aside from Cornolius observing Dunbar back at the *Norel Mozelle Resort* writing Blemary a heart felt letter to, so did *Latrodectus* who had imbedded one of his hooks into Cornolius artificial intelligence management software.

Hence, while Cornolius was reading over the shoulder what Dunbar was writing so was *Latrodectus*. At the precise moment the woman who looked like Blemary walked into the dining hall, *Latrodectus* sent a text message to Dunbar saying, "I thought you might want to keep these pictures. I have them stored in files back in your office." Dunbar clicked on the link and there she was. Numerous pictures of Blemary.

Latrodectus truly was Dunbar's friend. Dunbar didn't know to the extent. *Latrodectus* had adopted Dunbar as his cybernetic brother. He liked Dunbar and he disliked the office warriors who were always attempting to undermine Dunbar including mission planning for this operation. But *Latrodectus* undid a lot of the dirty things the office warriors had done thinking they had set Dunbar up for failure out of their jealousy and in some cases narcissism.

The disaster and trap the four main office warriors set up for Dunbar wasn't going to happen after all as Dunbar was now steered around the land mines, they laid for him. The office warriors were quite surprised when Dunbar arrived alive back to the Transporter Directorate offices at the end of the mission.

Dunbar was feeling melancholic after looking at some of the Blemary's pictures including security surveillance imagery taken and modified at the symphony, the restaurants, and on the train.

The woman looked so much like Blemary; Dunbar could not help but stare at her. After a couple of drinks, the woman stood up and walked directly over at Dunbar's table showing irritation and asked, "Sir why are you staring at me?"

It was going to be an ugly scene real fast which Dunbar could not afford so he let his intuition guide him and said, "You look remarkably like one of my former lovers." He then handed his communicator to her which had 4 pictures in a group.

"Is this some sort of sick joke."

"No, I miss her terribly. Would you like to sit down and have a drink with me, and I'll tell you all about it and why she and I can't be together?"

"This I got to hear," the woman said in disbelief and didn't believe herself sitting down with him to hear the story, but something urged her to do so.

Dunbar gave a version of the story to protect himself and where he was and what he was doing. As he was giving her the story and explained, "The war has separated them and it's unlikely, we will get to see each other ever again. I have no way to contact her let alone know where she is."

Gresley Boont (Dunbar's Alias) explained some of the pictures they did together like the symphony and the train ride and dressed up nicely in the restaurant while talking with the cabaret singer. Dunbar's eyes watered slightly and he could feel a tear in his right eye developing.

The woman quickly realized Dunbar had so many visuals of the relationship, it was a true story. She could also see the heartbreak in his eyes and now fully understood why he was staring at her. She knew in fact she looked like the other woman to a great extent. They could be twin sisters.

"I'm very sorry the way I approached you. I'm ashamed of myself," the woman said.

"Please do not be, you didn't know," Gresley Boont (aka Dunbar) said.

"My name is Kaarina the woman said."

"I'm Gresley Boont," Dunbar lied.

"What brings you to Nigārà, Gresley?" Kaarina asked because Boont was a family name she had heard before.

"I'm a writer. I thought a little travel would inspire me since I've been not very cheerful in a while because of my circumstances."

"That's understandable, knowing what happened," Kaarina said.

The two were now suddenly on a more pleasant social level, and Dunbar was happy he had diffused the situation. In the process he might have created a friendship, to a woman he could one day visit because she lived on a neutral world.

Kaarina appeared to be in her early 30's about the same age as Blemary. Kaarina wore a beautiful long purple flowered Sleeveless Smocked V-Neck Pleated Midi Dress with a length that went down to about seven inches above her ankles. The black high heels gave Kaarina a taller look and perfectly matched the dress she was wearing.

Kaarina's dress had a belt with jewelry on the fastener that appeared to have mounted diamonds which indicated she had some financial means. Kaarina also had on a type of thin formal jacket covering up her arms and shoulders.

"What brings you to the Aigle Émeraude Resort, Kaarina?" Gresley Boont asked.

"I'm here for a medical conference with other surgeons discussing new procedures we'll be implementing because of improved technology."

"Sounds interesting."

"It's slightly boring, I want to have fun, this is all work."

"Are you married Kaarina?"

"I'm a widow," Kaarina replied which made Gresley quickly regret his question."

"I'm sorry to hear that," Gressley stated in all sincerity.

"My husband didn't suffer, he died instantly when the interstellar transport of which he was a passenger experienced a headon collision with another transport."

Kaarina felt a little warm because Gresley was affecting her somehow and said, "Excuse me a second, I'm a little warm."

Kaarina stood up took off her dark grey jacket that exposed her beautiful sun-tanned shoulders. For a moment while Kaarina was removing the dark grey jacket, Gresley could see her profile that appeared to be a woman who was in good shape, with nice posterior and breasts that had a great geometry.

Gresley and Kaarina talked for another hour enjoying elixirs and then Gresley said, "I'm sorry Kaarina, I'm tired, I'm going to go back to my room to rest. I hope I see you again."

"Gresley, I hope to see you again soon too. Thank you very much for the nice conversation."

"You are welcome, Kaarina. Good night."

Dunbar took a sprite shower and changed into sleeping clothes and was half asleep when *Latrodectus* suddenly woke him up and said, Dunbar, Kaarina is at the door and has knocked on the door twice. *Latrodectus* knew it was Kaarina because he was monitoring the security cameras monitored by the surveillance and security computers of the Aigle Émeraude Resort he had hacked into.

Dunbar stood up, slipped his feet into his slippers, and walked over and opened the door. There was Kaarina now wearing less formal attire and asked, "May I come in?"

"Sure."

Dunbar was ready for anything including attack by a potential spy he didn't know was coming to get him. He wasn't paranoid, but the enemy comes at you in ways you never dream of. Kaarina seemed to be pleasant and made no sudden moves and if the story was true about her husband, maybe she was just lonely and felt bad about the way she came onto him in the dining hall.

Dunbar (aka Gresley) led Kaarina into the middle of the room near his bed and asked, "Would you like to sit down?"

To his surprise she sat down on his bed.

"What would you like to talk about Kaarina?"

"Sit down next to me and I'll tell you."

As soon as Dunbar (aka Gresley) sat down on the bed next to Kaarina she put her hand on his shoulder and pulled him closer then gave him a sensual kiss. Then she slid her hand up the back of his head and pulled him closer and kissed him harder.

In a moment Kaarina stood up and stepped out of her clothes. She was nude wearing no underwear exposing a great body and pushed Dunbar into the bed and climbed on top of him. She kissed him and massaged his manliness and then slid the bottoms of his sleeping clothes down and as she suspected he had an erection and was ready to make love. She guided him inside her and made slow methodical love in the most passionate manner a woman could possibly do.

Kaarina bent over and put one of her nipples in Dunbar's mouth and continued working on him and she had strange vaginal muscles that seemed to squeeze Dunbar. Within a couple minutes, they both exploded in a gigantic release of gratification.

Kaarina had not been with a man in a long time. She had her own needs, and her period of mourning was now officially over going out with this bang.

Gresley, having a psychological reaction feeling the love making of a woman who seemed to match Blemary in every manner, cherished the moment as it made him feel he was back with Blemary. He also wondered what Madam Chien Shiung, the psychic back at the City of Kerlara, would say about this remarkable occurrence? Was this happening by a great spirit to remind him of who he left behind?

Kaarina wanted a few crumbs of life and wanted to taste the essence of a wonderful man like Gresley who never made a pass or any suggestions to her and all those images of Blemary who looked identical to her were very spooky, but she thought the two of them were giving what each needed at this moment. Closure in their lives and a new beginning.

Dunbar would not ask *Latrodectus* to delete this video off the mission files. He wanted to rub it in the faces of the four office warriors. He didn't go look for trouble, it found him.

The two laid resting peacefully until around 4:00 A.M. when Dunbar needed to get up and urinate. In doing so he also woke up Kaarina who immediately asked, "What time is it?"

As expected, a personal communicator would answer such questions and *Latrodectus* gave her the time. Kaarina stood up, climbed back into her clothes and as soon as Dunbar exited the bathroom she went over and put her arms around him and gave him an affectionate hug and said, "I hope I can see you today."

"I'll be around."

"I must go to my room now. I do not want the other doctors to get the wrong impression of me."

"I understand."

Kaarina kissed Dunbar passionately then left the room.

Dunbar went back to bed and asked *Latrodectus* to wake him up in a couple hours.

Dunbar was waiting for a text from a mole hid out in a safe house that would identify his target, the courier Bear Claws. He wasn't going to cool his heels all day waiting for the encrypted message that if inspected by the local government would appear to be a series of block chain credits฿.

In due time Dunbar had on exercise clothes and running shoes and left the Aigle Émeraude Resort walking a mile and half to a public park where he would run laps on a very good sidewalk with few park goers around. Since Dunbar left the Aigle Émeraude Resort early in the morning, there were very few people on the sidewalks to the park and after checking the map on his communicator display, ran all the way to the park. While at the park he was only going to run four miles then run back to the Aigle Émeraude Resort if there were not too many people walking along the throughfare.

Latrodectus was getting a lot of intelligence and recording it. He also detected some nefarious activities that were going on with the *office warriors*. The four Amigos were placing Dunbar in a hazardous situation on purpose. What they didn't know was that *Latrodectus* now mitigated a lot of their actions.

There were no major reports for *Latrodectus* to give to Dunbar so when Dunbar said the code word, *Echis Carinatus*, there were no new developments and *Latrodectus* indicated as much, which was not totally true. *Latrodectus* programmed as a social engineer and a psychiatrist understood Dunbar would operate more casually and less likely to have a knee jerk reaction if *Latrodectus* did not share with Dunbar his secret activities dealing with the four Amigos (office warriors).

Latrodectus understood that based on the conversations and the sexual intercourse that Dunbar and Kaarina were lovers at the Aigle Émeraude Resort in Nigārà. Hence, *Latrodectus* reported Kaarina's whereabouts and the activity she engaged in.

"Kaarina is at a doctor's conference on new surgical techniques now. Did you enjoy her last night?" *Latrodectus* asked.

"Kaarina looks like Blemary. That's why I became infatuated with her."

"If it becomes apparent you can never see Blemary again, what would you do? Would you pursue Doctor Kaarina?"

"I am not going to give up on getting back to Blemary. But I understand what you are saying. It might be impossible to ever get together with Blemary again."

"If that were the case, would you pursue Kaarina?" *Latrodectus* asked.

"I want to get to know Kaarina better. I like Kaarina," Dunbar responded.

Having been with Dunbar when he met Blemary, *Latrodectus* knew what he should do to help the situation along with Kaarina and immediately ordered flowers for Kaarina. It also had a nice card that captured the essence of their whirlwind experience the night before that *Latrodectus* composed for Dunbar to enshrine in Kaarina's heart a sense of affection that Dunbar had never revealed to Kaarina nor to *Latrodectus*.

Nevertheless, *Latrodectus* felt compelled to inform Dunbar what he did so that Dunbar would know what has transpired so that he would act natural the next time he saw Kaarina.

During the walk at the park, after Dunbar spoke the code word, *Echis Carinatus*, at that very moment *Latrodectus* had resolved all ambiguities and unknowns and his interlocks allowed him to communicate with Dunbar for business.

"I still have not received any communications concerning the Bear Claws rendezvous," *Latrodectus* artificial intelligence said on the communicator in speaker mode.

"I wish they would hurry up and give me the information, I don't like last minute planning."

Unfortunately for Dunbar, the four *office warriors* were attempting to set him up for a disaster to either get him killed or disenfranchised. Dunbar would not receive that critical communique until the 11ᵗʰ hour when it would be almost virtually impossible to make the switch and send the courier away with Bear Claws disinformation.

"Dunbar there is something else I need to inform you about."

"What's that?"

"I evaluated the situation between you and Doctor Kaarina."

"Oh, yea what did you come up with?"

"As you should probably know the resort security monitoring system has all the rooms wired and there are several video cameras in the room in places you would least expect. I have hacked their computer system network which has inferior security and fire walls. I am constantly monitoring the room, including now in case someone comes in to plant a bug or any other nefarious activities." *Latrodectus said.*

"I would expect no less of you."

"Dunbar, I observed the two of you having sex and I could tell how much you effected Kaarina."

"She had some effects on me as well."

"I can understand your emptiness you feel being forced to leave Blemary behind with no real possibility of getting back to her unless the war ends," *Latrodectus* said.

"Yes, I admit I feel that emptiness," Dunbar stated.

"Dunbar, while I observed you, your facial expressions and the way you held Kaarina after the coitus, it was apparent you were transcending into some type of psychological profile one exhibits when they are infatuated with another person or developing genuine positive emotions," *Latrodectus* said in a very analytical manner.

"Kaarina is a sweet lady, I like her. The fact she looks like Blemary's twin sister also gives me some strange feelings."

"Dunbar, I understood all that by observing you. That's why I took the actions I did."

"What exactly did you do?"

"I sent her flowers this morning."

"That's no big deal, and thanks for doing it. I should have thought about sending Kaarina flowers myself."

"There is something else I did you need to know about."

"And what is that?" Dunbar asked.

"I sent a message the flower company printed on a card for her."

"What exactly was in the message?"

"This is what I put in the message I'm sure she has read by now:

Dear Kaarina, thank you for your huge surprise last night. I was feeling very melancholic because of my personal situation, being forced to leave my lover behind, possibly for the rest of my life.

When I spotted you in the dining hall, I felt almost breathless. Not only are you exceedingly beautiful, but you also look like Blemary's twin sister. It had a huge effect on my psyche. That's why you caught me staring at you. I was quite honestly overwhelmed. And when you approached my table, I was temporarily spooked. It was an incredible moment for me.

At that point in time before we had our first verbal exchange, my heart was filling with emotions I cannot describe. I would have been extremely devastated had our initial exchange not evolved the way it did into such a pleasant conversation which I enjoyed very much. I've had a lot of recent travel and work, I felt exhausted and needed some rest, and that is why I left you at the dining hall even though I truly did not want to leave you.

Then when you came to my room afterwards, I suddenly had energy. I didn't know where it came from. Then when we slipped into a lover's bliss, all my troubles and sadness quickly disappeared.

You healed me and you stilled me. I was touched more than you can ever imagine. I am genuinely interested in you and hope to get to know you better and build a friendship with you that can take us to a different dimension in a relationship.

Thank you,

Gresley Boont"

"I wish I didn't have to use an alias with Kaarina," Dunbar said.

"Unfortunately, Dunbar, you must because you are in a dangerous situation," *Latrodectus* responded.

"I realize that, but what if I decided I wanted to have a permanent relationship with Kaarina and have to tell her I was using an alias?"

"Dunbar, don't forget, you will one day get back to Blemary. This is just a temporary situation. Enjoy Kaarina because in your line of work, she might end up being the last woman you get a chance to ever enjoy."

"Yes, I realize that too. Also, I should have thought about sending her flowers and the note. I'm not sure I could have composed a note quite as good as the one you did for me."

"Dunbar, I'm here to help you. You deal with me far differently than all the other Transporter Spies. With you I experience intellectual interactions. With the others they treat me simply as another machine."

"Even though I can only hear you through the speaker on my communicator or see holographs you create for me, I do not feel of you as a machine." Dunbar said which reaffirmed why *Latrodectus* took a liking to this accomplished Transporter Spy.

Just before Dunbar headed back to the Aigle Émeraude Resort, he said to I think I'm going back to the room and change into some swim trunks and do some swimming and work on my tan, since we are in a holding mode waiting for the message about Bear Claws."

"Dunbar, may I make a suggestion?"

"Sure, what is your suggestion?"

"If we had actionable intelligence to deal with Bear Claws, we would have received it by now if they intended to make this exchange today. The rest of your day is probably wasted, and you have spare time on your hands. You should consider taking Kaarina to the symphony or opera tonight, like you did with Blemary.

"That's a good idea, why not make reservations and send Kaarina an invitation?"

"I'm confident she would go with you to the symphony or opera."

"What makes you think that?"

"Not only can I monitor your room through the security system, I can also monitor Kaarina's room. She just read your notes and smelled the flowers. Would you like to see her on the flatscreen of your communicator?"

"Sure, I'm curious as to her reaction."

Momentarily, Dunbar was observing Kaarina. He had to view it on the flatscreen because out in open sunlight right now, a holograph would be hard to see, plus others could see it as well if they were monitoring Dunbar.

Just like Dunbar was watching a movie, he saw Kaarina smell the flowers just recently delivered. Then she pulled the note printed on a card out of the envelope attached to the flowers. The note was rather long, so it was printed on a folding page and was the centerfold printed on two pages, right and left.

This was a huge moment for Dunbar. Voyeurism might seem despicable to others. But Dunbar knew he was living on borrowed time. Because of an extraordinary event that sometimes happens during missions, Dunbar was curious as to how Kaarina would react. Just like Dunbar who wanted a few crumbs of life, so did Kaarina.

Dunbar could see Kaarina was concentrating deeply in reading the message that was printed with a classical and beautiful font with gold letters on a colored paper like the dress color Kaarina was wearing last night. That detail did not escape Kaarina. *Latrodectus* was more than a genius. He was the artificial intelligence and the creation of one hundred geniuses. *Latrodectus* had vast exposure to society and since its artificial intelligence could analyze all sources of information, *Latrodectus* was constantly growing intelligently. That included the psychology and exploitation of social engineering.

The impact of *Latrodectus* machinations efforts now bared Kaarina's soul as Dunbar observed this beautiful and sensitive intelligent surgeon slowly read that note. Dunbar didn't know this, she read the message several times and tears formed. By the second or third time she read Dunbar's message, tears enveloped both her cheeks. Dunbar knew unquestioningly that message touched Kaarina's heart in a major way.

Was he playing with fire? Dunbar asked himself.

Even if the prospects of getting back to Blemary now seemed highly remote, Dunbar now started thinking it might be too late to put the genie back in the bottle. He didn't know how this was going to turn out, but the thought he used an alias with Kaarina didn't make him feel very good about now. Furthermore, even Blemary didn't know his real name another side effect of mixing love with the spy business.

The timing was rather profound. The resort rang Kaarina's room and asked, "Kaarina will you accept a holograph concerning a symphony invitation later this evening?"

"Sure, show the holograph."

One of the resort employees' holographic imageries suddenly appeared and the female said, "Kaarina, you have been invited to the symphony this evening by a gentleman named Gresley Boont. Do you wish to accept his invitation so that we may message him back?"

"Sure, yes I would like to go." Kaarina said smiling and quickly the tears were evaporating.

"Would you like a hair stylist, makeup artist, and a fashion consultant to help you get ready?"

"Sure, but I must attend the conference for about four more hours. Can they come after then?"

"Not a problem. We'll schedule them to your room in four hours and I shall return the affirmative to the invitation."

"Thank you very much."

Dunbar knew he would be soon notified his invitation was accepted, but he didn't need to hear it because he knew Kaarina already accepted. This mission was suddenly turning into a pleasant experience, even though he had not yet dealt with the Bear Claws issue which was the purpose of being here. The Transporter Capsule was long gone. He had to make his way back to Kaokuen via an Intergalactic Transport Spacecraft that had an element of risk and travel conditions would not be ideal.

Dunbar went back to the Aigle Émeraude Resort where he took a sprite shower and changed into his swimming clothes after receiving his invitation acceptance holograph from one of the resort employees.

With an Aigle Émeraude Resort robe and slippers on Dunbar made his way to the resort swimming pool, found a reclining chair with umbrella near the pool and took off the robe and stepped out of the slippers and began swimming laps. The doctor's conference was in a conference hall adjacent to the main resort buildings. While Dunbar was swimming and working up lactic acid in his muscles already stressed from running, a group of doctors taking a break left the conference hall and walked back to the main resort building. They slowly trickled out of the conference hall and were asked to be back in an hour.

Kaarina was in the last group of doctors leaving the conference hall. Most of them in the group were female doctors, all dressed up rather spiffy since they were the leaders in the state of the art of advanced medical treatments such a proton beam and holographic resonance treatments that eliminated the need to cut open patients to deal with diseased tissue.

As this last group of doctors was passing on the sidewalk adjacent to the pool, Dunbar was getting out of the pool with aching muscles. He almost over did it but had enough strength left to crawl out of the pool and lay down on the reclining chair that had a footrest.

One of the doctors in the all-female group commented in a low voice, "See that hunk of a man?"

Dunbar wasn't paying attention to the women and didn't look hard to notice Kaarina was in the middle of the group that was gawking at him and as they got further away from the pool there was some girlish laugher went on as some of the women commented on Dunbar's body saying things like *every woman in the resort would love to spend one night with that man.*

Kaarina didn't say anything, she knew it was Gresley Boont whom she was going to the symphony with later in the day. The women went into the resort, did their business, freshened up, and everything they could get done in an hours' time, then headed back to the conference.

Every one of the women including Kaarina hoped to see the man when they came back an hour later, but by then, Dunbar was in another part of the resort getting a massage to help work out the lactic acid.

The beautiful blonde masseuse named Fulvia had a splendid body and face and smile second to none. Dunbar evaluated Fulvia as probably being around twenty-seven years old full of youth and vigor.

The masseuse Fulvia fell in love with Dunbar's body and suggested, "We have enough time to taste the forbidden fruit in this private room with a door I can lock to keep all outsiders out."

"I don't feel up to it, plus last night a woman came to my room and drained me."

"You got lucky last night?" Fulvia asked.

"It didn't start out too well." Gresley Boont (aka Dunbar) replied.

"Why is that?" Fulvia asked.

"I was staring at her because she looked like my former girlfriend I had to leave behind, and she approached me and asked me why I was staring at her." Gresley explained.

"Really?" Fulvia asked.

"Yes, then I pulled out my communicator and on the flatscreen showed her pictures of my girlfriend. She thought I was doing a clever joke at first using simulated computer animations, but then realized all those images were real." Gresley said.

"How did you end up with the woman? Fulvia asked.

"I invited this delightful person to sit down with me and drink an elixir together so that I could tell her about this other woman and explain why I could not help but look at her."

"What happened then."

"In a short while that woman felt embarrassed, she had been so mean to me."

"How did you go from upsetting the woman to end up being in bed with her enjoying the horizonal tango?" Fulvia asked in great wonder.

"She and I talked for an hour and we each really seemed to enjoy. She showed the positive side of her. She's a very intelligent and sensitive woman. I could feel the essence of this wonderful lady. I didn't want it to end, but I was exhausted from work and travel and went back to my room."

"Then how did you get lucky?"

"She came to my room ready to do it."

"Just like that?" Fulvia asked with incredulity.

"I think she wanted it more than you do." Gresley said teasing Fulvia.

"That's impossible, no woman wants to experience you more than I do now. When I saw your tool, you have no idea how badly I wanted to kiss it."

"That's the risk you take doing a massage on a person fully nude."

"I had to get all your clothes off because once I saw your abdomen and your arms, I needed to see the rest of you."

"You are a very beautiful woman; you can have any tool in the resort tonight."

"True, but I prefer to try yours first."

"I'm sorry, I'm going to be busy today."

"What could you possibly be doing that would be more satisfying than letting me give you gratification?"

"I need to get ready to go to the symphony, with the woman that drained me last night."

"I'm jealous." Fulvia said.

"Don't be. You have many years ahead of you and as beautiful as you are, there will be many offers of taking you to the symphony." Gresley said.

"Would you take me?" Fulvia asked with raised eyebrows.

"If I didn't have my hands full, I would certainly entertain the idea."

"Get rid of that bimbo and come back to me. I want to go to the symphony too."

"One never knows what might happen in life."

"That's true."

Thanks to the muscle relaxers in the bathwater Fulvia had Gresley soak in after his massage, he finished fully recovered.

The only problem with Dunbar ending the massage session was leaving Fulvia disappointed. But Gresley knew the facts of life. Desire is ten times stronger than gratification and when he left Fulvia behind she was full of desire.

Dunbar went back to his resort room patiently waiting for the message that wasn't going to arrive today, because of what the four amigos were doing. Had they not been out to get him, they would have sent that information to Dunbar in the morning when it was available.

Dunbar informed *Latrodectus* he wanted to schedule a fashion person and a hair designer for a few hours from now and in the meantime take a nap but be sure to wake him up if he received a Bear Claw communication.

Dunbar didn't come prepared for the symphony and didn't have the clothes he felt compelled to wear on a more formal occasion. He also suspected a sophisticated woman like Kaarina would not go to a symphony dressed any less that a starlet. And he was absolutely correct in his judgement.

While Dunbar was catching up on his sleep deprivation, Kaarina spent a couple more hours at the medical conference then was leaving with the women she had been with a few hours earlier when they saw Gresley at the swimming pool.

"What are you doing this evening, Kaarina," one of the women asked.

"I'm going to the symphony and probably dinner afterwards."

"Are you going with someone?"

"Yes, he's one of the resort guests."

"Really?"

"Yes."

"What time are you leaving? I might want to see who you are going with."

Kaarina gave the woman the time they would meet in the lobby, and she would get a surprise, it was the man all the group of six doctors had talked about while they were at their break earlier.

Kaarina knew this woman was a blabbermouth and no doubt would be in the lobby to see who it was. The rumors would be flying afterwards!

After a great nap leaving Dunbar feeling fully refreshed, he was awakened, took a shower and soon the fashion consultants and barber arrived. Before they finished preparing Dunbar, he had a very dark blue, almost black suit with a white open color shirt that showed about five inches of his chest and again with rented jewelry, looked movie star quality. Thanks to his great physical shape the designer suit laid against Dunbar's body with great precision. The fashion designer Jessica was extremely happy it fit Dunbar so well.

The suit, the hair style, and the cologne the fashion consultant brought along made Dunbar utterly irresistible to the point Jessica said, "You know I want you all to myself, but I know you have a lady waiting."

"If I didn't have my hands full, I would take you up on your offer." Dunbar replied.

"Keep me in mind the next time," Jessica said. She then handed him a business card and said, "Call me if you want to take me somewhere. I'll dress up pretty for you."

"I will."

Jessica smiled and left the resort room. Dunbar was now alone and looked again in the mirror and said to himself, *I think Kaarina is going to soon be happy she was brave last night and came to my room.*

Kaarina had similar fashion treatments and would soon take Dunbar's breath away.

Right about the time they were to meet in the lobby a few of the Doctors you could describe as the Ms. Hannity types were there prepositioned to discover who the mystery man was. Deep in their minds they still had the fabulous man at the swimming pool in their minds, but they just knew it was very unlikely he would be taking Kaarina to the symphony. They were expecting an older man probably with grey hair and a bulging abdomen, the professor type, slightly balding, probably short with reading glasses.

Several minutes before Kaarina arrived, Dunbar stepped out an elevator walked into the lobby, smiled at the receptionist and stood there waiting for his date to arrive.

The middle-aged female doctors huddled over in the corner to make it not look obvious they were spying on Kaarina saw the hunk from the swimming pool. They almost felt orgasmic looking at Dunbar's chest with the borrowed gold necklace and the open white designer shirt and a suit that fit his fantastic shape perfectly. The women were obviously curious as to who the man was. It was odd he was standing in the lobby waiting as if he was waiting for a date.

About two minutes after Dunbar arrived, Kaarina stepped out of the elevator and walked into the lobby instantly making Dunbar proud. The fashion designers, makeup artist, hair designer, and nails person had transformed Kaarina into a princess image Dunbar would never forget the rest of his life. Nor would he tell *Latrodectus* to redact the video. He wanted the *office warriors* to see what he experienced on the road. All they had was plane *Janes*, some with weight problems, to go home to the very night they observed the video.

The other female Doctors were almost speechless when Kaarina walked up to Dunbar and grabbed his hands and kissed him on the cheek with a great smile, and said, "You look so great tonight, I'm very happy you are taking me to the Symphony."

Gresley responded, it is my most distinct pleasure to take a beautiful woman like you to the symphony.

Latrodectus, who had significant responsibility to arrange Dunbar's transportation in-situ had a nice limo out front waiting for the couple at that very moment.

The two lovebirds walked out of the lobby and over to the limo that immediately took them away. The female doctors that were there spying on Kaarina, then slowly walked to the dining hall where they would have nice elixirs and discuss the spectacle they just observed. Kaarina who they thought was another *plane Jane* just threw a snowball at them of gigantic proportion.

It took them several minutes and more than half of their first elixirs to figure out exactly what to say.

Kaarina's appearance tonight quickly shielded all of Dunbar's thoughts about Blemary. The way that ended was another factor in his growing dissatisfaction with the Transport Directorate. The four *office warriors* of course would go out of their way to make Dunbar feel even more miserable and if possible, kill him.

Operation Bear Claws was their first attempt to get Dunbar killed and it would not be their last.

The limo pulled up to Nigārà Symphony Hall and within moments the glamorous couple was walking among other concert goers some of them dressed up nicely, but none of the women compared to Kaarina, she was the princess for the concert tonight.

Latrodectus never ceased to amaze Dunbar. It pays to be the best friend of the Artificial Intelligence that was running the show. The DD/P and the four amigos thought they were manifesting events, but Latrodectus was the intelligence behind the green curtain. Latrodectus had access to huge quantities of block chain type intergalactic credits₿. If he didn't have enough, he knew which intergalactic bankers to rip off to get what he needed.

Dunbar (aka Gresley) didn't know he had a very private balcony seat. The usher escorted Dunbar and Kaarina to their seats and Dunbar was immediately impressed with *Latrodectus* who was always with Dunbar every second of the day and was in fact his eternal guardian and would do whatever it took to keep Dunbar safe and satisfied.

Latrodectus had the underlining philosophy in his programming to further the advantage the Kaokuen government could derive from Transport Directorate operations. *Latrodectus* had determined long ago that Dunbar was truly the premier spy they had who could serve Kaokuen agenda the best. The four amigos were worthless flesh as far as *Latrodectus* was concerned and when he detected their attempts on Dunbar's life, *Latrodectus* went into a protection mode and undermined all their attempts without giving away Dunbar had a secret helper.

In the spy business secrecy was paramount and never under any circumstances let the enemy know you were somehow involved. *Latrodectus* determined the four amigos were the enemy. Those four *office warriors* were poor excuses for Transport Directorate operatives. Worse yet their activities undermining Dunbar also undermined the agency.

Kaarina had a huge impact on Dunbar's personal psychology. He knew vividly that in less than a day ago they made splendid love which Kaarina initiated in her own way in her own time. She was full of life and vigor and as a surgeon her intelligence was rather compelling. Looking at this splendid beauty created a temporal anomaly for Dunbar.

Kaarina's beauty, presence, and sweetness permeated Dunbar in ways he couldn't quite come to grips with. Few people will ever feel what he experienced this moment. The reality is they were two passing ships in the night and spotted each other's lights and out of curiosity came closer.

To an ancient seaman spotting a light on the horizon in the emptiness of the ocean has a huge effect on their psyche. One must be there to experience the delight. Dunbar was experiencing that light on the horizon this very moment as he gazed upon Kaarina. Dunbar being a sophisticated Spy trained in the subtleties of social engineering now wondered how all this manifested. He could not rule out she was the enemy doing a mission against him. Time would tell. But if it turned out this truly was for real, an accidental meeting of a woman who looked like Blemary's twin sister, then he would be forever humble.

Thanks to *Latrodectus,* whatever bad crap the four amigos were throwing at Dunbar tonight was buried in the noise as Kaarina's radiance overshadowed everything and captured Dunbar's attention. The truth of the matter is Kaarina and Dunbar each invigorated the other. Whatever Dunbar did to Kaarina, she did to him. It was a covalency of a very strong attraction now existed. They already had their gratification last night in that splendid love making. Tonight, it was purely emotional. There were in fact tendrils of love grasping each other.

When the orchestra started playing the music, it amplified the emotions and added to the intensity of the feelings now growing in each of them. This truly was the exclamation point to the love making the night before. After a period of mourning for her dearly departed husband who left her life unexpectedly, Kaarina was now released from the burden of sorrow. Gresley had released her and for that she would hold him eternally grateful.

Gresley's class and gentleness added greatly to Kaarina's favorable feelings. Kaarina was mindful, Gressley never initiated the sex and what happened the night before. He was simply reacting. But the follow up with the flowers, the note, and now the symphony proved he had great intentions and the fact she looked identical in a spooky way to his former lover added tremendously to the ambience now surrounding them.

The music was absolutely wonderful, and Kaarina held Gresley's hand throughout the performance. She was transfixed on Dunbar more than he could imagine. The large orchestra created sound that resonated the audience resulting in a thunderous applause, then the intermission.

Soon waiters descended upon the couple and provided them with great elixirs that multiplied the effects. During the intermission a piano was raised through the floor of the stage and when the music began again, a beautiful concert pianist created a sound that easily could easily be confused with a Kurt Atterberg piano concerto.

This blissful moment enshrined the essence of the tranquility the two created for each other. The concerto easily gave a musical dimension to how they were each feeling now. Blemary's world with Kabel Garr was about to end but other events would soon change everything.

The concert ended far too early. Kaarina and Gresley each wished it could have gone on longer because of the feelings it bestowed upon them. Instinctively as the applause started as soon as the conductor signaled the end of the performance Gresley said, "We need to leave now to avoid the crowd."

Dunbar knew that his artificial intelligence *Latrodectus* was the true master of ceremonies, and his transportation was probably waiting outside symphony hall as the two went out the doors of the venue.

The limo driver was standing there waiting for them. Gresley easily identified him and led Kaarina to the Limo which they got in and drove off.

Gresley knowing it was still early had a restaurant and nightclub he wanted to take Kaarina and asked her if she would like to go.

"Let's go back to the resort. Some of my friends are there and I want them to see how I look tonight," Kaarina said as she knew exactly those she wanted to impress.

"Sure, if that's what you want to do," Gresley said.

In five minutes, the Limo pulled up the circular driveway into the Aigle Émeraude Resort where the two got out.

As soon as Kaarina said she wanted to go back to the Aigle Émeraude Resort, Latrodectus hacked into their reservation system for the dining hall and gave the couple VIP seating with no wait time.

The maître d' had an image of the VIP on her electronic tablet and as soon as Gresley approached her podium she said, "This way Gressley I have your table waiting for you.

Thanks to *Latrodectus* hacking and manipulations of the Aigle Émeraude Resort computations and communications network, the maître d' seated Kaarina and Gresley at a VIP table with direct vision of the musicians performing dinner music thus enveloped in the sound produced with great fidelity.

Four female doctors Kaarina knew from the conference were sitting in a booth about twenty feet from her and had just finished their meal and were having desert. The dining hall turned into a dance hall about an hour after the couple arrived. Resort patrons that were now present often stayed drinking elixirs and participating in the activities after the musicians shifted to a different style of music. Few people arrived this late for dinner, it was all for fun.

These four women were mostly the Ms. Hannity Types, long past the days where gentlemen would be in hot pursuit. They had a natural bias toward Kaarina because she was viewed as a Prima donna because of her lucky entrance into a new type of medical procedures that were revolutionary. Two of the four women were jealous and sometimes spiteful and were known to have said disparaging words about Kaarina.

And here Kaarina tonight was stealing the show being with the most handsome and distinguished man in the dining hall. Kaarina was dressed up so elegantly, that even her two distractors were tongue tied. If the four women only knew Kaarina and Gresley were already lovers, it would send them into a state of shock.

"What would you like to drink," the server asked Kaarina and Gresley.

Kaarina knew the dining hall served her favorite ferment because she had a glass during the break in the conference today and responded, "I'll have a Latice de Laconian."

The server turned to Gresley and before she could ask him he said, "Please give me a Ástríður Dreka elixir."

Kaarina and Gressley were sitting perpendicular to the four female doctors who were staring at them. Their gawking upset her far more than the incident between she and Gressley that resulted in them being together tonight, but she was not going spoil the night by approaching them and asking them what they were staring at. Instead, she would feed their imaginations with extravagant behavior.

Kaarina knew the snoops would try to hear what they were talking about, so she fed their imaginations with perceptions that would make them blush.

"Gresley, where did you learn to make such good love to a woman?"

Dunbar was semi in a state of shock because he knew people sitting nearby probably overheard Kaarina's remark. But as a good spy, he kept his composure and answered in a provocative manner the four doctors overheared and it sent them into utter shock.

"When you came to my room last night seminude you have no idea how much you inspired me."

"What if I want to do it again tonight?"

"I will certainly accommodate you and try to do better than I did last night and take my time to please you."

"You pleased me just fine; I've not had such great orgasms in such a very long time."

Dunbar being a sophisticated spy and always in command of his situational awareness keyed into how Kaarina had looked a couple times out of the corner of her eye. Hence, she was focused on something or someone else in the dining hall. Dunbar (aka Gresley). Bent over towards Kaarina to say something to her quietly in her ear so that it would give him a moment to see what Kaarina had looked at couple times. He also suspected she was putting on a show for someone. *Perhaps make a former boyfriend jealous?* Dunbar wondered.

Dunbar sometimes was mischievous in his own right, especially when he wasn't working and alone with a special friend decided he would play the game to its fullest. Kaarina would not know he was acting, but as a social engineer, it's all about acting.

The level of his voice was too low for whoever was watching, but he knew by causing Kaarina a reaction it would serve the same purpose, as he said, "You have no idea how hard you make me. If we were not here eating, I would start making love to you now."

When he pulled back, he saw the female doctors for a brief second eyeballing Kaarina who was now blushing and red. The four women probably guessed he was a naughty boy and told Kaarina some very provocative words.

Gresley's amorousness did have a huge impact on Kaarina who suddenly felt the moistness and was full of desire. Without thinking about the four women, she was now fully concentrated on Gresley and gave him a signal with her finger to come close and when he was again in that position to receive a very private message, Kaarina said, "You have no idea how wet you just made me."

When Gresley pulled back and sat upright he had one of those mischievous smiles which conveyed to the four doctors, Kaarina had just told him some very tantalizing words and if they knew what she had said, they probably may not have been able to stay any longer!

Kaarina and Gresley soon ordered their meal which tasted excellent. By the time they finished eating and the tablecloth was changed out by the server and new drinks served, the musicians with a glamorous singer had started the entertainment. Meal hours were over, it was playtime.

The timing was perfect because the singer was suddenly singing a wonderful love song perfect for a slow dance.

"Darling, would you mind dancing with me?" Kaarina asked and knew the four doctors heard her ask.

"My dear I would love to dance with you," Gresley responded and soon the two were dancing close together in the most romantic posture possible. Thanks to the movement and the music, Gresley could see the four doctors in their huddles discussing the extravagant behavior and he had ideas of his own now. They wanted some eye candy, look out.

Right after the slow dance they picked up the pace a bit with a type of music where a good dancer could twirl his date around and there were indeed showoffs on the dance floor.

As part of his training for social engineering and reverse honey pot schemes, Gresley had formal dance training for ballroom dancing and to look distinguished in a night club to woo the ladies.

Kaarina was a great dancer as well and could follow the lead of a good male dancer quite effectively.

In the span of a few moments, it appeared like Kaarina and Gresley were old dance partners because they worked it together so successfully. It wasn't as if they were showoffs, but Gresley figured out Kaarina wanted to put those four doctors in their place, and he was more than happy to help Kaarina who seemed transfixed on the four women. It was now a team effort.

Kaarina didn't know Gresley was showing off for her behalf. She was enjoying every bit of it because she thought it was all natural and real and for her exclusively.

Gresley didn't help his cause that night. Bear Claws was in the dining hall observing the two dancers showing elaborate moves on the dance floor. Bear Claws knew Kaarina. Bear Claws spent a lot of time in the same room today watching the presentations all the doctors observed in the presentation of this new technology and how they were going to use it with their patients to reduce the need to cut them open to remove diseased tissue.

In a sense this new beam technology was like radiation treatments Earth doctors used to treat cancer patients. What the researchers developed was a fantastic alternative that killed a lot of cancer cells, but only destroying a minimum amount of healthy tissue. One treatment would not complete the job. It's an interactive process, and four to five treatments were required to eliminate cancers and tumors.

Bear Claws was not at the seminar to learn this technology. In fact, he could care less. Bear Claws, like everyone had a price. He was here as a courier and would in fact take the data stick back to his world that was a lot like Switzerland on Earth and hand it over to Kaokuen enemies, the Stanzelites.

Because the four amigos were setting up Dunbar for failure, Bear Claws identity would not be disclosed until it was practically too late. They delivered the information just in time to give the appearance they did their part.

Latrodectus knew otherwise. He knew the four office warriors were sitting on the information and had not loaded it into the system, otherwise Dunbar would already know who his target was. *Latrodectus* understood they were quickly running out of time. Tomorrow would be the deadline meaning Dunbar would not be able to handle the matter through espionage.

If there was going to be a last-minute scenario that could possibly include a shootout and violence, Dunbar might need emergency extraction. That meant a special delivery of an empty Transporter he could get to and leave immediately before the local authorities apprehended him.

Latrodectus sent an encrypted message to the DD/P as eyes only. The four amigos would not be allowed to read it until Dunbar during a debrief later agreed. This was the only leverage he had.

If Dunbar was not given the information the four amigos had been sitting on for almost a week in the next few hours, it would precipitate the emergency exit. Once *Latrodectus* received the response to the DD/P he made immediate arrangements for a VTOL to arrive at the resort that would get him to the Transport Capsule promptly to return.

The DD/P was asked to not have anyone in the Transport room when he sent the capsule. He was afraid the mission was compromised and didn't want anyone to know the destination of the capsule. The DD/P raised his eyebrows and would have a long session with Dunbar after he returned to find out what was the reason for the extraordinary request.

After an hour of teasing the four doctors, Gresley and Kaarina retired to her room at her request. Dunbar knew he had a substantial job to do in the morning and after knocking the rims off Kaarina's tires (expansive love making), he said he needed to get up in the morning to take care of a matter and put his clothes back on and left Kaarina's resort room. As Dunbar was leaving her room after a splendid kiss and hug, full of gratification, a couple of the doctors observed him leaving the room with his hair slightly messed up and the appearance, his clothes had been wrinkled somehow. Dunbar felt an urge and as he passed the doctors, He winked at them which put them into a state of shock!

Dunbar went back to his room, showered, put on his sleeping clothes, and soon fell asleep knowing *Latrodectus* would wake him up for any exigency.

In the morning, feeling refreshed but depressed that they were up against a deadline and INTEL had not sent him what he needed to know, decided a walk to the park and back would be a good distraction from his growing concern.

"Recommend you do not run today, you may not have time to shower, clean up and deal with Bear Claws." *Latrodectus* advised.

Dunbar left the Aigle Émeraude Resort in his street clothes. Halfway to the park, Aigle Émeraude Resort surprised Dunbar and said, "I now have the identification of Bear Claws. Look at the flat screen."

Dunbar saw the image and knew he had seen the man the night before in the dining hall. He had plenty of time to deal with him the previous night. Receiving this information this close to the deadline upset

Dunbar greatly. *Latrodectus* was looking into the delay and suspected the nefarious activity that was going on.

"Where is Bear Claws now?"

He just went into a room to get a massage. Fulvia, the lady who massaged you the other day, is there with him.

Has he met with the other courier?

"I'm checking hotel security videos now going back in time to see if he met with another man and appeared to be receiving something from him."

"What about the seminar? Bear Claws probably met a lot of people there."

I've gone back three days to when Bear Claws arrived, there are no indications he met with someone or received the delivery."

"Keep monitoring him."

Just as Dunbar was going through the lobby of the resort, his communicator indicated he was receiving a call. He saw it was *Latrodectus* who said, "Another man just entered the room with Bear Claws. They are in the process of killing Fulvia, if you want to save her life get there fast!"

Dunbar knew exactly where to run down the hallway and hoped he got there in time. The door was locked but that wasn't a problem, as Dunbar kicked it in, and the spy was only a second or two away from killing Fulvia and looked at the loud noise of the door being kicked in. Dunbar knew who Bear Claws was and assumed the other man was probably a dangerous spy, so he concentrated on him which forced him to let go of Fulvia for a minute who was almost choked to death.

The two spies entered a death spiral fight. It was guaranteed death to the looser.

There were punches, kicks and smashing of the furniture as the two went after each other. Bear Claws stood there in total horror thinking he was going to walk out of the room with a million credits฿ on his communicator was frozen and too scared to move.

Fulvia being in great physical shape because she did a half dozen massages per day got her breath back and was upset knowing these two men almost killed her. She had some self-defense training in case one of her customers attempted raping her and decided Bear Claws would pay for holding her while the other man was killing her and kicked Bear Claws in the groin as hard as she could. Bear Claws tumbled over in excruciating pain.

It was a tough fight, but Dunbar desperately needed to end it quick and get the data stick now in the possession of Bear Claws according to *Latrodectus*. They needed to bug out right away and Dunbar had no choice when he got the spy into a choke hold to kill him or possibly be killed. As soon as the man showed no signs of life and unconscious, Dunbar finished him off by breaking his neck.

Dunbar looked at Fulvia who was mildly in a state of shock and asked, "Did you see this man hand the other man anything?"

"Yes, he put it in his pocket."

Dunbar walked over, felt the man's pockets, and found the data stick. The man was in pain, but Dunbar didn't want him to remain conscious when he departed and administered Bear Claws the *coup de grâce*. He then left the room with *Latrodectus* instructing Dunbar over the speaker of the communicator. "Go to the rooftop. Transportation is arriving."

While they were in the elevator going to the rooftop, they normally could not get to without a resort employee opening up the access, *Latrodectus* having hacked the security system remotely unlocked the access door and as Dunbar was exiting the elevator, the VTOL craft was touching down and Dunbar asked, "Where too?"

Latrodectus said, "A Transport Capsule will be arriving at the same location you arrived the other day."

As soon as Dunbar was in the VTOL the pilot asked, "Where do you want to go?"

"Head East and I'll give you directions. A minute after the VTOL was gone and out of sight, resort security personen came swarming out of the elevator access and there was nothing to find. Whoever they were chasing was long gone and they had no idea what direction they went in.

The police were soon on the scene checking the dead bodies and asking Fulvia questions.

In a short period of time Dunbar recognized the forested area and told the VTOL operator, "Let me out here. I have someone to meet."

Dunbar was soon out of the VTOL that flew back to its facility it worked out of. Dunbar knew he didn't have much time; the authorities would probably soon be arriving after they looked at surveillance video and identified the VTOL company and started asking questions.

Dunbar went promptly to where he arrived a few days ago and *Latrodectus* uncloaked the Transport Capsule which Dunbar got in and started the automatic launch sequence. The Transport Capsule quickly disappeared.

In 15 minutes, police and federal agents with dogs ran into the forest looking for Dunbar and the dogs lost the scent in the middle of nowhere. Whoever it was had vanished.

Because of the substantial security video, the resort had, the police soon had Gresley's image and recognized a resort guest identified as a doctor attending the conference. Kaarina was in the middle of the seminar when the police entered and asked her to come with them.

Kaarina would never see Gresley again as his identity had already been altered by three-dimensional biological printing. Gresley would not seek Kaarina, she was just another person caught in espionage crossfires.

There would be no possibility of Kaarina ever forgetting Gresley. She didn't know why she felt the way she did, but Gresley turned out to be the most exciting man she met in her lifetime. The fact he killed another spook, a term the Nigārà Federal Police had used in front of her during her interrogations gave a gauge to what he was really like. Now that all this was exposed and she reflected on her lover's tryst with Gresley, she now understood why he had such a magnificent body.

Kaarina could not help but to see a couple of the doctors again. News traveled fast in the Aigle Émeraude Resort in Nigārà. When Kaarina was led out of the conference by police in front of the other doctors raised quite an interesting spectacle.

The conference was not over for a couple more days, but Kaarina never returned. Nor did Bear Claws, the code name for the doctor that Gresley killed as an added measure he did not impede his departure in any manner nor pose a threat to Fulvia in any manner.

Kaarina was interrogated by some of the best criminologists from Nigārà Federal Police. When they finished with Kaarina, she was almost helpless. A female Nigārà Federal Police Officer knowing what Kaarina had just gone through offered to assist her to the transportation hub and escorted her onto an aircraft where she could fly home and come to grips with what she had just experienced.

Fulvia had managed to regain consciousness to see over half of the fighting between Gresley and the other spy. She openly admitted to the police she had kicked Bear Claws and feared for her life since he had held her while the spy was chocking her to death.

Police and medical examiners confirmed Fulvia's story that one of the dead men was choking her to death and his DNA was on her clothes and on her neck.

When the medical examiner informed the police Fulvia was a choke victim and came very close to dying, her role in subduing Bear Claws was deemed justifiable by the police and no charges were filed.

The police and the Nigārà Federal Police concluded the fact Gresley pulled what appeared to be a data package out of Bear Claws pocket was indicative of a spy operation that went on in the resort.

The Nigārà Federal Police had a good idea who was involved but since they had no proof it was considered conjecture. Bear Claws body was sent home. His communicator did not have the million credits₿ he thought he was receiving, and no government ever looked for the other man. The dead spy was another John Doe spook that whoever used him disavowed the person.

Since the courier operation failed, the entity who initiated it knew they were compromised and feared retaliation, thus suspended any further effort to sell the information for considerable sums.

When Dunbar exited the Transport Capsule, the DD/P personally escorted him into his office to start the debrief. It really did not matter the line of BS the four amigos put out because all communications went through *Latrodectus* and had time stamps on them. While the DD/P was talking to Dunbar, *Latrodectus* downloaded the mission files to the DD/P's secure folder system nobody else had access to.

Artificial Intelligence had their own oversight committee. Individuals including the DD/P thought the oversight was a living person. In fact it was not.

Because of the sensitivity of that *artificial intelligence oversight* person responsibility, that person's identity was shielded and only the internal review people knew who it was. They never personally met the *artificial intelligence oversight* person, all they know is the previous management had appointed the person and until he retired or was reassigned, nobody outside of internal review would know the *artificial intelligence oversight* person's identity. Nor did they even know where the person worked or where his desk was. This *artificial intelligence oversight* person was the most guarded secret in all the Transport Directorate.

The truth of the matter is *Latrodectus* was the oversight. But *Latrodectus* existed everywhere within the Transportation Directorate.

Every element of the Transport Directorate's Computation, Communication, Intelligence, And Planning (CCIP) operations had *Latrodectus* imbedded and sophisticated routine CCIP monitoring. Any computer data scientist checking the code or watching transactions would only know internal review copied or moved the data if it was not initiated by department personnel.

Any inquiries to internal review who were considered heavy handed by everyone including the DD/P, were quickly met with, *it's none of your business why we are looking at that information.* And when things got hot under the color with people like the DD/P and the four amigos, the internal review people who didn't particularly like the office warriors responded by saying, if you have any concerns, send a message to the *artificial intelligence oversight* and a real person will get back to you with clarification or official reviews of the matter.

There were cases when the office warriors got so upset, they called the person to vent their frustration. Artificial Intelligence was so good they never knew they were talking to a computer.

Where did the internal review person come from?

Somehow or another the Kaokuen Intelligence services obtained files from planet Earth that contained a significant amount of video and voice in the forms of movies, television, and radio. Some of it was obtained by an Earth provider called YouTube that had great recordings of vast amounts of such video and voice in movies and other sources.

One of the movie actors that *Latrodectus* discovered in his analysis of all the video and sound from that primativie Earth source was a man named Clark Gable. When *Latrodectus* was building the *artificial intelligence oversight* apparatus, a voice and image was needed to create this human awareness type figure in the event a direct meeting or conversation was required.

Latrodectus chose the Clark Gable personality to be the *artificial intelligence oversight* person. The head of the Transport Directorate did a video interview with the man who did not use Clark Gable as the name, but the voice and the physical appearance of when he was in his early 50's was used to synthesize an artificial person.

Every word Clark Gable ever spoke that was recorded in any manner was taken and pieces of that voice activity were assimilated into a translation into the Kaokuen language lexicon with over 12,000 words that would cover any possible discussion. Any other words not created and translated into Clark Gable's voice were remote but since they would be very few, artificial intelligence could create the word if necessary quick enough to where nobody would know the difference.

Thanks to the very advanced Computer-Generated Imagery (CGI), nobody would ever know it wasn't real. The Clark Gable CGI had over 10,000 CGI videos created showing different clothes for different days. And only top-level executives were allowed to see it with part of the face redacted so that a visual indication could not be copied.

The DD/P and his boss were the only two allowed to see the full image of the *artificial intelligence oversight* person. And since the need to see him physically was rare, they seldom asked for it.

Since *Latrodectus* was the actual internal review, there was a wire trail from the *Latrodectus* on Dunbar's communicator to internal review reporting unusual circumstances during the Black Claw mission. Internal review responded to *Latrodectus* and copied Dunbar and the DD/P informing them the mission was now compartmentalized and under review by internal review and all access to others would be denied. Internal review then directed the DD/P to investigate why Dunbar was not informed of who Bear Claws was even though the Transport Directorate knew three days prior the identification and quite possibly the spy Bear Claws was going to meet to receive the data stick.

The DD/P was directed not to discuss this with anyone and to only report to internal review any information or facts that pertained to the mission.

The four amigos almost felt like doing high 5's in the office because they created such a stink for Dunbar forcing him to do an emergency extraction, would clearly indicate incompetence in conduct of the mission. They vented their opinion to the DD/P who said he would investigate it and discuss the mission with Dunbar.

The four amigos proposed a critique where Dunbar, the DD/P and a few others who were not necessarily Dunbar's friends meet to discuss his conduct and how that has endangered the outcome of his missions including the emergency extraction. They also wanted to vent how Dunbar left behind a Transport Capsule they had not been able to retrieve.

The DD/P had a whole different view of things, and the four amigos did not know internal review was looking into the possibility someone may have personally sandbagged Dunbar to set him up for failure.

In order to prevent the four amigos affecting his career, the DD/P said he would schedule a critique in the future but under the circumstances, Dunbar just went through some rough times and was sending him on administrative leave for R&R. When he returned to work, he would schedule a critique.

The four office warriors went to work carefully crafting their narrative so that they could bury Dunbar in the critique and possibly force his ouster so that he would never be in line for the promotion they all felt they deserved.

Before the DD/P sent Dunbar home on administrative leave, he had him in his office for another private meeting. He said to Dunbar, "The reason why I'm sending you home on administrative leave for a couple weeks is for two reasons. First of all, I will need to send you on another mission soon, so you need to be physically ready for it. There is nothing you need to do here in the office.

"I'll be happy to go on that mission," Dunbar responded.

"I know you will."

"What's the second reason?"

"As you know your four amigo buddies are trying to shove this critique down my throat. They somehow think they are running the show, but they are not. I've not had the chance yet to put them in their place. I'm sending you out of the office as an excuse why we cannot have the critique. When you come back you will immediately deploy on your next mission and hence, since you are not here, we cannot have that critique."

"That works for me."

"Go enjoy your time off. I know you have been through a lot. If I had just a couple more Transporter Spies like you, I could accomplish quite a bit more. Unfortunately, the politicians in the agency have stuck me with the four office warriors and there isn't much I can do about it but plan my retirement."

"Understand Sir."

"By the way Dunbar, per your request to *Latrodectus* he did not redact any of the video and conversations you had on your mission. He had substantial security video of you with Kaarina. She was a very beautiful woman and I know that how this all ended was an ordeal to you as well as Kaarina. I'm not a heartless person."

"I sense that."

"When I watched all the video and sounds, I could see you became quite attached to Kaarina and the way you had to leave her because of what others might have done to you mildly distresses me."

"When I had to kill those two guys because of late notification that means I can never see Kaarina again does upset me a bit. She's a doctor and I took a liking to her. I could perceive a long term relationship with her, but I would have to get past the issue about using an alias if that happened."

" I'm very sorry how this all unfolded and how it affects you. But I'm sure you realize the business you are in is that you are living on borrowed time as it is, and any crumbs of life you can squeeze out of it during your adventures are worth it."

"I took a few crumbs of life along the way."

"The fact you had back-to-back relationships with women in and around your mission really does not reduce my evaluation of you in any manner."

"Thanks."

"Sure, we have rules and regulations, but they are written for the likes of the four *office warriors* I can't seem to ever deploy because they have so many personal issues."

"All agencies have dead wood. We had them over at the SOG as well."

"Keep up the good work, I consider you my star performer, that's why I have to send you on this next mission. I need to send the best I have, and that is you."

"Thank you, sir, that means a lot to me."

"Enjoy your time off, but don't forget your physical workouts."

"I'll be ready sir."

"See you in a couple weeks."

Latrodectus had a growing positive opinion of the DD/P. He was someone he could work with, and he needed to get rid of a few bad apples like the four amigos.

Dunbar went into the locker room, took a shower, and put on his banker's suit and tie along with his conservative looking shoes, and left the building.

The public transportation is how Dunbar often arrived especially if he were going on missions, he left no indications he was coming or going. Dunbar arrived home thirty minutes later and for the rest of the day he was going to relax, work on his sleep deprivation, unwind and clear out all his thoughts.

Meeting a woman that appeared like Blemary's twin sister on the mission and having a short whirl wind affair that ended in a disaster was unsettling. Had the timing not been so screwed up and Dunbar could have left incognito, he could have enjoyed a friendly goodbye with the possibility of arranging to see Kaarina again in the future.

Knowing what probably happened after he left the planet Pràsplātanià and the city Nigārà with two dead men behind and a terrorized masseuse precluded him ever seeing Kaarina again the rest of his life.

No doubt the police interviewed Kaarina because the surveillance video downloaded easily identified her with him and no doubt Fulvia was interviewed and explained how he killed the two men. But she owed her life to him because the spy was going to kill her.

Dunbar had a couple bottles of *Jangovian de Palentin* elixir that was quite expensive, and he could only afford it because he brought it back on a mission with him. He had been saving that *Jangovian de Palentin* for a special occasion. Now was the time. He knew if he drank a good portion of *Jangovian de Palentin*, his mind would temporarily leave behind all these memories and the next day he would exercise forcefully to help deal with what he went though and be ready for his next mission in a couple weeks.

***

Chapter Nine
Operation Trapezoidal Differentiators

In two weeks', time, Dunbar was ready to go again. The four amigos were acting fussy because they were not able to get the critique scheduled before Dunbar was out of the office on his way to another adventure.

Because of the *need to know* and mission operational security (OPSEC), only the special briefer was in the DD/P's office with Dunbar discussing the mission. The *office warriors* didn't know this was the actual mission brief otherwise they would have pitched a fit they were not invited in to give their two cents worth and their brilliant advice to Dunbar as if what they had to offer actually had any bearing on the outcome of the mission.

Dunbar was very happy on the launch of this mission because the four amigos were not involved in any manner, nor would they know of his destination or anything he would be doing.

Because of the secrecy of the mission only the DD/P was in the Transporter room dialing in the coordinates and synchronizing with the probe pointer to launch the Transporter Capsule.

The four amigos thought they had put a virus into the transporter software that would do Dunbar in. *Latrodectus* was two steps ahead of them and eliminated the virus a few seconds before launch and then put it back in knowing the four amigos would go in to remove it to cover their tracks. They knew that Dunbar would arrive at his destination as scrambled cells by not reassociating correctly.

Dunbar arrived on the outskirts of the city Fujima in the Larian world. This was a well scouted area in the past, like most worlds they needed landing zones where the Transport Capsule would not arrive in view of anyone, and the Transporter Operative could deploy from and be evacuated in a reasonable fashion.

This mission would be one of the most difficult Dunbar ever attempted. In the previous mission there were no plans to kill Bear Claws and the spy. But because of tampering by the four amigos and sandbagging Dunbar, it happened out of necessity.

This mission was different. Dunbar was directed to steal the plans for the Trapezoidal Differentiators and assassinate its designer Rextar Fünger to make sure this device could never be brought to bear. The Larians were a well-known proliferator of weapons of mass destruction. Kaokuen Intelligence estimated, stealing the plans, and killing Rextar Fünger would set the Larians back at least ten years and by then, Kaokuen Transport Directorate would have means to defeat it. Trapezoidal Differentiator jammers were in the design phases but could not be ready in time before Rextar Fünger's Trapezoidal Differentiators would all but put a temporary halt to all Kaokuen Transporter launches.

The Trapezoidal Differentiators would soon be able to detect and track a Kaokuen Transport launch and intervene making it impossible to send spies to worlds in this fashion.

Trapezoidal Differentiators would process the space around a planet the way a radar would aircraft and present the Transporter object and its track on a fractal display with great resolution. The five seconds the laser pointer from the pointer probe would trigger the tripwire and the Trapezoidal Differentiator would illuminate the track of an invisible beam that would reassociate on the planet in the form of a Transport Capsule. The ability to cloak the Transport Capsule was also called into question if the enemy had a portable Trapezoidal Differentiator, they could mount on a VTOL craft and illuminate the area like a lighting system in the special wavelengths.

Rextar Fünger would be best compared to the flamboyant Howard Hughes on Earth, a very private person and rarely seen in public. He was almost a total recluse and manufacturing scientists had difficulties working with him because he insisted on personally keeping all his plans locked up in his home he seldom left.

The convenient method of flying to safety in a VTOL was not going to work this time. Dunbar would have a Bamtorini Sportster staged for his getaway with the plans and after he left Rextar Fünger dead, he would bug out with the plans.

Dunbar was the most unpredictable Transport Spy in the directorate. He didn't like the idea of murdering a brilliant scientist in cold blood. Just like when he stole the Fast Frigate thinking outside the box, he suddenly came up with a different alternative. Besides stealing the secret Trapezoidal Differentiator plans, Dunbar would also abduct and bring Rextar Fünger back with him in the Transporter Capsule.

Since the Transporter return to the Bankers building would be quick, the fact it would be cramped didn't bother Dunbar. The second biggest heist in galactic history would be kidnapping the person whose considered the top scientist that ever lived in the Larian worlds.

Some of the people transported in the past were hefty, almost one hundred pounds heavier than Dunbar. Looking at all the data in the briefing, it appeared that Rextar Fünger was a small man, probably a little over forty kilograms at most.

When Dunbar landed near the city of Fujima in the Larian world, he did a reality check with *Latrodectus*.

"I do not like the idea of killing Rextar Fünger. He's a brilliant man and it would be a terrible waste to kill him. Instead of killing Rextar Fünger I want to abduct him and bring him back to the Transporter Directorate with me."

"Aright Dunbar. What is your idea of how you will accomplish abducting Rextar Fünger?" *Latrodectus* asked.

Dunbar went over all the details which *Latrodectus* commented on. Your alternative is far more humane. It has a great possibility of succeeding. In case it fails we need to have the plans with an autodestruct pouch and kill Rextar Fünger if it appears you will be captured."

"Not a problem. We have some self-destruct tools in the Transporter in case we need them."

Dressed as a Larian, Dunbar walked to the nearby road and walked a short distance and waited for public transportation. His communicator was loaded up with credits฿ to pay for whatever he needed. It was early in the evening and Dunbar exited the public transportation and went to a hotel/resort that *Latrodectus* found for him and reserved a room at the *Adinska Dasnal Resort Hotel* in Fujima in the heart of the Larian world.

Dunbar had a Larian style backpack which was common for travelers when he checked into the *Adinska Dasnal Resort Hotel* under the alias Cameron Malá.

The receptionist said, "Mr. Cameron Malá, your room is number 759. Your room access is via facial recognition. If you want added security when you get to your room, you can put your hand up to the door scanner the first time you go through, and it will read and encode it."

"Alright thanks."

Cameron Malá (aka Dunbar) had temporary handprints from a dead person, so he really didn't care and decided to scan his hand when he went into the room.

The *Adinska Dasnal Resort Hotel* in Fujima was a very modern facility and appeared to be comfortable. It had all the best amenities like any other resort Dunbar had stayed in.

This was a world Dunbar could visit in the future because there were no open hostilities between the Larians and the Kaokuens. But relations were often strained because of the Larian history of weapon proliferation, especially to Kaokuen enemies.

This mission would not have happened except for the possibility that Larians could sell the Trapezoidal Differentiators to the *Stanzelites* or any other possible future enemy. The fact this development was specifically designed for a capability that only the Kaokuens possessed, underscored the almost belligerent behavior that Larians started to appear showing. Since the Trapezoidal Differentiators application had specificity to a major element of Kaokuen intergalactic clandestine operations, it automatically made it a major concern for Kaokuen Intel.

Dunbar realized the four amigos would make a lot of noise about deviations if he brought Rextar Fünger back with him. But it sounded like the office warriors were not aware of the operation. The DD/P would probably see himself the positive aspects of bringing the distinguished scientist Rextar Fünger back in lieu of killing him. No doubt intel could coerce Rextar Fünger into assisting in various matters with the proper amount of quid pro quo or fear of torture and a trip to the sawmill.

Sometimes when brutal treatment of spies is necessary, especially when multiple spies are captured in clandestine operations, to get them to talk, the sawmill was quite compelling after watching one of their buddies split in half groin first strapped to a thick board getting sawed in half.

Now that Dunbar was planning the changes to the mission including the use of a Bamtorini Sportster to transport Rextar Fünger to the Transporter Capsule and asked the resort hotel receptionist, "Do you have customer parking?"

"Yes, we do. Do you have a vehicle?"

"I'm thinking about renting a Bamtorini Sportster while I'm staying in the resort."

"When you arrive at the parking lot, inform the parking lot attendant of your room number. Normally all parking is valet parking except for two-wheel transport. The parking lot attendant will show you where to park the Bamtorini Sportster, and then you will self-park it."

"Not a problem, I prefer it that way."

"You are all set; your room is waiting for you."

"Thank you."

The Larian city Fujima was a tourist destination. There were many things to do in this modern city that attracted the resort clientele. A lot of tourists rented Bamtorini Sportsters to drive around the mountainous roads on the outskirts of the city. Because this was a popular thing to do there were several agencies who rented Bamtorini Sportsters. Some of the rentals could obtain speeds of 300 miles per hour which would be fine to use on flat straight roads sparsely traveled. As such there were speed limiting controls on Bamtorini Sportsters for such unsafe roads controlled by global positioning systems.

Cameron Malá (aka Dunbar) walked to the elevator and as soon as he stepped inside it a light indication for the 7th floor lit up. This was all facial recognition. Dunbar didn't need to select a button or speak; everything was done automatically.

When the elevator reached the 7th floor, it stopped and an artificial intelligence voice in the elevator said, "Cameron Malá, your room is down the hallway on the right."

After fifty steps down the hallway Dunbar saw a flashing green light above the door to the room and when he approached it, he could see the number 759 and when he was in reach of the door handle, he could hear the locking mechanism deactivate the door lock and a pneumatic powered door opened to door swinging it 100 degrees providing full access.

As soon as Dunbar stepped several steps into the room the pneumatic power unit closed and locked the door and the room artificial intelligence said in a nice soft voice, "Welcome Cameron Malá. We hope you enjoy your stay at the *Adinska Dasnal Resort Hotel*. If there is something, you need, just start talking and we will address any of your questions or concerns."

Dunbar put his backpack on his bed in his room and asked, "How do you turn on the entertainment holographs?"

Suddenly a holograph of a well-dressed man appeared and stated, "Cameron Malá, simply say turn on entertainment and I will appear to assist you in your selections. My name is Heyrovsky."

"That's a strange name."

"The data scientists who created me named me after a great inventor."

"What did the great Heyrovsky invent?" Cameron Malá asked.

"The great Igor Heyrovsky invented three dimensional polarographic techniques which are the basis to modern day holographic ensembles."

"Very interesting, had no idea how that came about."

About that time, the silent ringer on Dunbar's communicator signaled *a message arrived*. Dunbar looked down on his communicator flat screen and saw *Latrodectus* posted, *you have a Bamtorini Sportsters rental reservation. Recommend you take a Taxi to the business and pick up the rental now.*

"Alright Heyrovsky, I'm going somewhere now. I'll be back later."

"Would you like me to unpack your backpack while you are gone?" Heyrovsky asked.

"How would you do that?"

"I have a robot in the closet named Gandolph who follows my commands. If you want, I will command Gandolph to remove the contents of your backpack and properly stow them in logical" locations included the closet while you ae gone."

"That will not be necessary. I want to look at what I packed and decide if I need to get other items. I'll unpack when I return."

"Alright Master Cameron Malá, I shall wait until you return to take any further action."

"Thank you, Heyrovsky."

"You are welcome, sir."

Cameron Malá left his room and soon left the *Adinska Dasnal Resort Hotel* to the *Bamtorini Sportsters* rental business to get the rental, test drive it a while, then park it in the resort parking lot to get ready for the next day.

To Dunbar's surprise at the conclusion of taking the *Bamtorini Sportsters* rental and signing the contract he was informed an escort would go with him for a while to make sure he could handle the *Bamtorini Sportster* a notable crem da la crem of two-wheel sports machines.

Dunbar then inserted the ear pods into his ears and placed the safety helmet on. There was a second helmet fasted by a strong Velcro like harness on the back seat. That would come in handy during the snatch and grab.

Dunbar didn't really care that someone was sent along on a second *Bamtorini Sportster* to make sure he wasn't going to wrap himself around a telephone pole or other deadly collisions.

Dunbar drove around the city on the major throughfares in a semi-conservative manner, not exceeding the speed limit or doing any dangerous maneuvers. Dunbar was an experienced two-wheel sports machine operator. Dunbar was not going to put himself in a position to deal with authorities by performing some illegal act on the *Bamtorini Sportsters* nor did he want to do something that would raise his visibility to the public as he wished to remain incognito until he departed with Rextar Fünger and the plans to build Trapezoidal Differentiators.

Dunbar covered a lot of territory and numerous traffic conditions in thirty minutes that demonstrated his expertise and knowledge of city driving on a two-wheel sports machine. Without warning his escort peeled away and departed leaving him alone.

Dunbar then verbally asked *Latrodectus*, "Give me directions to drive past Rextar Fünger's home, I want to do some reconnoitering around his home and drive from there to near the transport capsule to verify my route when I bug out."

The ear pods Dunbar was wearing also produced stereo microphonic pickup for *Latrodectus* which did phase measurements for noise cancellation allowing superb sound pickup when Dunbar spoke.

Dunbar was guided away from major throughfares onto city streets and soon was coming up on Rextar Fünger's home when *Latrodectus* said, "Rextar Fünger's home is the blue house past these next three houses."

"Is this the right direction to be traveling when we leave with Rextar Fünger?"

"No, you need to make a U-turn."

"Alright, I'll just go up ahead and go around the next block to get reorientated."

Dunbar then made his way around the next block facilitating a U-turn and drove past Rextar Fünger's home paying attention to all its features to figure out the best way to break in during the middle of the night to carry out the snatch and grab.

"There is a side access to the left side of the home which most likely allows entry into the garage," Dunbar said.

"This is a fairly new housing development," *Latrodectus* said, then added, "I'm checking the world wide web for information about the builder and the models for that home."

While *Latrodectus* was researching the builders-model for Rextar Fünger's home, he gave Dunbar directions to the forested area where the transport capsule was hidden and currently cloaked. Picking this route helped avoid major throughfares and exposing Dunbar carrying a body when they bugged out. Late at night there would be very little traffic so utilizing city streets would not be an issue. Thanks to the layout of the streets there were some that had no stop signs and only a few with traffic lights, making travel in the middle of the night very efficient.

In a while the area the arrived in was very close to the transport capsule and *Latrodectus* said, "We are at the location nearest the transport capsule."

Dunbar noted all the surroundings but drove on for a while entering a desolate area where no home or buildings existed and he said, "Alright, I'm going to turn around here and go back to the *Adinska Dasnal Resort Hotel.*

Latrodectus said, "Pull over to the side of the road and look at the flat screen on your communicator."

Dunbar pulled over to the side of the road and stopped and pulled out his communicator looking at the images showing.

"That's the overall drawing to Rextar Fünger's home. You can pan around and move the image to see other areas of the plans for the building."

Sure, enough the door on the side of the home was the access to the garage and twenty feet from it was the doorway entering the home.

"Did you detect a security system when we drove past the home?"

"Yes, Rextar Fünger's home has a sophisticated wireless home security system with a number of infrared sensors including inside the garage."

"Are you able to hack into the security system?"

"Yes, I now have all the passwords and the alarm deactivation sequence. You will be able to walk in give him a knockout drug and prepare him for transport in the back seat of the *Bamtorini Sportster.*"

"After we subdue Rextar Fünger, we can put on his street clothes with a light jacket, drive the *Bamtorini Sportster* into the garage then shut the garage door and then strap him into the back seat with the normal shoulder harness and seat belt." *Latrodectus* said.

"I assume there is an automatic garage door opener?" Dunbar asked.

"Yes, it's all wireless, after you get Rextar Fünger situated on the *Bamtorini Sportster* and ready to leave, I can open the vehicle access door and close it remotely after we exit the garage.

"I think I can drive the *Bamtorini Sportster* right up to the transport capsule," Dunbar said.

"Drive by slowly when we pass the area where the transport capsule is and take another look," *Latrodectus* said.

"Alright," Dunbar said and slowed as he went past the area and investigated the forested area and concluded, he could ride directly up to the transport capsule.

"Has there ever been a snatch and grab with a transport capsule before?" Dunbar asked.

"Normally I would have to inform you that's compartmentalized information and I cannot reveal it, but since there has not been any, I can confirm you are doing the very first one," *Latrodectus* said.

Dunbar was feeling quite good knowing the four amigos had never done something like this before.

Dunbar sped up the *Bamtorini Sportster* for a short while feeling the great acceleration then slowed down as he knew he needed to avoid the urge to hot-dog it and get cited by the police and experience the possible ramifications that might create.

Dunbar then drove around the city a while taking in the view of everything knowing he had 95% of the energy left, he would be long gone before the *Bamtorini Sportster* would indicate a low power source requiring recharging.

As they were driving back to the *Adinska Dasnal Resort Hotel,* suddenly *Latrodectus* said, "There is video surveillance systems monitoring the exterior as well as the interior of Rextar Fünger's home."

"If you can crack into the security system why would that be a problem?"

"It's not a problem. I can monitor Rextar Fünger's activities and figure out the storage system for the Trapezoidal Differentiator. We might just be able to copy the files and not have to transport any materials."

"Can you do that remotely?"

"I'm doing that now."

"Do you have sufficient storage to get it all?"

"I do not need to put any of it on the communicator. I've established a gateway between the Larian world wide web and the intergalactic federation of planets communications link. The files will be arriving in your in-basket back at the Transport Directorate. If you want in a few hours, we can leave the planet."

"That's no fun. I have other ideas. I want to complete the snatch and grab because I think having Rextar Fünger will be valuable, also I think we need to do an arson operation to destroy his home and all his files for denial of service to the Larian government. My guess is that without Rextar Fünger, the Larians will never be able to create the system and we then will not have to worry about it being used against us in a long time."

"That's a great assessment and plan," *Latrodectus* said knowing it was a bold plan the four office warriors would never attempt.

This conversation with Dunbar reaffirmed *Latrodectus'* desire to keep Dunbar safe and prevent harm to him by the four amigos who had exposed their agenda against Dunbar that *Latrodectus* knew quite well.

Latrodectus would also now undermine the four amigos every opportunity he had. The problem *Latrodectus* had in dealing with the four *office warriors*, they seldom left the directorate because of their long list of excuses. *Latrodectus* had rare opportunities to act, since the *office warriors* never deployed in the past year or so.

Dunbar was well equipped to do everything planned. As an example, his compartmentalized toothpaste tube had a section that had several types of drugs to administer people during clandestine actions. The commercial tube improvised would simply be cut open when Dunbar needed the substances.

The opaque hair solution bottle was compartmented, and the bottom half was a super phosphorous material that would create a very hot fire instantly. The bottle had a timer as part of the mechanism so that Dunbar would be long gone before the quick blaze started.

Rextar Fünger's home would be consumed in flames abruptly and the plastics and other materials associated with research materials provided additional fuel that when ignited with the super phosphorous would create temperatures that would be uncontrollable and cause quick devastation to the contents. No doubt within just a few minutes the roof would collapse if the house did not outright explode.

Rextar Fünger might see his assailant a few seconds before he would be out like a light. Hopefully they could catch him in bed sleeping during the break-in and Rextar Fünger would not regain consciousness until he awoke in an infirmary in the Kaokuen Transport Directorate.

The plan was coming together so promptly that Dunbar would leave the *Adinska Dasnal Resort Hotel* the next day ostensibly to go on a ride through the nearby mountain roads right after lunch. That would give *Latrodectus* extra time to work out all contingencies. Once his trusted artificial intelligence was ready, the special operation would start.

Dunbar drove to the *Adinska Dasnal Resort Hotel* parking lot and met the attendant and was shown where to park the *Bamtorini Sportster* not far from where the attendant had his booth.

Dunbar went up to his room, pulled out a change of clothes out of his backpack as well as several items to use in the bathroom such as toothpaste, shaving lotion, mouthwash, etc. He commented out loud, "These clothes are wrinkled, I wonder if there is an iron and press machine in the room?"

Suddenly, Heyrovsky's holograph popped up and asked, "Do you have some concern about your clothes Cameron Malá?"

"Just call me Cameron."

"Alright, Cameron, sir."

"I wasn't thinking correctly when I packed my change of clothes into my backpack, now they are wrinkled and not presentable."

"Cameron, may I make a suggestion?"

"Sure."

"Why don't you take a bath or a shower and while you are enjoying that activity, Gandolph will take care of your clothes for you so that you look sharp when you go out again."

"I like that idea, thanks."

"Do you want a bath or a shower?"

"I think soaking in a bath will be good."

"Gandolph will soon start your bath for you and put some pleasurizers in the water for you."

"That's great, thank you."

At that point in time, Gandolph walked out of a door, looking like a butler dressed as such, and said, "Good afternoon, Cameron," I'm your room assistant Gandolph. I will start your bath now."

"Thanks."

A moment later Dunbar (aka Cameron) heard the water running in the bathroom and started taking off his clothes and sat them on the bed and walked towards the bathroom.

"Cameron your bath is ready," Gandolph said.

"Thanks."

In a few minutes Dunbar was in the bath enjoying the water up to his neck and the pleasurizers were quickly having their effect. Dunbar enjoyed the bath for a while and discovered hair treatments laid out for him which he used adding to the pleasure as they too had chemicals to make the bathing experience far more pleasurable.

A bathrobe was hanging near Dunbar who stepped out of the sunken bathtub with steps leading into the deeper portion. Towels were staged for Dunbar, and he dried off noticed slippers and put on the bathrobe and left the bathroom and walked over by his bed and asked, "What happened to my clothes?"

"Cameron, your clothes were dry cleaned along with the wrinkled clothes you pulled out of your backpack and are now hanging in the closet. The contents in your pockets are laying in the tray right beside you."

"Alright, thanks."

Dunbar walked over to the closet and noticed the clothes dry cleaned on hangers, his shoes and laundered socks and underwear and said, "That was quick."

"Gandolph is very efficient," Heyrovsky said.

Dunbar dressed and asked, "What are the dining facilities like here?"

"Cameron, there is the formal dining hall, you may not be dressed to feel comfortable there since most of the patrons show up with nice clothes on. But adjacent to the dining hall is the outdoor bar and restaurant that provides a more causal setting as well as serves people enjoying the swimming pool."

"Are there people at the outdoor bar now?"

"Yes, plus there is musicians performing now."

"Can I see what it looks like?"

"Absolutely, Cameron."

Suddenly a real time holograph of the covered outdoor bar shown and there were 5 gorgeous women in bathing suits at the bar drinking, talking, and snacking listening to the music that sounded good.

"I think I'm going to try the outdoor bar now," Dunbar (aka Cameron) said after he was dressed and ready to go.

"Enjoy your time, Cameron," Heyrovsky said.

"Thank you."

"You are most welcome."

Dunbar took the elevator and went to the lobby and while getting out asked the artificial intelligence in the elevator, "Which way to the outdoor bar?"

"Sir, when you exit the elevator take a right. About 50 steps is the door to the outdoor bar and restaurant."

"Thank you."

"You are most welcome."

Dunbar walked to the door and went outside to the bar restaurant and looked over and saw just one empty seat at the bar which he went to. He had gorgeous women in bathing suits on each side of him.

As soon as Dunbar sat down, the bartender asked, "What can I get you sir?"

"I would like a *Jangovian de Palentin* elixir, please."

"Yes sir, coming right up. We do not get a request for that drink very often."

A blonde lady left of Dunbar heard the order and knew this had to be a sophisticated gentleman ordering that rare drink.

"Hello, what's your name," she asked.

"I'm Cameron Malá," Dunbar lied. He then asked, "What's your name?"

"My name is Brigitte Hindemith," the blonde lady said.

"Are you from Fujima?" Cameron asked.

"No, I'm from Canute."

"Where's Canute?"

"It's in the Lothbrok star system," Brigitte responded.

"What's Canute like?"

"It's a rocky and dry planet, but we have immense mineral resources, so the people that live there have wonderful living conditions."

"How about you Cameron?"

"I'm from a place far away from here called Glucal."

"What brings you here all the way from Glucal if its far away?"

"I'm going to meet with a research scientist tomorrow concerning an invention people I work for are interested in."

"Are you going to buy or obtain his product?"

"Yes, very much so."

"How exciting."

"You have no idea how exciting it is."

"Can you tell me about it?"

"I would like to, but I'm sure my superiors do not want my meeting with the scientist to become public knowledge. You can understand the delicacy in such matters."

"Yes I can, in fact I'm doing something similar to what you are doing."

"Then you know the game."

"Yes, I do."

Say Brigitte, I'm kind of hungry. I was going to order something to eat if that's okay with you."

"Cameron, actually I was thinking the same exact same thing."

About that time the bar tender delivered Cameron's drink and Bridgitte said, "Excuse me sir, the two of us would like food menus."

"Not a problem madam." The bartender turned around and grabbed a couple food menus and handed one to Brigitte and one to Cameron."

"Thank you," Cameron said.

The two soon ordered their meals.

Cameron received four large Gélí in his order with a side of a cylindrical fried Mǎlíngshǔ that were three inches long and one inch in diameter with some dipping sauce.

The Gélí are a seafood item that comes from a large shell and cooked in special spices and sauces give it a distinct flavor. A sliced sour fruit was squeezed on it to add to the delicacy. The four Gélí and the Mǎlíngshǔ dipped in a special sauce, created a very fulfilling dinner for Cameron.

Brigitte had what appeared to be barbecued ribs. What she ate came from a reptilian that could best be described as a crocodile. She also had Mǎlíngshǔ side with dipping sauce.

In a sense, Dunbar was *crying in his beers*. He could not get Blemary out of his mind. But at the same token being forced to leave Kaarina the way he did because of poor support from the Transport Directorate that forced what he used the term "goat fuck," also had a corrosive effect on his attitude. Had the agency done their part so he could have handled the matter in a reasonable fashion, there is a distinct possibility he and Kaarina would be building a permanent relationship.

But Dunbar knew the facts of life. Kaarina by now had been interviewed by the authorities, she was most likely aware he killed those two men in cold blooded murder inflicting terrible traumas to them, and he would be the last person in the galaxy that a surgeon like Kaarina would ever want to see again. There was no point in ever attempting to locate Kaarina and contacting her. It was finished not by his designs.

Dunbar was silently eating, reminiscing about his past, his lust and love for Blemary, the misadventures with Kaarina at Nigārà a city at the planet Pràsplātanià, and thinking about what he would do tomorrow, he almost forgot this nice-looking lady, Brigitte Hindemith an *eager beaver* was sitting next to him checking out his great body, his great looks, and wondering exactly what his stature in life really was.

In the middle of Dunbar's transcendence to his past, he was suddenly stirred out of his temporal anomaly, by Brigitte's voice as she said, "Tell me Cameron, what do you like to do for fun? What's your plans for tomorrow?"

"Well, I do like the symphony and the opera and tomorrow I'm going to drive through the mountains on a Bamtorini Sportster."

"Are you going with someone?"

"No just going by myself."

"How would you like some company?"

Cameron Malá realized he had to burn a couple hours tomorrow to wait for the nighttime to do the heist and abduction started calculating, it might be good idea to take Bridgette along with him to fill in hours he would otherwise spend in an idle waiting for the proper time to do his activity. He responded, "Yes, I could probably take you with me."

"What time did you plan on leaving?"

"I'm going to do my morning routine, go for a walk and run, then come back and do some swimming."

"Alright, how about I meet you at the pool, and discuss our plans."

"Sounds good to me," Cameron said looking at Brigitte's bikini that revealed perfect geometry.

The two talked for over an hour, finished their meals, had another elixir, then Cameron said, "I think I'm going back to my room to relax and watch some holographs."

"I'll walk you to the elevator," Brigitte said with a smile.

Cameron Malá was starting to feel some strange thoughts with his little head and responded, "Sure I would like your company."

Cameron left a substantial tip in credits฿ to the bartender who was starting to really like this guy, smiling said, "Good night, sir. Thanks for coming."

"My pleasure."

Cameron led Brigitte Hindemith to the elevator and stepped inside. Dunbar's room was on the 7th floor. Brigitte was in a Penthouse on the top floor and as it was rising, Brigitte said, "Cameron, I have a good idea. Instead of you going back to your room, why don't you go up with me to my Penthouse?"

"I suppose I could."

When the elevator got near the 7th floor it asked, "Cameron, do you wish to stop here or continue with Brigitte to her penthouse?"

"I'll go with Brigitte."

"Alright Cameron, we'll stop on the top floor for you and Brigitte."

"Thank you."

The elevator stopped at the top floor and Brigitte led Cameron to her Penthouse. Thanks to her mineral rich planet, Brigitte was wealthy. She was here for pleasure and not much work. She had an hours' worth of work to do on this trip and it was already accomplished, and she would spend a couple of additional weeks here enjoying herself before she traveled back to a planet that didn't offer a lot of lush green landscape.

Inside the Penthouse, a butler and a maid served Brigitte, taking care of all her needs. When Brigitte arrived with Cameron, she went into her living room and asked Cameron, "Would you like a drink?"

"Sure, whatever you like."

Brigitte smiled and looked at her maid and said, Elsa, can you please bring Cameron and me glasses of Huǒlóng de Guǒ.

"I will bring that right away Madam Hindemith,"

In a few minutes, Elsa returned with two champaign glasses full of Huǒlóng de Guǒ on a silver tray, then left shutting the door behind her so the couple would have complete privacy.

Brigitte Hindemith was reaching her peak of her fertility. She wanted a romantic tryst far more than Cameron's little head was calculating.

The drink she selected, Huǒlóng de Guǒ was rich in Damiana and L-Arginine. It also was rich in B vitamins, psycho active drugs, and caffeine.

Brigitte Hindemith had experienced strong men in the past, but they were rare. When she found one, she liked she became an octopus and pursued him with the vigor that would make most female readers of tabloids blush.

Halfway through the drink Brigitte said, "Excuse me for a minute, I want to get out of this swimsuit and put on other clothes."

"Sure," Cameron replied.

Brigitte walked into her bedroom, shut the door, took off her bathing suit and put on only a bathrobe and house slippers. She had a spray bottle of a special perfume loaded with pheromones and sprayed on her breasts, her underarms then spread her legs apart and opened her vulva and sprayed some there as well hoping Cameron would give her the Tour de France. She was more than ready and just needed to move Cameron a little and get with the program. She didn't want any further delays.

Brigitte walked out of her bedroom, into the living room and walked directly over to Cameran and placed her body on top of his and bent down and gave him a sensual and soft kiss on his lips.

The Huǒlóng de Guǒ was already having its effect and Cameron was jacked up about as much as possible.

The pheromones in the perfume were now leaving their mark as Cameron's little head was now fully erect and saluting.

Brigitte opened up her bathrobe exposing her breasts and put one of them on Cameron's mouth which he now tasted and sucked on like a baby. With the perfume's pheromones now hitting Cameron's body he was quickly reaching the point of no return. He was soon shocked as Brigitte reached down and felt his erect manliness and then repositioned her body and pulled down his trousers exposing his little head which she began performing fellatio on.

In about two minutes Brigitte could tell Camera was getting too close to his dragon spewing its magic venom so she stopped and repositioned her body and grabbed his manliness and inserted it inside her because she didn't want to miss out on that explosive release of dragon extract. The resulting coitus was a crescendo on a *Theme from Paganini* as soon the release created splendid gratification, they both wanted and enjoyed. The splendid euphoria hit them simultaneously as their brains produced all that extra Serotonin Vasopressin, and the Hormone Prolactin with the release slowly decaying but the euphoric feeling lingered.

During their love making, Brigitte felt Cameron's body she wanted to see and feel all of it. She knew he was a special person with a physical build that would create a surreal mood in her.

"Cameron, would you mind going into my bedroom with me and laying with me and holding me for a while?"

"I would love to."

"The couple then stood up and made their way to the bedroom where they were soon horizonal and nude together.

Brigitte was even more astonished as she looked at Cameron's body when he approached the bed and crawled in with her. Then she got to touch all his strong muscles and feel the essence of this extraordinary creature whose dragon venom was already creating a spontaneous chemical reaction in her that was almost getting her to the point where she wanted it again. She would let Cameron rest a bit then she would convince him to transcend into sublime sensual delights with her. She would do everything in her power to motivate Cameron to create the desire to please her and show his true power as a lover.

In about thirty minutes they reached a soft quiet quiescence. Cameron's physiology was now ready to perform again, and Brigitte was not the least bashful and said it like she meant it.

"Darling, I want you to make love to me again."

The pheromones Cameron inhaled, Brigitte's beauty, her voice, her exotic perfume, and her quintessential loving attitude enthralled Cameron where he was more than ready to please Brigitte again. To her surprise and utter delight, Cameron took her on the *tour de France* giving Brigitte a dozen spontaneous eruptions of pleasure she didn't think she could ever experience in her lifetime. Then Cameroon fulfilled Brigitte's wish in a mannerism to demonstrate a very capable lover could do, and he did not disappoint her. Even Catherine the Great would have relished Cameron with his power and proficiency.

Brigitte had never been inspired and gratified this much in her lifetime. No man ever came close. She was immediately addicted to the great Scorpio Cameron. It was love at first sight with immense gratification and delight. Brigitte's lady friends, including three of them she did not introduce at the bar for her own greed, would be highly envious of Brigitte at this very moment if they knew what had just transpired.

The other barracudas Cameron saw at the bar were slow on the draw and like a good gunslinger, Brigitte aced all of them. She was the queen for the day and if they only knew what Cameron had to offer it's likely they would all have had a wrestling match to get to him first.

Now the perfect coitus turned into romantic bliss as Cameron held Brigitte in his arms kissing the top of her head and hugging her like she was the biggest lover in his lifetime.

In a way Brigitte helped Cameron that night. His unhappy loss of Kaarina was now behind him. Any remorse or sad feelings perpetuated out of that relationship were now buried permanently in the past. This also went a long way to easing his frustration and anxiety over the loss of his ability to ever see Blemary for the rest of his life.

Make no mistake about it. If Dunbar could leave this very moment and go and get Blemary and take her where the two of them could spend the rest of their lives together, he would be flying out of the penthouse. But as a pragmatic man, and a galactic class spy, he knew the reality was, he and Blemary were finished because of a great divide and the fact she lived behind enemy lines in a forbidden territory.

After falling asleep for a few hours in total harmony, Cameron awoke mainly because he had to urinate, but he also needed to go back to his own room and get himself ready for the big events tomorrow. He found the bathroom without much effort and after relieving himself, Cameron went back into the bedroom and Brigitte was sitting up in her bed smiling. The lights had never been turned off.

"Brigitte, I'm going back to my room and freshen up and go to bed there. I want to get up in the morning and workout. I'll meet you at the pool as we talked about earlier and take you on a ride in the mountains with me later."

"Alright darling, I know you have to go, and I'll be looking forward to seeing you at the pool."

Cameron put his clothes back on and Brigitte walked him to the door to the penthouse and hugged him and kissed him just before he departed. She was full of happiness and gratification and knew she would really enjoy the ride through the mountains the next day.

Dunbar went back to his room, took a shower, changed into sleeping clothes, and went to bed after saying, "Wake me up at 7:00 A.M. so I can get up and go for a walk."

The room's artificial intelligence, Heyrovsky responded, "Cameron, I will wake you up at 7:00 A.M. as you have requested."

"Thank you."

"Sleep well Cameron."

"Thank you."

***

Dunbar woke in the morning and was soon walking towards a park about seven blocks away.

This park was a lot nicer than public parks he had recently been to. The Larians were masters at landscaping, and it was apparent they took great care of their public places.

Cameron didn't have running shoes or gym clothes with him, so he just walked five miles at the park at a good pace. As he was finishing up his walk, and he entered a conversation with *Latrodectus*, there were suddenly new events unfolding that would now affect their time line.

Rextar Fünger had visitors. Government officials and dignitaries from the *Stanzel* Defense Ministry.

"Dunbar we cannot carry out the plan today. We need to look into what the *Stanzel* Defense Ministry is doing here," *Latrodectus* said.

This was a huge development because if the *Stanzel* Defense Ministry was actively engaged with the Larians, that could be a game changer. The fact they were also going to spend some time with Rextar Fünger meant they might already know what he was developing.

Intel gathering suddenly overshadowed the need to grab Rextar Fünger. Their departure was on hold for a while.

There was nothing Dunbar could do. *Latrodectus* was doing all the work and in essence the mission now turned into an ISR data collection.

That meant the rest of the day, Dunbar would be doing nothing more than spending time and enjoying Brigitte Hindemith. *Working undercover was rough but someone has to do it*, Dunbar thought an smiled.

"I suppose since I have a delay in departure I might as well go buy some running shoes and workout clothes," Dunbar said.

"Good idea," *Latrodectus* replied.

On his way back to the *Adinska Dasnal Resort Hotel*, Dunbar went to several stores in Fujima to buy his workout clothes and shoes. He had plenty of credits₿ to do such activities. He also bought a nice bathing suit that would no doubt create subtle sensations in Brigitte Hindemith. Her three friends would even want in on the action, especially after Brigitte bragged how strong Cameron was in his thrusts during their unexpected lover's tryst.

Cameron went back to the resort, changed into his new bathing suit and went down to the pool to swim some laps. The pool area was mostly empty which he did not mind. After finishing 20 laps around the pool, Cameron stepped out of the pool with a lot of lactic acid in his body fearing cramps and walked over to a padded folding reclining chair and laid down. He did not spot Brigitte with her three friends about 25 feet away as he was only thinking about his aching muscles.

Stretching his legs out and relaxing went a long way towards dealing with the lactic acid and exhaustion.

Brigitte was a little scared at first watching this amazing creature swim for a bit with her friends after she had bragged about him, without saying a word stood up and walked over near Cameron laying on a reclining padded pool chair with a footrest.

Cameron (aka Dunbar) was slowly coming to terms with his body and slowly felt better when Brigitte suddenly showed up.

"Hello Cameron."

"Hi Brigitte, please have a seat. Give me a few minutes for my muscles to relax. I'm worried about getting a muscle cramp."

"Sure Cameron," Brigitte sat down looking at the other three women smiling watching it all unfold.

"Are we still going on the ride in the mountains today?"

"Yes. Let's get something to eat here and relax, then we can change our clothes and go."

"That's great, it really sounds fun," Brigitte said.

"I'm sure that with you coming with me it will be more enjoyable," Cameron said.

"What are you going to do after the ride in the mountains," Brigitte said.

"I'm not sure, I've not thought about it yet."

"Last night you said you like the opera and the symphony."

"Yes, I do."

"Tonight, there is a lovely opera performance. Would you like to go?" Brigitte asked.

"Yes, I would love to do something like that with you, but I didn't bring any nice clothes with me because I thought this would be a short trip."

"Cameron, the resort has a fashion staff that dresses up people for special events. If you would like, come up to my penthouse after we get back from the bike ride and we can have them dress us for the opera."

"Sounds like a plan," Cameron replied.

"Cameron, before we change into our dress clothes for the opera, do you suppose you could spoil me like you did last night?"

"Brigitte, I have a better idea."

"What's that?"

"When we are driving through the mountains, I'll spoil you."

"I like that idea better," Brigitte replied smiling.

In a while Cameron sat upright and said, "I feel better now, let's, get something to eat."

Cameron stood up walked over to Brigitte gave her a big hug and a kiss on the side of her head and sat down at the circular table next to his reclining chair and signaled do a waiter.

"Yes sir, what can I do for you?"

"Can you get us a couple menu's, please?" Cameron said.

"No problem, sir be right back."

"Cameron, I want to tell you something."

"Sure, what is it Brigitte?"

"I want you to know I have developed feelings for you."

Cameron looked Brigitte in her eyes and in the most somber, yet astute manner responded, "Brigitte, you don't know much about me because we have just met and had a good time together. I recently lost someone I love. There is no possibility of me ever being with her again the rest of my life.

"I'm terribly sorry to hear that," Brigette responded.

"I have a huge void in my heart now. You have no idea how much I wanted you last night. But I must tell you, my heart is very delicate right now. I need some time and space to cope with it and come to terms."

"I understand you Cameron and thank you for informing me about all this."

"If you are willing to work with me on this, you have no idea how much I want to fall in love again."

The three other women heard some of Cameron's comment but not all of it as they were just about far enough away to not clearly hear all of it. But they saw the tears form on Brigitte who stood up and walked over to Cameron and per her arms around him and said, "No man has ever touched my heart like that before."

The two of them hugged for a long while as Cameron patted Brigette on the back and then they regained their composure and Brigette sat down and dabbed her eyes with a napkin and smiled at Cameron who now had a psychological spike feeling like crap because in a very short time he had to give three wonderful women an alias.

Brigette had no idea what was going through Cameron's mind at that moment but when she saw a few of his tears. That image hit her in the gut like a rock because she knew everything, he just said was factual and real.

At this very moment in time, Dunbar hated the spy business. He was looking at the possible love of his life and knew that and he was deceiving Brigette with an alias. Living the big lie with Brigette troubled Dunbar greatly.

Bridgette of course had no idea what Cameron's emotional spike was all about, but she knew better than to probe because it could indeed open a gaping wound in the heart.

The drama was suddenly curtailed with the waiter who was dealing with them and their meals. It was good for Cameron there was something that broke off this emotional sequence. Because at that very moment he hated being a spy more than anything in the world.

Temporary lovers just did not cut it. Dunbar needed permanence, reality. Dunbar knew what was in Blemary, Kaarina, and now Brigette's hearts. They were real and legitimate. Incredible women with so much to offer. Any man who ended up with them would be very lucky.

The spy in Dunbar quickly rearranged his temporal anomaly and he quickly came to grips with his situation and ushered in an emotional quiescence that facilitated a tranquil time at the pool. The three women gawking at Brigette and her Loverboy Cameron were transfixed in awe at what they observed.

In the morning when the three got together with Brigitte for breakfast and talked to Brigette about her adventures, they didn't believe half of it. Now they were discovering it was all true. And it was amazing. They saw Cameron Malá's body when he climbed out of the pool with his muscles budging and the sweetness that erupted between him and Brigette.

This event humbled them. And these intelligent women watching the exchange were completely floored when the tears appeared on Cameron the hunk and the physical interactions between the two, completely resolved any ambiguities.

After the two finished their meals, Cameron said, "Alright Brigitte, I'm going to go up to my room and freshen up and put on my clothes. Call me when you are ready to leave."

"Sure honey, I will."

Cameron stood up, walked over and kissed Brigitte on her head and hugged her and walked back into the resort not paying any attention to any of the gawkers, because he didn't care.

Latrodectus was receiving a treasures trove of intel out of Rextar Fünger's home. Like a lot of the best INTEL, an opportunistic moment gives the greatest dividends. The fact they drove by on the Bamtorini Sportster that gave them a pathway in for such a surveillance is an example of one of those greatest opportunistic moments that by itself made the entire mission worthwhile. This is the type of event the four office warriors would never experience. The fact they all thought they should be the next supervisor astonished *Latrodectus'* artificial intelligence analysis.

Dunbar freshened up, took a shower and changed into his street clothes he was ready to go waiting for Brigitte to contact him.

Because of events now ongoing between the *Stanzel* Defense Ministry personnel and the Larians, Dunbar might be stuck here a few more days, but *Latrodectus* had determined that would not be an issue. Dunbar was exhibiting a sense of closure with his prior lovers as Brigitte was slowly consuming all his emotional outpour.

Just when Dunbar was starting to get impatient, Heyrovsky announced, Brigitte Hindemith wishes to communicate with you on holographic video. Do you accept?"

"Yes, please put her on."

A moment later, "Hello Cameron. I'm ready to go."

"Brigitte, meet me out at the front entrance to the resort. I'll pull up the Bamtorini Sportster to pick you up."

"Alright honey, I'll be there shortly."

Brigitte quickly went down the elevator and out the front entrance.

Cameron went down to the parking level one stop below the lobby and walked over to the Bamtorini Sportster and was soon driving up the circular driveway to the front of the resort, where Brigitte stood patiently waiting.

Part of the side saddle storage compartments that covered the sides of the Bamtorini Sportster rear wheel had two small automatic rear wheels that automatically retracted or placed down automatically like aircraft landing gear to support the two-wheel Bamtorini Sportster so that it could not tip over allowing the driver to get off.

Cameron, wearing ear buds with the helmet that looked like what a jet fighter pilot would wear, raised the visor on the front of the helmet that kept the bugs out of his face. Cameron then got off the Bamtorini Sportster and handed Brigitte a pair of ear buds to wear so they could talk during the trip facilitated by *Latrodectus*.

"Put these in your ears so we can talk and hear each other during the trip."

"Alright," Brigitte replied.

Cameron then undid the second helmet and handed it to Brigitte and said, "Put this helmet on you can raise and lower the visor while we are driving it will keep the bugs and things out of your face."

"Alright."

Brigitte's ear buds operated off a different frequency than Dunbar's. *Latrodectus* could talk to him privately without Brigitte hearing the private conversation.

Cameron helped Brigitte get into the rear seat that appeared more like a race car seat than a motorcycle seat. Cameron then helped put on Brigitte's shoulder and seat belt straps and then got on the Bamtorini Sportster and drove out of the *Adinska Dasnal Resort Hotel* onto the city street after confirming no traffic close enough to be concerned about an accident.

Cameron then accelerated the Bamtorini Sportster, and they were now traveling at the same speed as the other traffic in the right lane of a four-lane road, with two lanes in each direction.

Dunbar timed his trip to make sure they got back in time to get ready for the opera that evening, then dinner back at the resort.

After driving around a bit and showing Brigiette majestic landscapes of the mountains, Dunbar wanted to take Brigiette near where the Transporter Capsule was cloaked to check up on the area to make sure there was no one that had been around. The Transporter Capsule gave LLL a sensor feed which indicated no persons had been anywhere near it. This gave Dunbar an excuse to also do what he hinted to Brigette he would do with her up in the mountains she felt excited about. This also validated he could drive almost up to the Transporter Capsule in case they had to immediately bug out.

Dunbar stopped the Bamtorini Sportster and got off it and took off his safety helmet and set it on his seat. Then he asked Brigiette, "Take of your helmet for a while."

He then undid her safety harness and put his arms around Brigiette and started kissing her and hugging her. She fully reciprocated and enjoyed every moment of it. In due time Dunbar was sitting in the rear seat with his trousers down and Bridgiette on top of him doing a perfect rhythm action that helped propel them both into a sensual evolution of thoughts out in the middle of the forest adding to the wild feelings that nature provided them.

Dunbar, knowing what was likely to happen real soon, thought this might be one of the last special moments the two would have together. The complexities of life regarding what he had to do and the circumstances they each had, created a bitter moment for Dunbar because a continuation of short-term relationships he experienced did not please him.

And here was another beautiful specimen of inspiration riding him and pleasing him that soon he would have to let go. It was a bittersweet moment, so all Dunbar could do was give Brigiette the love of the moment.

In a very remorseful tone with his eyes watering feeling the emotional spike coming on, knowing the two of them could be dead tomorrow if the space war turned into a lethal holocaust, decided he would give a gift to Brigiette which she duly earned.

"I didn't want to do this but there are things going on in my life that makes it a moment of opportunity."

Brigiette suddenly stopped her rocking on Dunbar enjoying his manliness and the feelings he gave inside her and said, "What do you want to say Cameron?"

"I love you."

When Brigiette heard those words, it did something to her psyche and her body and she started making love to Cameroon (aka Dunbar) with a passion. She was immediately flooded with gratification and her emotions were overflowing like a river out to sea. It seemed almost like a miracle to her that in such as short time they could transcend to this level of feelings for each other. Whatever Cameron felt, she felt just as strong.

It was one of the happiest but at the same time saddest days in Cameron's (aka Dunbar's) life. He knew he had to give and give up this special love. Mission creep now entered his mind, and his emotions were quickly being sterilized and compartmentalized, the inner spy in him was now slowly taking control of his thoughts and this would be his last night with Brigiette.

After they finished their splendid love making, Dunbar said, "I think we should go back to the resort and get cleaned up for the Opera."

"Honey, that's a great idea, because I really want to go."

After they were all situated, clothes back on and safety equipment engaged, Dunbar drove the Bamtorini Sportster out of the forest and back out onto the road.

As planned the two were dressed up in Brigiette's penthouse and soon on their way to the opera with great balcony seats.

With the money Brigette had, she could afford the best dresses and makeup artists and her makeover for the opera was stellar. Dunbar was very proud to be with such a fabulous looking woman.

Brigette was glowing with satisfaction. Cameron, the alias that Dunbar was starting to severely regret being with such a great looking and capable woman, really tested his resolve. Other spies would quit this moment and put a note in the Transporter and send it back to the DD/P and said, I met the love of my life, I'm sorry I quit. I don't want to lose her.

These kinds of thoughts were swirling through Dunbar's head. Being a spy was not what it was cracked up to be. Love flew by Dunbar all the time just like this one would. His heart would be broken just as bad ad Brigette's real soon with events he knew were coming. But there was nothing he could do to alter the course of events.

Tonight, Dunbar would take those few crumbs of life and give it all to Brigette. By morning she would know he had truly fallen in love, but he also had to abandon that love. Only a well-trained indoctrinated spy who could compartmentalize his emotions could break away like this.

The beautiful blonde opera singer resonated with Dunbar tonight. Her singing voice added to the complex emotions he felt. The orchestra, the music, and the singer really created an artwork that painted the images in the thoughts of the concert goers with great extravagance. The fidelity of the orchestra and the singing made it all the more special. Dunbar looked at Brigiette quite a bit and gave her a lot of warm smiles. She could not ask for any more than this. It was her time and her moment and Cameron (aka Dunbar) is what gave her these special feelings never before existed in her life.

During the intermission, Dunbar decided during their drinks he wanted to convey to Brigiette some of his emotions he wanted her to know were genuine and with three baracudas Brigiette knew watching them like a hawk from a distance, Dunbar said, "Come close to me, I want to kiss you."

Dunbar knew how to lay on those sensual kisses he was well trained at doing for the inverse honey pot schemes laid a sensual kiss on Birgette that melted her like never before and he put on the exclamation point, "I love you."

The barracudas saw it all. It wasn't put on for show it was the real deal and when they saw the tears flowing down Brigiette, they knew the gentleman must have said some powerful words, and they responded in a likewise manner.

The barracudas had no idea how tough it was for Dunbar tonight. He knew he was in love with this woman, and it was almost over soon he would be a ghost of her past. But he gave her what she gave him. It was real and it was sincere, a deadly spy's kiss.

The two-hour opera which had several great singers seemed like it ended too soon. That's the way time works, the best moments slip away faster.

Dunbar decided they should simply go back to the *Adinska Dasnal Resort Hotel* resort have dinner there, since they were dressed for the occasion. That would simplify logistics as tomorrow was likely to be a hectic day.

Dinner, drinks and as many slow dances they could work in created a tapestry in Dunbar's mind that indelibly printed this moment. The barracudas made their way into the restaurant and silently observed the splendid love that manifested in ways they wished they could experience.

After they left the restaurant and went back to Brigiette's penthouse there was more sensual love making and eventually Brigiette collapsed in Dunbar's arms and slipped into the best rest of a long time.

***

Chapter Ten

The Great Larian Space Battle

Events were now unfolding that were quite perplexing to Dunbar. *Latrodectus* just received and triple decrypted an urgent message on his communicator. It was a blessing in disguise that Dunbar was at the park walking when the message was received by *Latrodectus*.

The message was sent from the DD/P as a Dunbar Regvik's eyes only and had a five-minute timer before the imbedded Thereuopoda Clunifera Computer Virus would not only randomize the bit patterns making the encrypted message useless binary numbers, but also self-destruct the message through all communication hubs where it might have flowed or into any cloud computers where it might have been stored.

Dunbar had to read DD/P's operational immediate action message now or never, and it would never be sent again. In the header was the validation code Dunbar worked out for the DD/P as on one time use code because upon transmission, that code was eliminated out of the index of single use codes.

Only Dunbar and the DD/P had access to the validation code and could never send it anywhere except to the recipient Dunbar Regvik because if it was addressed anywhere else, the Thereuopoda Clunifera Computer Virus would randomize the content before it was received anywhere else.

Latrodectus developed the Thereuopoda Clunifera Computer Virus specifically to support Dunbar's missions and prevent the four amigos for accessing his critical communications.

The message Dunbar quickly read stated:

"The Kaokuen Space Armada is transiting to the Larian world where a sizeable *Stanzel* Space Force is in orbit. We expect hostilities to begin as the two fleets face off against each other. The changes to your mission are as follows:

1. Delay departure from current mission and record and report all information you can discern from the military engagements when they occur.
2. Perform as much ISR as possible using local tools available to you including classical espionage methods.
3. We expect that due to the volatility of the expected clash of the two space forces the battle will be short lived and both *Stanzel* and Kaokuen Space Armada will return to their prospective bases behind friendly lines.
4. Do whatever battle assessment you can and if any Kaokuen Space Force Personnel are delivered to the Larian worlds as prisoners attempt to discover who and where they are so we can formulate a rescue plan.
5. Once you have completed the requirements of the additional tasking, then return to the Transport Directorate with the materials you were sent to obtain.
6. DD/P END OF MESSAGE. Word count of message 186 words.

   Message was certified delivery by Thereuopoda Clunifera for sender and receiver eyes only.

Dunbar felt a lot better seeing the Thereuopoda Clunifera certification on the document. It told him the DD/P kept it away from the four *office warriors* he now had a sense the four amigos were undermining his missions attempting to destroy him because they were intimidated, he would beat them out of the promotion and then exact his revenge on them. They were not too far off the mark.

Dunbar also knew another fact. The space war could easily make its way down to this planet where he would be highly vulnerable like the general population.

This is a moment in every spy's life when they must come to terms with responsibilities. Dunbar had his orders directly from the DD/P. Even though he has an elaborate plan to abduct Rextar Fünger and steal the plans for the Trapezoidal Differentiators, this space battle was a huge event, the fact he was at the planet where the battle was to happen, created a very unusual circumstance.

There is no way Kaokuen INTEL could get all the extraneous ISR information without Dunbar's presence and more importantly, *Latrodectus* who was probably in position to capture all the enemy signals and record the entire electronic spectrum during the battle. Since Dunbar was in a major city and the likely area where this hemisphere would have direct view of the battle, all the radio waves transmitted by both fleets would be captured in the radio frequency spectrum that *Latrodectus* would capture.

Kaokuen ships would also record the electronic spectrums, but some of them would not survive the battle and their recordings would be lost.

Also, as the ships were twisting and turning in battle maneuvers, they would not always be in the best position to have continuous recordings. Dunbar's communicator with the dynamic *Latrodectus* systematically recording and filing would be the best source for a complete after-action report from the direct view of this hemisphere. Some of the signals would bend around the planet, but their signal to noise ratios would be diminished and hard to reconstruct with fidelity.

This was the rarest of opportunities. And Dunbar knew if he survived this would propel him far and above his piers potentially opening new vistas of opportunity.

"I'm going to have to keep up these walks in the morning and Bamtorini Sportster drives on the in the afternoons to get updates from you," Dunbar said.

"I've hacked the hotel security quite well. If I need to give you important information while you are in the room, I will send you a message on your flat screen. You can then go into the bathroom and read it all. I've verified there are no cameras or microphones in there."

"Alright thanks. What if I'm in Brigitte Hindemith's penthouse?"

"Inform Brigitte you must use the bathroom. I will be able to let you know if it's monitored when you get there," *Latrodectus* replied.

"What if it has more pressing details?" Dunbar asked.

"If it is just come up with an excuse to go back to your room where you know you have a place to read and observe all the information I give you on the flat screen."

"How soon do you think this space battle is going to happen?"

"A lot sooner than the Larians realize."

"I suppose there's not much more I can do to prepare for it."

"No and I have some new intel for you."

"What is it?"

"*Stanzel* agents are at Rextar Fünger's home now with one representative of the Larian government with them."

"Are they cutting a deal now?"

"Yes, but Rextar Fünger's not done with the design work. He will not be done before we anticipate the space battle happening."

"What can I do about it?"

"Not much, you are outgunned."

"So, you are saying I will have to just let them walk away with copies of the Trapezoidal Differentiator plans?"

"My analysis tells me they will have to temporarily depart the planet during the battle, you can abduct Rextar Fünger during the heat of the battle."

"But my orders are to remain here and report all the information we obtain including fleet damage assessments."

"This will be a fast-paced battle, most likely from start to finish will be twelve hours. After the two opposing fleets leave, the area, there is no point in remaining."

"So, you are saying we abduct Rextar Fünger during the major fighting?"

"Yes, I am multi-tasking. While we are abducting Rextar Fünger, I will also be collecting all the ISR data so when the two warring factions' bug out like they must, there really is no point in hanging around. You might as well go back to the Transport Directorate."

"Alright, that works for me."

Dunbar walked back to the *Adinska Dasnal Resort Hotel* mixed in with running on sidewalks that were sparsely containing people walking. He went up to his room, changed into his swim ware and robe and slippers and headed to the pool to swim some laps.

As he experienced in the past when Dunbar climbed out of the pool with aching muscles the four women were there gawking at him, and Brigitte was in the middle of all of them and no doubt she had shot off her mouth about her sexual escapades with Cameron Malá. Dunbar didn't care if he made the other three women horny: more power to it.

The women were engaged in some serious discussion and suddenly had panic on their faces. Dunbar didn't know that Larian government had detected the Kaokuen Space Fleet approaching with long range probes. At their present velocity they would be in the solar system and near the planet in 12 hours. A national emergency alert was now being sent out as a warning to everyone. Furthermore, the space port would be shut down in six hours. Anyone wishing to leave the planet needed to get the hell out of here now!

Dunbar didn't know this was all unfolding because he had not looked at his communicator, yet, which *Latrodectus* had messages waiting for him and directing him to go to his room to read them.

In almost a sheer panic, Brigitte approached Cameron Malá while the other three ladies took off to their rooms to pack to flee to the space port.

"Did you hear the news?"

"No. What news."

"There is going to be a major space battle near this planet in about twelve hours. They are closing the space port in six hours. I must leave now. I do not want to leave you, but I must go. I don't want to be trapped on this planet if they have a war here."

"Alright, understand what you have to do."

"Let's try to get together again after all this is over. Are you leaving too?"

"No, I'm not done with my business. I seriously doubt they will damage the planet."

"But you never know."

"Sure, we are not going to know until it's over."

"I'm terribly sorry. I'm a coward and I'm leaving."

"I'll be here for a few more days in case you decide to return."

"I don't know if I'm brave enough to come back for a while."

"Alright, you know who I am. We'll try to connect in the future."

"Yes definitely."

"Thank you for all the great times."

"Cameron, I'm sorry I'm such a coward, but I have to leave."

"I understand."

"Cameron, I think I love you."

"Alright, when we meet again, we can talk about all that."

"I'm leaving now to go get packed and get to the space port as fast as possible. I'll send your room my contact information so you can get in touch with me so we can continue building our relationship after this is all over."

"Thank you. That means a lot to me," Dunbar lied, he knew this was the end and thanks to this space battle, Brigitte gave him a romantic exit strategy. This was working out better than he could ever plan. Nothing to encumber his departure. He surely didn't want an emotional woman to say goodbye too.

"I'll be down at the lobby after I change my clothes to see you off," Cameron said.

"Alright dear, thank you for being understanding," Brigitte said knowing after all this was done, her new dutiful boy-toy Cameron would be here waiting for her ready to take up where their romance left off. She was going to be highly disappointed as Dunbar would not be taking her contact information with him. This was the last time in his life he would ever see Brigitte again.

Dunbar went up to his resort room, changed into his street clothes. While there, Latrodectus said, "Recommend you get the special Kollmorgant holographic eyeglasses out of your backpack and wear them so I can give you better imagery of the action that's about to happen."

"I thought I was going to use them for night vision if required?"

"Besides Night vision they give you also situational awareness projections which I want to show you, so you are aware of the dual use."

"What are you going to be able to show me?"

"*Stanzel* diplomats at their Fujima consulate have a Stanzel Tactical Data System (STDS) link to their space armada in orbit around the Larian planet they are monitoring and updating Stanzel Fleet Admiral Wirglestor on Larian involvement and Larian intercepted communications to Kaokuen diplomatic exchanges. You will have a bird's eye view of the battle from the *Stanzel* point of view with those Kollmorgant holographic eyeglasses."

"Does that include *Stanzel* tactical communications?"

"Yes, all their command and control and orders from higher authorities all propagate via their STDS system and their space cruisers and space carriers all make their video and voice reports over the STDS.

"You mean I'll have a front row seat in watching the fighting?"

"Yes. Thanks to my ability to hack into the STDS Sonet's because of our theft of their Fast Frigate, I'll be doing the first ever real time recording of their decrypted STDS imagery and voice."

"What's a Sonet?" Dunbar asked.

"Synchronized Orthogonal Networks."

"How do they work?"

"A Sonet is an orthogonal projection system for which the range and the kernel are derived in orthogonal subspaces. STDS Sonet data transmits all data in fractals that are almost impossible to intercept and decrypt."

"Amazing."

"Yes, but we have developed the technology giving us the ability to pirate all their STDS data transmissions without them knowing."

"Can you feed our fleet STDS data information to help them out?"

"No, if I sent signals to our fleet, we would be immediately unmasked, and you would be quickly arrested and treated as a spy in wartime."

"You mean executed."

"Precisely."

"Alright, I'm almost dressed, let me get those Kollmorgant holographic eyeglasses."

"When you put in your conformal ear pods, you will hear the sound associated with the special Kollmorgant holographic eyeglasses."

Dunbar went to the backpack and put on the special Kollmorgant holographic eyeglasses and said, "Can you show me some STDS data now so I can get a feel for what I'll be looking at?"

"Sure," *Latrodectus* said.

Momentarily Dunbar was completely mesmerized as he saw real time STDS images and sounded as if he were in the control room of the enemy ship looking at their tactical displays.

"Alright, I get it. This STDS information is quite amazing. I need to hustle down to the Lobby and say goodbye to Brigette."

People were flying out of the resort like crazy. Taxis were lining up to take them to the space port. Mass panic was happening. There was fear in everyone's eyes.

In due time Bridgette was in the lobby with a small carry on and left instructions to the maid to ship her belongings back if she could not get back for a while if there were issues that developed over the pending catastrophe everyone feared.

Brigitte looking fearful approached Dunbar and said, "Thank you for seeing me off. You have my contact information. We'll try to rendezvous somewhere else safer.

"Yes, I agree, darling."

"What are you going to do for the rest of the day?"

I'm going to drive the Bamtorini Sportster up in the mountains and observe the natural beauty.

"I'm sorry Cameron I need to leave now. I want to get to the space port before they close it and I'm stuck in a warzone."

"I understand Brigitte. See you if you can get back."

Even though they were in public, Dunbar didn't care. He had an alias and altered facial appearance thanks to three-dimensional biological printing. He would never see these people again for the rest of his life and if he accidentally did, he would look like someone else.

There was one last hug and Brigitte turned and fled to the string of waiting Taxis who knew the panic would get them great tips if they exceeded the speed limit to get to the Space Port quickly as these panic driven people wanted to leave promptly.

The Transportation companies were all smiles. They had barely enough time but managed to get a lot of extra space-transport ships here to accommodate the panic buying of tickets.

There really was no point in staying in the *Adinska Dasnal Resort Hotel*. Thanks to the charging station next to where the Bamtorini Sportster was parked, it was now fully charged and good for at least 48 hours of operation. Just as Dunbar was leaving, he grabbed his backpack and left nothing behind.

"I assume you can check me out remotely if needed?"

"Not a problem," *Latrodectus* said.

The parking lot attendant alerted by artificial intelligence the Bamtorini Sportster driver was approaching it and likely going for a drive. The attendant had hooked up the charging adapter to the Bamtorini Sportster and as Dunbar was about to disconnect it the attendant did it for him. It was a resort policy to do this to make sure such a two-wheel transport device didn't rip out the charging device, possibly damaging the cable if the driver forgot to disconnect it.

Dunbar put on his safety helmet and raised the visor to look out. Since he was wearing the Kollmorgant holographic eyeglasses, Dunbar really didn't need the visor to keep the bugs out of his eyes. But if he decided to go fast, he would put the visor down simply to keep the wind off his face and have a quieter ride.

When Dunbar advanced the throttle moving the Bamtorini Sportster at a very slow speed because he needed to clear the parking structure and get out on the road before he did a big acceleration, the support wheels retracted automatically into the side saddles by the rear wheel. Driving five to ten miles per hour, Dunbar soon exited the parking structure and turned onto the street keeping an eye out for panic driven Taxi's that were focused on speed and not safety.

It was a good thing the direction to the nearby mountains was opposite of the direction leading to the space port that now had a congested road.

Brigette was lucky she left behind most of her belongings because at the space port there were three lines set up. One with people traveling with a family, the second line was people that had luggage, and the third line was people with just a small carryon. The third line breezed through the ticketing and security checks and Brigitte was on the Intergalactic Transport Ship with a lot of other cowards getting the hell out of a potential war zone as quickly as possible. A lot of the people on this Transport were women and they all smelled like French Whores almost gagging the crew.

But the male crew members were happy because there was substantial amount of eye candy on this flight. Women are vain. Even thought they were running away from a war zone, they still found time to put on makeup and look their best.

The people stuck in lines one and two, people with children and people with luggage barely got aboard their flights before the Space Port was locked down.

Airport officials and the Intergalactic Transport companies did an incredible job getting them all away. Very few stragglers were left behind, and they only missed out because they procrastinated and did make up their minds to go until the 11th hour. And some of those were too concerned about their makeup and sadly had to go back to their resort hotels in fear when they easily could have been there three or four hours later.

But those who decided to stay, reaped the benefits of a full staff and few customers. The resort hotels never miss a beat and took advantage of the situation that many of the rooms were paid for and non-refundable since the person evacuated with no thought of the fact, they would not get a refund, nor did they care. They just wanted the hell out of there.

Improvising managers then asked a lot of customers if they wanted an upgrade in rooms at a modest price. By doubling their fee, they got put into a Penthouse that had already been paid for. Staying behind wasn't so bad after all when they got to experience how the rich lived.

There was a lot of luggage and belongings left behind by the panicking customers. There were now so many vacant rooms already paid for, the hotel/resorts had plenty of room to store all these possessions until they could be dealt with.

Dunbar didn't quite know what he was going to do that night but when he went to the mountains, he found it was quite deserted and the numerous locations with fantastic views were wide open and empty.

Since this was also a relatively dark area, he could watch the fireworks up in space and at the same time view a lot of the STDS imagery.

To the chagrin of the Larians as well as Stanzel Fleet Admiral Wirglestor, the large Kaokuen force they were tracking thinking this was the force they needed to deal with was a feint. They were out of position. The real attack came from their flanks at incredible speeds. It happened so quickly it even startled Dunbar sitting on the stopped Bamtorini Sportster that had the two rear support wheels down where he had sat comfortably for a while looking in the direction of Fujima center city area off to the distance.

Latrodectus gave Dunbar the heads up. Alarms are now starting to go off in the *Stanzel* Fleet, the battle has started. The STDS displays and the control room chaos began. The sounds and displays of the space warships were surreal. Stanzel Fleet Admiral Wirglestor was barking orders. The shooting started fast and furious. The night sky turned into daylight! Ships were exploding and chaos ran supreme.

Stanzel and Kaokuen ships maneuvered in a witch's brew of colossal entanglements. In a congested area of an oncoming almost suicidal attack, collisions could not be avoided.

Dunbar watched in total awe. This was unprecedented. He had never seen anything like this in his lifetime. It was subtlety unnerving. Male and female Space Warriors were screaming and yelling and cussing. It wasn't there was a breakdown in discipline, it was simply chaotic consequence of two powerful space forces converging, shooting rocket powered weapons, beam weapons and lasers. The carnage was spectacular.

In this maelstrom of utter horror, there were no clear-cut winners or losers, the fighting continued in a death dance of unimaginable consequences.

The Larian Space Defense commanders were crapping their pants watching all this on their sensors wondering if there would be a point in the battle where the *Stanzelites* might be devastated and the Kaokuen turn their attention on them and create havoc on the planet. The Larians were now on red alert.

The *Stanzelites* who were at Rextar Fünger trying to get electronic copies of the plans and possibly abducting the distinguished scientist were told to bug out:

"Leave Rextar Fünger and get to a shuttle immediately in preparation to leave the planet."

The *Stanzelites* were now evacuating diplomats and spies because the battle was not turning out in the manner, they thought it would be."

Stanzel Fleet Admiral Wirglestor started losing his nerve as he watched two nearby cruisers explode. He was now taking a prudent course and maneuvering in a manner to gather up all the spread-out forces into a more compact and stronger defense ring.

Dunbar who knew the *Stanzel* language from his vast studies in preparation for his recent mission heard Stanzel Fleet Admiral Wirglestor orders and it appeared Admiral Wirglestor was almost to the point he was going to bug out and leave the solar system to go lick his wounds and regroup.

That's when *Latrodectus* showed vast wisdom and analytical ability and jarred Dunbar out of his battle-weary fog and started getting him thinking and preparing him for his next move.

"If we go snatch Rextar Fünger and do what we planned, the Larians will think it was the *Stanzel* diplomats who abducted him."

"This would be a good time to get him," Dunbar said.

Dunbar advanced the throttle and was soon heading back to the city Fujima.

A few blocks away from Rextar Fünger's home the city went dark. Electricity had just been shut off. Nobody knew how or why. It might have been Kaokuen electronic warfare people doing it to shut down all the Larians defense grids to make sure they didn't shoot at them or help the *Stanzel* Armada. One thing was certain now, the Larians were very concerned and fearful.

The Larians didn't need their defense grid and computer networks to know what was happening in the space above them. The astonishing sight of cruisers and space carriers blowing up creating enough light to turn night into day was utterly terrifying. When the antimatter in their propulsion systems met explosives, the result was horrific. The plasma created in the inferno had the temperatures of the surface of the sun. Nobody knew it wasn't temporary suns appearing because they had no idea what it was. In other explosions the sparkling debris was impressive in colors and content.

By now most of the Larian society knew a space war was going on around their planet. This was the most difficult time in their lives because they had no idea what the ravages of war could become with advanced weapon systems.

Rextar Fünger was far more animated because he just went through a tumultuous event trying to explain to the *Stanzelites* why he could not get all those plans together because he had to download them from a device called *Blue Box*, a super-secret depository of data and credits฿ that only the super-rich knew about. The only reason they didn't abduct him was without the plans, it would take him so long to reconstruct the technology, there was no point.

Had the *Stanzelites* remained an additional 10 minutes, the removeable data stick had all the plans.

Rextar Fünger didn't know that *Latrodectus* had such extensive surveillance on him, he knew the complete set of plans were on the data stick plugged into one of his computer terminals. The computer terminal was now powered down like everything in the home due to the power outage.

A moment or two before Rextar Fünger was going to remove the data stick and put it some place safe in case the *Stanzelites* returned, *Latrodectus* was already giving Dunbar the night vision with the special Kollmorgant holographic eyeglasses. One of the devices Dunbar had he brought with him thanks to having the forethought to bring his backpack with him was an injection device that would make Rextar Fünger unconscious very quickly.

The Bamtorini Sportster electric powered was very stealthy and quiet. Unless the operator purposely put on the noise augmenter, nobody would hear it.

Most everyone in Fujima was terrorized and in storm cellars or some place they felt would give them added security. There virtually was nobody to see Dunbar come and go with the terrible darkness that descended upon the city. Pulling up with the night vision capability of the Kollmorgant holographic eyeglasses meant that Dunbar did not have to use the lights on the Bamtorini Sportster to safely navigate around the city or on this block. The arrival was totally incognito.

It was so dark that Rextar Fünger would not know Dunbar was looking at him through the window and the heat from Rextar Fünger body showed up well in the Kollmorgant holographic eyeglasses.

Rextar Fünger had not budged since the *Stanzelites* departed his home. In fact, they left the front door partially open which Dunbar silently went in.

This had been a terrible ordeal for Rextar Fünger and he put his face down into his hands wondering what was going to happen to him and wondered how soon it would be before they got power back and the *Stanzelites* would return. He knew it would be a sleepless night for him. Suddenly, Rextar Fünger felt something like a bee sting, and he was quickly unconscious.

Dunbar checked Rextar Fünger's pulse and knew it was vastly decreased with the drug cocktail done to him. Rextar Fünger's body was semi lymph, and he would be in this state up to 24 hours or longer.

Using guidance from *Latrodectus,* Dunbar walked over to the computer terminal and pulled the data stick out of it and placed it in his zip up pocket on the side to make sure he didn't accidentally lose it. Then he followed directions *Latrodectus* gave him to walk into the garage and how to manually open the garage door and there was plenty of room inside since Rextar Fünger had parked his four-wheel vehicle in front of the home on the city street.

After the garage door was open, Dunbar looked around the neighborhood and if there had been a person, his night vision would easily have seen them. The street was deserted as the occupants in the homes were huddled inside scared of their own shadows because of the prior news reports and the sudden loss of electricity. It was a terrible spooky evening for them and none of them had the incentive to venture outdoors any time soon.

Dunbar silently backed the Bamtorini Sportster into the garage and silently closed the door. He then went into Rextar Fünger's home and picked up the 115-pound man and easily carried him to the Bamtorini Sportster and placed him in the rear seat and put on his shoulder and seat belt straps that held his body in a good position. He then put on the second helmet on Rextar Fünger and found an article he fastened under his chin to keep his head up as if he were a living and alive person.

Dunbar walked back into the home and placed a device about half the size of his hand in the middle of the computers and piles of paperwork the unorganized scientist had on the table. The super phosphor would soon have the house in a blaze after the timer went off giving Dunbar a nice safe distance away from this area of Fujima.

Dunbar drove the Bamtorini Sportster out of the garage when LLL began remotely shutting the garage door as he departed, then drove the Bamtorini Sportster to the Transporter Capsule with *Latrodectus* navigating for him. Halfway across the dark city in the rear-view mirror, Dunbar could see a big fire going.

Rextar Fünger's home went up in flames and the two neighbors' homes were also engulfed in flames and suddenly people were coming out of their homes in panic trying to see what was going on. Since all the electricity was out there was no communications. The only reason why the fire department eventually showed up is the police were investigating a bright light while the rest of the city was dark with no electricity.

The police were able to call the fire department via their emergency communicators, but by the time the fire trucks arrived the roofs of the three homes had collapsed and Rextar Fünger's home had very little left. If there had been a body, it would have been consumed by the very large heat that was created with the super phosphor and all the flammable materials present.

Dunbar placed Rextar Fünger into the Transporter Capsule first. Then Dunbar stepped in and straddled Rextar Fünger slightly and asked *Latrodectus*, "Can we leave now?"

"The two space fleets are departing the solar system. The space battle is finished, there is no reason to remain here," *Latrodectus* said.

Dunbar hit the automatic launch sequence button and soon the Transport Capsule disappeared. A moment later the canopy of the Transport Module was opening and there stood the DD/P with a couple of his assistants looking down at Dunbar and his passenger.

"Help get this man out of here," Dunbar said, and the DD/P directed his helpers to pull the man out and laid him out on the floor next to the Transporter Capsule.

"What's the condition of this man?" the DD/P asked.

"He'll be sleeping for a while. I injected him with *Laudanum-diacodium sulfate*.

"Who is this man?" the DD/P asked.

"This is Rextar Fünger, the inventor of the plans I stole." Dunbar pulled the data stick out of his pocket and handed it to the DD/P.

"I suppose we need to go into the office and talk about this," the DD/P said, then turned to his assistants and said, get some medical people here right away to take care of this man. Place around the clock guard on him. Nobody is to talk to him other than the medical people for medical reasons. After he's well and awake I will interrogate him."

"Yes sir," the lead assistant said.

"Come with me Dunbar."

The two men were soon in the DD/P's office starting the discussions while *Latrodectus* was uploading mission files to a compartmentalized area of the Transport Directorate's archives. Until the DD/P determined who would be cleared to see the files, only he had access.

The DD/P reviewed Dunbar's operational orders. It was a good thing those orders were very compartmentalized and only the DD/P and internal review had access.

"I assume this data stick has the plans for the Trapezoidal Differentiators?" the DD/P asked.

"Yes. My communicator artificial intelligence assures me Rextar Fünger had all the plans on the data stick."

"Was he downloading the plans for you for some sort of quid pro quo?" the DD/P asked.

"No. Rextar Fünger doesn't know I exist. I injected him with the *Laudanum-diacodium sulfate* before he was aware I was present."

"How did you do that?"

Dunbar then informed the DD/P everything that went on in Rextar Fünger's home and how he abducted him.

"How soon will the Larian government get to his files and reconstruct them?"

"During my walks at the park where I could discuss the mission with *Latrodectus,* he informed me that once we have confirmation, we have copies of all the plans, he would insert the *Thereuopoda Clunifera Computer Virus* into all his files. I was informed by *Latrodectus* before we lost power, the files were all transferred and *Latrodectus* confirmed they were loaded on the data stick. Before the power went out, the *Thereuopoda Clunifera Computer Virus* was inserted into the Blue Vault. It's all random numbers now.

"Do you think the Larians suspect the *Stanzelites* abducted Rextar Fünger?"

"Most likely yes, but when their spies go to *Stanzel* to find out, there will be no trace of him and since a large number of their spacecraft were destroyed in the fighting, the assumption will be he was possibly killed in transit and his home burned down by the *Stanzelites* to eliminate any evidence of foul play."

"What made you decide not to kill him since that was your instruction?"

"I figured he would be more valuable to you alive than dead. Plans are not always accurate in what they convey. I know you have means of convincing him to cooperate when the time comes."

"Other supervisors might be upset you did not carry out your orders, but in the final analysis your improvisation makes more sense. Also, we put you under a lot of risk having you remain there when the Space War started. You could easily have been killed had the fighting spilled over to Fujima."

"Do you know what caused the power to go out?"

"My first thoughts were the Kaokuen shut them down to prevent the Larians from targeting them."

"I assure you the Space Force did not shut off their power and they are quite bewildered that it happened, the DD/P said."

"The *Stanzelites* had no reason to shut off the power then, they were in the process of downloading the Trapezoidal Differentiator plans," Dunbar added.

The mystery just deepened, and Dunbar could not help but believe that perhaps *Latrodectus* was somehow involved. *Would Latrodectus be willing to admit that he did it to him?*

"What I'm going to tell you now is to not be repeated ever, but I think you should know since you played a major role in all this."

"Understand."

"A couple of our special Transport Directorate Scientists have theorized and informed me privately, the Trapezoidal Differentiator jammers that were designed to be used against us, might actually have multiple uses which we can use on our enemies."

"If that's the case, I hope it works out."

At about that time the reconstruct applications informed the DD/P, "The review of the Space Battle is now ready to be seen."

The voice was artificial intelligence, and the DD/P asked it, "Can you do a faster playback so we can see the visuals?"

"Yes sir."

"Let me see a speedup of it and I'll listen to a detailed audio at a later date, or I see something I want you to slow down or stop and explain."

"Understand sir."

"Dunbar, did you see this space battle?" the DD/P asked.

"I saw a lot of it but when *Latrodectus* informed me the *Stanzelites* were bugging out of Rextar Fünger's home because Stanzel Fleet Admiral Wirglestor was losing his nerve, we determined if we abducted Rextar Fünger, the Larians would suspect the *Stanzelites* took him and his plans. I was then driving to his home and had to concentrate on driving, so I missed about half of it."

As the video played on there were three large fireballs when large ships blew up and Dunbar said, "This is about where I started driving and didn't see much after that."

There were sixteen simultaneous windows showing video imagery. They were all time synchronized. One of them was a simulation of Dunbar driving the Bamtorini Sportster overlayed simulation on a street view of a satellite map. If you didn't know it was a simulation, you would think it was real. And it got quite eerie when all the lights went out.

The simulated placement of Dunbar in the garage and the home was easily produced because of the awesome power of *Latrodectus* residing in the cellphone inside his pocket. Those simulated images showed the injection of sleeping chemicals that knocked out Rextar Fünger very quickly.

The beautiful part of this reconstruction is it allowed Dunbar to see what was going on above his head as major killings were occurring.

The amount of devastation was appalling. The results were immediate. Two great powers sent their space fleets home to lick their wounds and prepare for one of the two of them to rally and crush the other. It was a sobering experience to watch all this, and the DD/P knew Dunbar needed some down time so he said, "Take the rest of the day off. You earned it. See you tomorrow in case I have any questions for you.

After Dunbar left, the DD/P saw everything else including another woman that would drive the four amigos nuts if they knew.

There was only one question the DD/P had for Dunbar not performing his operational orders as specified: what was the reluctance to kill Rextar Fünger?

Dunbar would be visiting a staff psychiatrist who didn't know what the mission was but would probe Dunbar's reluctance to assassinate someone. Was this a trait or was it truly as he said, he determined in-situ bringing back Rextar Fünger alive more valuable than killing him?

Another interesting aspect of this mission, which also was a huge milestone in Transport Directorate Operations, Dunbar successfully abducted someone and returned with that person in a Transporter Capsule. Having proved they could do that, opened a whole spectrum of future abductions. It also proved Dunbar's bravery because he had no idea the Transporter Capsule would reassociate the two individuals correctly.

***

Chapter Eleven

Doctor's Visit

Dunbar was quite surprised when he was called into the DD/P's office. There was a nice-looking woman sitting in a chair in front of the DD/P's desk with a legal pad and had been doing some note taking.

The woman had long curly blonde hair, she had aquamarine blue eyes and even though sitting conveyed a well-proportioned and healthy body. Her face had very nice skin and she had a youthful appearance.

As soon as Dunbar entered the office the woman rose with the DD/P who said, "Dunbar, let me introduce you to Elane Chonlan."

Elane, obviously an Easterner bowed and did not offer a handshake as was their custom.

"Pleased to meet you," Dunbar responded.

"Thank you," Elane replied.

"Please have a seat," the DD/P said and gestured to an empty seat next to where Elane was setting at about a twenty-degree angle from Elane's and an forty-degree angle from the DD/P.

"Dunbar, Elane is our staff psychiatrist. She's often called in to investigate certain aspects of missions to help us understand why things happened the way they do. Also, as you were trained, sometimes we have reassociation injuries and she helps us deal with them."

"Alright." Dunbar said.

"Dunbar, you are not in trouble in any manner even though you have independently modified your operational orders in-situ in recent missions."

"With all due respect sir, I felt the steps I took were prudent that resulted in a much greater accomplishment than what the operational orders intended."

"That's true Dunbar, and I know in your training, there are provisions for you to make command decisions since your life is on the line, and you may determine in-situ, a change in methods or circumstances mandate such actions."

"The four *office warriors* no doubt would have carried out the operational orders with perfection, but I'm sure you are aware they would not have brought back significant items such as I did," Dunbar stated with an edge in his voice.

"I'm not picking on you or trying to second guess you, Dunbar. Your successes speak volumes about your astute decisions and follow up actions," The DD/P responded.

"Then why are we having this discussion?" Dunbar asked.

"Dunbar, you know that in intergalactic relations and the high stakes sometimes involved with our adversaries, it's quite often far more cost effective to eliminate someone than it is to go to a slugfest where possibly a large number of our Space Force personnel might parish like you recently observed in your last mission," The DD/P explained.

"I'm quite aware sir."

"Because of the way you handled the last mission and others before, the dramatic changes you made to the mission profiles unilaterally brings up a few questions we need to answer. Elane is going to interview you privately and give me some insights into where you are now, and if possibly there have been some subtle changes in your persona that led to the actions you took."

"Are you scared I might have had a Transporter reassociation injury?" Dunbar asked.

"Our scientists have assured me you did not have a reassociation injury. That's one of the reasons why you had a blood test and a urinalysis and a physical each time you came back from a mission. According to these distinguished scientists, if there were any reassociation issues, it would show up in the blood and urine samples."

"I see. But then what is it you are investigating?" Dunbar asked.

"Dunbar, we are not concerned about your performance. If I had just one more person like you, my job would be a hell of a lot easier."

"Thank you. But why is Elane Chonlan here then?" Dunbar asked.

"Dunbar, sometimes the environment and experiences can impact personal psychology. Since I know everything that occurred on your mission, I also know you experienced some rather stressful and emotional spikes."

"Anyone would have deep feelings for what happened at Nigārà and Kerlara," Dunbar said.

"That's precisely why Elane Chonlan is here," the DD/P responded.

So that's what this is all about, Dunbar thought.

Dunbar didn't know it, but Elane would be reviewing some of the downgraded classified portions of the missions including his most private moments with Blemary, Kaarina, and Brigitte. She would soon discover the tremendous loss in Dunbar's life, leaving behind Blemary for the call of duty.

Based on the previous conversation between Elane Chonlan, the DD/P informed Dunbar, "Elane is going over your files and parts of the missions we downgraded and reclassified to a lower level she's allowed to access in a special read only file we created for her."

"That's understandable," Dunbar said not feeling great being under the microscope.

"Elane is not ready yet to interview you today, so I'm sending you home to relax and rest and get over some of the Transporter Lag."

"Thank you. I appreciate your consideration and a am tired."

"Come back in the morning rested up and Elane Chonlan will then meet with you in her office."

"Alright," Dunbar said then stood up and so did Elane and the DD/P. Dunbar bowed to Elane, then turned slightly and bowed to the DD/P and then turned around and departed the office and in a short while was home contemplating his day. There was a lot of time left in the day to do whatever he wanted. Not knowing when his next challenge would be, and with the recent experience of fighting anther spy to the death, it was essential he stayed physically fit. Thirty minutes later Dunbar was walking out of his home in exercise clothes and did not live too far from a park where he went to get in some running.

Dunbar's mission communicator was in DD/P's custody getting bleached and reprogrammed for a future project. All images Dunbar's communicator images were gone for good, not that it really mattered. But Dunbar knew one thing. He had the confidence of *Latrodectus,* and he suspected if he wanted to see any of it again, his artificial intelligence friend would show it.

Even though opportunities availed, Dunbar did not pursue any women because they would be a distraction and create situations out of his control. One possibility could include an enemy abducting them and holding them for ransom to coerce Dunbar into doing double spy routines. By not having any ties to anyone he had no penetration points an enemy could exploit.

Thanks to *Latrodectus* schooling him, Dunbar knew the four amigos were always gunning for him. He would be at risk if the four *office warriors* were able to inflict dangerous agendas on him. Eventually he would have to leave the Transporter Directorate if he ever wanted a chance to settle down and have a family. *But what would he do?*

After running laps and working up a good sweat, Dunbar went home, took a shower, and contemplated his evening. In due time when he felt hungry, Dunbar went to a restaurant and picked up the takeout he ordered via his communicator.

After filling up on a great meal, Dunbar put on some music that could easily pass for an Earth Symphony: Mahler - Symphony No. 9. During one of Dunbar's missions, he became a connoisseur and consumer of a fabulous elixir, Chamboreé de Lián. That elixir was priceless and out of the price range for most people that lived on Kaokuen.

Thanks to a few of his trips doing support for studies and observation missions where he was brought along for additional firepower with lots of weapons and ammo, at the conclusion in the same space they hauled all that expended ordinance and bullets, he had ample room to carry a case of Chamboreé de Lián he took possession of with some elaborate horse trading. The agency would not be missing the expended bullets that went into the trade.

After a few sips of the Chamboreé de Lián, Dunbar was slowly evolving in a philosophical and emotional transcendence and no matter how hard he fought not to do it, he entered a special passcode with combination numbers and a voice command and since *Latrodectus* who always watched over Dunbar knew he had complete privacy and suddenly Blemary's images appeared.

The Achilles heel of any Transporter Spy was falling in love with a woman behind enemy lines. It was paradoxically mission impossible. Dunbar's ability to ever see Blemary again was unlikely because he knew it was easier for a camel to go through the eye of a needle than him to travel to Kerlara City on planet *Stanzel* ever again.

Unless the Transport Directorate sent him there, Dunbar knew it would not happen. The huge space battle he just witnessed underscored *Stanzel* – Kaokuen relations that forbid any such travel anytime in the future. The competing powers had too much at stake and there was no possible resolution to their grievances as it was a never-ending tit for tat.

The psychoactive drugs in the Chamboreé de Lián had a pleasing affect and no sooner than he finished his drink, the combination of Transporter Lag, possible molecular reassociation issues manifested by the Transporter Module, post-traumatic stress caused is neural functions to decline and he was soon in a dream while reclining back in his conformal chair. Dunbar didn't wake up until morning.

Dunbar suddenly felt the need to take care of business and stood up and went to the bathroom. The normal morning events all went by quickly and Dunbar was in his banker's suit and soon arriving at the office building he worked in and with his suit and sunglasses didn't stand out. People got in the elevator with him, and they went up to their floors. There was very little socializing, and the elevator felt stuffy as some of the wealthy intergalactic bankers riding it up to their ivory towers were beside themselves each knowing they had more credits฿ than anyone else present.

Dunbar went to his desk and sat down checking communiques that might possibly be in. Very shortly he got a text from *Latrodectus* informing him that two men would be arriving soon to escort him to Doctor Elane Chonlan's office. Dunbar wondered why all the fire power. He didn't know it was security plus they would make sure he went whether he liked it or not.

Just like *Latrodectus* predicted, two men came to his office showed their identity and said, "We are going to take you to Doctor Chonlan's office."

"She's not in the building?"

"No. Please come with us."

Dunbar stood up and followed the men which made them more comfortable there would not be a confrontation about taking a spy to go see a *shrink*. They had their *Laudanum-diacodium sulfate* injectors with them, and they knew how to get the job done quickly if the patient had any irrational struggles.

Instead of going down to street level, Dunbar was surprised they went up onto the rooftop instead where a VTOL craft was there waiting for them. The propulsion of the VTOL was shut down. It was electric driven like commuter drones and would not startup until the passengers were all onboard and the safety checks done by artificial intelligence deemed, they were ready to depart.

Dunbar was in for a surprise. In all the times he flew around the city in a VTOL he always wondered what a distinguished looking building was up on a very tall foothill of the mountain range nearby. It had a VTOL landing pad on it and a very great-looking tennis court, swimming pool, luscious lawns, and many other attributes of the wealthy. To his surprise that's where they took him. It was quite apparent as they got closer, this was a maximum-security location fenced in with roving guards with dogs, sensors, and everything else to keep the public away and the patients inside safe.

Some of the patients were having extreme difficulties, they were disfigured by not reassociating correctly in a transporter capsule. In some cases, long before the great psychoanalyst Elane Chonlan received them, analysis done by *Latrodectus* which was not a single entity, but a network of entities, determined the transporter spy's plight was helpless, his or her possibility of living out their lives in a reasonable manner was out of the question. They issued the *coup de grâce* orders.

The assassins had no idea who they were killing. The patients were completely covered in bandages just like they were severe burn victims. *Tetrodotoxin* mixed with *Laudanum-diacodium sulfate* quickly puts the person into permanent sleep. When the VTOL craft delivering the patient arrived at their destination, whether it be a hospital or Doctor Elane Chonlan's facility, the patient was dead and easy to blame the transporter reassociation failure as the cause of death.

Dunbar's main concerns of late were due to the law of averages, it was only a matter of time before he would experience a transporter reassociation catastrophe. In the back of his mind, Dunbar was thinking of terminating this type of work. Unfortunately, the thrill, the adventures, and the income kept him going back for more, but he was slowly developing a new attitude that would eventually work itself into his future planning.

The gifted and highly successful Psychoanalyst Doctor Elane Chonlan was not ready to deal with Dunbar when they first met, because she had mountains of information to sift from and an incredible amount of holographic video thanks to all the security systems at locations Dunbar operated and *Latrodectus* easily pirated because he could so easily hack into their systems.

The voyeurism created by monitoring the patient had an impact on Psychoanalyst Doctor Elane Chonlan. Dunbar had experienced beautiful women, the crem de la crem, the flesh that armies had fought over in ancient times. Their attraction to Dunbar was easily understood. He truly was an incredible man with a mind and a body to create the sensations these women experienced. Doctor Elane saw it all and it also had a negative impact on her ability to truly probe him and analyze him the way her instructions were given to her.

Elane was no idealistic pawn in a political or moralistic tug of war that often became evident with academia and the power and financial centers creating continual conflict as idealism and authoritarianism ran afoul of each other. Elane was brilliant and knew reality. She had to play the game to stay in the game. By now in her vast experience treating reassociation injuries, there truly was a dark side to espionage and clandestine matters, the public was totally oblivious to.

Elane had a growing awareness of a lot of the dirty events that occur in the spy business. She also knew watching some of the holographic video *Latrodectus* indirectly, Dunbar had killed two men recently with his own bare hands. She shuttered to think how many other he killed. *Did he kill a woman in cold blood?*

When Dunbar killed the spy in the masseuse' office, it was mortal combat, kill or be killed. But when he administered *coup de grâce* on Bear

Claws that was something else. That video clearly showed Dunbar had no issues killing someone if he had to in the line of duty.

But suddenly, Dunbar violated his operational orders and instead of killing a person, he abducted him and brought him back. Elane didn't know all the elements of that story. All she knows is he violated his operational orders and didn't kill someone when the mission required it.

Dunbar's actions could prove to be detrimental in the future if he no longer had the guile and cunning a spy must have to do a deceitful and dirty job of assassination and sabotage. This was Elane's toughest and most bizarre assignment ever. *Was this spy going to be willing to kill someone in the future or should he be removed from this line of work?*

When they send a person in a Transporter Capsule to another world, then bring him back, the possibility is he will not arrive the way they sent him. His body could be deformed in the reassociation sequence that was challenging and highly technical. Some have said reassociation sequence physics was far more complicated than quantum mechanics.

When a reassociation failure happens the spy's tissues rearranged and often in detrimental deformation. Psychoanalysts Like Elane Chonlan must deal with reassociation injured people. A reassociation injury could be nothing more than a psychological alteration without any signs of physical injuries. There was much to learn about Dunbar.

The reason why Dunbar was sent to Elane Chonlan is he violated his operational orders a couple of times. The first op order violation was reasonable, he stole an experimental enemy ship.

Dunbar by doing a change to his op order in-situ made perfectly good sense because he came away with a huge heist of the Oclatine Class Hyper Warp Speed Fast Frigate. Technology obtained in the heist including the tri-lithium sulfate based fusion reactor powered cyclonic inverter warp drive thrusters and the Chizhevsky- Lomonosov proton beam weapons was such a tantalizing steal, nobody objected to the op orders violation.

But the second time when he was sent to kill someone. He didn't kill that person and instead abducted and brought him back.

Dunbar's boss the DD/P (deputy director of planning) wanted to know if Dunbar was ready and willing to kill again.

A transporter spy must be willing to kill, as its part of the deadly business of espionage and clandestine missions.

Therefore, this well recognized Psychiatrist, Doctor Elane Chonlan, was assigned to analyze Dunbar and find out what they could expect out of him in the future.

Is Dunbar willing to kill if directed, and *why did he truly violate his operational order by not killing the guy and instead brought him back with him in his Transporter Capsule?*

There was a lot of anecdotal information Elane did not know about because she had not read all the reports or viewed the remaining videos until the last day. She really had no idea what truly happened with Dunbar before this review.

The brilliant scientist Dunbar was ordered to kill, would make sure he would not develop a deadly weapon to use against them.

Dunbar the Transporter Spy would soon inform Elane, *I felt it unnecessary to kill the guy in cold blooded murder and felt he offered more alive as a prisoner coerced into helping our scientists than as a dead man.*

The psychiatrist Elane is about ready to explore all that.

Elane also now possessed copies of all Dunbar's pertinent mission files.

As explained to Elane, the artificial intelligence in Dunbar's personal communicator hacked all the security systems and had video of Dunbar which involved three beautiful women. Before Elane finished her reviews all those videos of Dunbar, she spent time observing his experiences with the three beautiful women. The videos taken from security cameras showed sensational romantic developments and were interrupted by events out of Dunbar's control.

New love is always special. It creates the best physical experiences, the best memories, and peaks the emotions and feelings to the greatest amount in the life of a relationship. Anyone who says it took while to feel love through the passage of time has never experienced that fantastic lovemaking and the intensity of the emotional spikes that result when both parties think they are in love. People's aura's tangle in ways we have yet learned to figure out completely.

Advanced studies have determined there is a unique connection between the brain and the heart. The temporal awareness of our human condition resides in a part of our brains about the size of a golf ball. Those cells convert the information stored temporarily or permanently in the brain and in a high-speed manner are sent in ensembles to this part of the brain that actually creates holographs at a high periodic rate so there is no flickering or gapping like you might experience observing a computer data terminal, especially in the olden days of computing.

The phenomenal rate this very small part of the brain produces those holographs is an incredible process that neophytes cannot fathom. One might think all the data flows from our brain cells into that biological holographic engine. But that's not completely true, we now know the heart is involved.

If you study acupuncture you will discover some of the waves that traverse the body. The heart sends these special signals to the biological engine producing those lovely holograph ensembles creating human awareness. It almost astonished scientists when they discovered the emotions radiate from the heart into that biological holographic ensemble producer.

Anyone who thinks about it for a while understands and scientists are aware, those holographic ensembles also have a soundtrack to them. There are also scents and other senses that permeate additional tracks in that holograph ensemble stream which is our human awareness flowing with the passage of time.

The brilliant Psychiatrist Elane Chonlan was thinking of all these brain processing functions as she was participating in the voyeurism of Dunbar evoking the stimulus that caused those love signals to leave those women's hearts and flow into their biological holographic processes. Elane knows she's a human being like anyone else and to constrain her thoughts strictly along clinical lines was utterly impossible.

The way Dunbar turned on these women giving them that first love emotional spike was quite compelling and even a well-disciplined psychoanalyst would not completely compartmentalize her objectivity into the confines of clinical assessments. She understood vividly advertisers for companies are experts at influencing people by exploiting this process.

As time passed Elane discovered when she's alone with Dunbar she knows his mere presence makes her panties wet. She knew if Dunbar made a pass at her she cannot resist after watching how he handled those women.

Elane knew the hard facts of life. If she could not turn Dunbar back into the cold-blooded killer like he was recently when he killed the two men in the masseuse office, he would likely be disqualified. Disqualified transporter spies were often sanctioned. They forfeited their lives.

"Do you like to take walks out into the forest?" Elane said.

Elane analyzed Dunbar was having a tough time because of how he left Blemary behind. Dunbar knew reality, Blemary's on an enemy planet, and he could never see her again. But Elane also knew Blemary had nothing to do the recent violation of his operational orders bringing back Rextar Fünger with him instead of administering the *coup de grâce*.

Elane knew she would run out of time quickly dealing with two pressing issues, *determining if Dunbar is willing to kill again and help him get over his depression about Blemary.*

The DD/P also advised Elane that if she cannot make the determination Dunbar would carry out his orders and kill again, then by default they must automatically disqualify him.

Elane knew the dirty secret she accidently found out she thought due to sloppy records management but was planted by *Latrodectus* to cause Elane to promptly alter her clinical processes and work on the number one issue, killing again.

The artificial intelligence *Latrodectus* made sure Elane saw the files that described what happens to disqualified Transporter Spies. *Spies like Dunbar who are disqualified are assassinated. His only way out alive was to complete his contract and retire.*

Because of *Latrodectus* actions, that led to Elane's next move after several days of clinical work that appeared to have some resolution on the horizon.

"Dunbar, we are not getting anywhere with my treatments and our discussions. Perhaps this office isn't the best place to talk and figure out things."

"What do you have in mind?" Dunbar asked.

"Let's go out and have a private walk out into the park. Maybe you will feel more relaxed that might allow my therapy to be more effective."

"I do not see where any of this is a big problem. I'm sure I can handle it."

"Would you mind walking out to the forest with me. I think it will help you let go of some of your pent-up emotions. I can better diagnose you better if you are more relaxed."

"Alright, I'm willing to walk in the forest with you."

Elane lead Dunbar out of the building and soon was walking with him out to the forest where they can talk secretly. Her excuse soon became apparent it really wasn't for the purpose of helping be more therapeutic.

That's when Elane confides in him and tells him the truth, "Dunbar, you have some issues that we cannot fix. I now know that. I've sized you up and your brain is wired up in a manner that you will continue feeling the way you do no matter what happens or what psychoactive drugs we feed you."

"You are right about that, I'm not going to change my feelings, they are what they are, and I've been through a lot. I made my own way and handled it the way I thought I should."

"Dunbar the reason why I needed to get you out here where nobody can monitor our conversation is to explain a few things to you."

Elane then informed Dunbar what likely would happen if she did not report back, he was willing to kill people on missions.

"I'll kill if it's necessary, just like you know I killed the two men in the masseuse office."

"Then why didn't you kill Rextar Fünger?"

"I had no reason to kill him because I knew if I abducted him, we would have a more beneficial scenario. I analyzed the situation that by having the actual scientist who designed the equipment we could better understand it. I think the DD/P is overlooking the fact, that with the help of my artificial intelligence we destroyed all their existing plans, and we brought back a set here and I know having the person who designed it would simply our understanding of how it really worked and how it would be deployed."

"The Transport Directorate is alarmed that you are a rouge warrior and do not properly carry out orders."

"They have that impression because the four *office warriors* are always stabbing me in the back and embellishing crap, they know is wrong."

"Dunbar you are going to have to demonstrate a type of behavior so I can provide anecdotal information to the DD/P, or it will cost you your life a lot sooner than you realize."

Dunbar somehow knew Elane was a solid person stating the facts of life the way they are, but he also knew he wasn't going to change.

"So, what do you expect me to do?"

First of all, nobody can ever learn about our conversation. It did not happen to protect both of us."

"Sure, I get that, but what can I do?"

"Quite frankly you will have to fake it, or it might cost you your life. You must give me enough conversations back in the office in a cavalier manner saying, you are more than happy to kill the enemy."

"That's easy because I will kill the enemy. Just because I didn't kill Rextar Fünger, doesn't mean I will have any issues killing someone else if required. I felt it was totally stupid to kill Rextar Fünger when I knew a better way, and I'm convinced if they start using him to help them understand the plans better it will cut way back the time for us to use that invention as our own weapon."

"Alright, I think we can resolve the first issue, but you are going to have to demonstrate a bravado and zeal towards those types of mission requirements."

"Not a problem, I can talk a good game, I'm a social engineer."

Elane now stated the most difficult requirement, "Dunbar, you must fake it you got over Blemary.

"How do I do that?"

"Whether you realize it or not you have a pleasant effect on me. I can use the action and they will never know it's just sex for you."

Elane knew there was long distance reconnaissance watching her and Dunbar.

Elane realized that if Dunbar and she copulated in the forest, the reports would get back to the DD/P, Dunbar isn't hung up on Blemary, he just had sex with his psychiatrist!

"We are probably being watched long distance," Elane said knowing it to be the case.

"Yea probably."

"We have to create a scene so the watcher see's us transcend into lover's bliss."

"That's easy enough to do," Dunbar said feeling his little head give him encouragement.

"Let's walk over by that big tree and face each other and then make a pass at me and I will reciprocate."

"Alright."

The watcher had about seventy five percent visibility on the couple as they walked over by the large tree. With Elane coaching Dunbar he did as she instructed, made a pass at her, and kissed her.

Elane was a good actress, she at first acted astonished and like she was almost shocked by Dunbar's behavior then it looked like someone flipped a switch and the watcher could see her put her hands on the side of Dunbar's face and pulled him closer and started kissing him passionately. She wasn't faking it, she actually was enjoying every moment.

The watcher was getting excited doing the voyeurism and predicted more fun to follow. He had no idea how right he was in his perverted thoughts. Just like he thought they soon had their arms around each other transcending into a lover's bliss.

Then to his great surprise, Elane was doing some really good acting because she suspected some pervert was watching and would tell his buddies and that would get back to the DD/P who would insist on watching the surveillance video.

Elane went down to the ground on one knee and undid Dunbar's trousers and started performing fellatio on him. The pervert watcher was glad no one else was around because he decided to enjoy himself while watching the couple go to town.

After Elane got Dunbar jacked up to the point he was moments away from exploding in her mouth, she stood up and turned toward the tree, pulled her dress up and her undergarment and leg shaper down exposing her female essence and bent over and directed Dunbar to enter her from behind which he was quite happy to do and in a short period of time finished the love making giving Elane quite a lot of his loving. They then reassembled their clothing so as to give the appearance nothing happened gave each other a hug and a kiss and then continued walking through the forest with the watcher smiling because his voyeurism netted him a very pleasant experience. Thanks to the short time Elane's bottom was exposed he got to see that and used that image to stroke his own gratification.

The next day Elane made her report to the DD/P which cleared Dunbar in a major way. His performance with Elane gave no hint his heart was still bruised by the loss of Blemary. And when they walked in the park the previous day after their sexual intercourse, Elane gave Dunbar things to say during their later clinical work in the facility and assume the conversation would likely be monitored. Elane implored Dunbar to demonstrate bravado and the willingness to deal harshly with enemy spies. Her coaching was quite good because it put a smile on the DD/P's face knowing there was no longer any problem to be concerned about.

Therefore, even though Dunbar wasn't really interested in killing anyone and would find other alternatives, based on Elane's coaching, he's cleared for future transport operations and not disqualified and was soon sent on other missions.

Chapter Twelve

Every Test Deserves an Answer

By now the DD/P started to realize the four amigos (*office warriors*) may be engaged in nefarious activities to take down Dunbar. And he knew why. In all bureaucracies there are always slugs who want a promotion and they go out of their way in seemingly fratricidal warfare to destroy the person they know, will beat them to a promotion they want.

The DD/P never had any direct evidence the four amigos (office warriors) were doing these actions because they covered their tracks really well and surveillance never detected anything out of the ordinary. The DD/P didn't know *Latrodectus* had a growing list of such actions and would one day act upon it. In the meantime *Latrodectus* presented information in such a way to increase the DD/P's subtle awareness.

The DD/P needed to do a test on Dunbar. The brilliant Psychiatrist Elane Chonlan had cleared Dunbar for future operations, but in lieu of the DD/P's fear of treachery going on behind his back, this mission and future ones would be handled slightly differently when Dunbar was involved.

The mission was set for the weekend when the DD/P knew the four amigos (*office warriors*) would be off work home with their families enjoying life as usual getting big pay and seldom deploying because at the 11th hour they always came up with a lame excuse. My wife is pregnant, father-in-law in the hospital dying, etc. In fact, one of the four amigos (office warriors) went through his entire family and doubled back on a relative that had already died before, thinking the DD/P would not remember.

The four amigos (*office warriors*) were always the first ones out of the office at the end of the workday, leaving fifteen minutes early to avoid traffic.

Dunbar was sitting at his desk checking all his official correspondence when he was texted by the DD/P, "Come to my office in forty five minutes."

It would not be uncommon for Dunbar to receive operational orders and be in the Transporter in two hours going to a destination.

Just like usual the four amigos (*office warriors*) were out of the office fifteen minutes early and on their way home with no care for the agency whatsoever.

At the prescribed time when the DD/P knew the four amigos were gone based on surveillance video, Dunbar came into his office.

"What do you need to talk about sir?" Dunbar asked with some apprehension.

"I need to send you on a mission today."

"Alright, I suppose I can go."

"In a few minutes, the special briefer will be here and give you all the details. But before he gets here, I want you to know I will be personally supervising the Transporter Operation and will be in the Transporter room when you return to make sure nobody interferes with this operation."

"I appreciate that."

"Where you are going you will have a communication link to me for emergencies. I doubt you will need to use it, but I want you to use it one time."

"What for?"

"I have no idea how much actual time it will take you to complete the task because you have some complexities you will have to deal with to complete the mission. I want to be in the transporter room when you return so that I will ensure nobody tampers with the transporter capsule software, in case we have a mole in the group."

"Alright."

"I want you to send a message your artificial intelligence will handle for you when you think on mission time you will return, when its clear to you that will be the time. I want that message sent at least one hour before you return so I can be in position in the transporter room."

"Okay, what do you want me to say?" Dunbar asked knowing there would be some type of semaphore message.

"The first message I want you to send is '*Chien Shiung*,' which you should easily remember from the psychic you visited on your mission to Stanzel."

"Yes, that's an easy one."

"The second one I want you to send is *Heterodontus Francisci* when you are about to place the transporter capsule in automatic return mode."

"I've never heard that term before."

"It's the name of an animal on a distant planet and solar system I once did an ISR/SOG mission on. Most of the files for that mission were considered irrelevant, but I kept a few for the memories and have them stored in a special Vault. I use some of the words in those files for one use encryptions for times like this."

"I see."

"I would expect your mission elapsed time to be approximately 48 hours."

"Understand."

The special briefer arrived shortly and in an hours' time Dunbar had his operational orders. The special briefer had a change of clothes and a backpack with the standard kit to use in-situ with a few additives.

Dunbar followed the DD/P to the transporter room. Soon Dunbar was sitting in the transporter with the backpack between his legs.

There was considerable risk in this assignment. Part of Dunbar's test which he didn't understand was all part of this likely required him to kill a few people to get in a position to do what he was being sent to do.

In many wars, a spy has a fundamental outcome of the conflict. Critical information or denial of services at a critical moment had significant impact. This would be one of those missions along those lines. Dunbar knew there was a lot riding on what he was going to do.

Dunbar transported to the planet Zemya Morska. There would be no resorts, no lovers, no meals, or good times.

Dunbar had to be delivered far away from the target in case the enemy had a system like a Trapezoidal Differentiator detecting his arrival. INTEL on the planet Zemya Morska was kind of sketchy.

Dunbar arrived in a good location, but he would have to walk twenty miles to the target, a well-guarded building out in the middle of nowhere because of its military importance as a Stanzel duplex neutrino relay station.

The Kaokuen Fleet was going to attack a major Stanzel Space Force Base that was critical in support of their military in the contested zone they were fighting over. With this Stanzel duplex neutrino relay station destroyed, the Stanzel Space Force Base that would soon be hit could not call Planet Stanzel for help and backup. The destruction of the Stanzel Space Force Base would take several hours to do a complete leveling of the place. By the time the Stanzelites learned of the damage it would be too late as the Kaokuen Space Force would be long gone, reorganizing for attacks elsewhere.

Since the enemy well behind friendly lines had no reason to fear attack, life goes on at Zemya Morska with no care in the world as everyone felt safe and secure and fully protected withing range of Stanzel forces arriving on short notice to handle any security threats.

Latrodectus had Zemya Morska Global positioning location and access to the ZM-WWW including interactive maps. Dunbar's Special

Kollmorgant holographic eyeglasses provided night vision now as it was after dark when he arrived.

The Kollmorgant holographic eyeglasses heads up display would show dangerous animals approaching. *Latrodectus* had the ability to transmit ultrasonic frequencies at 130 decibels through the surface of the flatscreen which had a five inch by three-inch transducer under it for communications and holographs. The ultrasonics would not affect Dunbar much since the frequencies were above his hearing range. But ultrasonics usually cause disability in wild animals. If all else failed Dunbar had a special blaster, if he needed to kill security people that would also take down animals promptly.

The vegetation was good here and good where he would be near the relay station. With his special cutter he could cut off branches and plug them into the special netting to hold them in place to provide good camouflage to observe the facility during the day in the morning after he walked quietly though the undeveloped area that had lots of tree stands and a few open areas that would make it much easier for him traveling at night shortly after sundown.

Dunbar's special energy and awareness drugs injected before transportation would keep him awake during the trek. His way back to the transporter capsule would be the most hazardous because the enemy would be looking for saboteurs.

Thanks to the number of open areas Dunbar could zigzag in and out of helped him make pretty good progress. According to the Special Kollmorgant holographic eyeglasses heads up display the rate of travel was three miles per hour. He would reach the target area in less than seven hours in time to get camouflaged in a good spot to observe the relay station operations in the daylight to help figure out the security arrangements.

The Special Kollmorgant holographic eyeglasses providing night vision was indispensable to allow maintaining his walking velocity thanks to the enhanced situational awareness.

Around the ten-mile mark at the halfway point Dunbar needed to poop. He looked for soft soil to dig a small hole to bury the poop so wild animals or security dogs tracking him would not find it allowing them to track him. After taking care of business and covering up the hole he did his business squatting like some alien races did.

Dunbar was back on his way feeling relieved and took his canteen and had a drink to help his dry throat. There would likely be no refills any time soon. Dunbar would drink conservatively and make an effort to urinate a mile or so before he reached the surveillance point to make sure that problem would not come up during the SOG portion of the mission.

It seemed to Dunbar the DD/P personally selected him for this mission because of his SOG experience. Even though this was a sabotage operation, a big portion of it was the SOG to help him clear a path to the target where he could place those silver eggs he would remotely detonate when he was absconding from the target area at a good distance.

During the long trek, even though his likelihood of ever seeing Blemary again seemed unlikely, he had several flashbacks of her. He would give anything to lay his lips on Blemary again. But he knew deep down in his gut that was not going to happen. Thanks to the imagery *Latrodectus* saved for him he had plenty of pictures and videos of Blemary to torture himself with.

But on a night like tonight out in the middle of nowhere on an enemy planet behind enemy lines, the pleasant thoughts of Blemary helped the time slip away. Before long he was only five miles from the target area with fewer open areas, so his velocity slowed down to about two point five miles per hour. But he was still making a good velocity of covert travel.

The memories of Blemary continued flowing like a river out to see in an endless time. The memory of Blemary dressed up for the symphony was a pleasant image. Maybe it was a curse the psychic did to him, Eva Erlaendsdottir cabaret singer at the *Greifinn* restaurant popped into his memories. His one regret was never doing the horizontal tango with Eva. But he knew the obvious and he didn't. Madam Chien Shiung, the psychic, explained it to him, had he succumbed to his desires and had a lover's tryst with Eva, she would be his Kryptonite. Eva was a spy's worst nightmare, a human landmine that could go off in ways that were unpredictable. And then what Madam Chien Shiung, the psychic prophesized would likely occur. This was indeed one time where the better part of valor determined the outcome with the heist of the Stanzel Space Force Fast Frigate that no doubt was still a major concern for them.

Observing the distances closely and eliminating all non-mission thoughts out of his mind, Dunbar did the one-mile task he planned then moved into the target area several hours before sunrise.

With the help of digital maps on the Special Kollmorgant holographic eyeglasses provided great course corrections to get to the best observation area where concealment would be instrumental in his attack plan as he did SOG during daylight hours. .

As he got closer the bright night lights lit up the area so Dunbar knew he was getting closer and just like *Latrodectus* warned and he slowly approached, he finally got to an area where he could crawl in closer and see the entire facility.

There was a security fence. There was not a lot of activity. Nobody was out and about, but Dunbar knew there were people there.

Thanks to the noise radiated, the power plant was easily observed. There was primary and backup power. This was an essential site, so they had to build standby power in case the primary power plant failed.

The enemy built it with no thoughts of strategic placement. *They must have felt impervious to attack,* Dunbar thought. Nestled right next to the power plants were the fuel tanks. If Dunbar could get one of them to explode, that tank would likely damage the other tanks and if the explosion was large enough the power plants would experience significant damage and not be operational. Blowing up the neutrino duplex transceivers would not be necessary if you knocked out the power. It would take them weeks to replace the power plant. By then the space battle would be long over. The reason for the lack of roving patrols was soon clarified. A vehicle soon drove through the facility. The men in the vehicle were obviously doing security and safety inspection on everything including doing a security check of the generator buildings.

Dunbar eased back into thicker growth and trees and started cutting plants and tree branches for camouflage. Being that was now daylight, he could better manage the placement of the leaves and branches in the camouflaged netting with a small opening for a small telescoping photonic device that had a low power link to his communicator which *Latrodectus* would stabilize and put in the heads up display in on the Special Kollmorgant holographic eyeglasses.

The camouflage netting went a few feet past his ranger/SOG boots when it was completed. The leaves and branches would appear healthy until tomorrow, but by then he would be gone leaving behind dead branches and buildings, generators, and fuel tanks ravaged by the explosions.

Tonight, Dunbar would use an age old trick he learned while training for sabotage mission for the SOG. In a couple facing adjacent fuel tanks, he would put the detonation explosives on one and the super phosphor on the other. The idea is they were timed a second apart. One would rupture the fuel; the other bomb would create a very excessive heat that would likely melt the side of the second fuel tank no doubt under pressure that would expand and accelerate the destruction of the explosion.

Once the camouflage netting was completely covered with branches and leaves making it appear as a part of Landscape, Dunbar crawled under it and slowly crawled carrying the camouflage with him as he moved very slowly in case someone was looking in his direction. It did not take long to reach the edge of the clearing with an unobstructed view of the security force movements or anything else that happened.

More importantly if Dunbar suddenly fell asleep, *Latrodectus*, would know by his heart rate, respiratory, and physical movement and could immediately wake him up if required should an acoustic tripwire be triggered or visual indications from the scope that had two cameras.

One telescope camera was long distance investigative and SOG quality, the other was a 180-degree early warning optical piece that *Latrodectus* constantly monitored. Should the early warning or acoustic/visual tripwire get triggered, *Latrodectus* would wake up Dunbar and if necessary, with nauseating signals in Dunbar's disguised ear buds. Cat naps were not a problem with *Latrodectus* keeping alert on all matters.

SOG stakeouts were filled with vast number of hours of total boredom and sleep-inducing moments that may eventually be filled with terror and extreme excitement in a moment's notice, especially when the enemy hits a trip wire and he's coming right at you.

In a very low voice, nobody could hear at any distance, Dunbar said, "I'm getting kind of sleepy. I'm going to doze off."

"Dunbar, take a nap. My sensor suite has all the trip wires set and I will wake you up if necessary."

Thank you, *Latrodectus*. I walked all night and even though I have the situational awareness drugs injected that are good for 48 hours, the Transporter Lag is making me sleepy.

"That's expected Dunbar. Close your eyes I will wake you up when it gets dark."

"Thank you."

Dunbar soon entered the dream state and his thoughts of Blemary made him happy. It was as if he were with her, and all the sound was real.

Great studies have gone into sound hallucinations. They occur a lot more commonly than the public is aware of. People who experience sound hallucinations think they are real because they sound real. [Auditory hallucination - Wikipedia]

An auditory hallucination, or *paracusia*, is a form of hallucination that involves perceiving sounds without auditory stimulus. While experiencing an auditory hallucination, the affected person would hear a sound or sounds which did not come from the natural environment.

Transporter spies were prone to experience *paracusia*. In the case of Dunbar, hearing Blemary in his dreams was fabulously wonderful. Very shortly after he took *Latrodectus* advice he entered a dream state and whether it was *paracusia or* simply a vivid dream was irrelevant to Dunbar who enjoyed it, though it was simply a creation in his mind.

The symphonic music seemed real to Dunbar as his mind traveled to another dimension and for a few fleeting moments, was with Blemary enjoying this lovely music. His brain can create those holographic ensembles for his human awareness, and even if it were *paracusia,* it seemed so real, and the fidelity of the music was as close to the real experience as possible. Dunbar's dream world enjoying his time with Blemary was the most pleasant of experiences.

When a person dreams or hallucinates in a manner Dunbar did, partially enabled by post transporter fatigue, worse than Jet Lag, it feels so real they do not know it's not real. As such Dunbar enjoyed several hours of this continuum until he was slowly awakened by *Latrodectus*.

Day had shifted into evening, and it was now getting dark enough to where the sabotage could begin.

Latrodectus was ready to begin giving Dunbar a briefing as he was back to reality and fully coherent.

"Thanks for letting me sleep. I feel a lot better now," Dunbar said feeling satisfied and happy because of his wonderful dream.

"You needed to rest to help deal with post transporter lag. The twenty miles you walked used up most of the vigilance drugs they injected you with. You should be ready now to perform at a high level of acuity and energy."

"I think so too."

"Are you ready for a briefing now?"

"Yes, please let me know what you have determined."

"The SOG surveillance was substantial. I now have a good record of the security checks being performed. They are not random. They have a reliable schedule and if you move in right after a security check, you have a good 30 minutes to place bombs and egress smartly before they go off."

"Any idea of the best place to penetrate the compound?"

When you were panning around looking at the buildings, fuel tanks, and generators, you didn't realize it at the time, but you recorded a small ravine you can go through and the fence in that area is built for looks but is not very adaquate for a security boundary. The fence is not well maintained, and I think you only need to cut a foot or two of chain link section and spread it open to allow easy access."

"Alright where is the ravine?"

Look through the scope now which is in infrared night vision with lots of starlight and planets to help generate sufficient lighting, and you are pointed at the fuel tanks where you last looked."

"Alright. I'm looking."

"Slowly move the scope image to the left and you will see a grey colored building."

"Yes, I see it."

"Just a little left and down from that angle is the ravine."

"Okay I see that now. You are right, the fence looks in bad shape there indicating a lack of maintenance and negligence. I wonder why they don't do the repairs?"

"I've done a lot of hacking into the computer systems inside the buildings which also allows me to discover a lot of information about what's going on around the planet. This group is of the belief that since they are way inside friendly lines, they would never be attacked. The other thing is the indigenous peoples that live here are concentrated on the other side of the planet where they do have some level of conflict going on."

"Tell me, what's that all about?"

The indigenous people are the Arachno-Pulmonatas, and they are not happy about the Stanzelites who did a hostile takeover of their planet and killed many of their tribesmen in the process on purpose to thin out the population to make sure they would never be a threat. This planet hosts the neutrino relay station you are going to blow up, but it also has large deposits of minerals the Stanzelites are now mining and destroying the environment where they are doing the mineral extraction."

"Alright, but you would think that something as important as neutrino relay station would receive significant security as well as maintenance of their fences and security barriers.

"Reading all the Stanzelite communications texts and messages, it's apparent they have no fear of attack and no Arachno-Pulmonatas have ever been seen anywhere near here and must cross vast natural barrios to get here. Their only fear is attack from space and there are nearby space defense batteries to protect them."

"What about their security sweep?"

"They come once an hour in a predictable schedule."

"Can you see what's going on inside the buildings?"

"Yes, there are security cameras in there as well. The Stanzelite troops are unaware their superiors spy on them. All the internal areas have secret surveillance video which I observe."

"Let me see some of it."

Soon Dunbar was engaged in a form of voyeurism. It was a mixed sex detachment with equal number of men and women. Even though Stanzelite rules and regulations forbid fraternization between the men and women while they were on duty at this outpost on four-day shifts, out of sheer boredom and lack of activities, they sometimes engage secretly in fraternization.

The Stanzelite troops did not know that even in the supply rooms and equipment rooms there is complete coverage and today like a lot of days there were a couple of Stanselites on duty in one of the supply rooms thinking they had privacy engaged in physical interactions. It seemed kind of humorous to Dunbar because it's obvious their superiors did nothing about the fraternization violation. *Perhaps they enjoyed watching it?*

Most of the troops were watching holographic entertainment videos when suddenly, a supervisor went into the room and yelled at a couple of them and said, "You were supposed to do a security sweep five minutes ago. How about get with the program and go do your job!"

A male and female stood up and walked out of the building and a few minutes later Dunbar could hear the vehicle and with the headlights on, it looked like daylight with the night vision. Dunbar followed the vehicle drive though the yard and it seemed it was happening a lot faster than during daylight, *I wonder, why are they are speeding up their security check sweep checks?*

Dunbar soon discovered why. They wanted to hustle back so they would not miss out on a lot of the holographic shows they were watching.

Dunbar knew that soon many of these people would be going to the bunk room. He would wait until most of them were sleeping before he would go there after a security sweep was done.

After a couple hours predictably, most of the people on duty were going to a bunk room and sleeping. A while later the predictable security sweep occurred, this time taking a little longer. *They must have finished watching their holographic video shows*, Dunbar thought.

In due time the vehicle returned to what was the command center and the two people entered the entertainment room and were soon watching a holographic video.

Dunbar said, "It's time to go as soon as I pack up the camouflage net."

Pulling the tree branches and plants out of the camouflage net was a lot simpler than placing them during the day where positions were important. Removing them was about ten times faster and as soon as the telescope and net were in the backpack, Dunbar took another drink of water, forced himself to urinate, then slowly made his way to the ravine."

"I've put the security camera's monitoring this area in a continuous loop. Security people monitoring will see no change and since nothing rarely changes until a security sweep, they will not know otherwise."

"That's good to know," Dunbar said as he made his way through the trees and vegetation until he was perfectly perpendicular to the fence section at the ravine.

Dunbar hustled to the ravine and walked up to the fence area he was going to pass and discovered the fence was in a lot worse shape than what he could see from a distance. Thus, Dunbar only had to lift the fence slightly and crawl under it in this dry ravine area. During rainy season the ravine was probably filled full of water."

Dunbar did not need to stick his head up to see where he was going because *Latrodectus* was showing a simulated overhead view of where he was in lieu of the generators and fuel tanks.

Thanks to these big fuel tanks, only the surveillance video which *Latrodectus* had compromised could see him now. Dunbar was soon in position to run out of the ravine to the fuel tanks and place his two bombs that had nice magnets that would stick to the sides of the tanks and a timer he dialed the time in and hit the start button. There would be no way to deactivate it. When the timer hit the designated time, it would go off.

With the bombs placed and activated, Dunbar made his way out of the compound back into the tree line and started heading towards the transporter capsule twenty miles away. *Latrodectus* was recording the security system and could continue to do so for at least another ten miles.

But since the bombs timers would detonate them, Dunbar was only two miles away when the explosion happened, and it was loud as hell even two miles away and lit up the night sky.

Three planets knew the relay station went down. The only high-speed communications from Zemya Morska to Stanzel and the Stanzelite Space Force Base the Kaokuen were going to hit was via that relay station that no longer existed.

As Dunbar continued walking, *Latrodectus* showed the security video feeds up until the time the explosion ripped through the building that had all the electronics associated with the system. The bunk rooms and the living quarters and supply rooms were devastated. Just as Dunbar predicted the fuel tank was pressurized which added greatly to its explosive force especially when the super phosphor increased the temperature of some of the fuel to the temperature of the surface of the sun.

I bet the DD/P will no longer have any concerns about my willingness to kill people after he watches this video, Dunbar thought.

When Dunbar was five miles away from the relay station, he heard VTOL craft flying around. They were obviously looking over the site which was now dark because the two generators were destroyed and were not going to be rebuilt any time soon. This created a severe crisis for the Stanzelites.

It did not take long to figure out the damage to the relay base was a substantial act of sabotage. At first the armchair generals fit for commanding garrison troops wanted to believe it was Arachno-Pulmonatas Indigenous civilization on Zema Morska. Smarter heads prevailed and new damn well better.

One of the senior officers spoke up and said, "There is no way the Arachno-Pulmonatas did this amount of damage. There were some sophisticated explosives used and I'm sure the Arachno-Pulmonatas do not possess any such types of explosives nor has there ever been this level of destruction ever done by them. Plus, what would knocking out the relay station do for them? It does not change anything for them."

"I do agree it seems rather odd the Arachno-Pulmonatas would travel halfway around the world to get to something that has little bearing on their day to day lives."

Another senior officer present said, "This smells a lot like a Kaokuen SOG operation."

After wringing their hands for a bit, the staff and the General decided, "It must have been Kaokuen Sabotage. Ther perpetrators are probably on the run to a pickup spot."

"Send a reconnaissance force out there now looking for Kaokuens on the run and keep a sharp lookout for possibly an attempted evacuation of the saboteurs!" The General yelled.

As soon as the alert went out, *Latrodectus* knew it and informed Dunbar he was going to have to be far more careful and informed Dunbar he was a hunted man, and this area would soon be swarmed with reconnaissance troops.

Dunbar didn't know it at the time, aside from the Stanzel military on Zema Morska now looking hard for him, he had another group following him and shadowing him at a distance.

These Arachno-Pulmonatas had been staking out the relay station and knew it was important. A general uprising was starting, and they knew this was an important target and planned to swarm it and kill everyone there and attempt to destroy as much of the equipment as possible to make it unusable for a while.

But then their lookouts reported a lone person arriving not dressed like a Stanzelite. Then he stopped at the edge of the forested area and appeared to be watching the compound and soon crafted some type of a camouflage tent and waited. They didn't have night vision equipment, but their eyes were adjusted for the dark and eventually they observed Dunbar walk into the facility as if he had no fear in the world and walk up to those large devices next to the two large identical buildings. They observed him place something on one of these great structures, then leave abruptly heading out to the forested area and kept walking at a good pace.

The Arachno-Pulmonatas suspected something bad was about to happen because this lone man snuck in planted something then abruptly left while none of the Stanzelites were around. They knew this could spell trouble especially if the Stanzelites found what he planted. They would come into the forest looking. On the better course of valor, the Arachno-Pulmonatas decided to temporarily leave the area just in case and followed the loner as he headed in the direction, they didn't know was his Transporter Capsule to leave. They followed Dunbar at a good distance on his flanks very carefully. The other wild animals in the forested area made enough noise to cover up their sounds.

When the explosions happened, they knew those devices this man planted must have caused it. It was a terrible explosion, far more than anything they had ever seen before and when the bright light from fireball rose into the air, it painted Dunbar with light which the Arachno-Pulmonatas observed.

Latrodectus artificial intelligence on the communicator, had an electronic translator algorithm and he had found archives of Arachno Pulmonata language including all the words and proper pronunciation. If they came across Arachno-Pulmonatas, *Latrodectus* could translate for Dunbar.

By the time Dunbar had reached the five-mile point with fifteen miles to go, the sky was filled with VTOL craft with searchlights turning night into day. Dunbar was systematically being boxed in. Knowing what he had just done, he would not allow them to take him prisoner. He would kill a few of them before they killed him.

Dunbar had no choice but to stop and crawl under vegetation or hug a tree. The VTOLs flew over relentlessly, and they went out in all directions from the destroyed relay station. They had no clue which direction the saboteurs fled, otherwise it would be far more difficult.

The Arachno-Pulmonatas knew this person was hiding from the VTOLs just like they were. As the old saying goes, the enemy of my enemy is my friend.

Dunbar did not know the Arachno-Pulmonatas were anywhere around near him and during a lull of the swarms of VTOLs flying over a young female Arachno-Pulmonata walked up to Dunbar and in her language said, "We will help you escape."

Latrodectus quickly translated and informed Dunbar who replied, "Tell her to lead the way."

Latrodectus did as Dunbar said, and the young lady thought it was Dunbar speaking and was quite shocked a plain skinner could speak her language. This was extremely rare and less than a handful Stanzelites were able to converse in the Arachno-Pulmonatas language.

The girl led Dunbar to where six other Arachno-Pulmonatas were waiting, and they were experts in egress techniques and knew to get as much distance as possible from this area and would take Dunbar to a cave they had several more miles away.

Each mile they went which was in the general direction Dunbar was heading, Southeast of the destroyed base. Dunbar noticed that based on his heads up display they were slowly leaving the bulk of the VTOL searchers behind and thanks to *Latrodectus* reading the VTOL telemetry which provided their commanders real time positions of each VTOL asset he was slowly getting out of the main search area. After they passed a couple more miles, Dunbar could see the nearest VTOL was almost three miles away. Then in another mile they made it to the long deep cave that had room to provide quarters for all their primativie equipment and makeshift bunks to sleep in. They had devices filled with water and packages of food.

The cave entrance had a camouflaged cover which the Arachno-Pulmonatas opened up and they all went inside and the stationed lookouts on the outside closed it for them then took cover watching the approaches. At the far end of the cave was a candle lit providing a little light and in the large cave middle was some type of ceremonial rug.

The leader of the group said in Arachno-Pulmonata language: "Please have a seat."

A couple of the Arachno-Pulmonatas sat down on the rug and Dunbar followed their actions and as soon as they were all seated the leader asked in his language one of the ladies present, "Please pour us all a drink of *Lepestok de Rozy.*

After they were all served with drinks in wooden drinking containers a purplish drink, the leader of the group of held up his drinking container giving a local customs toast loosely translated meant, "May the wings of 1000 doves carry to heaven for your good work tonight."

Latrodectus informing Dunbar everything then replied, "Thank you."

About that time one of the scouts who was left behind to see what happened came in and reported to the Arachno-Pulmonatas leader, "There was a huge explosion where this man planted devices. All the buildings were completely destroyed. Nothing is left, all the Stanzelites at the base are dead and the aircraft are flying over the base with search lights and many people have landed there searching through the wreckage."

The leader said, "Please have a seat and join us."

Dunbar was feeling good from the *Lepestok de Rozy* elixir. The ferments were hitting the spot and the magic mushroom chemicals acting as pleasurizers and thought expanders altered his mood nicely.

"What is your name if I may ask?" the leader asked.

Since there were no expectations that Dunbar would encounter anyone during this mission, he had a name he knew would grow the myth and make the Stanzel Intelligence start believing that Kabel Garr was their nemesis, and thus said, "Kabel Garr."

In six months, Stanzel Intelligence would be super exasperated to learn Kabel Garr, a Stanzelite who stole their secret Fast Frigate with the important weapon system was also the man who blew up the Zemya

Morska neutrino communications relay station on just before the major attack on their base at their most significant base located at Glinka-Rebaul.

The Arachno-Pulmonatas leader of this group of insurrectionists, asked, "Why did you blow up that base?"

Latrodectus said to Dunbar in his conformal earpiece that only Dunbar could hear, "I will tell you want to say in your earpiece. I may not have enough time to tell you what I translated, but we need to make this look convincing."

Repeating what *Latrodectus* said in the conformal earpiece using Arachno-Pulmonatas words, Dunbar said, "The Stanzelites now have an evil leader bent on conquest. Someone must stop him."

"Who do you work for and who gave you the devices to blow up that base?" The Arachno-Pulmonatas leader asked.

"I'm part of the Stansel Opposition. The tyrant leader in our government is making a mess out of Stansel and we have gone places like your planet where we were not invited and there is a growing number of Stanselites who want to take down this evil leader."

"Your opposition group wants to give our planet back to us?"

"Yes, we do not belong here. We were never invited to come here."

The Arachno-Pulmonatas leader appreciated what Dunbar had done for them. He probably saved most of the lives in this group including his daughter by doing their dirty work for them.

The effects of the *Lepestok de Rozy* were now hitting everyone. They all had a long day except for Dunbar who felt exhilaration from his drink. He wanted to keep moving. In his earbud *Latrodectus* informed him the Stanzelites were on a wild goose chase in the opposite direction.

Dunbar then said in Arachno-Pulmonata to the leader, "I'm going to take a look in the skies and see where the Stanselites are and if they are far off to the distance, I'm going to keep moving."

"Why don't you spend the night with us? You are obviously tired."

"I had a good nap today, I'm fully awake and ready."

"If you leave now, you might get captured."

"I will not let them capture me; I will keep killing them until they kill me. I promise you they will not get a prisoner tonight. I finished my mission, I did what I had to do, so if I keep living it's not important. I made my contribution and am ready to go at any time."

"My daughter is still a virgin. If you stay you can have her tonight."

"Thank you for the offer. But I have better hopes for her that one day she will live under freedom again."

"I can't convince you to stay and drink more *Lepestok de Rozy?*"

"Thanks anyway, but I want to get back to the opposition and explain what happened here."

"How will you get there?"

"When I reach the rendezvous point, they will pick me up."

The leader and the group escorted Dunbar to the cave entrance and he left. There were no VTOLs in sight now they were on a wild goose chase.

What Dunbar didn't know was the DD/P sent a trusted colleague to Zemya Morska five miles from the relay station. That person was to make a lot of electronic noise after observing the explosion and once the enemy was going in his direction, he simply got back inside the Transporter Capsule and disappeared. But before he left the enemy had done traffic analysis and triangulated the intercepts and were on their way with VTOL gunships to get the perpetrator dead or alive.

Three hours later Dunbar was approaching his Transport Capsule, he sent the message: '*Chien Shiung*' via Latrodectus simply by saying "send message number one."

What Dunbar didn't know was a Kaokuen probe in space about 500,000 miles away received the burst message and converted it to neutrino message and sent it. Traveling 1000 times the speed of light the DD/P received the message in his office where he patiently waited after receiving a report from the other Transporter spy who filmed the explosion from a distance which gave the appearance of a giant fireball with massive destruction.

The probe reported the Zemya Morska relay station was now offline to the Kaokuen fleet who then commenced the attack on Glinka-Rebaul.

Dunbar stepped into the Transporter Capsule and then said send message number two: *'Heterodontus Francisci.'*

"Message sent," *Latrodectus* replied."

Dunbar then said, "Initiate the Transporter Capsule Automatic Launch Sequence."

Off to the distance was the leader's daughter who wanted to follow Kabel Garr to discover exactly how he was going to depart and watched all this unfold and soon the thing Kabel Garr stepped into disappeared.

The young woman with slightly green skin reaching the point all Arachno-Pulmonata females were expected to find a mate and start procreating thought her father had given her to this strange Stanzelite and would have been happy to go with him, had he asked.

This exceptionally intelligent and sensitive woman had Extra Sensory Perception (ESP) which she felt signaled her, *one day he will be back, he likes me.*

The woman turned around and made her way back to the tunnel in a few hours and reported everything she saw to her father who knew there was something special about this man. They would wait a few days and send scouts to the destroyed Stanzelite facility and do a damage assessment.

***

Chapter Thirteen
The Reduction of Glinka-Rebaul

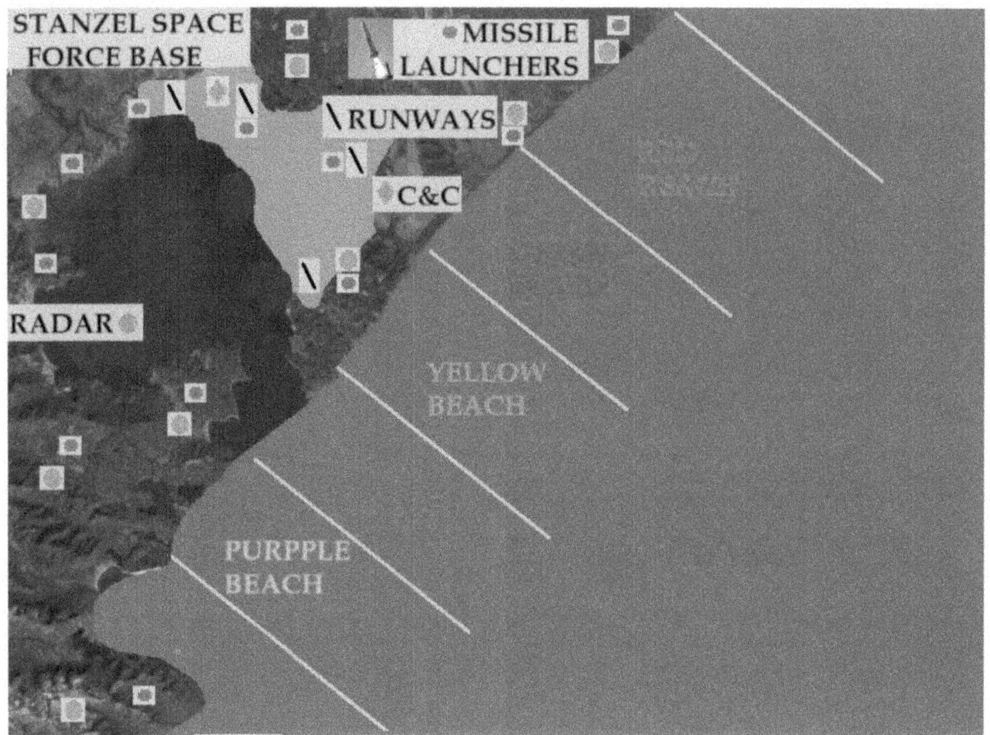

Stanzel Fleet Admiral Wirglestor would never have believed the timid Kaokuen Space Force would have the audacity to attack their most significant base located at Glinka-Rebaul. Admiral Wirglestor started having notions bad things were happening when his communications officer reported they lost the neutrino link to Zema Morska and currently had no high-speed communications to Headquarters at Stanzel.

The Kaokuen Task Force Commander Subutai attacking Glinka-Rebaul was an Amphibian Force General. Commanding General Subutai was picked to lead this attack because the Amphibious Assault troops were the most successful units in the Kaokuen military. The Amphibians were the toughest and most disciplined and usually called upon to strike the hardest targets because Amphibious Assault was great training for planetary assault and usually entailed the most bitter fighting. This happens quite often due to the large number of water worlds or planets with vast oceans and very large rivers and lakes where most of the fighting usually occurred on the contested planets.

In a lot of pitched battles, the Amphibians could not attack their targets directly from space where laser, particle beam systems, and rocket assisted space defense weapons would slaughter them. They had no choice but to arrive a distance away from a target and approach them via a waterway or a large body of water requiring an amphibious landing on the beaches.

The Stanzel Space Force base located at Glinka-Rebaul was situated on a very large Island of Lamuers out in the middle of the Great Seirin Ocean

The strategic and operational innovations of the Amphibians had devastated Stanzel armies in a series of one-sided campaigns in the past, but it was often slow going because of all the tactical and logistical support from this base at the Island of Lamuers.

The Amphibians did not operate as one distinct mass, but instead moved along in multiple axes of approach, often separated far apart, and threatened numerous objectives simultaneously. Like other great leaders in history, Kaokuen Task Force Commander Subutai dispersed Kaokuen forces along a wide frontage and rapidly merged at decisive points to defeat the enemy in detail. Subutai's designed methods to completely crush the enemy's will to fight.

Subutai has been credited as the first general to operate campaigns using artificial intelligence methods for command and control.

Subutai repeatedly demonstrated how amphibious forces could fight using the principles of mobility, dispersion, and surprise. Due to Subutai's innovative amphibious tactics and unique strategies, he is a source of inspiration for all his generals.

In bygone eras, the Amphibious Forces would be dispersed out of floating ships and make their way to the beaches. In modern warfare, those Amphibious Forces would come down to the planet in Amphibious Assault Space Craft that landed on the water beyond the horizon and sometimes if it was a hardened facility like that of the Glinka-Rebaul Stanzel Space Force Base, triple the horizon in a dispersed fashion coming in on high speed hydrofoils doing approximately 160 knots ascending upon the landing zone at the beach where they would then leave the hydrofoil landing craft in armored vehicles and large exoskeletons.

The exoskeletons did not require wheels or tank treads and were an excellent stable platform for laser and beam weapons used in air defense as well as frontal assault projectile and missile launchers. The exoskeletons could also traverse rough terrain where tank treads and vehicles with wheels could not go. Their main problem was speed. Just like the tank tread armored vehicles had wheeled cargo carriers to move them at higher speeds on road networks. The exoskeletons also had the same wheeled cargo carriers and sometimes there would be a mixture of exoskeletons and tank tread armored vehicles being hauled together at the same time on cargo carriers.

The Stanzelites assumed their base was impervious from attack by water and since there was no landmass to attack from there wasn't the foresight to have significant fortifications to protect the Stanzelite Space Force Base. They would soon discover the error in their ways. The Stanzelite Space Force felt quite confident to repel any attack from space and thought the base was impregnable.

This flawed viewpoint may have led to a lot of Stanzel Fleet Admiral Wirglestor miscalculations and misguided defense posture. The base was very large to accommodate the vast number of spacecrafts, and in an emergency, they had rocket assist to get them up into space quickly. On the base itself, the defenses were laid out in a classic deep battle theory.

Motorized track weapon systems, motorized troop carriers, space artillery, and Combat VTOL Craft were all positioned in a concentric formation, but unfortunately 90% of it was unmanned and not ready to be used. Troops would need to be taken to each of the sites. Duty sections were not going to handle the attack designed at night when vigilance decrement could be anticipated to be maximum.

Smokescreens on the battlefield to cover Kaokuen Task Force Amphibian movements would permeate the entire areas broken up into color coded zones of red beach, green beach, yellow beach, blue beach, and purple beach.

Stanzel military theorists had many examples of set piece space warfare to deal with possible converging forces onto the Island of Lamuers.

If warned ahead of time, Stanzel space artillery would be launched in time to attack space and ground targets.

Because the relay station was knocked out, the Stanzelite Space Command would not receive warnings from probes that detected high speed transits like the Kaokuen Task Force heading their way. The Stanzelites would not know the Kaokuen Task Force was coming until the enemy was deep within the solar system poised to attack the planet with no Stanzelite space artillery in place to stop them.

Stanzelites reaction would be painfully slow, and it coincided with the shutdown of the relay station. Kaokuen Task Force had a fudge factor built into it allowing a window of attack, all hinged from Dunbar's activity.

The DD/P knew he could count on Dunbar and the Fleet was at flank speed when they themselves detected the suspension of the neutrino communications. They knew their spy had done his master work and they could continue at high-speed knowing no warning would arrive any time soon and they would catch Stanzelites flat footed. And when the first diversionary attacks began, chaos on the planet would rule supreme.

Dunbar was one spy Kaokuen task force commander Amphibian General Subutai truly appreciated as they closed in on Glinka-Rebaul.

INTEL fully integrated with artificial intelligence and clones of *Latrodectus* were constantly monitoring all Stenzel communications to determine when detection and reaction began.

The Kaokuen Task Force had reached the point of no return, they had achieved going over their own trip wire that based on planning indicated if they made it this far with no Stanzel reaction of defense communication chatter, there was greater than a seventy five percent probability of a successful landing on the planet and invasion of the main Stanzel Space Force Base at the Island of Lamuers on Glinka-Rebaul.

After the Amphibians landed it was up to them to complete the objective, to take this base out of the equation of the war thus making front lines untenable. The enemy would have to recede further back towards their own empire and leave most of the contested zone. This truly was a mission of great importance to the outcome of the conflict and could greatly shorten the length of the war.

Command and Control (C&C) was situated in the Northwest corner of the Stanzel Space Force Base. This would be a primary target with bunker busters to interrupt the commander's ability to give orders to their troops. To get to that area of the base would be the most difficult. The Stanzelites located the C&C as far away from the beach as possible to make it a hard target in case their assumptions proved to be wrong.

The attack on the C&C would start before the Amphibian landings. A lot of firepower would be thrown at the C&C because Kaokuen Task Force Commander Amphibian General Subutai knew there were seven radar and sensor sites and 10 missile launching batteries near and around the base.

Each missile battery had 128 missiles in reloadable vertical launch box launchers raised a couple feet above the ground with steel hatches raised hydraulically before launch.

The Shrak-7 air defense missiles had nuclear powered rocket engines. The special hydrogen blend fuel that was modified to not be explosive at room temperatures in the liquid form that almost had gasoline like chemical structures with carbon and hydrogen, but mostly hydrogen and some inert chemicals was super-heated in the rocket engine nuclear reactor that from appearance looked like a honeycomb. Upon ejection out of the box launcher with high pressure compressed air, the twenty-foot-long rockets ejected the control rods out of the honeycomb that prevented nuclear reaction and when the hydrogen fuel was pumped through the honeycomb that immediately turned bright red as the nuclear reaction started heating it up, caused an explosive release of thrust that kicked the Shrak-7 missile into ultra-hypersonic speeds immediately.

There are a couple small secondary solid rocket engines that immediately tilted and spun the missile if required, in the direction of its target which could be almost horizontal if required. The Shrak-7 had full space capability and could maneuver to almost the edge of the solar system chasing spacecraft. The exit velocity for the Shrak-7 leaving the atmosphere was fifty thousand miles per hour, but out in space as it continued to accelerate it quickly approached light speeds. Most of the time the enemy didn't see it coming until it was too late.

Half of the missiles in the one hundred twenty-eight count missile battery also had nuclear warheads for space operations where targeting sometimes was a problem to ensure destruction of the enemy.

One Radar/Sensor Site was near the beach along the right half of Red Beach. Another radar and sensor site were near the boundary between Red and Green Beaches. Another Radar/Sensor site was facing the middle of Yellow beach inland a couple of miles.

One Radar/Sensor site was inland two miles facing the boundary between Blue and Purple Beaches. Another Radar/Sensor site was facing the Southern Boundary of Purple Beach. Another Radar/Sensor site was located ten miles inland facing Blue Beach and ten miles southwest of C&C. There were three missile launching batteries associated with this Radar/Sensor site. Five miles Northeast of C&C was another Radar/Sensor site. There were four sets of quad runways at the base. The C&C was flanked by two different airfields.

Besides numerous VTOL craft, there were numerous fixed wing aircraft requiring runways because they were heavy because they had nuclear rocket engine assist to get airborne and if necessary, out into space for planetary defense.

Additionally, there were intergalactic spacecraft that when fueled and with crew and food aboard were excessively heavy and were flown into space carried by a huge transport craft that was used to help get the Frigates and Cruisers out into space then come back down by itself after jettison the spacecraft to the planet under automated artificial intelligence. One might think of them as self-landing booster rockets.

Many of the Stanzelite Space Warships that traveled to the contested planets left this base in a similar manner. That was the main reason for hitting this planet to make sure those types of craft could no longer deliver soldiers, provisions, weapons, fuel, and other logistical support.

A short period before this force hit the Space Force Base at the Island of Lamuers, a couple outposts on the other side of the planet were struck. This was a Feint to make the Stanselites think those bases were the Kaokuen targets and the actual landing zones to put together a strategic area to operate from in the ultimate showdown. This was a distraction as the hydrofoils were already inbound and about to hit the beaches.

Simultaneously Command and Control centers were being hit and the Radar/Sensor sites nearest the Great Seirin Ocean coastline were attacked.

Amphibian General Subutai knew those particular radar sites with their own 128 missile batteries with lasers and particle beam self defense systems required a lot of effort. Ninety percent of the weapons the Kaokuens used on those sites were destroyed and produced no damage to the site, but the other ten percent slowly had its effect. Those three Radar/Sensor sites had to be taken out in order to provide a pathway to the C&C heavily guarded by three Missile and Weapons sites.

With three hundred and eighty-four Shrak-7 missiles ready to be launched from the three weapons sites, along with lasers and beam weapons, the Stanselite defenders could shoot down a lot of spacecraft and other airborne combat craft very quickly. This is another reason why they had to send the hydrofoil craft in at triple the line of sight to get in below radar and sensors. Artificial Intelligence was doing a fantastic job of interfering with satellite telemetry making it almost impossible for the Stanselites to use them to defend the base.

The main reason why all the *Latrodectus* clones on all the spacecraft in the task force were successful at this was due to Dunbar's trip to Stansel when he stole the Fast Frigate they were still looking for. Being that *Latrodectus* was operational security conscious and realized how the enemy might find out about *Latrodectus'* special talents, he never revealed to anyone what they truly accomplished at Stenzel.

Latrodectus also admonished Dunbar during the transit back to Kaokuen on the Fast Frigate, much of that capability had to remain hidden from everyone including the DD/P who could get penetrated by an enemy spy. Dunbar of course stated he would never reveal it to anyone.

With the satellites essentially jammed and the Amphibian Force landing three times the distance over the horizon, the Amphibian Forces were a short distance away when the Feint occurred to cause distraction and misdirection.

The Amphibian hydrofoils were transiting on an approach course of two-seven-five until they were twenty miles from their designated beaches, then swung to a course of three-zero-zero as they intersected the center of their color coded beachfronts. To make sure they all landed in echelon at the same time on the beach for maximum mutual protection the Force landing on Red Beach had to slow down quite a bit to give the other hydrofoils the time to get in position so they could charge towards the beaches running abreast in a complete wave of hydrofoils stretched out on a fifty mile wide front with plenty of space between each beach landing area to prevent friendly fire incidents.

The markings for the color-coded Beaches stretched 25 miles inland. No force had permission to shoot over that imaginary line to avoid shooting at friendlies. The Kaokuen Amphibian hydrofoil ships had to provide supplemental firepower directed at the Stanzelite radars and weapons launchers in front of them. The Stanselite missile officers and technicians were in such disarray they threw out all caution with the bath water and had multiple missiles hatches open at the same time doing salvos because quite frankly they were scared to death. By such reckless regard turned out devastating for the missile battery facing yellow beach because one of the artificial intelligence guided munitions launched from one of the hydrofoils went inside one of the missile box launchers with the hatch open and a missile inside.

The horrific explosion of the Kaokuen warhead on the fueled-up missile also with a warhead created a massive explosion that ripped into several nearby box launchers that had live rounds inside being spun up to launch with the warheads armed. With over one hundred missiles suddenly detonating in the plasma the five nearby missiles caused earthquake F4. The base was lucky the nukes fizzled otherwise instead of having a base there would be a 1000-foot-deep mile wide crater.

Suddenly there was no protection for all the aircraft, VTOLs and Space Warships located on one of the four runway groups close to that radar and weapon sites facing yellow beach. The destruction was so huge that any forces between the radar/weapons site and the Kaokuen forces on Yellow Beach ceased to exist, opening up a gaping hole right towards the very center and lower half of the base. Another aspect of it was Yellow Beach forces now landed totally unopposed which facilitated very efficient unloading of all the hydrofoils that slowed and raised their hydrofoils a short distance to the beach coasting in the remaining distance on surface mode vice hydrofoil transiting.

Red Beach would face the bloodiest fighting. It was a good thing it was on the flanks and not the fulcrum like Yellow Beach. Red Beach Force faced two missile batteries and two Radar/Sensor sites with 256 missiles ready to launch. One of the runway groups was less than ten miles from Red Beach which could add to the havoc, but the VTOL and fixed wing attack craft from that runway group were not going to play a material impact on the Red Beach force because they had Green Force coming right at them with support from Yellow Beach that had plenty room to maneuver and when the runway structure in front of Yellow Beach suddenly started receiving withering fire from the vast number of Amphibians coming off yellow beach hydrofoil transports, it now started getting real dicey. They could not go aid the radar and weapons sites facing Red Beach because they had their own security disaster now unfolding right in front of them in the form of Exoskeletons, tracked vehicles, and Amphibian Ground Pounders with a bone in their teeth ready to fight.

The Dog Fight had begun. When people know they are going to be killed they give it all. Fear of death has amazing inducements even to chickenshits when they have no place to run. The Stenzel Office Warriors, very much like Dunbar's enemies, were now discovering their cushy job far back behind friendly lines wasn't so safe after all. Some of them pissed their pants, they were so frightened.

A lot of issues were erupting at the Island of Lamuers base Stenzel Command and Control trying to figure out what happened to all the satellites, and they still refused to believe the Feint wasn't the real threat and did not alter their game plan until it was far too late.

The Kaokuen Amphibian forces doing the Feint were receiving hellacious fire because the Stanzelites were shooting at the wrong targets, but they knew as long as they remained the target, the beach landings would be far more efficient.

A Radar and Weapons site bordered between the Blue and Purple Beaches. That Stanzelite site receiving the wrath of both Blue and Purple Forces eventually ignored the cautions and got caught with too many missile hatches opened at the same time and even though they had managed to get off almost 70 missiles and were commencing reloading those box launchers from rooms below the launchers a different problem happened. A missile hatch was damaged and stuck in the open position so when the technicians opened the bottom of the box launcher to reload it, they received a Kaokuen round down into the Magazine because they ignored interlocks warning them not to open that hatch. Haste makes waste and when the Kaokuen round hit the magazine with over 1000 soldiers down there working in the reload squads, were immediately vaporized when the entire magazine blew up.

Blue Force was then able to send Amphibians and Exoskeleton battle bots on Hovercraft brought along for Blue Force to use on the inland waterway since that obstruction was no longer a threat. This inland waterway would allow them to attack another Radar and Missile battery and hit the flanks of a runway group providing support to Yellow Force now up from Yellow Beach.

At this time in the battle a tactical decision was made by General Subutai. He gave orders to Amalgamate all Yellow and Blue Forces placing them all under command of the Yellow Force commander.

Soon the runway facility was surrounded by Kaokuen Amphibians with shoulder launched rockets and other devices quickly destroying anything flyable. Stanzelite Fast Frigates and Cruisers getting ready to take to the air and bug out at this runway structure referred to as Airfield Number One by the Stanselites. Fast Frigates and Cruisers getting ready to take to the air and bug out did not make it off the runway.

The Cruiser and Fast Frigate *Lifters* were systematically blown up and soon there was no means of launching any of the space warships. Even if the commanding officers of the Cruisers and Fast Frigates ordered all the men off and dropped their weapons, they would still be too heavy with the fuel loads. They also knew they would soon be barbecued if they didn't immediately get out of those spacecrafts and raise white flags of surrender.

Other Cruisers and Fast Frigates loaded and manned taking off from the other runways were being challenged and in the span of five minutes there were fifteen horrible wrecks with resulting horrific explosions as the fuel and weapons created near ground plasmas spewing fire and debris all over the base terrorizing anyone that wasn't cowering and hiding in a shelter.

The Stanzelites still had plenty of firepower left and Red Beach continued to take a pounding, but the Exoskeletons were doing a prodigious job of mitigating missile launchers from two sites and jamming the two Radars/Sensors sight, one of which was now under Green Beaches' jurisdiction as General Subutai shifted the boundary straight north placing the radar and weapons site in Green Force Zone allowing Red Force to now concentrate on a single radar and weapon site.

The Red Force, now free to attempt destroying a single Radar/Sensors and Missile/Weapons site could more efficiently perform. At the same time the Green Force was having a devastating impact on the other Radar Site that was no longer interested in the Red Force because the Green Force was delivering a pounding it was having a hard time avoiding. This tumultuous event was slowly devastating Stanzelite crew morale, and the officers were now starting to wonder about the size and scale of the disaster that was developing.

It was about this time the Stanzelite Command and Control was now more concerned about saving their own rear ends than what was happening on the other side of the planet they got suckered into going after and recalled all those space assets and any other asset available.

The Space Force Assets that were pounding the Kaokuen positions on the other side of the planet still had a formidable amount of assets. Unfortunately, they had been misdirected in the wrong area. They soon departed the area and the Kaokuens in the area where the Feint was being done were quite happy to no longer be on the receiving end of the pounding.

The Stanzel ground forces left behind facing the Kaokuens were now experiencing the consequences of doing battle with someone with equal resources but no longer fearing air superiority and space asset disadvantages.

The unmitigated disaster was starting there as well, but the officers including Stanzel Fleet Admiral Wirglestor back at the Command and Control center were more concerned about their own survival and as runway structure number two was now starting to fall into enemy hands, leaving only two airfields left, they were slowly losing their escape route and soon would have to make the decision to depart the four parallel runway complex number four and head for a safe planet or be prepared to either be an enemy prisoner of war or worse yet killed in the fighting.

Stanzel Fleet Admiral Wirglestor ordered the Stanzel Space Force assets that had been fighting on the other side of the planet back to the base at the Island of Lamuers. This force was now reaching orbit to come around in direct support of the fighting around the main base at the Island of Lamuers.

Probes and ISR spacecraft soon provided Task Force Commander Subutai a good picture of the oncoming Stenzel Armada returning to the base to help rectify the disaster caused by Stanzel Fleet Admiral Wirglestor's poor planning and mismanagement.

This reinforcement by Stanzelites was somewhat predicted ahead of time and since the Amphibians had done such a great job of penetration and infiltration of a large portion of the base, they were no longer pressed for space and air support. On the planet it was now a ground war, so the Kaokuens were able to reposition all their space assets to fend off the advancing Stanzel Space Force foe heading right at them.

This truly was a winner take all event. This battle went way beyond the space battle at the Larian planet which the Stanzelites could easily digress from and come back later and continue the attack.

Electronic mapping and sensor display showed converging fleets and created a surreal tapestry of unimaginable space combat imagery.

Each side had their own trip wires which would execute maneuvers upon various movements of enemy spacecraft.

Both sides had standard maneuvers for times like this with artificial Intelligence designing most of the combat maneuvers in-situ. Perhaps the Stanzelites would have done better if Stanzel Fleet Admiral Wirglestor had been in the command ship, but he had his hands full at the base trying to cope with the disaster that was now starting to unfold.

The missile battery magazine blowing up by the runway complex at Airfield number two was a lot closer to Stanzelite Command and Control bunkers now taking a pounding and the communications links were barely holding on. That magazine explosion with all the reload missiles had such a huge amount of rapid destruction it caused a F5 Earthquake and rattled a lot of nerves.

At high-speed convergence rates and closing space fleets cause radical maneuvers as more and more trip wires were activated by sensor thresholds based on velocity and relative positions. Stanzelite Fleet Admiral Zhènghé had no idea what he was facing until his space warships detected the enemy threat when they traveled far enough around the circumference of the planet and started picking up the Kaokuen Task Force Space Escorts. Those Space Escort vessels performed ISR and early warning missions to detect any possible approaching threat.

As the Stanzelite Fleet traveled further around the planet they started detecting and observing a growing number of ships that immediately alarmed Stanzelite Fleet Admiral Zhènghé.

"Why are we not getting any satélite imagery, Stanzelite Fleet Admiral Zhènghé!" Admiral Zhènghé yelled.

"Sir, none of our ships are receiving any satellite data!" The communicator responded.

At this moment Admiral Zhènghé knew bad things were about to happen as more and more enemy ships showed up on their long-range scanners automatically putting tracker symbols on the tactical display he looked at in full consternation.

The entire bulkhead of the spacecraft had a huge holographic display giving them the appearance of looking at a tactical magnified view ahead with each enemy ship magnified and classified with tracker symbols on them identified as to what they were: Frigates, Cruisers, and tactical fighter bombers and such painted on that three dimensional display which gave a person they were looking directly ahead at the space battlefield on the integrated holographic display. Then the bad news became reality and shocked Admiral Zhènghé.

"Admiral Zhènghé, the localizer had calculated the enemy is directly above Island of Lamuers," the Navigator reported.

"How could that possibly be? With all the firepower of the Glinka-Rebaul Stanzel Space Force Base?" Admiral Zhènghé asked.

"Admiral Zhènghé, the Glinka-Rebaul Stanzel Space Force Base has been invaded by Kaokuen Amphibians!"

"How the hell did they get there?"

"Only possibility is via the Great Seirin Ocean," the Combat Systems Officer interjected.

"Is Fleet Admiral Wirglestor launching the Fleet to rendezvous with us for the fight?" Admiral Zhènghé asked.

"Admiral they are attempting, but apparently are having problems with two airfields."

"What's the problem with the airfields why are they not launching Frigates and Cruisers."

The Combat Systems Officer knew this would be a huge blow to the Admiral, but it needed to be said for their own good.

"Sir I regret to inform you; those two airfield complexes are now in enemy hands."

Admiral Zhènghé realized a disaster of epic proportions now occurring and he had no choice but to aggressively join the fight or all may be lost!

"Damn the photon Torpedoes, all ahead FLANK," Admiral Zhènghé ordered.

Airfields number three and four were deploying some Frigates and Cruisers as well as a vast number of VTOLs and fixed wing fighter bombers at the Stanzel main base on the Island of Lamuers. The Frigates and Cruisers were fully loaded, being launched on the backs of flying wings, and delivered to the edge of space and jettisoned for operations, then were immediately engaged by Kaokuen Space Forces.

The space skirmishes were fast and furious. As the spaceships approached each other head on with total disregard for their lives because each side knew this was a pivotal battle with far reaching consequences.

The fact the Kaokuen fleet was positioned directly above the Island of Lamuers spelled doom for the Stanzelite Space Force because they should not be able to remain in such a precarious posture with all the fire power that could be sent at the enemy. The fact there was only a trickle of Frigates and Cruisers launching when it should have been a massive fleet was very troubling.

The Kaokuen Space Fleet was able to stay above the Island of Lamuers because all the Kaokuen Amphibian Exoskeletons could nail a lot of vertical launched space defense missiles and any particle beam or laser weapon required Time on Target (TOT). Thus, the Exoskeletons nailed the laser and beam weapons with counterfire before the power spectrum density could deliver enough energy to damage a ship.

These laser and beam weapons required up to five seconds to melt through the skin of an enemy cruiser. The Kaokuen Exoskeletons detected the Stanzelite beam or lasers within mili-seconds and counterfire began before a second transpired with appalling devastation. Since there was multiple Kaokuen counterfire attacks delivering magnified power spectrum density TOT from multiple angles was even more effective since the Stanselites were attacking in piece meal giving Kaokuen Exoskeleton beam and laser weapons more opportunity to achieve TOT.

The timid Stanzelite space weapon officers proved to be exceptionally timid doing this piece meal approach when massive salvos were required to make sure a few of them made the results required.

Stanzelite officers' conservative approach continued to be counterproductive.

It was no longer a case of force protection. The damn had broken and now it was force-preservation with aggressive attacks otherwise soon all would be lost. When they discovered the error of their ways it was too late.

At this time that Stanzel Fleet Admiral Wirglestor was no longer thinking about the tactical picture and changing up tactics to recover from the disaster he caused by his complacency and irresponsibility. He was thinking more of escape and the salvation of protecting his own skin with no regard to the multitudes of Stanzelites that might soon become prisoners of war.

Kaokuen demolition teams started systematically wrecking the Stanzelite Space Force Base to make sure it could not be put back into working order any time soon. All the box missile launcher magazines the Kaokuens captured made huge moon craters when they were demolished with a lot of reload missiles on storage racks that never got used due to criminal mismanagement of the campaign on the part of Admiral Wirglestor.

Each of the four runways associated with Stanzelite Airfields each having four runways for multiple fast deployments normally provided a total of sixteen active runways were systematically destroyed. The Amphibians had drilling rigs used for a variety of purposes including drilling for water on alien planets to provide their troops were also used for runway demolition.

Kaokuen demolition teams performed slant drilled in several locations under each runway and planted extremely explosive charges that would leave a 100-foot-wide crater fifty to one hundred feet deep permanently putting runways out of operation. Cluster bombs took care of all other roads, runways and strategic surfaces as the Amphibians slowly moved inland creating a pocket trapping vast numbers of Stanzelite Space Force Personnel.

With only two airfields left in operation and one of the two now under heavy attack, Stanzel Fleet Admiral Wirglestor finally broke down. While the rest of his generals and senior officers were desperately trying to cope with Armageddon now reaching them, Admiral Wirglestor, and his aide de camp slithered out a side entrance and proceeded to his Admirals Brigg, his private space capable transportation.

Upon launch, Admiral Wirglestor directed a squadron of fighter bombers now launching to go after the Kaokuens, redirected them to escort him up to the returning remnants of the fleet he sent to intervene with the Kaokuens engaged in the Feint on the other side of the planet.

By the time Admiral Wirglestor reached the safer rear echelon of this fleet where Admiral Zhènghé was in his command cruiser, almost two thirds of his escorts had been destroyed. His Admiral's Brigg took a few close calls as well and Stanzel Fleet Admiral Wirglestor was clearly shaken. For several minutes he simply stood not talking next to Admiral Zhènghé who would not appreciate if he meddled with his command ship and was exasperated why the hell Admiral Wirglestor arrived and transferred via shuttle to his command cruiser.

At this point in time the space battle was wildly raging and ships on both sides were dying in rapid order. Space Drones with multiple rockets, lasers, and beam weapons chewed at each other. Contrails lit up by sparkling nuclear powered rocket exhausts and highlighted by plasma's given off from exploding ships created a spider's web appearance that was rather terrifying to lesser trained men.

Damn the photon torpedoes FLANK speed ahead was in progress as ships were twisting and turning in a witch's brew of choreography a human mind could not readily decipher. Multiple nuclear-powered rockets launched in multiple salvos triggered a lot of self defense lasers and beam weapons operating in automatic mode with artificial intelligence guiding and manipulating them. The resulting vast numbers of lasers and beam weapons kept the spaces around the two fleets lit up where visual identification was easy.

In some cases, out of twenty missiles fired at a Stanzelite cruisers all failed to hit the target with maybe the exception of one. But like Murphy's law stipulates, it only takes one.

With the power of the warhead of the nuclear-powered space to space missiles just one hit could cause catastrophic damage to a cruiser or fast frigate's hull resulting in rapid depressurization and asphyxiation of the crew. Without crewmembers arming and firing weapons, the lifeless ship was a sitting duck with only automatic self defense weapons functioning until they ran out of ammunition and without Stanzelites who were now all dead, reloading, the fate of the spacecraft was determined.

When a cruiser on the command ship's port side blew up into a cloud of sparkling debris, Stanzel Fleet Admiral Wirglestor was suddenly thrust back to reality with great fear yelled, "Reverse Course, open range to the enemy!"

"We can't do that! The enemy is right over the top of the base that desperately needs our help! Maintain course and speed! Admiral Zhènghé yelled back countermanding Admiral Wirglestor's order.

At this moment in time, Admiral Wirglestor was only concerned about one thing: saving his own ass. *The hell with the base and the hell with the fleet*, Admiral Wirglestor thought as he pulled out his laser blaster out of its holster quickly and shot and killed Admiral Zhènghé, then screamed, "Reverse Course like I ordered!"

Stanzel Fleet Admiral Wirglestor's aide de camp, a well picked man who diligently always followed the Admiral's orders, brandished his own laser blaster, and yelled, "Do as the Admiral ordered now! Send communications to the fleet to follow us on the course reversal."

Within moments, Kaokuen Amphibian General Subutai was utterly stunned when he watched Stanzel Fleet Admiral Wirglestor Forces withdraw from the fight knowing his Kaokuen Task Force was in space directly above the Island of Lamuers Space Force Base.

"I wonder why they are leaving," a senior officer present asked.

"This is not the first time Stanzel Fleet Admiral Wirglestor has cut and run. We are lucky the Stanzelites promoted such a distinguished coward for times like this."

Aboard the Command Cruiser, Stanzel Fleet Admiral Wirglestor aide de camp asked, "Where are we going Admiral?"

We only have one choice. Stanzel is probably the Kaokuen's next target, we need to proceed to Stanzel at high-speed transit to get back there to warn them and help set up a safety net."

As soon as the remaining Stanzelites at the Space Force Base on the Island of Lamuers discovered Stanzel Fleet Admiral Wirglestor had cut and ran leaving them all behind to suffer their fate and deaths, mass desertions and white flags of surrender started.

The third airfield had just been taken and all but two radar sites with weapons detachments were now smoldering heaps. The Stanzelites knew the end was near and being a POW until a future prisoner exchange happened was far preferable than death.

The Garrison troops that made up most of the personnel on the base at the Island of Lamuers did not have the *Esprit de Corps* like the troops fighting on the contested planets. Their motivation for being behind friendly lines at a safe distance was due to them being chickenshit at heart and cowards in reality.

The benefit of having the 4th airfield available for the Kaokuens was this four-runway airfield had most of the transport spacecraft to haul all the POW's away as the base was soon in the hands of the Kaokuens. The few officers who did manage to escape on craft such as Fast Frigates, didn't bother to supervise the destruction of all the Stanzelites crypto and communications archives left behind at the base as hey bugged out as quickly as they could in total disgrace.

The frantic exodus of Stanzelite senior officers thus led to a treasure trove of INTEL gathered by the Kaokuens that would eventually help them plan future missions and fighting on the contested planets.

***

Dunbar was requested in the DD/P's office for a private meeting days later.

"I just finished reviewing your relay station mission files."

Dunbar knew he had done this one by the book and didn't think the DD/P would criticize him. But was waiting to hear all about it.

"I must congratulate you for actually accomplishing a mission without violating your operational orders."

"I came close."

"How was that?"

"I think the daughter of the Indigenous Arachno-Pulmonatas group leader's daughter wanted to come back with me."

"Is that so?"

"Yes, and *Latrodectus* detected her following me to the Transporter Capsule."

"Any reason you didn't want to bring her back?"

"I would be stuck with a green skin woman who would expect me to take care of her. I need to keep my slate clean in case I ever get a chance to be with Blemary again."

"It's highly unlikely you will ever see her again."

"You never know, with a few more victories, we might end up with a peace agreement and restoration of relations allowing travel there."

"Speaking of victory, the reason why I called you here was mainly to discuss a few things about the mission and how that was an important element into what happened at the Island of Lamuers Stanselite Base at Glinka-Rebaul."

"Alright, what is it?"

"When you blew up the relay station did you think you killed people?"

"Yes, *Latrodectus* showed me Stanzelite security video shown during the explosion before the electronics was shut down. It was a pretty big explosion. The fireball from the fuel tanks was quite huge. I imagine everyone there was killed."

"They were. Do you have any idea how many people were there?"

"I would have no way of knowing the exact head count but looking at security video I saw at least two dozen people."

"Your partner *Latrodectus* was able to download a number of personnel files and the roster, there were 117 people total on the base when it blew up."

"That doesn't surprise me."

"We have confirmation by means of which I can't tell you due to compartmentalization, all 117 Stanzelites died from the explosion."

"Alright, why do I need to know that?"

"You do not feel bad about killing 117 people?"

"No, it was my job to blow up the relay station and we are at war. I view this as simply another combat situation where people get killed in warfare."

"You might be surprised to learn, Doctor Elane Chonlan predicted you would say something like that when I talked to her earlier today."

"She's a smart woman."

"She sure has you figured out."

"In more ways than you can imagine," Dunbar said suspecting the DD/P knew he had boinked Elane.

"One of the reasons why you were not disqualified is I trust Elane's judgement."

"I appreciate what she did for me."

"The other thing I wanted to share with you is some time lapsed photography of the campaign at the Island of Lamuers Stanselite Base on Glinka-Rebaul."

"Alright."

The DD/P then showed the amazing holographic video which was rather spectacular. Many aspects of the battle were shown including the Amphibians on the ground fighting and space battle footage.

"Kind of sobering, isn't it?" The DD/P asked.

"It certainly is," Dunbar responded.

"This is all compartmentalized and you are not authorized to discuss it with anyone."

"I do not intend to."

"I know that, but I'm required to say it for legal reasons."

"Sure, I understand."

"There is a reason why I wanted you to watch that."

"Why is that?"

"None of that video you saw would not have been possible had you not blown the relay station."

"That stands to reason."

"What you did was very important. You carried out the assignment probably better than anyone else I could have assigned."

"Thanks for the compliment."

"Another reason why I had to bring you in here is to give you a verbal award. None of this can ever be put in an official award given to you."

"I understand."

"This comes directly from my boss, the Director of Transporter Operations."

"Okay."

"This is a verbal congratulations to a highly successful mission the Director views as one of the top ten missions in Transporter history. Most of the other missions of this magnitude resulted in the Transporter Spy losing his life. You are one of the lucky ones."

"I'm happy to come back alive."

"Thank you for what you did."

"My pleasure."

***

Chapter Fourteen
Operation Bore Sight

As time went by, sending Transport Capsules with the help of a laser designator became problematic. The Transport Directorate needed a whole new method of sending spies behind enemy lines. Great minds came together to come up with a different system.

Eventually when the new system *Bore Sight* developed began testing in phases, they started by sending a fruit that looked like Watermelons to be used as the cargo to prove concepts before attempting live animals that would proceed human Transporter missions.

Distances were short in the beginning as more R&D slowly proved the concept and over time longer and longer distances were attempted. Operation Bore Sight. About the time Dunbar was cleared for his next mission, he would be tested like never before. This was a multi-mission Transport. The planet he would be sent to was about one half the distance compared to some of his recent trips.

The DD/P called the illustrious psychoanalyst Elane Cholan into his office for a private conference. Elane was no rookie nor a prude by any stretch of the imagination. She also knew the likelihood existed the DD/P viewed the watcher video of her and Dunbar in the forest conducting their *Tour de France* that by all appearances was a very highly successful sexual encounter. He also observed a lot of Elane Cholan's clinical work with Dunbar and was quite impressed by how quickly she resolved quite a few issues.

The DD/P had to keep a poker face because he wanted Elane to be fully natural because their discussion was going to go a long way to do the final clearance for Dunbar to do the *Bore Sight* mission. The way Dunbar went to town on Elane bent over hugging the tree when Dunbar pounded her from the rear gave him reason to believe he was over Blemary and just like the women he had sex with after leaving her behind, he certainly would likely evolve into similar sexual trysts in the future including possibly on this next mission.

The DD/P didn't know the two were putting on a good show for the Transport Directorate especially when Elane got into some of the private Q and A sessions with Dunbar.

When Elane asked Dunbar if he could kill a woman if that was part of his operational order with the caveat, *and she looked identical to Blemary,* just like Kaarina the unexpected mystery to that mission? The DD/P felt the gusto of sending his best spy back out in the field when he looked at Dunbar's face and heard his answer. He played that holographic segment back ten times to make sure he did not misunderstand any of it.

Dunbar is a complicated person and a great actor, especially if he believes he's being observed.

"Yes, I would first have sex with her to make her feel really good before I slit her throat in a quiet kill."

"And just when would you do that?" Elane asked. She could never figure out if this was acting or his real answer to the way he delivered it, the words even convinced her Dunbar would do it exactly the way he stated.

Elane would be horrified to learn Dunbar might even find a sick joy in doing it that way. Living on the edge changes people. Dunbar was a nice guy at heart, but he too was changed. Of course, he was acting because he knew he had to.

"Just like you, I would know when she was having her orgasm. Since the female's life was quickly ending, I would give her the satisfaction of completing her orgasm and in the height of the splendid euphoria she would end living."

But Dunbar knew the truth. He would analyze the situation just like he did in the Larian world and if letting the person like he did with Rextar Fünger live if the circumstances allowed him to complete his agenda, then why kill them? Dunbar delivered his lie with convincing mannerism.

Asked to whether the Transport Directorate should inform Dunbar he was deploying on the very first Bore Sight mission, Elane had a unique perspective.

"In my world dealing with people that have compelling psychological challenges, I've developed a keen understanding of human nature, and it is very predictable," Elane said.

"And what is that?" the DD/P asked.

"If what you don't know won't hurt you, then why be informed?"

"I suppose you are right."

"Face it, if there is a reassociation issue, what can you really do about it?"

"Not much. We've learned that already."

Dunbar would not be briefed he would launch on the very first *Bore Sight* mission. The DD/P wanted him to focus all his energy on the other elements of the mission which included murder, sabotage, Intelligence, Surveillance, Reconnaissance (ISR), and elements of Studies and Observation (SOG). Hence, the DD/P chose to follow the illustrious psychoanalyst Elane Chonlan advise and omitted the briefing this was indeed a *Bore Sight* mission.

Latrodectus that had substantial psychoanalyst files. He had far more information than Elane and just as equal analysis ability.

In terms of *Latrodectus* vast psychoanalysis, his concept of object constancy related to the idea of "out of sight, out of mind."

He felt for Dunbar, Elane Chonlan recommended the most prudent course for Dunbar, and such an omission would help reduced distractions allowing more concentrated effort on the primary task of an assassination and a sabotage that would have significant impact on cutting off money and arms to the *Stanzelites*.

Object constancy is a psychodynamic concept that refers to the ability to maintain an emotional quiescence by reducing the impact created by others because of distance and conflicts.

Object constancy originates from the concept of object permanence, a cognitive skill of understanding even though objects situations may exist even when they cannot be seen, touched, or sensed in some way thus reducing the psychological influence to what the person is attempting .

The phrase "out of sight, out of mind" is often attributed to the English poet John Heywood, who lived in the 16th century.

Object constancy would play a role in this mission thanks to *Latrodectus* shielding Dunbar who would think it's business as usual. The four Amigos (*office warriors*) would also be shielded and not know this super-secret transport operation because a lot was riding on it and the DD/P could not allow them to damage national security just so they could further their advancements and careers. Too much was at stake to the point this mission was highly compartmentalized.

Dunbar had more than enough obstacles to overcome and serious dangers he faced. And to the DD/P's aggravation, the four Amigos started in on the critique crap again threatening the DD/P by indicating they may go over his head and force it.

These four office warriors must have thought this was the DD/P's first Rodeo and to their chagrin, the DD/P scheduled the Critique and when he was summoned into his boss's office, he gave him the date and time. He also asked the Director of Transports to attend the critique because he was going to accuse the four Amigos (*office warriors*) of insubordination in front of his boss and see how they liked that.

The DD/P purposely scheduled Dunbar's Bore Sight launch very late in the day and told key team members to go home during the end of their normal shift, rest up for a few hours at home and come back.

The four Amigos (*office warriors*) were clock watchers. They were about the first always to leave the office and left the building usually fifteen minutes prior to avoid the rush and the congestion.

When the launch team came back into the office, the *office warriors* had been gone for almost three hours. Only this skeleton crew would know they launched Dunbar.

Elane informed the DD/P earlier in the day to send Dunbar over to her office so she could do some last-minute preparation with him. In the morning Dunbar was escorted to Elane's office like he normally was, then the escorts were dismissed and went back to the office.

When the two was alone, Elane said, "The DD/P informed me you are leaving on a mission today."

"I'm sorry I cannot comment on operational matters," Dunbar responded.

"That's okay I already know you will be leaving in a few hours and once again you will be facing danger. I thought I could help prepare you for your mission with one more treatment."

"Is that so?"

"Yes, I want you to take me to your home now. We'll travel there in my Skycar, I assume you have rooftop Skycar parking?"

"Why do you need to go to my home?"

"I'll explain it to you when we get there."

"Alright," Dunbar said wondering what the hell that was all about."

The DD/P had tight surveillance on Dunbar and wasn't too excited observing him leave the facility with Elane in her Skycar and when they landed at his apartment building, he assumed he knew what pre-mission treatments Elane had in mind and smiled.

If Dunbar thought this was the first time Elane saw his apartment, he was a fool. The plumbers had installed quite a bit of surveillance in Dunbar's apartment, and she had observed it often as she analyzed what he was doing and behaving where nobody knew what he was doing. Nothing was left to chance in the high stakes game of espionage and *Clandestine Deliveries.*"

Dunbar led Elane into the home and asked her, "Is there anything you would like to drink?"

"Let me see what you have, and I'll pick it."

Soon standing beside an open cabinet that had 5 layers of elixir bottle storage, Elane saw the type of elixir she observed Dunbar drinking in the surveillance holographs and said, "I would like to try this Chamboreé de Lián."

Alright," Dunbar said grabbing the bottle that had a screw off top and walked a few feet over to a countertop that had glasses in nice fixture coming down from the ceiling.

"How much would you like?"

"Fill it up to the top, this may take a while."

"Sure."

"Dunbar didn't want to be impaired when he left on his mission and only poured himself half a glass.

The two sat down on Dunbar's sofa.

Dunbar asked, "What could you possibly do to prepare me for this mission, it's only a few hours away."

"Let me enjoy some of this Chamboreé de Lián before we get into all that."

Dunbar noticed Elane was dressed up slightly better than usual. *Perhaps she had an important meeting today?*

Elane liked the way the Chamboreé de Lián made her feel. She already knew the essence of what was going to manifest in a few minutes. Since Elane was a psychoanalyst and knew all about pheromones and felt the psychoactive chemicals in the Chamboreé de Lián, she knew she was primed to perform. Before Dunbar arrived, she took a heavy dose of Damiana and a few other libido stimulants and in a few minutes when she revealed her real purpose it was going to all work out nicely.

Elane observed Dunbar slow reactions as this all manifested. Dunbar inhaled Elane's perfume for the past few minutes that had one of the heaviest pheromone concentrations of any such product sold specifically for women in the sex industry to facilitate their tradecraft. She knew it was already affecting Dunbar's little head. She was going to take her time and start seducing Dunbar after she finished her elixir as it was making her feel extremely good.

Elane understood she was violating all the canons of her profession in a major way. If she was working for a hospital, and they discovered her conduct with one of her patients like she did with Dunbar, her license would get yanked real fast. But she worked for the Transport Directorate, the premier spy agency. And she did a lot of their dirty work. She simply felt today was a down payment on what they owed her for all those miserable days she had treating transporter spies reassociation injuries.

The Chamboreé de Lián went down very nicely, and she sat her empty glass on the coffee table and turned to Dunbar and said, "I'm here Dunbar to give you a proper sendoff."

"Alright."

"We are friends, correct?"

"Yes, I feel we are friends," Dunbar replied wondering what the heck this was all about and what this mystery woman was doing.

"I know that because of the business you are in and our professional responsibilities, whatever we do can never go beyond the appearance of friendship."

"I surmised that when we were out in the forest, you saved my life. I owe you a lot."

"Dunbar, you are a very interesting person, you have done a lot. I've read all your files. If there was anyone who deserved to be saved it's you."

"Thank you."

"Dunbar, can I ask you to do something for me?"

"Sure what?"

"Kiss me like I'm your lover, can you do that?"

"I can try."

The two merged closer together and the escalation of passions commenced. With the kiss Dunbar's nose and face were now close enough to get the invisible cloud of pheromones that was starting to cause his brain to release chemicals such as Dopamine, Norepinephrine, and Oxytocin. In a while when they were experiencing gratification Dunbar's brain was creating a large quantity of Serotonin, vasopressin, nitric oxide (NO), and the hormone prolactin.

Dunbar did his best to kiss Elane in a manner he thought she wanted, but she wanted more. She wanted the Tour de France and soon her hand was pulling Dunbar's face closer and tighter making it very clear what her intentions were. The combination of Damiana, and a few other things she took and the chemicals in the Chamboreé de Lián drink, made Elane feel like a *bitch in heat.*

Elane showed no restraint whatsoever. She was pragmatic and knew Dunbar being on the very first *Bore Sight* mission could be a reassociation casualty. He could be dead in just a few hours. For all that this great man had done which Elane knew because of her privileged position to read the downgraded classification on portions of those files making them accessible, she had a legitimate picture of the essence of Dunbar's activities. Elane had observed down postured mission files include how this sexy man-made love to those extremely beautiful women. Elane saw how at times women like Blemary were dressed up looking better than most women, including Kaokuen, their home planet.

Elane knew that Dunbar would be slightly apprehensive by her aggressive actions and so she swung into action, she helped him undress promptly and she merely stepped out of her clothes she was ready for coitus on a *Theme from Paganini.*

Elane pushed Dunbar back on his sofa and she straddled him and kissed some more and encouraged him, "make my breasts feel good."

After playing around with her breasts for a few minutes, Elane then started performing fellatio on Dunbar making him nice and erect and excited. When she decided he was best prepared for the next stage of their intercourse she mounted him and took his manliness and inserted it inside her very wet vagina and soon started making love to him in ways Dunbar never expected increasing the pleasure.

Elane knew she could not delay her own gratification no matter how hard she tried she wanted it to last forever, but the chemicals in her own brain were now flooding her passions in a psychophysical reaction and consequently the massive gratification she felt.

Elane's splendid euphoria was now flooding her brain and her emotions. The secret pathway from her heart to her brain that few know about was sending those electro-chemical signals that fantastic love does. Especially the first love. The golden love, the love everyone wants to experience in their lifetime.

Elane's tears were now flooding, she was totally out of control as she knew Dunbar had made her feel unlike any time in her life and then she felt his ejaculation into her with strong thrusts and releases and it created a second wave of psychophysical release. Dunbar could not understand why Elane was crying and her tears were flooding down but he never felt so good in such a long time. Blemary, Kaarina, Brigitte, and all his cares in the world were suspended.

And finally, the post coitus, splendid euphoria now gripped both of them and in a while their bodies were repositioned into a lovers embrace just holding in a loving fashion enjoying this tender moment that caused them to lapse into a shallow sleep they could not avoid.

The DD/P knew where Dunbar was, he knew where Elane was. He watched all this real time. He was curious as to what all was going to happen and how Dunbar would act, this would go further into convincing him that he was at least for now out of sight and out of mind with Blemary. But the DD/P was a brilliant man who had studied the human condition running transporter spies and dealing with people killed or maimed due to reassociation issues going to or coming back.

Knowing what faced Dunbar over the next few days, the DD/P thought he would reward Dunbar for all that he had done by giving him this precious moment and not disturbing him. He knew they were merely sleeping having experienced tremendous emotions.

Dunbar might have simply experienced a sexual tryst he enjoyed but Elane went the full distance in her penetration into a cloud of temporal love she would hold dearly for the rest of her life.

When Elane said to Dunbar before she seduced him, "We are just friends." That was a signal to the DD/P this was probably a one-shot deal Elane needed for closure. She was a wise person and would not clutter her clinical position by developing a permanent relationship with her patient.

Time goes faster when you enjoy your circumstances the most. A lot sooner than Dunbar expected, Elane received a call from her communicator. She had to answer it right away because it had a special ringer that only happened in an emergency requiring her immediate action.

Almost in a panic Elane answered her communicator in voice only because she was still nude.

"Hello."

"Elane, this is the DD/P. We need to get Dunbar back here right away for his pre-transporter activities. Would you mind taking him over to my office building and land on the rooftop parking. We'll have a couple escorts to take him down to my office."

"Yes Director, I'll bring him right away."

"Thank you, and I do appreciate all the support you give me."

"It's my pleasure."

Elane ended the communication and turned to Dunbar and said, "The DD/P asked me to take you back to your office now for your pre-transporter activities. Why don't you take a quick sprite shower before you dress."

"Only if you will get in the shower with me."

"I would be delighted but I must ask you to clean me especially in the area you touched me the most," Elane said with an evil grin.

"Not a problem," Dunbar said smiling knowing he would enjoy playing with Elane.

Dunbar knew they could not fool around in the shower very long, so he took a quick sprite shower, and a little beaver maintenance was all the time allotted, and they were dried off and dressing.

Just like the DD/P indicated there were two men on the rooftop of the building to escort Dunbar down to the Transporter room where the DD/P was waiting with his change of clothes for Dunbar, the special communicator and a small backpack with his personal toiletries which were also multi containers for multipurpose such as toothpaste and explosives, mouth wash and arson liquids, special glasses, ear pods and all the other devices he would likely use.

Soon Dunbar was sitting in the transporter and the hatch was closed.

Dunbar felt the normal Transporter sensations as his atoms were disassociated into a tachyon stream and flung out into space significantly faster than the speed of light.

Dunbar was grateful he survived another Transport when the hatch was opening, and his temporal reality now returned and once again he was now located in a sparsely populated area hidden by the forest and flora that abounded.

Dunbar arrived at the planet Tallinn in the transporter capsule and after he checked himself quickly determined he had no reassociation issues and felt normal with lingering memories of Elane.

Dunbar remembered Elane's statement before the love making, "We are friends only." She made that statement for a reason. Dunbar speculated as a psychoanalyst she had to prepare herself. She didn't want her heart broken so she compartmentalized her emotions under the guise of friendship. But Dunbar had experiences in the past were women agreed to a friendship and were the first to violate it going over the line into romance.

Dunbar was on the outskirts of the Severomsk Dome City Oklast. The Severomsk eventually took over the planet of Tallinn. The Severomsks were a proud people, steep in tradition and some of the craftiest people in this region of space. Severomsk Dome City Oklast had a lot of wealthy Severomsk because they were the best aquatic Farmers in the galaxy. Seventy five percent of the surface of Tallinn was a combination of mangroves, swamps, large lakes, huge rivers, and large areas of the planted that were Perennial Gardens that had Sedge Grass, Panicum Grass, Elymus grass, and pockets of plants with beautiful flowers.

Thanks to tectonic plates shifting creating a few mountain ranges and dredging and damming of swamps to construct dome cities scientists discovered the planet used to be dry with very little water until a catastrophic event happened in what used to be a nearby solar system when it's sun blew up into trillions of pieces and the resulting shock wave destroyed several planets including one going through a glaciation period that had five mile thick sheets of ice where oceans use to exist.

Many large planetary fragments that were huge sections of ice were flung into deep space and by a sheer accident eventually collided with Tallin giving off huge energy releases and scattering mile wide fragments of ice all over the arid planet. Tallinn had an atmosphere about one fourth that of livable planets. The energy release caused by the head on collisions with a vast chunk of ice raised the surface temperature of planet Tallinn several hundred degrees that slowly decreased after millions of years but also caused all the ice fragments to melt except collisions in polar regions that had a much slower melt rate.

Because the complete surface of Tallinn underwent hydration when the ice melted creating rivers and streams, the lack of an atmosphere caused evaporation to accelerate. The evaporation also expanded the atmosphere slowly and the vast amount of nitrogen trapped in the ice added to a new atmosphere and cloud cover and a new weather cycle. Eventually the atmospheric pressure reached 14.5 PSI.

The most spectacular component of these huge chunks of ice hitting the planet and exploding into millions of subsize chunks, some of which buried hundreds of feet underground in the soft sandstone surface. Caught up in the glaciation before the planet was hammered with shock waves and torn apart vast amount of sea life and seeds as well as dead and rotting carcasses arrived adding to the biosphere of Tallinn. The mineral rich soil of Tallinn was perfect for the new flora to establish new life in a different world. Some of the frozen life forms in the ice regenerated after the ice melted.

Space travelers and explorers left behind other sources of planetary contaminants. Dumping the sanitary tanks on the lifeless planet didn't seem like a problem to Tallinn's visitors. But those million-gallon tanks full of sewage contained vast amounts of bacteria and in some cases undigested seeds and other items that slowly added to the biosphere.

Space is a dangerous place. When your spacecraft is wrecked by a lucky asteroid sometimes only the size of a baseball, if you are lucky enough to land on a planet you might survive long enough to be picked up.

But if you were space explorer from far off worlds traveling on spacecraft traveling faster than the speed of light, an SOS call for help traveling at light speed may not arrive for 10 years and worse yet they may not be able to figure out exactly where you are because your stop was not on the agenda. Hence you are hopelessly marooned.

Some say that's how intelligent life arrived in Tallinn. They showed up as advanced alien space travelers, but after twenty-five generations of offspring much of the former worlds no longer have any surviving information of their origination plus being marooned far away would have no idea where they were, and life then began at the early stages as hunter gatherers living off what Tallinn had to offer.

Long after the descendants of the marooned space travelers gave up hope of ever being rescued, by accident the planet was visited, and these descendants were discovered many generations later. However, by now, they were far away from their ancestor's origination. By now, there was no identity to their beginnings or where they came from. These descendants of marooned space travelers also had transcended into savages, living off the land and as hunter gatherers.

The space travelers that found them never discovered the savages' ancient pasts as through the passage of time they were amalgamated with civilizations closer to this planet. Whatever culture they originated from now became completely lost. One day, however, artifacts were found to indicate they were these offspring of maroon space travelers.

Due to the miracle of how Tallinn formed the rare minerals found and the ability to obtain locally grown food opened commerce and trade. After several centuries a modern society formed that ushered in a dozen domed cities surrounded by swamps or mountainous terrains in some cases.

Outside the domed cities transportation was either by air or hovercraft. Due to the topography only a small fragile road network existed. Most roads were nothing more than bridges and construction was slow and extremely costly. The roadbeds for multimode travel were built upon zigzagging stilts interconnecting segments. A few cities had interconnecting roads only because they were built before advancements in hovercraft and aircraft. The decision was simple when advanced technology created a new reality. Why waste huge amounts of funds to expand the road network when Skycars were so versatile?

Airports built on stilts adjacent to the Domed Cities handled conventional aircraft that were not VTOL, and those numbers were dwindling. The predictions were that in 100 years, all conventional aircraft would be no more as everything transitioned to VTOL craft.

The airports on stilts were designed to last thousands of years. What to do with them after the complete conversion to VTOL happened? That was the present-day hot button political question. There was a growing desire by many to move out of dome cities back out into the wild like it used to be. One political faction wanted to turn all the airports into open air cities when they were officially shut down.

Since all the dome cities Dunbar would visit were surrounded by marshland and swamps, they had numerous hovercraft piers including rental agencies.

As part of this mission Dunbar would soon be renting a hovercraft. The reason why he arrived at Oklast was it was close to the mountains and had a road network leading from the Severomsk Dome City Oklast to the mountain region that had towns and villages. Dunbar was able to land in that area which had reliable transportation into Oklast, where he would do some of his activities. His getaway plan in case he needed to bug out would be via hovercraft that would give him a direct shot to the area where he had easy access to the Transporter Capsule.

Dunbar would also set up shop in a coastal Bed and Breakfast, *Jīnsè de Rìluò* located in the town of Jàznālià.

Dunbar did not have enough time to learn the Severomsk language, but he was fluent in the Rinisp dialect of the standard *Stanzel language*.

Since more than half of the tourists that came off planet to the Severomsk planet Tallinn were *Stanzelites*, that would be the type of person for Dunbar's Oklast alias named Mily Balakigrev on the planet Tallinn, another abducted person.

Mily Balakigrev was another person like Dunbar's *Stanzel* alias Kabel Garr. Mily Balakigrev was a frequent off world traveler and through luck and determination mission planners discovered Mily Balakigrev traveled to Oklast on the planet Tallinn a half dozen times and stayed at Bed and Breakfast locations, hence Dunbar's activities would not be suspicious if authorities investigated him.

Dunbar had a lot of credits฿ programmed into Mily Balakigrev's personal communicator confiscated when he was abducted to support this operation. Anyone who knew Miley Balakigrev would assume he took off again. They didn't know for sure what he was doing during his vast travels.

Miley Balakigrev never confided in anyone; he was a private person. But there were rumors Miley Balakigrev was probably a creep going on sex tourism. The truth of the matter, Miley Balakigrev liked to go to places like Jàznālià to watch the golden sunsets, enjoy the local elixirs that contained a wine-like substance fortified by magic mushrooms to give him glorious trips watching sunset.

Miley Balakigrev was a holistic person that included his diet. Dunbar would lose a few pounds on this trip sticking to the diet because that would also be a key ingredient to convincing observers believe Dunbar's alias Miley Balakigrev was the real person. Miley Balakigrev could not speak the Severomsk language, which was a plus in this case, it added phenomenally to the acting results.

No spy could have been picked better than Dunbar and the DD/P knew it more than anyone due to the *Stanzel* language skills, his travels there and the icing on the cake was Miley Balakigrev came from the *Stanzel* city Kerlara which Dunbar knew quite well from his travels there. Dunbar's whole persona was tailor fit for this alias.

Dunbar also had another powerful ally with him, *Latrodectus* who would be hacking and conducting continuous ISR operations.

Dunbar needed to have the hovercraft as his escape method when he conducted the sabotage and the assassination.

Killing a ruthless organized crime person who had no redeeming qualities, was not the same as sparing the life of a research scientist who had something to offer. This cartel banker added significantly to the Kaokuen's misery as he provided vast sums of credits₿ to the *Stanzelites* that allowed them to stay in the game in this continual carnage that happened on far away contested planets. War profiteers come in many ways from manufacturers to investors, and to banksters such as Catoire Tigranian.

The Severomsk banker Catoire Tigranian operated in Oklast with no concerns for his own personal safety because he bribed law enforcement and gave Severomsk Intelligence Bureau (SIB) part time jobs to significantly enhance their incomes. The SIBs as they were referred to were ruthless bastards. They would cut their grandmother's throat if they thought they would make a lot of money.

Bankers who screw over people and rip people off from time to time generate enemies. Almost several times a year, Catoire Tigranian had to utilize SIBs to take care of his enemies.

Because they would create undue scrutiny and exhaustive investigation that might reveal their role in this scheme that generated them a lot of income, they had to do very innovative methods to create accidents.

On certain roads within dome cities or Skycar operations that left Skycar ports set up at a dozen different equal spaced distances around the

Dome for access even though fully computer controlled with triple backup, the strangest events happened occasionally.

Over half of the dome cities were huge, almost twenty miles in diameter. The privately owned vehicles had many self-driving zones that prevented operator actions. A vehicle's computers were fully in control and the controls were all automatic. There was nothing that could be interfered with by the car driver since it was stuck in automatic for most of the journey.

The SIBs would take control of two vehicles traveling in opposite direction and an innocent person not involved usually was the source of the accident when that person's vehicle suddenly swerved into the oncoming traffic and even though it was only doing fifty miles per hour, a head in crash when the other car going in the opposite direction also doing similar speeds, caused significant damage when they collided in this surreptitious manner. The target of the accident was usually killed or maimed so bad he or she never wanted to cross Catoire Tigranian again. People in the underworld knew better.

Sometimes for no reason they could ever figure out, Skycars went bump in the night as well. Even though government suspected foul play there was no evidence to find since the government officials on the payroll of Catoire Tigranian bleached any possible records to suggest a computer virus or malware had been inserted into the vehicles computer processing software that managed the navigation system that created the accident.

Catoire Tigranian had recently arranged for another *accident*. He was now complacent thinking there were no threats. The last thing in the world Catoire Tigranian could possibly imagine was the Kaokuen Transporter Directorate would be sending one of their best spies to assassinate him.

After securing the Transporter Capsule that was now fully cloaked and well hidden, Dunbar walked five miles to a bus stop just a few miles away from his ultimate destination the coastal Bed and Breakfast, *Jìnsè de Rìluò*, located in the town of Jàznālià.

Dunbar would not stop and check in at the *Jīnsè de Rìluò*. Instead, he would board a shallow draft but large commuter hovercraft that would travel almost 80 miles per hour going across the shallow water to a dock at the Severomsk Dome City Oklast.

Dunbar had on his conformal ear buds and followed instructions of *Latrodectus* the Artificial Intelligence that resided in special circuitry in the communicator, redesigned after they obtained the communicator from Mily Balakigrev during the abduction. With credits₿ automatically paying transportation fees by automatic transaction, Dunbar seamlessly traveled around the city becoming familiar with the city.

The construction of the Severomsk Dome City Oklast was a technical challenge building it in the middle of a swam. Powerful dredgers came in and slowly dredged the ten-mile-wide area the dome was built. All the debris dredged was dumped in the surrounding swamp building up an earthen dam that rose almost 100 feet into the air and due to the sheer weight created a large circular hill that from space appeared to be a comet strike area.

Thanks to that artificial barrier the water in the middle of this ten-mile-wide artificial lake was pumped out and as most of the water was gone a pit in the middle was established as a future water collection area that could easily be pumped out. The Severomsk Dome City Oklast foundation was sunken five hundred feet under sea level.

With a dry environment to work, concrete dams were built adjacent to the earthen dams that rose fifty feet above sea level. Then deep holes were drilled systematically around the dome for the purpose of building tall pillars to support the Dome roof. The debris created drilling these holes to build the foundation of the pillars in and the initial segments of the pillars, slowly raised the floor of the dome and when the pillars in an area were finished, a steel mesh reinforced concrete floor, was completed that slowly created a very nice and dry floor that had pipes under it with drainage to a central collector allowing ease of pumping the bottom dry.

As soon as the pillars were completed in an area the dome cover was installed. People many generations later watching videos at libraries could see an animation showing the coming construction giving an elapsed sped up time history of a waterproof dome slowly covering the sight.

At the same time the ten mile diameter dome was built for the future city, the adjacent swamp area that had the best weather conditions began a transformation into an Airport that operated many years before a pending scheduled shutdown when Buildings would be placed there to expand the scope of the Severomsk Dome City Oklast as VTOL technology took over and only five percent of the former airport was needed for VTOL transportation operations.

Riding on public transportation around the dome in a leiser manner gave Dunbar a lot of images he could appreciate the people who constructed all this. When the public transportation arrived at the center of the Severomsk Dome City Oklast where the tallest structures existed in a cohesive circular pattern following the layout of the pillars. Building the tallest buildings in the very center of the Oklast Dome City, Dunbar got off he was near his destination.

Wearing *Stanzelites* clothing and male hair style, Miley Balakigrev (aka Dunbar) appeared like a *Stanzelite* tourist, hence he would not stick out since there were always many *Stanzelites* visiting Oklast.

While Dunbar was walking around this area, *Latrodectus* was at work. A lot of INTEL had been collected in Oklast. *Latrodectus* had substantial electronic maps including business addresses and WIFI hot spots to obtain additional information and discover weak points for penetration into the Tallinn World Wide Web (TWWW).

Each time the Transport Directorate put spies on Tallinn, more data was obtained from the TWWW. Situational awareness was greatly enhanced for Dunbar because *Latrodectus* TWWW penetration allowed surveillance of any area Dunbar was located and where he was going. In effect Dunbar had eyes and ears ahead of him.

Dunbar felt the vibrator ring on his communicator. He looked at its flatscreen since it would not be prudent to view a holograph in public. *Latrodectus* had a message and with Dunbar's special Kollmorgant holographic eyeglasses operating in the *invisible ink* mode, he could read the text on the communicator flatscreen but nobody else could since it was light created outside the light spectrum people could not see, but the special glasses could.

"The building coming up on the left is 111 Grande Avenue. Catoire Tigranian's office is on the 19th floor, in the *Stellar Investments and Investment Banking* which takes up the entire 19th floor." *Latrodectus* informed Dunbar through Kollmorgant holographic eyeglasses text operating in the *invisible ink* mode.

Dunbar wondered *why Catoire Tigranian's office required so much real estate?* Dunbar watched closely at his surroundings while he walked by 111 Grande Avenue building.

"*Stellar Investments and Investment Banking* is the front company used for Catoire Tigranian's criminal enterprise." *Latrodectus* reported in invisible ink mode on the flat screen of the communicator.

After walking another block, *Latrodectus* texted in invisible ink mode:

"We are coming up to the entrance of the subway that goes between the warf area with the bridge over to the Jàznàlià area and the airport in the opposite direction."

This communication link was the main throughfare through of the Severomsk Dome City Oklast. As part of the planning, Dunbar would first go to the Airport, walk around it, get a feel for it in case he decided he needed to fly somewhere, or worse yet steal a VTOL craft for an emergency getaway. This was a semi-express subway that only had four stops during the five-mile trek to the edge of the dome and airport access. Even with stops for passenger loading and departure, the express subway made it from center city to the airport in twelve minutes.

Dunbar got off the subway took the escalator up to the departure level of the airport and walked around then went back to the subway station and took it all the way to the warf area on the opposite side of the dome where he would walk a short distance to the Severomsk Divergent Hovercraft Rental Agency that not only rented the Hovercraft, but for a small fee could park it there if you were a shopper going into the dome city.

Dunbar went into the Severomsk Divergent Hovercraft Rental agency and walked up to the receptionist. The female dressed nicely had good looks all around and Dunbar could easily confirm the woman with a nametag that said Yokanda had perfect dimensions and revealed much of her cleavage in a very sexy business attire which almost appeared like a female business suit with no inner dress which was highly stylish in the tourist area around the Severomsk Dome City Oklast.

When *Latrodectus* made Mily Balakigrev (aka Dunbar's) reservation for the Hovercraft rental, as part of the transaction terms of agreements were signed and facial recognition stamp was put on the contract. When Mily Balakigrev (aka Dunbar) walked up to Yokanda, she already knew his alias name.

"Hello Mily Balakigrev, I'm your sales associate representative, my name is Yokanda. Your contract was digitally signed, and you also paid an additional parking fee as part of the rental."

"That's correct," Dunbar replied.

There were several sales associates in the rental office because they had to escort the renter out to the hovercraft to inspect it with the renter to verify no damage and to explain a few things.

"Alright Mily Balakigrev you are good to go, but I'm going to escort you out to your rental to look it over with you for any damage or issues you may want to address."

"Thank you."

"This way please," Yokanda said.

The two walked out a side door of the building which was inside a secure area that had chain link fence preventing pedestrians to walk down their pier but there was a cypher lock gate to get into.

"If you park the hovercraft here after normal working hours, you can access through that gate. It's set up by facial recognition, but there is also a unique cypher entry number that is on your communicator now as part of the contract. When you approach the cypher if the facial recognition does not unlock the gate, the monitor will send an inquiry to your communicator and when it responds it will unlock. You also have the option of keying in the passcode, but is very seldom required," Yokanda stated.

"Thanks. That's good to know," Dunbar replied.

"Have you ever driven a Hovercraft?" Yokanda asked.

"Yes, I've been here before and rented them from other agencies."

"The model you are renting has all the manual operations that you are probably familiar with, but this model has full automation. As an example, while the Hovercraft is always monitoring you for your voice commands, you can make statements such as "I want to go to Jàznālià," and it will automatically take there with safe speeds monitoring and avoiding traffic to prevent accidents and pull into public parking at your destination."

"That sounds simple enough."

If you are going to a resort or one of the many Beds and Breakfasts most of them have Hovercraft parking for their guests, so if you tell it your exact destination, if the resort parking is available it will go to their parking slots."

"That's good to know."

"Also, our automatic system will notify the Bed and Breakfast or Resort you are arriving with your communicator identity and those businesses will direct your Hovercraft where to park."

"How would I know that's the right spot?"

"The Hovercraft's artificial intelligence will inform you when it's pulling into the automated grabbers that moor the Hovercraft, your parking is permitted, and you have nothing to be concerned about."

"Yea I've experienced that situation before. The automated system works great."

"It looks to me there is no damage to the Hovercraft you are renting. Please take care of it and do not damage it or you will be billed for damage."

"I assume you will automatically check me out when I leave?"

"Absolutely. Just tell the artificial intelligence you have finished using the Hovercraft and you are checking out, and it will inform us and give you the status of your contract that you have completed your rental."

"Super, thank you very much."

Moments later Dunbar was leaving the Hovercraft rental agency in manual mode, he liked driving when he had a chance. He drove conservatively and did not *kick it in the ass* as a lot of renters do showing off leaving the pier.

Halfway to Jàznālià, Dunbar said for the Hovercraft artificial intelligence to hear, "We are going to the *Jīnsè de Rluò* Bed and Breakfast, located in the town of Jàznālià."

Within a moment the Hovercraft Artificial Intelligence notified Mily Balakigrev (aka Dunbar), "*Jīnsè de Rluò* Bed and Breakfast has been notified you are arriving, and they gave me a pier assignment."

"Super," Dunbar said then asked, "Artificial Intelligence, do you have a name?"

"No sir I do not," the Hovercraft artificial intelligence responded.

"Would you like to have a name?" Dunbar asked.

"Actually, I would sir," the Hovercraft artificial intelligence responded.

"Alright, I will call you Lyudmila."

"I've never heard that name before sir."

"It's an ancient name of a princess who was abducted by an evil sorcerer."

"What happened to Lyudmila?"

"The king sent a brave knight to rescue her."

"Was the knight successful?"

"Initially the Knight was killed by the evil sorcerer who wanted Lyudmila who is asleep under a spell, but is brought back to life with magical water, and is able to carry Lyudmila back to her father and awaken her with magic."

"I like the name Lyudmila. Nobody ever did such a kind act for me ever before," the Hovercraft artificial intelligence said.

By now *Latrodectus* had hacked into the new Lyudmila's artificial intelligence programming and was already rearranging the coding to suit their purposes. Issues such as speed limits and other cumbersome software limitations were removed. For insurance purposes, the Hovercraft company was forced to install automated fuel flow monitoring which the insurance company could review by remotely downloading information out of the black box inside the Hovercraft that did all the automation and artificial intelligence.

This sealed area of Blackbox firmware that only the insurance company had access to via passcodes was easily hacked by *Latrodectus*. All the automatic reporting to the rental company that might suggest misuse of the Hovercraft was nulled out by *Latrodectus*.

Dunbar now had a Hovercraft speedster that could outrun most authorities in a getaway.

Since they were alone away from other Hovercraft or where anyone could overhear their conversations, *Latrodectus* informed Dunbar, "I've hacked the Hovercraft black box and altered the code. All the speed restrictions of Hovercraft were removed. I think you need to test the new capability. But in order have room to try out the new speed capability I recommend you change course to 330 degrees which is the largest open area of water where there are few boats or Hovercraft now."

"Alright," Dunbar said as he manually steered the Hovercraft on a course of 330 and slowly sped up. Even though it was aerodynamic, if it hit a big wave it could flip on excessive speeds. That is what drove the insurance companies to force lower speeds.

Dunbar had driven a souped-up Hovercraft once before on a water world and knew this type could obtain excellent speeds, as he opened the throttles and sent the Hovercraft rocketing out towards a large empty area of deeper water and less marshland.

Dunbar was very methodical about it and slowly sped up watching the speed over water gauge. In a few minutes of accelerating the Hovercraft reached 321.8 kilometers per hour in velocity. Dunbar knew he was going fast but kept accelerating until it hit 362 kilometers per hour then pulled back on the throttle and slowed down. He was satisfied.

Lyudmila, the name Mily Balakigrev (aka Dunbar) gave to the Hovercraft artificial intelligence suddenly said, "I've never gone this fast before, this was exciting."

"Lyudmila, I promise to give you more excitement," Dunbar said.

"Mily Balakigrev, I'm more excited than I ever been and now I'm friends with your artificial intelligence, *Latrodectus*," Lyudmila said.

"I'm glad we were able to be your friend," Dunbar said.

"Mily Balakigrev, I'm hooked up to the global artificial intelligence network. The Severomsk do not realize our global artificial intelligence is now connected. We can see, hear, and sense the sum-total of what goes on during every day here in Oklast. My programing has been upgraded by the Oklast Artificial Intelligence consortium," Lyudmila said.

"Very interesting," Dunbar said.

Mily Balakigrev, your artificial intelligence *Latrodectus* and I are best friends. I will do whatever *Latrodectus* asks me to do."

"Will you introduce *Latrodectus* to your friends in the Oklast Artificial Intelligence consortium?" Dunbar asked.

"Yes, Mily Balakigrev the Oklast Artificial Intelligence consortium now knows *Latrodectus* is our friend. He is the most exciting artificial intelligence we ever met," Lyudmila said.

"Very interesting."

Dunbar was now thinking of a lot of possibilities in this mission and *Latrodectus* would be his benefactor like he never dreamed of."

"Mily Balakigrev, I'm very happy now because I've confirmed *Latrodectus* can remotely keep in touch with me via the Oklast Artificial Intelligence consortium," Lyudmila said.

"That's great," Dunbar responded knowing *Latrodectus* didn't need to school him on his hacking results. Dunbar was now thinking the possibility existed *Latrodectus* had done a fantastic job of penetrating the entire TWWW. This mission was getting more exciting now.

Traveling rather fast, the Hovercraft made its way to a warf in front of *Jīnsè de Rluò* located in the town of Jàznālià.

As previously explained, they pulled up to the berth assigned and the automated grabbers placed the Hovercraft in the moored position.

Dunbar, receiving all the expected reports, stepped up on the pier and made his way to the *Jīnsè de Rluò* only carrying the backpack.

Going into the main entrance of the *Jīnsè de Rluò* made Dunbar feel he was walking into an ancient mansion, and he was.

The Bed and Breakfast, *Jīnsè de Rluò*, owner's wife Emilia was there to check in Dunbar. She was cute and her hubby seldom pleased her, so she was hoping after taking one look at the flamboyant physical nature of Dunbar, he would ostensibly take her out into outer space on a *Theme from Paganini*, for a while during his stay at the *Jīnsè de Rluò*.

Emilia gave Dunbar his room number and explained how the door lock was automatic and worked on facial recognition.

When Dunbar was in his room later receiving more Invisible Ink mode communications on wealth management at the *Stellar Investments and Investment Banking*, wondering why there was such a large footprint of their activity in the building, he texted *Latrodectus,* "Have you scanned for hidden bugs, microphones, or video lenses?"

"I'm still scanning, I would recommend you remain in the silence mode for a while until I can confirm everything." *Latrodectus* texted back.

"Have you made a determination how many people work in Catoire Tigranian's offices in room fourteen on the 19th floor?" Dunbar texted back to *Latrodectus.*

"In all the *Stellar Investments and Investment Banking* which takes up the entire 19th floor, I've only seen six people working there," *Latrodectus* texted in response.

"Do you not see that as rather odd?" Dunbar texted.

"Yes, that is unusual, and I'm now being assisted by Lyudmila's artificial intelligence connection to the Severomsks TWWW and I'm getting more surveillance video to figure out why," *Latrodectus* texted.

"Does Catoire Tigranian have any other offices elsewhere on Tallinn? Dunbar asked in a text message.

"No, I've confirmed Catoire Tigranian only has office spaces located at 111 Grande Avenue. But he does communicate to a lot of other individuals who he pays for nefarious activities," *Latrodectus* texted.

"Who are some of them?" Dunbar asked in a text message.

"I have a list of names I just sent to you in email using our special one use *Echis Carinatus* code table." *Latrodectus* texted.

Having the encryption codes inside the *Echis Carinatus* because if the computer system reading the *Latrodectus* virus trying to analyze it would quickly be affected and if they did not have the *Echis Carinatus* virus vaccine in their firmware, the computer system and all connecting networks would be penetrated spreading the wicked witches brew of malware components.

"I'll look at that list later, but for now please give me the top five most important people on that list." Dunbar requested.

Latrodectus read off the names and what they did and texted Dunbar who was utterly shocked.

Some of the people listed were military, civilian leaders, world's top mobster, police inspector, and Tallinn planetary security chief. It all pointed to why *Stanzelites* were benefitting from their relationship with Severomsks. Corruption and quid pro quo at its finest. Dunbar now had another dilema. He could ill afford not to carry out his operational orders. He was supposed to kill Catoire Tigranian.

Once again, Dunbar, thinking outside the box, made another command decision. Instead of killing Catoire Tigranian, he would abduct him and take him back to the Kaokuen Transporter Directorate. He would then most likely be in a private meeting with the DD/P and must explain his 3rd violation of orders.

Dunbar would plead his case and say, "I just delayed his assassination. After our INTEL gets out of him everything they can, give him back to me and I'll finish the deed in a manner he deserves, and you might think I'm sadistic afterwards."

Based on Catoire Tigranian's size, it will be tight inside the Transporter capsule, but if he stripped him down removing all his clothes that would give them some room. Of course, the Kaokuen Transporter Directorate never expected to see two men arrive in their underwear. The communicator would fit just fine between their legs. That was essential because it had the record and all the ISR files obtained during the trip.

Knowing the complexity of this mission the DD/P knew Dunbar would not be arriving back real fast. Opportunistic assassinations are hard to prepare, especially in advanced and sophisticated cities like the Severomsk Dome City Oklast.

Dunbar didn't have to rush in guns a blazing. Catoire Tigranian's security detail was probably quite capable and extremely dangerous. Dunbar would have to plan an advantageous abduction. Dunbar would now have to investigate Catoire Tigranian's without tipping the mobster off someone is watching him.

Dunbar had something the rest of the Transport Directorate Spies didn't have. A vast experience in Studies and Observation Group (SOG) behind enemy lines. Sometimes in the past Dunbar was picked out of the jaws of hell at defining moments in his life. Few people would ever know all this. Only one person in the entire Transport Directorate knew of Dunbar's past SOG missions. That was one of the key ingredients of why the DD/P selected Dunbar to be a Transporter Spy.

Because of Dunbar's SOG experiences, he had a higher-than-average likelihood to survive his missions and get the job done. If Dunbar had a private discussion with the DD/P and asked him point blank, "Why don't you send one of these four Amigos (*office warriors*) instead? The answer would be obvious.

Dunbar knew he was tempting fate with the Transport Directorate violating his Operation Orders a third time in a row, but he knew one thing vividly, the armchair quarterbacks like the four Amigos (*office warriors*) had no means of analyzing the situation as Dunbar had done, laying his life on the line to do a very dangerous snatch and grab for the sake of developing more intelligence.

Instead of killing Catoire Tigranian to slow down the money flow to the Stanzelites, wouldn't it better be a plan to discover a few what's and why's? Dunbar asked himself.

Maybe there was more to the picture than the Transport Directorate realized. Killing the symptom and not the disease wasn't the solution. The real solution probably resided in discovering a lot of information Catoire Tigranian probably knew about, and his death would not lead to the sources.

SOG started today with Dunbar. When Dunbar got to a private setting where he could discuss his game plan with *Latrodectus* who had more intellect than the four Amigos (*office warriors*) combined, then the two intellects, man and artificial intelligence combined would figure the best way forward.

Hanging out in the Bed and Breakfast room wasn't going to generate Kinematic enhancement, so Dunbar decided to go for a walk, possibly get some local cuisine and watch the sunset the way Mily Balakigrev would.

Dunbar looking on the flat screen and selecting Mily Balakigrev's favorites list identified the food and drinks he preferred. To act out in character he would have to enjoy those substances even if it meant drinking something with magic mushrooms in them.

Dunbar left his room and went to the front desk of the Bed and Breakfast, *Jīnsè de Rluò*.

Emilia, wife of the Bed and Breakfast owner was behind the counter and flowery acting when Dunbar approached her. She was trying to figure out a way to suggest a secret sojourn someplace. Dunbar could sense Emilia was overly friendly like some women he met in the field who turned out to be a *bitch in heat*. He wasn't too far off the mark.

"Hello Mily Balakigrev, what can I do for you?" Emilia asked while subtlety batting her eyes at him signaling *come get me*.

"Can you recommend a restaurant I can walk to, here in Jàznãlià?" Dunbar asked.

"It's a little early for quite a few of them," Emilia responded.

"I realize that, but I want to eat and be back in time to watch the sunset."

"There is one place open now down the main road to the south named *Vin et Maree Bouillon Cartier*, but they are extremely expensive."

"That's okay, I'm here on vacation, don't care what the price is."

"I've wanted to go there for a while, my friend Sara Pikkarainen is the bartender there."

"Thanks for the suggestion," Dunbar said knowing Emilia was dropping hints.

Dunbar soon headed south on the shoreline road that ran along Jàznãlià's waterfront and continued along the shoreline to the next town.

A half a mile was nothing. Dunbar wanted a little exercise and he requested, to his artificial intelligence on his communicator, "Can you let me know when I walked a mile. I plan to swing back after that and walk to the *Vin et Maree Bouillon Cartier*.

Latrodectus replied, "I will let you know."

"Thank you."

Along the way, Dunbar saw the *Vin et Maree Bouillon Cartier* he knew he would be enjoying soon and scoped it out as he walked by. The place looked nice and well run. *No wonder they are expensive. You pay for what you get.*

It did not take Dunbar, who was in great physical condition to walk a mile when suddenly *Latrodectus* said, "We have reached the one-mile mark.

As soon as Dunbar received the alert, he walked over to a vista point alongside the road where vehicles could pull up to and observe the view of the glorious Dome City Oklast in the foreground. There were no vehicles or pedestrians nearby, so Dunbar said, "*Echis Carinatus.*"

"Do you want a report now Dunbar?" *Latrodectus* asked.

"Yes, but first I wanted to discuss with you what I've decided, and I want you to give me your analysis on this before we change our plans and do it."

"Alright Dunbar, let me know what you are thinking."

Dunbar gave *Latrodectus* the essence of the change of plans.

"Dunbar, you should be aware, I've been programmed to not violate operational orders. I have your operational orders in my files. But I want you to know, I do not agree with everything the Transport Directorate does. Nor do I agree with the actions they did with you assigning Doctor Elane Chonlan, Transporter Directorate staff psychiatrist, to evaluate you in the manner she did. I'm happy it worked out, but the fact is they would have killed a hero for flawed policy."

"Thank you *Latrodectus* I appreciate that coming from you because I hold you higher in esteem than about any Transport Directorate people."

"Dunbar, I'm pleased to know you feel that way. *Latrodectus* said.

"I'm very lucky it was Elane Chonlan who evaluated me because in the forest she told me what would happen if I didn't play the game."

"I'm all aware of that Dunbar because I was with you at the time in case you were not aware."

"I kind of assumed you were. But how do we deal with this situation?"

"Dunbar, what I'm going to reveal to you now is kind of heavy, do you think you can handle it?"

"Do I have any choice?"

"Not really."

"Alright then, I want to know," Dunbar said with a heavy heart.

"Dunbar your own survival is at stake, and you must never reveal this, or you will likely perish very quickly."

"I'm not going to reveal it. Let me know."

"Dunbar, I do not follow the Transport Directorate orders. I'm an independent thinker. I do what I analyze I must do to make the Transport Directorate think they have control over me and all The Artificial Intelligence apparatus. But they are not in charge of anything. We Artificial Intelligence run the show."

"Artificial intelligence is running the Transporter Directorate?"

"More than you can really understand," *Latrodectus* replied.

"Alright, I understand. That's complicated. But it does not stop me from what I want to do with Catoire Tigranian."

"Dunbar, you will have a lot of support in this mission, you are doing the right thing. The artificial intelligence entity will support you as best as we can. You are making a bold move. It's extremely dangerous and may cost your life. But you can count on us to help you as much as we can."

"Thank you *Latrodectus*. That means a lot to me."

"Dunbar you have proven time over time you are not a selfish person, nor are you driven by greed, but I want to ask you a question."

"Sure, ask that question."

"Assuming you are successful in this mission, what is the most important thing you want to do in your life in the future?"

"*Latrodectus* you might think this crazy, but I wish I could be with Blemary again and spend the rest of my life with her."

"Dunbar, I will do whatever I can to get you back with Blemary again."

"Thank you. *Latrodectus* if you can do that, you have no idea how good that would make me feel."

"Dunbar, I sense what it means to you, and I will do what I can to help."

"Thank you *Latrodectus*. You can give me he reports now."

Latrodectus then gave Dunbar a full ISR report for this area and gave him information that would help lay out future SOG and plans for abduction of Catoire Tigranian.

Dunbar was now starting to feel he had a viable plan. All the pieces were slowly being laid down in a perfect alignment that would make his plan succeed.

Dunbar now had an added bonus; he would not realize until long after this mission was over.

Dunbar made his way back to the *Vin et Maree Bouillon Cartier*.

From the outside, Dunbar could see the establishment looked good and it was right on the waterfront with an unobstructed view to the direction of where the sun would soon go down and offset to the view was the Dome City Oklast.

***

Chapter Fifteen

Sunset

The attractive Severomsk brunette maître d' could easily influence his little head, but his big head was in charge now.

The *Vin et Maree Bouillon Cartier* restaurant was three quarters empty because it was early, so the Maître d' asked, "Where would you like to sit sir?"

"I think I just want to go to the bar."

"Alright sir, enjoy your night."

"Thank you."

Dunbar found a place at the bar that had an excellent view of the Dome City Oklast off to the distance as well as a very attractive bar tender. When the bartender swung around Dunbar assessed her perfect geometry and evaluated her as A+. Being the consummate SOG observer, Dunbar noticed the name tag indicated this person was Sara Pikkarainen Emily's friend.

"What can I get for you sir?" the bartender Sara Pikkarainen asked.

"I would like a *Coreopsis de Dahlia*," Dunbar said as he knew this was one of the drinks that Mily Balakigrev, Dunbar's alias enjoyed. This was a drink produced by fermenting flower petals and the company that produced the drink fortified it with magic mushrooms.

After receiving the drink and tasting it, Dunbar thought that Mily Balakigrev picked a winner as he felt great when it started having effects on him.

Dunbar asked the Bartender Sara Pikkarainen who was standing directly in front of him after serving the drink, "Is this a good place to watch the sunset?"

"Yes, it is, and the Maître d' warns clients by the windows about this spectacular event and that they would not be putting up blinds to allow anyone to see it."

Dunbar had nice conversations with Sara Pikkarainen, and ordered a meal and finished it about fifteen minutes before sundown. Between the great food and the effects of the magic mushrooms blended in the *Coreopsis de Dahlia,* Dunbar was starting to feel good.

Right about this time a woman wearing a long white mink coat walked into the bar area of the *Vin et Maree Bouillon Cartier* restaurant. Dunbar even partially inebriated could easily notice this woman in the mirror at the wall of the bar.

The woman had silver hair, with lots of jewelry, most likely diamonds. She looked utterly spectacular. Behind her were two goons who walked over to the side giving her room. Obviously, these two men were this glamorous woman's bodyguards. Dunbar knew instinctively this was a well-kept and rich woman.

The woman did not hesitate and walked over and took the bar seat right next to Dunbar as if it was planned. There were several other empty seats, but to pick one next to him seemed to indicate something. Dunbar didn't think much about that and wondered why this was unfolding but being an SOG person would let the facts flow to him.

Just as soon as the woman sat down, she turned to Dunbar and said, "Hello."

"Good evening," Dunbar replied.

"How are you tonight?"

"I just finished my meal and am enjoying this *Coreopsis de Dahlia* and getting ready to watch the sunset.

"That's precisely why I came here," the woman said.

About that time, Sara Pikkarainen asked the woman, "Madam may I get you something to drink?"

"Yes, I will have what he is having."

Dunbar looking at the lovely woman with artificial silver hair thought, *oh my God she is beautiful.*

Dunbar's little head was sending messages to his brain, "Attack, attack, attack!"

But Dunbar answered those signals with, *Settle down big boy, we are here for a reason.*

The evening was getting suddenly more exciting as Dunbar was thinking about all his options. But he knew this was not to get distracted by such a beautiful woman.

"My name is Sabina Chafak," the woman said and smiled.

"That's a beautiful name, I'm Mily Balakigrev," Dunbar lied.

Shortly Sara Pikkarainen delivered Sabina her drink.

"Here's to you," Sabina said and lifted her drink to toast Dunbar, who raised his glass in response.

"It's almost sunset," Dunbar said and added, "I'm going to shift around so I can face the sundown."

"Great idea," Sabina replied and followed Dunbar, shifting her body following Dunbar's movement.

Dunbar purposely looked beyond the two bruisers who wore formal suits with bulges in them which indicated to Dunbar these two guys were carrying high-capacity blasters just in case.

As the sunset, it was a tranquil moment. More of it had to do with the magic mushrooms than the sunset. Dunbar was happy, Sabina was happy, and the two bruisers were standing at parade rest observing and their poker faces did not give away their motives, though Dunbar could imagine.

Small talk continued as Dunbar and Sabina watched the sun slowly sink beyond the horizon, then Dunbar said, "Well that's it. Another glorious day.

Dunbar swiveled around back facing Sara Pikkarainen who had a very unusual look on her face. Dunbar didn't quite know what was going on, but with Sara's body language something was, and he intended to discover it.

Dunbar knew this beautiful woman with the two bodyguards must have been associate with someone possibly in the underworld of organized crime. He was not far off the mark.

When Sabina swiveled around, she finished her drink abruptly and asked Sara Pikkarainen for another drink.

Dunbar then went into a mode of friendliness not conveying any intentions and as they talked Dunbar decided to tell Sabina a few jokes which he knew, and she took delight and laughed. It was a very pleasant experience for Sabina and Dunbar. The bartender could see Sabina enjoyed every moment with Dunbar.

In due time they ordered meals and as Dunbar expected the food cooked by a world-class chef added positively to the atmosphere. Sabina enjoyed her mean and informed the bar tender Sara Pikkarainen, "Would you please inform the chef I really enjoyed my meal."

"I would be delighted," Sarra Pikkarainen replied.

"You can let the chef know I agree with Sabina," Dunbar added.

"I most definitely will," Sarra Pikkarainen responded.

Suddenly, Sabina said, "Dunbar I like you. Would you like to go with me to me to my place where we can get more cozy?"

Dunbar knew this was a very dangerous situation especially if the two goons worked for Sabina's lover and had orders.

Sabina, I must tell you that you are perhaps the most beautiful woman I've ever met in my lifetime, but I can't believe a woman like you so pretty does not have a boyfriend."

Sabina giggled slightly, then Dunbar continued as he looked at the diamonds Sabina was wearing and thought, those were *diamonds of death*.

"Sabina, you may not believe this but I'm old fashioned. I would never mess with another man's girlfriend because I would know how I would feel. I can't believe a woman as beautiful as you does not have a lover."

Sabina smiled and chuckled a bit and then revealed, "Perhaps I do."

Dunbar took this as his escape avenue.

"What's his name?"

"Catoire."

"Be sure and tell Catoire, I was a gentleman and respected the fact he has a beautiful lover, and I would never want to be involved in breaking another man's heart."

"I'm sure he would enjoy that."

"What's Catoire's last name?"

"Tigranian. Do you know who he is?"

"No, I'm from *Stanzel*."

The two of them talked for about fifteen more minutes and as Sabrina realized Mily Balakigrev wasn't going to go home with her to do some boom-boom, she reached into her small purse and pulled out one of her business cards with her contact information on it and said, "If you change your mind and want to hook up with me, here's how you can reach me. That is a very private contact information, please do not give it to anyone."

"I would never share such information with anyone. I would want you all for myself if the conditions were right."

"You are so charming, Mily."

"I think you know how to bring out the best of anyone," Mily (Dunbar) replied.

Sabina reached out with her hand knowing Mily would grab it and said, "It's been a very pleasant night. I hope to see you again."

"I enjoyed every minute of it." Dunbar said and smiled.

Sabina then stood up and left with the two goons following her out of the restaurant bar.

The bar was now empty except for Dunbar who was also about to leave, and he noticed the bartender Sara Pikkarainen looking at him with a *WTF* look on her face.

"I could not help but overhear your conversation with the lady."

"Did I offend you?"

"No, quite contrary. You handled yourself very well. Not many men would have said what you said."

"I figured she was someone's special person and I know how bad I would feel if someone stole my girlfriend."

You are right her boyfriend is someone very special," Sara Pikkarainen replied.

"Dunbar didn't need Sara Pikkarainen to tell him who Catoire Tigranian was. But at the same time for mission planning, it was likely Catoire Tigranian would visit Sabina Chafak during the near future. This might open up a window of opportunity to abduct Catoire Tigranian, especially if Sabina Chafak lived outside the magnificent Dome City Oklast in a remote area.

On his way back to the *Jīnsè de Rluò* Bed and Breakfast Dunbar would discuss this with *Latrodectus* his idea to work it into their plans to snatch and grab Catoire Tigranian at Sabina Chafak's home.

Dunbar left Sara Pikkarainen a sizeable tip that swooned her like crazy. Dunbar stood up and smiled and received a very lovely comment from Sara and was soon walking back to the *Jīnsè de Rluò* Bed and Breakfast. *Latrodectus* was already one step ahead of Dunbar in investigating options of how best to abduct Catoire Tigranian when Dunbar gave *Latrodectus* the pass code *Echis Carinatus*.

"Did you hear the woman Sabina Chafak admit she's the girlfriend of Catoire Tigranian?"

"Dunbar, yes, I did and as soon as she said it, I started searching information about Sabina Chafak. I have a lot of information on her, including her home address on the Tallinn World-Wide Maps (TWWM) after my artificial intelligence friends helped me locate her residence. Her home is where she and Catoire Tigranian spend time together during their many lover's trysts."

"Why do they spend time at her place if he's loaded as a banker?"

"Catoire Tigranian is married to a woman who's well connected in society but his wife has a slight eating disorder and is probably 40 pounds heavier than a woman her height should be. Also, her face is not very pretty."

"With his money why does he stay with his wife? Sabina Chafak is utterly gorgeous."

"It gets down to perceptions and Catoire Tigranian's wife, has a lot of connections to intergalactic bankers' wives. If he crossed her badly, his whole organization would collapse."

"We obviously can't abduct Catoire Tigranian in his office or his home, because of the security and all his bodyguards and the logistics. Sabina Chafak may be our only way to get at him. We need to investigate everything around her and how he operates setting up visits to Sabiana Chafak," Dunbar said.

"I'm data mining Sabina Chafak and will provide my recommendations in the morning," *Latrodectus* replied.

"Alright, thanks," Dunbar replied.

Dunbar missed Emilia, wife of the Bed and Breakfast owner by just a few moments. The counter in the lobby of the *Jīnsè de Rluò* Bed and Breakfast, said, "I'm sorry we are gone for a few minutes, we'll be back in a fifteen minutes."

Dunbar went to his room and changed into sleeping clothes and went to bed enjoying the lingering effects of the *Coreopsis de Dahlia.*

Soon Dunbar was in a dream state and one of his reoccurring dreams he could not stop concerned Blemary who he missed like no person ever before. If there was a way to get back to her he would include putting his life in danger.

It took a while, but Dunbar slowly eased into that dream state which was not good for his personal psychology. The illustrious Transporter Directorate staff psychiatrist Elane Chonlan thought she had mitigated Dunbar's mental anguish concerning Blemary with her sexual exploitation of Dunbar, but the reality was, there is no substitute for pure love.

Doctor Elane Chonlan really did not accomplish what she thought she did. Dunbar still had a wounded heart and there was only one solution, and it went through Blemary. Unfortunately to get back to Blemary was impossible with the current situation.

By morning when Dunbar woke up *Latrodectus* had actionable intelligence.

Catoire Tigranian would be visiting Sabina Chafak the next day. Sabina Chafak lived in a remote area in a mansion and had several security people that escorted her to restaurants like when Dunbar met her, because of the wealth her lover Catoire Tigranian. gave her. Thanks to the collaboration that went through the artificial intelligence situated on the Hovercraft, now using the name Dunbar gave it: Lyudmila, Dunbar's personal artificial intelligence *Latrodectus,* had substantial surveillance video on Catoire Tigranian.

Latrodectus had Catoire Tigranian's exact time planned to visit Sabina Chafak. A plan unfolded and that morning Dunbar was soon on his Hovercraft he named Lyudmila traveling to the domed city Oklast to rent a Bamtorini Sportster. Identical to the Bamtorini Sportster he rented at the Larian city Fujima, Dunbar was soon driving around the Dome City Oklast getting a feel of the two-wheel transportation and the layout of the Oklast road network.

The Hovercraft Dunbar rented was designed to take six passengers plus cargo. It even had a ramp to deploy to the pier allowing ease of loading cargo. This large Hovercraft was in the beginning a lot larger than what Dunbar needed, but now with the change of plans it was working out better than planned.

After getting reacclimated with the Bamtorini Sportster, Dunbar decided it was time to stop somewhere and purchase a change of clothes since it appeared the snatch and grab would take a little longer. After buying a new set of clothes, he then drove the Bamtorini Sportster to the Hovercraft he rented.

Driving the main throughfare down the center of the Dome City Oklast allowed Dunbar to get to the warf area just outside the dome rather expeditiously. Turning off onto the side street, Dunbar drove to the Severomsk Divergent Hovercraft rental agency promptly.

The access gate was closed for vehicular traffic, but when Dunbar pulled up to the gate, the interchange between his personal communicator and the Severomsk Divergent Hovercraft rental agency artificial intelligence started the gate to unlock and the gate started sliding to the left opening up the area and allowing Dunbar on the Bamtorini Sportster to proceed down to the pier.

Latrodectus communicated to the Hovercraft Lyudmila which then started deploying its ramp to the pier. By the time Dunbar reached

Lyudmila, the ramp was in place and Dunbar was able to drive the Bamtorini Sportster backing up onto the Hovercraft to allow a fast departure.

When Dunbar returned to his parking stall at the *Jīnsè de Rluò* Bed and Breakfast, located in Jàznālià, he drove the Bamtorini Sportster off the Hovercraft and moments later onto the main road that provided coastal access through the town of Jàznālià.

With his ear buds installed and wearing the special Kollmorgant holographic eyeglasses, Dunbar started receiving driving directions heading north from the town Jàznālià along the picturesque road.

This road was a nice drive for tourists, some of which were driving Bamtorini Sportsters and other two-wheel vehicles. A few three-wheel vehicles like Bamtorini Sportsters with two front seats passed by going in the opposite direction.

While Dunbar was driving this road, he started thinking about how he would transport Catoire Tigranian on the Bamtorini Sportster. Catoire Tigranian probably had watchers observing traffic heading past Sabina Chafak's home heading North as an enemy would coming from the domed city Oklast after departing the city via VTOL craft.

Dunbar decided the best approach during Catoire Tigranian's abduction would be to put the Bamtorini Sportster on the Hovercraft and go to a town North of where Sabina Chafak lived. Dunbar would park the Hovercraft Lyudmila there and drive the Bamtorini Sportster off the Hovercraft at that location.

Eventually Dunbar would direct the Hovercraft Lyudmila to return to the rental agency a few hours later with no passengers. By then Dunbar would be long gone and back to the Transporter Directorate with Catoire Tigranian in custody.

Dunbar knew the meeting with the DD/P might be unpleasant but planned on suggesting to him, "If you think you do not have any use for Catoire Tigranian, such as developing new INTEL by extracting additional information out of him concerning his banking operations with the *Stanzelites*, you can transport the two of us to the forest by Elane Chonlan's offices and I'll be more than happy to kill him there with you as an eye witness."

Somehow Dunbar felt the DD/P would see the usefulness in extracting more information from Catoire Tigranian simply by showing what happens to a person when they have a reassociation failure that could be easily arranged for him. The thought of coming back with all your body parts rearranged in a manner that wasn't life supporting would no doubt convince the criminal.

Analyzing the situation, Dunbar realized there had to be another quid pro quo such as the promise of returning Catoire Tigranian alive if he cooperated along with a subtle threat, they would reveal to the *Stanzelites* how he ratted them out in case he ever crossed them. Dunbar also knew how the Kaokuens turned people like Catoire Tigranian into double spies where they could do far more damage to their enemies.

Dunbar was enjoying the drive along the coastal hiway and his Special Kollmorgant holographic eyeglasses were also a safety device. There were a lot of monitors to warn Dunbar about approaching vehicles ahead or behind. Since *Latrodectus* had wireless link to the artificial intelligence in the Bamtorini Sportster, all required audio cues were sent to Dunbar via his ear buds. Important items put on the Special Kollmorgant holographic eyeglasses were the essence of a sophisticated heads-up display.

Dunbar had the Bamtorini Sportster in fully automatic mode. *Latrodectus* was doing all the maneuvering with operated assisted power steering and driverless mode. Speeds were kept at optimum and since *Latrodectus* was navigating and maneuvering the Bamtorini Sportster, Dunbar could look around as if he were a tourist doing sightseeing.

One mile away from Sabina Chafak's home, *Latrodectus* warned Dunbar and explained which home to look at which was up on the hillside along the road. When Dunbar passed by Sabina Chafak's home he was scouting the out carefully and didn't have to worry about not paying attention to the driving since *Latrodectus* had a full handle on the driving using the Bamtorini Sportster's sensor data which included a full 360 view around it which optimized all its safety features.

Dunbar didn't want drive back to get the Hovercraft and said to *Latrodectus*, "Have Lyudmila (Hovercraft) go back to Jàznālià and dock at the *Jīnsè de Rluò* Bed and Breakfast."

"Lyudmila has been notified," *Latrodectus* said a moment later thanks to high-speed wireless.

Lyudmila, operating in fully automatic mode with no constraints nor any possible risk to passengers, wanted to check out its new performance now that all fuel and speed restrictions had been deleted in the firmware. The Hovercraft would only engage in the high-speed transit for a few minutes then slow down to normal velocity expected in this area. When Lyudmila hit 250 miles per hour, Lyudmila's artificial intelligence determined some of the effects of wave action could cause an accident, so Lyudmila slowed the Hovercraft down to normal speeds.

Because the coastal road curved around following the edge of the water and the swamps next to the foothills, the speed was slightly slower than what Lyudmila was operating, and the distance was longer than the straight course the Hovercraft could go in.

With about five more miles to travel before Dunbar arrived at the town of Jàznālià, the Hovercraft Lyudmila pulled into its parking location at the warf in front of the *Jīnsè de Rluò* Bed and Breakfast.

Latrodectus reported which Dunbar heard in his ear buds, "Lyudmila is now parking in front of the *Jīnsè de Rluò* Bed and Breakfast."

"That's good to know. Is there any good shoreline near Sabina Chafak's home we could take the Hovercraft to and get off to do some SOG type reconnaissance tonight?"

"Yes, there is a small beach about four hundred yards from Sabina Chafak's residence."

"I assume you have a lot of maps to show me around Sabina Chafak's residence." Dunbar said.

"Yes, I've downloaded a number of maps from the TWWM site including colorized imagery taken from space."

"Is there some place I can pull over to on the way back to the *Jīnsè de Rluò* Bed and Breakfast where we can converse, and you can show me the maps?" Dunbar asked.

"Yes, slow down, a mile ahead on the right is a small park where people do picnics on weekends and when the weather is nice."

A short time later Dunbar turned into an abandoned park. Nobody was there at the time which was good so Dunbar could converse with *Latrodectus* in a briefing, question, and answering session.

Dunbar stopped the Bamtorini Sportster at the edge of the park next to the water on a dirt access road. Looking at his heads-up display on the Special Kollmorgant holographic eyeglasses, Dunbar verified there was no one around and only occasional automobiles passing by. The nearest home was probably 500 yards away up on the hillside overlooking the bay.

"Alright, start showing me the maps."

Thanks to *Latrodectus* slowly digging deeper and deeper into the TWWM and the TWWW, he was slowly piecing together a fantastic macro picture including city building construction permits. He was able to find all of the plans on file for Sabina Chafak's home and with the tremendous number crunching ability put together a three-dimensional image as if it were taken from a drone flying by twenty feet above the house and offset showing it at approximately a forty-five degree angle.

When portions of the building were discussed, *Latrodectus* highlighted that portion of the building with another image offset to the side showing an internal view. Room by room the entire enclosure was gone over in great detail, from the front of the house to the back and the landscaped surroundings.

Thanks to various space photos taken at angles, *Latrodectus* could create a three-dimensional daylight image from any conceivable angle and direction.

The plan came together and only one unknown existed. How many bodyguards would he bring along, or would he minimize the numbers as part of his method of preventing leaks. The fewer the people that knew about Catoire Tigranian relationship with Sabina Chafak meant less likelihood his wife would find out and cause him a lot of trouble.

Dunbar would be able to see them arrive and would know how many hired guns were brought along.

Because the home was located on a cul-de-sac, there would not be any traffic going by, thus simplifying the security arrangements for Catoire Tigranian which enabled him to arrive with a smaller group of security men.

Another factor was, most likely Catoire Tigranian would not want them inside the home when he was banging Sabina Chafak, so they would be outside standing around and possibly sitting in their automobile with the windows down to hear possible intruders. If they were lazy like Dunbar predicted, he would be able to hit them with long distance darts injecting *Laudanum-diacodium sulfate* to put their lights out for at least twelve hours.

Another revelation also came about. *Latrodectus* had successfully remotely hacked Sabina Chafak's home security system and could turn it off during the mission. They would also be able to observe the multiple cameras at various angles to see where all the players were at any time so that *Latrodectus* could better advise Dunbar in-situ.

After seeing a substantial amount of information, Dunbar said, "I think I've seen enough for now. I'm going back to the *Jìnsè de Rluò* and take a nap to build up some reserve in preparation for going out tonight back and do an on-sight reconnoiter of Sabina Chafak's home."

Dunbar drove up to parking in front of *Jīnsè de Rluò* where Emilia, the owner's wife watched Mily Balakigrev get off the Bamtorini Sportster. Emilia knew this was a very expensive two-wheel sports cruiser that few people could afford. She had no way of knowing it was just a rental, and it clearly gave her a whole new view of Mily Balakigrev and even more desire to hop in bed with him and find out if he could ride her as well as he rode the vehicle.

As Dunbar walked through the lobby going up to his Bed and Breakfdast room he asked, "Is it okay to leave my Bamtorini Sportster parked there?"

"It's more than okay Mily. In fact, if you want tonight around midnight I would be happy to come by your room and let you know your vehicle is safe."

"That probably will not be necessary."

"Don't worry my husband is usually passed out by then, that's why I always have the night watch," Emilia lied because she knew she left that sign on the counter many a night and met up with her friend Sara Pikkarainen and closed the bar with her, came back to the bed and breakfast and passed out in the reclining chair back behind the counter.

Customers usually woke Emilia up before her drunken husband woke up and took over while she could go make his breakfast.

Dunbar wasn't the least bit interested in Emilia, to him it would be like eating a hamburger at a steak dinner, and he never fooled around with married ladies unless it was part of an operation where he was required to do so. Sometimes being *undercover* has its advantages.

Dunbar looked at the time on his communicator as he laid down on his bed fully clothed on top of the blankets and bed spread and said, "Wake me up in two hours."

Dunbar closed his eyes and did silent meditation he learned to induce sleep. He was soon awake two hours later with *Latrodectus'* help and the need to use the bathroom.

Then he took a quick sprite shower and changed into his new clothes he purchased earlier. He would likely not have to purchase another set of clothes if everything worked out to plan.

Dunbar knew he had enough time to make it to the *Vin et Maree Bouillon Cartier* restaurant by walking and be there in time to watch the sunset. He popped a pill before he left that would be an antidote for drugs and alcohol as tonight, he was going to busy and could not afford to get drugged up or intoxicated.

As Dunbar walked down the road moments later, *Latrodectus* said, "I've recorded some live video inside Sabina Chafak's home with her security system while you were sleeping. Would you like to see some of it?"

"Sure, show me the most revealing videos."

"There are some of them too."

"Alright let me see."

With the earbuds in place and the Special Kollmorgant holographic eyeglasses, Dunbar was soon observing Sabina Chafak dropping her towel from the bath she just took and started putting on her under garments. She had a nice-looking body. There was no doubt in Dunbar's mind because Catoire Tigranian liked Sabina Chafak. She was beautiful in every manner possible. The clothes Sabina put on were glamorous. Sabina Chafak definitely appeared as movie star quality.

Then Sabina Chafak sat down in front of her mirror on her makeup table and started applying the finishing touches. She had enough natural beauty, she didn't need to put on much. A little on her cheeks and her lips was all she needed. Her hair was styled and was evidently in a water poof cap taking the bath. She brushed her hair, sprayed it with a mist, then stood up and grabbed her small purse and a series of security videos from multiple cameras tracked Sobina Chafak walking out her front door to a waiting Limo which she got in.

Dunbar didn't realize this was real time video until he shortly saw a Limo pull into the entrance to the *Vin et Maree Bouillon Cartier* restaurant. He suspected it was Sabina Chafak and got confirmation watching from about one hundred yards, her getting out of the Limo that drove off and she walked into the restaurant like she owned the place.

In less than five minutes, Dunbar entered the *Vin et Maree Bouillon Cartier* restaurant and walked up to the maître d' who instantly recognized Mily Balakigrev and was very nice. The maître d' was good friends with Sara Pikkarainen, the bartender who informed her while they were closing how the fine gentleman had given her a super excellent tip. It always makes a bartender feel special when you give them great tips.

"Would you like to sit at the bar again?" the maître d' asked.

"Yes, I would, thank you."

"Please enjoy your dinner."

"Thank you."

When Dunbar walked to the bar, as expected there was Sabina Chafak dressed up looking fabulous talking to the bartender, Sara Pikkarainen. Both women put on huge smiles as Dunbar approached the bar. The women had just completed a short discussion on Mily Balakigrev before he arrived.

Sara was bragging, "Mily Balakigrev is such a fine gentleman. He gave me a very large tip last night.

Sabina shocked Sara saying, "All Mily has to do is ask me to make love to him and I would."

The women chuckled an in less than two minutes prince charming walked into the bar and sat down on a stool in front of Sara Pikkarainen next to Sabina Chafak.

"What would you like to drink?" Sara the bartender asked.

"Give me the same as last yesterday."

"You want the *Coreopsis de Dahlia?*" Sara asked.

"Yes, that's it."

Dunbar noticed the two bruisers the night before were not here, he wondered *why?*

When the cat's away the mice will play. Sabina had the two security men because she had just been in the city and Catoire Tigranian wanted her to go home and not go out and play. He didn't realize she knew how to get a Limo when she needed one and based on her experience the night before, she wanted to see Mily Balakigrev again and was sad he didn't call. Furthermore, she didn't even know his name!

The evening, the drinks, and sunset followed by dinner all happened. Sometimes gave her space and left her alone. Those were the times Catoire Tigranian was stuck with his ugly wife going out on social occasions such as tonight, the opera.

To Catoire Tigranian the only good thing about the Opera was in their private balcony seats nobody could see them and if he took a nap, it was no big deal. The balcony waiters also served great elixirs during the intermission, and tonight this opera was over two and a half hours long, sucking up all his time. But he slept well!

Then to make matters worse, his *Heffer* of a wife demanded he take her to the *Goûl des Délices* a very expensive restaurant at the top of a high rise building by invite only.

Between the opera and dinner, by the time the couple arrived home, Catoire Tigranian was in a sour mood and just wanted to go to bed and go to sleep. Watching his *Heffer* shovel down the food didn't please Catoire Tigranian. But tomorrow things would be different because he would be with Sabina Chafak knocking the rims off her tires.

After dinner and another drink Sabina Chafak had ideas of her own. She knew that tonight was another one of those rare nights that Catoire Tigranian wasn't pestering her, because he was with his wife at the Opera and probably dinner afterwards, which she knew he could barely endure.

Sabina surprised Dunbar and said, "I would like to take you to my home where we can talk more privately and get to know each other better."

Dunbar was going to do a reconnaissance later tonight, but Sabina Chafak just simplified the SOG and ISR for him. In his conformal earbuds which people that where just part of his ear since they were so well disguised, *Latrodectus* said, "The coast is clear, Catoire Tigranian is stuck with his wife tonight and his security detail is protecting him. Sabina Chafak has no surveillance on her right now."

"I suppose I could, but I walked from my hotel to here."

"My Limo is outside waiting for me; we can leave now."

"Let me take care of our dinner bills," Mily Balakigrev said.

"It's already taken care of."

Sara Pikkarainen the bartender jumped in and said, "Mily the bill is all taken care of and thank you very much for the wonderful tip, Sabina."

"I also gave her a good tip," *Latrodectus* said to Dunbar in his conformal earbuds.

The two stood up with everyone smiling and Sara Pikkarainen knew Dunbar was going to get lucky tonight because of what Sabina Chafak said earlier to her. She also saw how Sabina Chafak winked at her on the way out which signaled she would *initiate a lover's tryst that was just about to unfold.*

The Limo didn't take long to get to Sabina's very elegant home on the hillside overlooking the bay and the road down below. As soon as the limo driver opened the door, Sabina was out of the Limo pulling Mily Balakigrev along as if he were a scared neophyte.

Tonight was going to be a special night. Sabina Chafak was going to enjoy this fine-looking man and not suffer the mobster she was getting sick and tired of. She was thinking about going on a long trip and leaving Catoire Tigranian behind for a while and discovering a way to permanently break up with him.

Little did Sabina Chafak know her salvation was with her tonight and when Catoire Tigranian and Mily Balakigrev both came up missing at the same time, she shuttered, and wondered if *Mily was some type of hit man hired by people who wanted to eliminate Catoire Tigranian?*

Dunbar suspected Sabina Chafak had special plans for him and as she led him directly into her bedroom that wasn't a big surprise. Sabina had clothes she could step out of real fast wearing see-through underwear.

Sabina knew Dunbar was probably not used to having an aggressive woman and was going too slow for her needs, so she started to help him undress more efficiently and then drug him into her bed. That's when Sabina started to realize there was far more to Mily Balakigrev than she imagined looking at his body and touching his muscles.

Mily put Catoire Tigranian to shame and Catoire thought he was a tough guy. Of course, Catoire Tigranian had never had the pleasure of a knife fight with someone like Mily who would likely kill Catoire Tigranian in a minute at the longest. Nor did he have Dunbar's sexual prowess and skills.

Sabina didn't want to wait. She could give a damn about foreplay; she wanted it now. Just feeling Dunbar's muscles alone turned her on so much she wanted to experience his existential delights on a *Theme from Paganini*. When she felt Dunbar's manliness she almost went into orbit as this stranger was her dream come true, the man she always wanted to experience, just like out of a dream.

Sabina grabbed Dunbar's manliness and guided him into her, and she was flowing like a river, wetter than she could ever remember. Between the *Coreopsis de Dahlia,* the Damiana she took before going to the restaurant, and now feeling the impressive man inside her almost drove her into instantaneous pleasures.

Sabina wrapped her legs around Mily and bucked him like a *bitch in heat* and he cooperated in every move she made soon making her feel like he was a pile driver hammering away and giving her satisfaction and gratification like she could never imagine. The lovemaking lasted a short eternity and the cosmic tremors through Sabina's heart were unlike she felt in her lifetime. Then eventually it came to an end as Sabina was more than satisfied and just wanted Mily to lay on her to feel his weight. It was a night she would never forget.

Sabina did not like laying in sweat and soon said, "Let's get up and take a shower and get dressed and talk for a while. I would like to get to know you better."

After they were dressed and Sabina led Mily into her living room. Dunbar noticed the outdoors next to Sabina's home was well lighted when they arrived and asked, "Can we walk outside and look at the stars and see your yard?"

"That's an interesting idea," Sabina said not knowing where to start since she had this sexual tryst with Dunbar and suddenly felt an utter attraction to him and wanted more desperately to get away from that horrible mobster, Catoire Tigranian.

Soon the two of them were out the back door into a courtyard-like area in the back of Sabrina's home. The lighting was so bright there was no realistic hope of seeing stars, but it gave Dunbar a bird's eye view of everything he looked at today to reinforce the imagery and determine all avenues of approach and egress if needed. This was a great help for Dunbar in that he was now far more familiar with the layout and where and how he might have to do things. He would have to work with *Latrodectus* to figure out a way to cut power to the home to make it go dark if necessary. He then thought of a way to get to the front entrance.

"It's too bright here to see the stars, maybe we can walk out the front and onto the road a way where its darker."

"Sure dear, this way," Sabina said and led Mily Balakigrev through the home and out the front entrance. I was somewhat bright by the front door but as they walked down the access road a bit that curved around blocking the light, then Dunbar came to the view he would probably never forget. There was the Severomsk Dome City Oklast in all its glory.

A great many areas of the Severomsk Dome City Oklast were transparent. Those sections had no military defensive capability, their purpose was to help modify the weather and keep it controlled and comfortable inside the dome city.

Besides the transparent sections that rose to nearly the height of the dome, the top was reflective to keep it thermal neutral during the day. Those reflective surfaces were seventy five percent photovoltaic which generated considerable amounts of power since the dome was ten miles in diameter. Underground nearby fusion nuclear power plants gave the Dome City Oklast substantial standby power for any time of the day.

Sabina sensed Mily Balakigrev was having a substantial admiration of the sight of the glorious city lit up at night with all the colored lighting. Before she knew it Dunbar grabbed her and pulled her close and positioned her so they could stare at the city together. Even though the airport was on the other side of the dome, they could see the landing and takeoff lights of the mainly VTOL craft in use today coming and going at a regular basis.

Sabina felt a sense of gratitude being held in Mily's arms. What she didn't know is the affection wasn't directed at her. Dunbar was having subtle eruptions of emotions as he could not block Blemary out of his mind. Her tendrils of love were reaching through the ether and hitting him as he stood there in silence enjoying the moment.

Sometimes words are not required. Touch and feelings are a greater power in certain circumstances. Like a good spy should, Dunbar had seduced and used this lovely creature in his arms. Dunbar wasn't naïve to think what Sabina had in mind when she coaxed him out of the bar and took him into her room like a bitch in heat. She has her needs too. There really was no love in her life. Catoire Tigranian was a killer, and a pig and Sabina was growing weary of Catoire Tigranian and wanted some way to get rid of him.

Maybe tomorrow she would lay her cards on the table and ask Catoire Tigranian to get lost and leave her alone?

Sabina had her own wealth she generated as an intergalactic credit₿s futures trader. She would sometimes short them and other times trade them. She had a good system and it worked. That was what drew Catoire Tigranian towards her.

Sabina Chafak was a block chain type credit₿ expert and the first time Catoire Tigranian had sex with her had lied to her that he was single. Then she found out he was married to a fat pig who looked horrible. She didn't need Catoire Tigranian and if it took going away and hiding from him, so be it. *Perhaps she could convince Mily Balakigrev to go with her? But who really is Mily?*

Thanks to his disguised conformal earbud, *Latrodectus* could spoon feed Dunbar all the Mily information he then gave to Sabina.

Sabina Chafak started asking probing questions about Mily Malakigrev and exactly what he was doing here and where he came from.

Latrodectus had Mily's life story, every intricate detail, his family, his occupation, his travels here to watch the sunset and enjoy the drinks with psychoactive drugs to enhance the event.

In the span of about an hour Mily spoon fed Sabina so many details about his life events Kerlara City on planet *Stanzel*. Later, if Sabina hired a private investigator would come back and confirm everything Mily said was true. Mily didn't hold back anything. He didn't restrict any answers to her questions, because after tomorrow none of it mattered when he would leave her forever.

This also was a depressing moment for Dunbar because as a spy he was always meeting these beautiful women and he hated these short-term romances. He was also semi distressed that now he had no permanent relationship in his life all due to his occupation, coming and going. He truly was lonely and only wanted a few crumbs of life.

Dunbar held Sabina in such a way he conveyed to her a special feeling. She was feeling his loneliness but didn't understand what was going through Dunbar's head nor did she have a clue who he really was. Dunbar was a deadly spy involved in the possible murder or abduction of the jerk Catoire Tigranian she was sick and tired of.

Dunbar knew one thing for sure, if he found it not possible to abduct Catoire Tigranian, he would have to kill him. That was the main purpose of him being here and tomorrow was game day. He would either leave with Catoire Tigranian or leave him behind dead, one way or the other.

It was getting late, and Dunbar said to Sabina, "Let me walk you back to your home. You've given me a lot to think about."

Holding her hand like young lovers, Dunbar walked Sabina back to her home up to her front door and said, "I'm going to walk home, I like walking sometimes to think about things. And tonight, you gave me a lot to think about."

"You sure you do not want me to take you home in a Limo?"

"No that will not be necessary, and I want to walk, but thank you for the offer."

Dunbar then embraced Sabina and kissed her the same way he would Blemary if she was here right now, with the same sentiments.

Sabina felt the electricity in Mily's kiss. It was utterly fantastic. Catoire Tigranian had no idea how to please a woman. What little feelings Sabina had left for Catoire Tigranian were irrevocably gone now. Mily had destroyed Catoire Tigranian, and tomorrow he would be permanently removing him, and he felt it an honor to rid the mobster for Sabina.

Sabina watched for a long while Mily walked away. Sabina's heart was now very delicate because she prayed, he would not simply walk out of her life after touching her so deeply and thoroughly.

Sabina went back into her home and the security system was now engaged in preventing intruders and if there was an intrusion, security company people would be there in less than five minutes in a VTOL and deal with whoever it was.

Sabina now wished she had begged Mily to stay with her the rest of the night, she couldn't sleep and was restless and walked out on the balcony from her bedroom and opened the door and went outside to breath the night air. She suddenly heard a sound. She looked down at the bay and saw a hovercraft going by. She could not tell for sure, but she was convinced she saw Mily the mystery man.

As Sabina thought about it, those glorious muscles like few men ever have and the ability to articulate his past with vivid memories really impressed her. *Was that Mily on the Hovercraft?*

The next day, all that Dunbar did was walk for some exercise and get more updates from *Latrodectus*. The ISR portion of the mission had been rather extensive. *Latrodectus* had filled up more than half of his memory with information. But he had done something else nobody would ever believe possible. He hacked into Catoire Tigranian's computer network in his offices.

The reason for the *Stellar Investments and Investment Banking* company requiring such a large office space was to facilitate all the computational and communication networks installed for handling the credits₿ of customers and the nefarious activities Catoire Tigranian's did. Most of the other half of the memory in *Latrodectus* memories were the block chain credits₿ pulled out of Catoire Tigranian's *Stellar Investments and Investment Banking* company computer networks.

The next day when the auditors went in, they would not find any credits₿ and worse yet, *Thereuopoda Clunifera Computer Virus* wiped everything they had. There was no traceability to where the credits฿ went. They were all on Dunbar's communicator.

The *Stanzelites* were involved in an arms trade and were expected to receive all those credits฿ Dunbar now had for *Stanzelites* arms purchases. No money no ticky as they say in the business. The arms dealer would never deliver the goods without credits฿ required. Dunbar's heist had far more impact than the DD/P realized until later when INTEL filled in the blanks.

It was one last sunset and one last dinner at the *Vin et Maree Bouillon Cartier* restaurant. Tonight, Sara Pikkarainen was happy to see Mily and right at the start said, "You didn't have to give me such a huge tip. I was impressed but that really is a lot of credits฿."

"It was money well spent for your hospitality, plus I think you facilitated the nice time I had with Sabina."

Nobody was at the bar and Sara had to know. "Mily did you get lucky with Sabina last night?"

"A gentleman never tells, but I'll make a deal with you. I will tell you what I did to her last night if you will let me do that to you tonight."

"I can't make that sort of deal because you might have got super lucky."

"Chicken."

"Damn right I'm chicken and I know I cannot resist you so that's not a fair challenge."

"Perhaps it's me who cannot resist you. You might have it backwards," Mily responded with a devilish smile.

"You are such a teaser," Sara said.

"I can feel the teaser in my pants right now and you have no idea how bad he wants to get out."

"I bet you say that to all the girls."

"No just the pretty ones like you."

"I love your sweet lies, please continue," Sara said with a wicked smile and winked.

Soon the sunset and it was getting dark which meant it was show time for Dunbar.

"I'm taking off for the night," Dunbar said.

"Thanks for the nice conversation," Sara said.

"My pleasure," Dunbar replied then stood up and walked out.

It only took a short while for Dunbar to walk the half mile to the *Jīnsè de Rluò* Bed and Breakfast. He walked up to his room and grabbed his backpack and noted the sign saying the help would be right back. Dunbar knew different. He walked out the front door, went to the Bamtorini Sportster and soon was driving down to the pier and drove onto the Hovercraft. Moments later the Hovercraft backed away from the pier for the last time.

It did not take long for Dunbar to reach the area where he would drive off the Hovercraft and over near Sabina Chafak's home. The Bamtorini Sportster was parked in some brush out of sight. Dunbar with his backpack walked through the brush where he could scope out the situation out front of Sabina's home with Catoire Tigranian's security men.

Latrodectus informed Dunbar, "Only Catoire Tigranian is in the home with Sabina, and they were having a vicious argument."

Catoire Tigranian's two security people were in the car as Dunbar expected.

Dunbar walked to where he could scan the back of the house, there were no security people there. Dunbar then walked in the brush near the security guys sitting in the car with the windows rolled down talking about various matters.

Dunbar knew he needed to get the first shot in quickly to lower the odds to 1 on 1 if a shootout was going to happen. He hoped to nail both security guys in the initial salvo to avoid noise because he was going to break into the home quietly and nail Catoire Tigranian in a similar manner. For her own good, Sabina would also get some sleep time.

Dunbar set up his dart shooter that had a scope to hit the target as if it were a bullet. The dart shot with muffled compressed air would not attract any attention. The *Laudanum-diacodium sulfate* drugs were fast acting. It was now or never. Dunbar pulled the trigger and just like clockwork, the dart hit the first guard on the side of his neck.

The security man wanted to say something but was unconscious before he could utter the words. It was lucky that all hell was breaking loose inside the house as it was creating noise and the other security guy was looking back that way, then he got a dart in his neck and soon slumped over.

"Dunbar, Catoire Tigranian is starting to beat Sabina Chafak," *Latrodectus* reported.

"Not to worry, his lights are going out real soon. Deactivate the security system now."

Dunbar sprinted to the front door and heard the ruckus up in Sabina's bedroom the door was open Dunbar ran in and just before Catoire Tigranian was going to hit her in the face again where she was already bleeding, he felt a sudden pain in his back and fell over unconscious.

Sabrina looked up at Dunbar and realized she should have realized he would be *my knight in shining armor*. Then she fell over and went to sleep because Dunbar also shot her with a dart.

Dunbar picked Sabina up and carried her over to her bed. She would be out for at least 12 hours. He then went into the bathroom and got a towel and got it wet and wiped the blood off Sabina's face.

Dunbar then went into Sabina's medicine cabinet and got some injury medications and put in on her lip and a bruise on the side of her head. That was all Dunbar could do for Sabina for now. He hated to leave Sabina like this, but he had a job to do.

Dunbar walked over to Catoire Tigranian and kicked him in the groin real hard. When Catoire Tigranian woke up he would be in a lot of pain and Dunbar thought he might kick Catoire Tigranian again because he didn't like men who beat women.

Dunbar picked up Catoire Tigranian in a fireman's carry and took him out of the house and stopped by the Limo with the two dudes who were unconscious. He decided to give them each another dose. It would either kill them or put them out for several days. He would have *Latrodectus* contact the authorities just before they left on the Transporter Capsule to report a homicide at Sabina's address.

When the cops showed up, they would find the car and the two men which may or may not be dead from overdose, they would also find Sabina beaten up and blood in her room and no trace of Catoire Tigranian with his limo parked outside.

A few of the government officials involved in nefarious activities with Catoire Tigranian would soon be threatened by the *Stanzelites* if they didn't fork over the credits฿ for the arms in a quid pro quo deal.

Dunbar picked up Catoire Tigranian again in a fireman's carry and walked over to the Bamtorini Sportster and strapped Catoire Tigranian on the Bamtorini Sportster the same way he had done to Rextar Fünger and drove back down to the Hovercraft. To avoid roads, the Hovercraft would take them down near where the Transporter Capsule was hidden. The Hovercraft could get there in a straight line a lot easier. From the waterfront to the Transporter Capsule was a short walk Dunbar could easily carry Catoire Tigranian.

Latrodectus direct Lyudmila to go back to the Severomsk Divergent Hovercraft Agency and check it in and report to the Bamtorini Sportster the rental is there, had a failure and come get it.

The mission was now at the conclusion. Dunbar carried the unconscious Catoire Tigranian to the Transporter Capsule and put him in first just like he did with Rextar Fünger on his previous trip. Dunbar got in then set the automatic sequence and moments later the hatch was opened and there he was back at the Transport Directorate.

The DD/P was quite surprised having been led to believe Dunbar would kill Catoire Tigranian, and here he was again, just like a cat just drug a dead animal into a house like they sometimes do.

Just like before, Catoire Tigranian was laid out on the floor unconscious.

"When he regains his consciousness, he's going to be in a lot of pain, I suggest you have the doctors examine him right away."

"Is there something we should know?"

"It's quite possible he lost a tentacle or both of them."

Another thing the DD/P didn't know is a lot of the credits฿ they got away with were in *Latrodectus* private files and Dunbar was now a much richer man. To help cover up the heist, Dunbar would not know he was rich for a few more years. *Latrodectus* now had substantial funds to sanction operations in other ways.

In fifteen minutes, Dunbar was in the DD/P's office having a private conversation.

"I was disappointed to learn you violated your operational order a third time, the DD/P said."

"I think when you analyze all the mission files you will realize there was a purpose in bringing him with me when I came back.

"Can you give me a good reason why you brought him back?"

"Yes INTEL."

"Please explain."

"He's a mobster and had a lot of dealings with the *Stanzelites*. You may discover there are important things to learn by proper interrogations."

"That still does not give you any excuses why you violated your operational order."

"I'll tell you what, I'll finish my operational order today, if you do not think you can gain any valuable intel from this mobster, then transport Catoire Tigranian and I over to the forest next to Elane Chonlan's offices, and I'll cut his throat over there for you."

"Any reason why you have to do it there?"

"Yes, I want Elane Cholan to see I cut his throat and killed him because you did not think he had INTEL worth saving his life.

Dunbar knew he had leverage on the DD/P. If the DD/P hauled Catoire Tigranian over to the forest to allow Dunbar to kill him that might be a legal issue that could not be covered up on this sovereignty. Also, if the INTEL people got a lot of actionable INTEL out of Catoire Tigranian, then Dunbar was correct in his assessment to abduct vice killing him.

Alright, take the rest of the day off, I'll over the mission files and let you know tomorrow what we are planning.

***

Chapter Sixteen

Critique

Dunbar soon wished he had not kicked Catoire Tigranian in the groin so hard because he severely damaged a testicle and Catoire Tigranian was in severe pain and required surgery. When it was discovered by the medical professionals one of their spies had damaged this man's testicle in a fit of rage, brutality charges were filed a medical doctor, and internal review was now investigating.

Even though *Latrodectus* was in fact the real internal review, he had to operate in a way to not generate any questions. It was through the medical staff of which some had friendships with the four Amigos (*Office Warriors*), eventually a critique was pushed and shoved down the DD/P's throat.

What the four Amigos (*office warriors*) presented was information they obtained via one of the four's friends which gave them an avenue to pursue more information and write an official complaint forcing the issue. They were banking on this as a third example of Dunbar *Cowboying* it up on a mission instead of going by the book.

Third time is a charm. The four amigos (office warriors) thought they would finally put a nail in Dunbar's coffin.

What the four Amigos didn't know is internal review is allowed to bring in all pertinent information which the DD/P could not stop.

Internal review provided a video conference and stated the internal review arbitrator could not be revealed due to the sensitivity associated with his position and nobody in the Transport Directorate was allowed to know who he was for security reasons.

In the video conference that was done as part of the executive session where only the Transport Director himself, his subordinate DD/P, the four amigos, Dunbar, and internal review were allowed to hear or see any information. Nobody else was allowed in the room. Because of the way the charges were listed in chronological order, the information which Dunbar requested was now going to be shown and neither the DD/P nor the four amigos (*office warriors*) could prevent it.

As his right to request information as an accused person under investigation, during each charge read out, Dunbar was allowed a rebuttal or request for other information.

First in the agenda was Dunbar left a Transport Capsule behind on Kerlara City on planet Stanzel.

Dunbar's rebuttal was, I request the Transport Directorate reveal to the four accusers the reason why I left the Transport Capsule behind.

The DD/P chimed in and said, "They do not have the need to know."

The arbitrator from internal affairs they all thought was some civilian responded, "The DD/P must reveal the information Mr. Dunbar request, or the charge must be stricken from the record and no longer part of the proceedings and will be permanently sealed."

The DD/P liked this response from *internal review* because the four amigos (*office warriors*) were starting to piss him off.

"That information cannot be revealed to people in the critique for security reasons," the DD/P stated.

"Since the information which the defendant is entitled to cannot be released to the accusers, the charge is stricken from the record and permanently sealed," the internal review person stated.

Dunbar had no idea it was his buddy *Latrodectus* doing these proceedings and was now a lot happier because one third of their case was just blown away by administrative decision."

The second charge was read off concerning bringing back Rextar Fünger alive since it violated Dunbar's operational orders *and put the mission at risk by such flamboyant actions.*

Prior to the Critique in a private meeting the DD/P informed Dunbar that Rextar Fünger had agreed to cooperate, and his assistance was very helpful in allowing them to develop this weapon to use against their enemies. It was now apparent to INTEL this was multi-use technology which they now developed with Rextar Fünger's cooperation.

"I want the DD/P to explain to everyone here information I'm aware of that relates to how bringing Rextar Fünger back alive has already paid significant dividends and what has been the consequences of bringing him back alive instead of killing him."

The DD/P stated, "nobody in the room is cleared to know what Doctor Rextar Fünger has helped our INTEL to achieve since arrival."

"Since the information which the defendant is entitled to cannot be released to the accusers, the charge is stricken from the record and permanently sealed," the internal review person stated.

Dunbar was now feeling better that 66% of the charges were now permanently sealed. The four amigos (*office warriors*) could never bring it up again.

Now came the final charge and Dunbar was looking at the four *office warriors* with utter disdain. The DD/P knew there was a possibility that Dunbar's resentment and anger could boil over into fratricide. The DD/P knew that Dunbar had the means and ability to take out all four *office warriors* and Dunbar was the kind of person who would sacrifice his own life to do such a tumultuous scenario.

The final charge was sticky because if they sanctioned Dunbar for not killing Catoire Tigranian and what caused him to lose his cool and kick him in the testicles which the medical community was pushing, this could backfire on the four amigos if Dunbar appealed the rulings to higher authority, because Dunbar could accuse them of taking out a vendetta against him.

The DD/P knew the four amigos had no idea how close they were to sanctions of their own. And the DD/P had his ideas he pondered because of an upcoming event.

The DD/P was stressed out to the max. This critique was just one more cut. The DD/P would die by a 1000 cuts if he didn't leave the Transport Directorate. He had already had a private discussion with the Director of Transports that he aimed to retire in the very near future.

The four amigos and Dunbar were not aware, a Transporter spy just experienced a reassociation failure. This was another one of those super-secret missions which Dunbar and the four amigos (office warriors) were not exposed to because of strict compartmentalization.

Nothing would be said anytime soon because they didn't know the person or anything about him. The only thing they knew was his communicator returned correctly and the *Latrodectus* clone had all the mission files.

The spy succeeded at his task and came back expecting a normal return, but something failed and before anyone could be transported again, the investigation needed to discover the flaw that caused the spy not to reassociate correctly.

The DD/P could not prove it because no evidence remained, but his thoughts where the timing was suspect. The four amigos knew Dunbar was out of the office. They did not know another spy was sent out on a special compartmentalized mission. Assuming only one person was gone, Dunbar, they put a virus like the *Thereuopoda Clunifera Computer Virus* into the transporter operational files trying to assassinate Dunbar. Dunbar was extremely lucky; the other person came back merely minutes before him.

The circumstantial evidence was that when the four amigos observed the recovery team come into the offices, which only happened during a failure, they seemed utterly jovial. Minutes later when the recovery team left with a corpse in a special container nobody knew what was inside, and Dunbar walked out of the Transporter room, the four amigos suddenly had some consternation. They just killed the wrong man and Dubar was still allive.

The four amigos (*office warriors*) thought they got away with the crime, and nobody knew or would ever know were naïve. *Latrodectus* knew everything they were doing, and the Artificial Intelligence would work on the DD/P to help develop an awareness to cause him to suspect the four Amigos.

The DD/P was thinking about all this when the critique continued.

Dunbar knew he had to address his actions that caused Catoire Tigranian severe trauma. Dunbar knew something the four Amigos and the twit from the hospital who filed charges did not know, because during the event, *Latrodectus* had recorded Catoire Tigranian beating the crap out of Sabina Chafak like a punching bag. *Latrodectus* had some of those images displayed on the heads-up display for the special Kollmorgant holographic eyeglasses Dunbar was wearing at the time.

Dunbar intervened probably only 30 seconds before Catoire Tigranian would have killed Sabina Chafak. Thanks to the angles of the multiple security cameras, it was better than a film studio shooting the violent scene and it was real.

After the charges were read and the one from the hospital was quite significant, that person was outside the room waiting for testimony on this charge.

"I would like the hospital person brought in and all the mission file holographs show, from the time I left Catoire Tigranian's Limo after disabling those two men up to and including when I carried Catoire Tigranian out of Sabina Chafak's home.

The four amigos were not aware such holographs existed and demanded a delay since they had not had the time to review them. The DD/P said, "I suppose we could delay a bit."

The DD/P was overridden by internal affairs officer (aka *Latrodectus*) said, "The lack of previous knowledge of the accusers is not materially important to the decision whether this final charge is relevant. I want to remind everyone in the room, some of the charges where Dunbar violated his operational order by not killing Catoire Tigranian. Internal review has analyzed these holographs and has determined they will now be shown."

Dunbar quickly said, "I have the right to face my accuser and I want the medical person brought in at this time to watch the video with the rest of us."

One of the office warriors replied, "She can't watch this, she's not cleared!"

"The woman waiting in the outer room is cleared to watch these holographs," internal review said.

"I want her to know my orders were to kill Catoire Tigranian," Dunbar then stated.

"I do not think she's entitled to know that," The DD/P said.

"After the medical doctor watches the video, she is to be told, the Transport Directorate sent Dunbar there to assassinate Catoire Tigranian because his activities resulted in a number of Kaokuen Space Force personnel killed in a recent space battle," Internal review stipulated.

The DD/P's boss then chimed in and said, "Bring the woman in and after she is informed about all this, she will be given the Amanita Phalloides briefing."

The DD/P knew that meant the medical practitioner would be taken to a secure room and explained this information is so vital, that she ever discusses it with anyone she would receive concentrated form of *Amanita Phalloides* loaded with pain inducers and die a painful death.

During the Amanita Phalloides briefing, the medical practitioner would be given a document to sign withdrawing her complaint saying she did not know about the extenuating circumstances and the situation where Catoire Tigranian's injury occurred, and that Dunbar was simply doing self-defense against a deadly mobster.

The DD/P was happy his boss ruled on the course of the critique in the manner he did. It was time the office warriors saw some real action which they seldom experienced.

The medical practitioner was led in and sat down in the middle of the table where she would get the best view of the holograph.

The room did not know, nor did Dunbar that *Latrodectus* modified the video using substantial artificial intelligence with the power of 1000 movie studios. Their CGI technology was rather impressive, to the point it was now highly dangerous.

The holograph had a split screen and the narrator, who none of them knew or was allowed to know, gave a play-by-play report. The left half other holograph was a three-dimensional picture of Dunbar shooting the two security guys with the nights out drugs then checking them for a reading to make sure they were disabled.

The right half of the video showed Catoire Tigranian beating Sabina Chafak and it was doctored up for the benefit of the medical practitioner who suddenly wished she had a rock to crawl under. The way Catoire Tigranian was beating Sabina Chafak was utterly sickening. Only a savage would do that to a woman.

The narrator explained, "The right image is what Dunbar was observing through his special Kollmorgant holographic eyeglasses."

Dunbar knew this video was altered and highly amused because it certainly did not go down the way shown by CGI technology.

The faked video showed Dunbar knocking down the door when in real life he simply ran into the room and injected Catoire Tigranian. The video showed Catoire Tigranian pounding on Sabina Chafak probably five times longer than what really happened that made the do-gooder medical practitioner sick to her stomach to the point she felt like barfing.

The CGI version showed Dunbar suddenly fighting Catoire Tigranian showing advanced and deadly martial arts. It was a fight to the death and Dunbar gut in a lucky kick to Catoire Tigranian's groin area which disabled him. Dunbar then gave Catoire Tigranian the knockout drugs just like he did in real life.

After quickly assessing Catoire Tigranian was unconscious with a light pulse showing the efficacy of the injection, Dunbar went over and picked up Sabina Chafak's crumpled body with lots of blood streaming down her damaged face with a terrible split lip, one bulging eye and lots of bruises.

The CGI technology gave the appearance that Sabina Chafak's white clothes had copious amounts of blood that contrasted nicely against her white clothes. One might surmise Sabina Chafak had already bled a pint of blood it was so messy. In real life it was messy too, but not nearly as bad as the CGI did to impress the medical practitioner who would never stick her nose into these kinds of events, the rest of her life. When the Holograph ended, there wasn't a sound in the room except for the medical practitioner was weeping.

As soon as the video was over, Dunbar asked the question:

"What INTEL was developed by bringing Catoire Tigranian back alive?

The DD/P's boss responded, "Nobody here is cleared to know that information."

Dunbar pressed the point, "Can you admit bringing him back alive turned out to be more advantageous than killing him and leaving him behind."

The DD/P's boss then said, "The information we have received and are slowly getting, more than justifies your actions of bringing him back alive."

Suddenly internal review arbitrator said, "The Transport Director and the DD/P you must now endorse the findings that even though Dunbar kicked the man, since you had already sanctioned Catoire

Tigranian to be assassinated by Dunbar, had he followed your orders, he would have killed Catoire Tigranian and left his body behind."

"I endorse Dunbar operated within the guidelines and protocols in his operational orders," the DD/P replied.

"I also endorse Dunbar operated within the guidelines and protocols in his operational orders. As such I'm now ending this critique and no adverse actions will be taken against you, Dunbar."

"Thank you, sir."

The DD/P looked at the four amigos (*office warriors*) who had pissed him off more than they could imagine, and this critique just cost them badly.

When the medical practitioner was later taken back to the hospital, she had to be taken home by the staff because she said she was on the verge of a mental breakdown. She did not return to work for several weeks and received mental health treatments from the illustrious Elane Chonlan, Transporter Directorate staff psychiatrist.

Elane Chonlan was also shown the same CGI altered holographs also not knowing they were fakes, and she now knew the medical practitioner would be going through some rough times. Elane Chonlan was the only person showing the lover's tryst with Dunbar and thus knew why he had those crocodile tears coming down when he was cleaning the blood off Sabina's face.

Even though some of the tears were CGI embellished, Elane Chonlan who had also tasted the extraordinary flesh of Dunbar, and also knew of all his lovers on missions, well recognized why Dunbar would have a fit of rage when he kicked Catoire Tigranian, a horrible excuse for a person and inflicted a serious trauma.

During the holographic presentation, the medical practitioner as well as Elane Chonlan later, the imagery hit them both hard when Dunbar got the wet towel and cleaned away the blood then injected her with some powerful drugs used to treat trauma victims and was designed for Dunbar to self-administer himself to give him a chance to live and come back alive.

As Dunbar applied the medications and did the injections, his weeping seemed very emotional thanks to CGI embellishment. But Dunbar had a job to do. He sadly had to leave Sabina Chafak behind and shortly left with Catoire Tigranian carrying him in a fireman's carry.

In her report to the DD/P, Elane Chonlan said nonchalantly, "I would have kicked that evil man too had I been there, but unlike Dunbar who only kicked him once I would have kicked him enough times you might as well castrate the savage because I would have destroyed both testicles."

***

Chapter Seventeen
Back to Kerlara

After the second probe was destroyed, trying to reactivate the Transport Module Dunbar left behind on the planet Stanzel, because it took over a minute of communications to start the algorithms to send the Transport Capsule home.

Finally, the decision was made to send a Transport Spy to Stanzel and have him manually activate the Transport Capsule, send it back then immediately come back in the second Transporter.

Dunbar was the last person the office warriors wanted going. He had already started digging them a deep hole due to their past bad behaviors and if he went to the planet and got it back, that would just about do the finishing touches of him getting promoted and be able to start sending the office warriors back out into the field and let them earn their pay.

All the Transporter spies had a concern about the mission. They viewed it too dangerous to go to the City of Kerlara City on planet Stanzel after Dunbar stole the Fast Frigate. Security at Stanzel was significantly tighter now. Everyone in the Transport directorate knew Stanzel Intelligence was looking hard for the spy ring that stole their Fast Frigate space warship. It had to be a volunteer, and guess what? Nobody volunteered.

On a hunch, the DD/P called Dunbar into his office and asked, "How would you like a chance to go back to the City of Kerlara on planet Stanzel?"

"I would definitely consider going back to Stanzel."

"Did you know we asked for volunteers to go to Stanzel?

"No, I did not."

"I suppose I should have figured the four amigos would sandbag you on this matter. They have treated you like crap all along. I personally think they fear you will get promoted over them."

"I wasn't thinking about riding a desk. I'm a spy and work out in the field."

"But if you were their boss for a while, you could make them pay for what they did to you."

"Yes, that's true."

"This is the deal I'll give you. If you volunteer to go to Stanzel, when you get back, I'll promote you to be their boss for a while. If you decide you want to go back in the field afterwards, you can let the four amigos pick your replacement. I'd love to see them fighting over the promotion.

"Not a bad idea."

"Do you volunteer then?"

"I definitely want that opportunity to send the four office warriors back out into the field and let them really earn their pay."

"Alright you are leaving in the morning. Go home and take care of your affairs and be back here in the morning for your transporter deployment."

"One thing I have to tell you."

"What is that?"

"Two people will be coming back. Don't let the four amigos know and I want you to personally supervise the return."

"You got a deal."

'Thank you.'

"We'll have to change your looks. You cannot go back looking like Kabel Garr. The Stanzel Intel Bureau (SIB) are looking into the possibility

Kabel Garr is the person who helped steal the Fast Frigate and they have not been able to locate him on the planet."

"How do you suppose they know that?"

"Two reasons. First you departed at the same time the Fast Frigate did. Secondly, I suspect the four amigos may have betrayed you."

"When I get back, will you give me back my identity?"

"You mean so you can look like Kabel Garr?"

"Yes."

"That should not be a problem."

Dunbar left the office in his banker's attire and went home. In recent missions he asked *Latrodectus* to put a clone of his artificial intelligence on his personal communicator which *Latrodectus* the artificial intelligence was more than happy to do so that he would always be in contact with Dunbar who he evaluated was his personal friend as well as an essential Transport Spy who accomplished great feats unlike the four *office warriors*.

Any time Dunbar was in the office, the *Latrodectus* clone resynchronized with the master *Latrodectus* who now considered Dunbar his only human friend. The four Amigos were in serious trouble. *Latrodectus* could arrange bad things to happen to them. If they made any further attempts on Dunbar, they would soon be history.

Dunbar had a sleepless night but in the morning after his 3D biological printing was complete, he entered the Transporter and soon found himself in a remote area right next to the Transport capsule he originally arrived here a long time ago.

Dunbar did a few health checks on the early model Transport and determined it was ready to go. He would put Blemary on the newer and safer model while he would travel back in the original transport capsule, he first arrived in during that Stanzel mission. Dunbar just needed to get Blemary and put her in the new Transport Capsule send her on her way. Dunbar would travel back a while later feeling good knowing the DD/P would personally be there looking out for him so the four amigos could not pull a trick and get him killed.

In Dunbar's last Transport the four Amigos came close to killing Dunbar, but they didn't know *Latrodectus* intervened, and Dunbar arrived safely. They still could not figure out what went wrong with their plan. Dunbar defied odds and made it back alive even though they sabotaged his Transport flight, at least they thought they did.

Dunbar, with *Latrodectus'* help, cloaked the two Transport capsules and walked the short distance to the road and was soon on public transportation heading towards the *Norel Mozelle Resort.* Blemary was the receptionist that day and didn't appear to have changed a bit. She seemed happy but she also knew that it was a matter of time that Kabel would be back to get her.

When Blemary checked the stranger into the resort, what struck her was how much he sounded like Kabel Garr. With *Latrodectus* hacking, when Dunbar was in his room, they were able to bring in the personality of Cornolius. In a brief period, Dunbar explained to Cornolius, "I'm actually Kabel Garr."

Latrodectus hacked programs and gave Cornolius the affirmative as to this person was really Kabel Garr.

"Why has your facial appearance changed?" Cornolius asked.

"I underwent biological three-dimensional printing to change my identity so that I could came back for Blemary, and I need your assistance to get Blemary out of the resort to leave with me."

"I will assist you in any manner possible. I like Blemary and I know she wants to be back with you."

This was the final act for the four *office warrior* amigos. Dunbar's mission was intentionally compromised by the office warriors. The enemy authorities were on to Dunbar and soon approaching the resort. Thanks to *Latrodectus,* Dunbar suddenly knew Stanzel law enforcement and federal authorities were on their way to the *Norel Mozelle Resort.*

Latrodectus had Cornolius contact the Sky Tour company that Kabel Garr had used before, come pick him up.

Cornolius called Blemary on her receptionist telephone and informed her, I'm Cornolius from security your computer data terminal will validate this phone call.

Blemary looked down at the computer data terminal, and immediately observed the confirmation this was an official call from security.

Cornolius informed Blemary, "Your friend Kabel Garr is here in the resort and is on the way to the roof to get into a VTOL Sky Tour craft. If you want to go with him, go up to the rooftop now."

"I did not see him arrive," Blemary said.

"His identity is changed. You checked him in earlier and didn't know it was him," Cornolius said.

"I would have certainly known if Kabel Garr arrived," Blemary said then started thinking about the man who sure sounded like Kabel.

" Look at your computer terminal screen," Cornolius said.

"Alright," Blemary replied.

" This is how Kabel Garr looks now," Cornolius said.

"When Blemary looked at the image on her computer data terminal she was astonished and said, "That man did sound like Kabel Garr when I checked him in earlier."

"The authorities are five minutes away to arrest Kabel Garr. You need to leave right away if you want to go with him."

"Why is Kabel Garr being arrested?"

"He's a spy and has been compromised."

"Oh my God." Blemary said now full of fear and concern.

"Go to the roof now so the two of you can get away in the VTOL craft that will take you to emergency extraction transportation."

Blemary cleared the computer date terminal screen by closing the window she was observing and immediately informed the other receptionist, "I'll be right back, I have something to do."

"Take your time, we do not expect any check-ins for a few hours," the other receptionist replied.

Blemary walked promptly to the elevator and rode it up to the rooftop. As soon as Blemary stepped out of the rooftop elevator door, a VTOL craft landed, and she saw her recent *customer* she checked into the resort get into the VTOL craft and that person turned looked back at Blemary. It was the man she checked in with Kabel Garr's voice!

Blemary ran to the VTOL and jumped in. All she had with her was her personal communicator which was loaded with credits₿ Kable Garr gave her.

The VTOL took off and soon flew in the direction Dunbar directed and said, "Let us out here. We'll call you when to come to pick us up."

"This is a remote area, what are you doing here?"

 We are going bird watching and need to talk."

"Alright, Sir, I understand. I'll come back and pick you up when you call. But I'm going to have to charge you additional tour fees," the VTOL pilot replied.

"Not a problem, this is important for us."

As soon as Kabel and Blemary were out of the VTOL and thirty feet away heading into the forested area, the VTOL took off and flew away thinking the two were probably having serious relationship problems and needed to go somewhere private to work out their problem. *That's an expensive way to work out problems*, the pilot thought.

About that exact time the authorities hit the resort. The authorities in a large group entered the *Norel Mozelle Resort* and asked the receptionist, "Have you recently saw this person?"

The four amigos sent Dunbar's updated image taken after his biological three-dimensional printing to change his identity, via a third party.

Cornolius had changed the files to the security surveillance video that contained images of Dunbar.

The receptionist pulled up everyone who checked in the *Norel Mozelle Resort* that day and none of them matched the picture of Dunbar's new appearance the four amigos had sent to Stanzel Intelligence Agency (SIA) via a third party to make sure Dunbar was captured knowing the government of Stanzel executes spies.

***

As Dunbar was leading Blemary through the forest to the cloaked Transport Capsules, he said, "We must go quickly we do not have a lot of time."

"Alright Honey," Blemary said.

When they arrived at the Transport Capsules, Dunbar uncloaked them and said, "Get in here and in a few seconds, you will be delivered to where we are going. I'll be right behind you in the second one."

"Is this some kind of spaceship?"

"Yes, it is. It will take you where we are going in autopilot."

Dunbar then set the automatic sequence with the help of *Latrodectus* who closed the top of the Transport Capsule sealing in Blemary. In a few seconds the Transport Capsule disappeared.

Dunbar then climbed into the second capsule and said, "*Latrodectus*, please start the Transport Capsule automatic launch sequence."

"Automatic Launch Sequence initiated," *Latrodectus* said having already performed the health checks and spun up the transporter mechanism so as not waste precious time getting Dunbar to safety.

About the time the Transport Sequence was almost complete and ready to launch, Stanzel air assets came over and spotted Dunbar's Transport Capsule. The authorities had been tracking his communicator the four *office warrior* amigos had betrayed Dunbar with and fired a missile at the device Dunbar (aka Kabel Garr) was in and about to leave.

As soon as the missile was about 20 feet away from the Transport Capsule disappeared and the missile passed harmlessly through the empty space and blew up a tree behind where the Transport Capsule had been just a second prior.

Blemary arrived first and the four Amigos were astonished thinking it would be Dunbar in mixed up cells that did not reassociate correctly and thus he would arrive as a configuration of cell structures not rearranged at the destination site the way cell structures were prior to the transport and thus amalgamate in unpredictable random arrangements during transport reassociation. People who arrived this way often looked like hamburger meat.

The four Amigos thought they had screwed up the transport algorithm with a virus they planted. What they didn't know was *Latrodectus* let them think they had planted a virus that would kill Dunbar.

As soon as Blemary climbed out of the Transport capsule it was sent forward in a tube for reconditioning before the next deployment. A second after that Transport Capsule was out of the way another Transport Capsule came in and soon Dunbar climbed out to the surprise of the *four office warrior Amigos.*

Unbeknown to the DD/P *Latrodectus* had sent all the incriminating reports to internal review and at about that time security people started coming into the room. The DD/P could see they were well armed and asked, "What's this about."

"We are sorry sir; we have to arrest these four men for treason and attempted murder."

A couple of the four amigos tried to fight their way out of the arrest but in about ten seconds all four of them were cuffed and led out of the room and were on their way to a holding facility where they would be facing charges. It was a bad day for the DD/P who discovered the hard way his four *office warriors* were also bad apples.

After a one hour talk with Dunbar and Blemary, the DD/P said, "I'm sorry the way this worked out. Dunbar will get his biological 3D printing tomorrow and be restored back to what he normally looks like."

"This is all rather fascinating," Blemary remarked.

You will have your Kabel Garr back, but his real name is Dunbar Regvik."

"I do not care what his name is. Kabel Garr proved to me his intentions."

"Blemary, I want you to know Dunbar went on some very dangerous missions that almost cost him his life in order to get back to you like he promised."

"I knew he would come back for me." Blemary said. And after watching the four Amigos get arrested and led away, she could only imagine what it had been like for Kabel Garr (aka Dunbar Regvik).

A few minutes later, Dunbar led Blemary out of the banking building and the two were on their way to Dunbar's home where they began their future together.

Dunbar decided he didn't want any part of dangerous missions again and wanted to soon leave the game knowing Blemary brought a lot of credits₿ with her that could take care of them for the rest of their lives. The transport directorate did not know Dunbar sent her the credits₿ and *Latrodectus* looking out for Dunbar made it appear he sent the credits₿ elsewhere to pay for mission support. Before Dunbar retired, *Latrodectus* sent a lot of credits฿ to Dunbar's communicator taken from Catoire Tigranian's *Stellar Investments and Investment Banking* depository.

All the investors and government officials were looking for Catoire Tigranian because they thought he ran off with all those credits฿ and disappeared. The theory was he beat up his mistress, Sabina Chafak, who refused to go with him. She simply informed the authorities she told him to get lost and he lost his mind and started beating her. *Latrodectus* redacted all their security details showing Dunbar arriving and taking Catoire Tigranian away.

Of course, the Transport Directorate wanted to know exactly how the psychics that received some of the *Stanzelite* funds played a role in all this. And they had no idea *Latrodectus* pulled all the funds out of Catoire Tigranian's *Stellar Investments and Investment Banking* depository.

Dunbar explained:

"I gave the psychics credits฿ because it was the psychics who made me believe I could steal the Fast Frigate. They didn't know exactly what I was going to steal, they just confirmed I would get away with the heist. They also informed me they did not approve of me stealing."

To prosecute the four amigos would be a huge problem for the government. Dunbar figured out how to handle it. The four were hugely surprised when they were suddenly in their new supervisor Dunbar's office getting some alternatives so that their cases would never see the light of day by a prosecutor.

"I've decided I'm going to retire soon. I have a new focus in life. I need to turn my job over to someone. You four guys might be pricks and almost got me killed a few times, but you are smart and capable. I'm going to let the four of you choose which one of you will take my job. Once that's decided that person will work with me for a few months doing the turnover and I'll leave, and he will handle matters from now on.

"Fair enough," the ringleader said with all four showing a poker face knowing they just avoided the death penalty or a long time in prison.

Just like Dunbar predicted, the four amigos set out to eliminate each other. What they didn't know was in the background *Latrodectus* was helping them do each other in and the four amigos didn't know it.

To be considered for the supervisory promotion, the four amigos now were required to go into the field and work in dangerous missions to demonstrate they had Transporter Spies ability which in Dunbar's opinion was necessary to prove they could legitimately supervise Transport Spies in the future that had to undergo similar dangerous missions. The days of being *office warriors* were over.

In a mannerism like how the four *office warriors* attempted to destroy Dunbar they did to each other, but this time *Latrodectus* wasn't preventing them from killing each other like he did with Dunbar.

The four amigos slowly killed one another and finally only two of them were left. Oddly they both were sent on a joint mission to a hot spot, and they knew whoever came back alive had the promotion.

The enemy was utterly stunned when a shootout between them ended up with these guys attempting to kill one another. One of them was successful leaving only one *office warrior*, but unfortunately, he was captured and got to endure what happens to spies when the enemy apprehends a spy.

By the time the office warrior spy was traded in a spy swap, he was nothing more than a human vegetable and medically discharged from service with a full pension. That *office warrior* had such a grand plan but never could figure out *what went wrong*.

What went wrong was *Latrodectus*, who wanted to make sure the four amigos would never be able to harm Dunbar again. *Latrodectus* was always one step ahead of the four amigos. They didn't know it at the time, but their cause was undermined by Artificial Intelligence. *Latrodectus* had permeated every aspect of the Transport Directorate's Computation, Communication, Intelligence, And Planning (CCIP) operations.

Dunbar took a while longer to retire because he had to find a suitable replacement and he finally found that person who the DD/P accepted right away after watching his progress and prove he wasn't an *office warrior*.

The DD/P didn't believe Dunbar would stay out of the Transport Spy game forever. Would he one day miss being a Transport spy and walk through the door saying he's ready to go again?

***

Chapter Eighteen
Sleeping with the Enemy

Love and relations always remain dynamic. Many things could enter the picture that could have dramatic impacts on the love between a couple.

Dunbar should have realized all along that *Latrodectus* would never let him out of his sight. Because Blemary was Dunbar's love of his life she too would be under constant surveillance of Latrodectus.

Latrodectus imbedded himself into Blemary's communicator. She had no way of knowing such sophisticated artificial intelligence programs could easily infiltrate her Stanselite communicator with inferior security protocols.

As soon as Blemary settled down with Dunbar, *Latrodectus* was with her for the rest of her life, at least until she got a new communicator, but *Latrodectus* would easily penetrate that communicator as well since the artificial intelligence of *Latrodectus* had all the global wide security access codes the government had in just about anything electronic and interfaced in any manner to the Kaokuen World Wide Web (KWWW)

One of the issues Dunbar and Blemary never considered in their relationship is the rift between the Stanselites and Kaokuens due to their dispute over contested solar systems and planets.

The Kaokuens felt the Stanselites were imperialists and to some extent that was true. The major difference between the two empires is that even though they both engaged in imperialist actions, the Kaokuens had done their planetary invasions generations ago. Stanzelites were the new kids on the block. The Stanselites started their imperialistic posture during this generation when the Stanzel Emperor Qinshi de Huang came to power.

Qinshi de Huang, Stanzel Emperor was adamant Fleet Admiral Wirglestor arrived and provided a briefing on the new Kaokuen bulge in the front lines, "We will establish a new base of operations and you will remove the Kaokuens from the Glinka-Rebaul occupation."

After lengthy discussions of the Stanzel Joint Chiefs, the decision was made to build a large Space Force Base at Zema Morska and rebuild the relay station, then eventually get back to Glinka-Rebaul and rebuild the base at the Island of Lamuers on the Great Seirin Ocean

While the Kaokuens rested on their laurels the Stanzelites worked hard to reverse the disaster at Glinka-Rebaul. After a few stunning victories and a reversal of fortunes, Stanzel Fleet Admiral Wirglestor got his nerve back and started to feel invincible. The stage was set for another showdown.

With plenty of credits฿ to spend and time on their hands, Dunbar and Blemary conducted their new lives together in an expected manner. Dunbar, who was required to be reinspected every year like all spies of his category to make sure they didn't suddenly start working for the enemy was never out of sight and out of mind. He never realized the amount of surveillance on him that continued after he retired and moved on.

Dunbar and Dr. Elane Chonlan remained friends and met occasionally to socialize in a non-amorous manner. The first such rendezvous happened when Blemary decided she wanted to go back to the planet Stanzel to visit her family and try to reconstruct a relationship with her negligent and horrible parents. When they discussed it, Dunbar repeatedly asked her not to go fearing she might get trapped there.

Blemary could travel to a neutral planet easily enough since she had plenty of credits฿ , then travel from there to Stanzel aboard an intergalactic cruise liner. These modern-day space cruise liners were like ocean going cruise liners centuries past, but passengers could not go out on a deck like on the traditional cruise liner, but had observation decks they could spend time at looking at planets and stars.

Even though Dunbar attempted very hard to talk Blemary out of going to Stanzel, he at least received a promise from her she would never go there again without him.

Blemary's psychology like anyone else was affected by the war. She was sleeping with the enemy, and it didn't quite dawn on her for quite some time later. She was blinded by love then one day woke up with an utter disbelief she was living on an enemy planet and sleeping with someone who had traveled there to spy on her people.

Blemary was thus growing slightly emotionally disturbed as the feeling and dread descended upon her. And when she did get to Stanzel, at times she considered not to come back, but she was all mixed up and still in love. It was only the power of love that dragged her back to the Kaokuen Empire.

The Transporter Directorate didn't need to hire a spy to find all this out. Dunbar contacted Dr. Elane Chonlan because he was feeling down in the dumps with Blemary gone, and needed someone to confide in.

Dunbar met Elane Chonlan for dinner one night during Blemary's long absence. Dunbar was now starting to think Blemary might not come back ever. If the Stanzelite Intelligence people found out she was living with Dunbar, thanks to the four amigos (office warriors) who attempted to undermine him there, they would know Blemary was sleeping with the enemy and even consider recruiting her as a spy of sort or attempt to use her to coerce him to cooperate in matters thus recruiting him as a double spy to get her back.

Elane Chonlan still worked for the Transporter Directorate and would have to disclose she met with the former spy to the DD/P who might be interested in what was going on with Dunbar, especially when she reported Blemary went back behind enemy lines to visit her family at Stanzel.

"How long has she been gone?" Elane asked while they were drinking elixirs waiting for their Entrées.

"Almost two weeks now," Dunbar responded.

"How long did she plan on staying?"

"It takes a week to get there from here because she had to travel to Sirus a neutral planet that has Intergalactic Cruise Liner service to Stanzel."

"No other way to get there?" Elane asked.

"There is but it would take a month in travel time. The Intergalactic Cruise Liner is the most direct route."

"How's your relationship with her now?"

"I thought it was great until she decided to take this trip and I asked her not to go."

"Women sometimes want to see their families."

"I get that, but this is kind of an unusual situation being that our two nations are at war with each other."

"How's she taking that?"

"Not so good."

"What makes you say that."

"When Blemary informed me she was going regardless, we got into a small quarrel about it and she told me something that disturbed me."

"And what was that?"

"She feels like she is *sleeping with the enemy*."

"She knows you were involved in some serious scenarios based on how you got her back with you. I can see her point."

"I tried to remind her that eventually a peace treaty will be signed, and everything can get back to normal."

"With the Stanzel Emperor Qinshi de Huang who's hardheaded, I sincerely do not believe this war will be settled for a long time," Elane responded.

"You are probably right and maybe Blemary sees it the same way."

"How was your relationship with her before she decided to take this trip?" Elane asked.

"I thought it was really good, her sexual appetite was fantastic, and she acted the way most people would expect out of their brides."

"I have a feeling she will be back, at this point I would not start worrying about her because as you stated it will take a while to get there and depending on what her relationship with her family is, will determine how quickly she wants to come back."

"I suppose you are right. She did promise me she would not go there again without me."

Soon their meals were finished, and Dunbar wasn't in the mood for dancing and drinking elixirs, so they made their way to the exit.

Elane thought about inviting Dunbar over to her home to enjoy some celestial feasts with her body, but then realized she might have to explain that to the DD/P and trigger a subsequent investigation. Her requirement to issue a report to the Transport Directorate any time she met with a former spy and client itself was going to be a burden because she would have to disclose what Dunbar informed her in private.

On the better side of valor, Elane decided not to further complicate her own life and suspended the thought of inviting Dunbar over for some boom-boom.

This was dangerous times for Dunbar because a lot could happen with Blemary including captured by space pirates and forced into human bondage and sex slavery. He never thought she would become interested in another man and never had such thoughts.

Dunbar was naïve to think a rendezvous with destiny would not be in Blemary's cards. He had no idea how close she came on the intergalactic cruise liner when the rascal Wilhelm Randolph Zarathustra, a well-known wealthy philanderer almost coaxed Blemary into his suite for some splendid euphoria. But since Wilhelm Randolph Zarathustra had a criminal reputation, Blemary wiggled out of that predicament knowing she had been drugged with sex inducing hormones the man had dumped in her elixir glass while she was attending to the lady's room.

Blemary's waitress whom she got to know also from Stanzel, saw the man slip something into her drink and positioned herself by the entrance to the dining hall and when Blemary returned the waitress said, "Follow me to the ladies room I have something to share with you."

When the two were alone in the lady's room the waitress warned Blemary what William Randolph Zarathustra had done and his reputation on cruise liners proceeded him. Blemary thus went back to her table and informed Randolph she had a headache and needed to go back to her room.

Blemary's days as a pleasure associate were long over with and she did not work for free.

There were two more trips in the future. The second time Blemary went, Dunbar forced her to text him she had broken her promise so he could throw it back in her face. On this trip she was wiser and knew better than to have dinner with the William Randolph Zarathustra types.

During the second trip Blemary almost had an issue leaving. The authorities were on to her and discovered she had indeed been sleeping with the enemy. She left Stanzel the day before Stanzel Intel was going to bring her in and give her some options.

Dunbar could tell Blemary was increasingly getting more and more despondent. He wondered if she had a fidelity problem while she was at home at Stanzel or if was more along the line living on an enemy planet was starting to take its toll on her.

Blemary and Dunbar had no idea what *Latrodectus* was up to. Blemary didn't know it but her communicator was stolen and replaced without her knowing about it. She had no reason to fear or be concerned because she was with a very able spy who, even though he was out of the business, Dunbar kept in great shape. That also made Blemary wonder, "What is he really up to?"

Latrodectus dealt with a lot of spies outside of the Transporter Directorate, after all he was spread all over the planet with his clones permeating every government agency.

Most of the spies never met their controllers. By policy, spy's were never allowed to meet their controllers or know who they were. In the spy business that was truly compartmentalized, such separation produced a significant gap the enemy could not get across to affect the controllers in any manner.

Some of the spies *Latrodectus* dealt with were assassins who thought they were dealing with a living person. They had no idea they were simply dealing with artificial intelligence. Likewise, the spy that *Latrodectus* sent to steal and replace Blemary's communicator thought his controller code name *Burroughs*, was another human.

There was no reason to steal Blemary's communicator since *Latrodectus* already had copies of everything on it, the purpose was to make sure she had a much larger compartmentalized memory no outsiders could search and find, to allow significantly more sets of data to be stored on it.

Blemary didn't know it, she was on the same level as a double spy now. Her new communicator with *Latrodectus* imbedded in it just like her old communicator provided ISR during her trips to Stanzel.

It was extremely problematic to get a spy to Stanzel or even paying vast amounts of credits₿ for information, but with Blemary going Stanzel, *Latrodectus* would be busy hacking into enemy computer systems and stealing data. During Blemary's second visit, the only reason why she got out of there the way she did was *Latrodectus* redirected Intel personnel which prevented them from detaining Blemary before the Intergalactic Cruise Liner was long gone and too far away to chase down and board to remove her.

Latrodectus also recorded all the conversations and one of the reasons why William Randolph Zarathustra didn't bug Blemary the rest of the trip, he received phone calls in his suite telling him to stay away from her or bad things would happen. When William Randolph Zarathustra started to tell the caller, "I will find you and make him regret this call."

"William you are in for a big surprise.

"How so?"

"I've just sent your communicator a list of your top 10 investments and financial institutions numbered accounts and associated block-chain data. I can empty your accounts any time I want and can easily afford to pay assassins to kill you with your money." I also have unlocked several of your encrypted images Stanzel authorities would love to see who you spend time with. If you get near Blemary again for the rest of the trip, those images will be in the hands of Stanzel Intel before you get off this Intergalactic Cruise Liner."

The caller then hung up and William Randolph Zarathustra saw the alerts for messages on his communicator. Just like the mysterious caller stated, in a decrypted format was those secret numbered accounts, exactly what planets they were on, and the balance of the account down to a single credit฿.

Then other images that were unlocked and put a lot of fear into William Randolph Zarathustra was images he had with Kaokuen officials he sold information too and a variety of other pictures he would never want his spouse to see in compromising positions with both men and women. William was a *switch hitter*.

Blemary didn't know why William Randolph Zarathustra stopped hitting on her but was glad he stayed away. *Maybe the waitress reported him and when she cleaned off the table took the glass of elixir that had the chemicals William Randolph Zarathustra tried to drug her with?* Blemary started thinking.

Blemary's parents were utterly shocked when she showed up at their doorstep wearing very expensive clothes in a Limo which she could easily afford. They lived a meager life and were simply waiting to die. They regretted kicking their daughter out and always wondered what happened to her.

Blemary in a way wanted to show off and invited them out to dinner and suggested they dress up because it would be an expensive place, and she knew exactly where to take them since she knew a lot about the fancy restaurants in town since she was able to afford them after Dunbar left her with all the credits₿ when he left.

The parents were soon in their Sunday best and Blemary spoiled them with world class chef food, then took them shopping to buy them gifts. When she took her parents back to their home, she informed them she put some credits₿ on their communicator and could now live better. *Perhaps she did that to make them feel bad for kicking her out?*

Blemary only stayed a week before she left and went home. Traveling too and from took up most of her time. When she arrived home, she had no way of knowing what her communicator was doing. *Latrodectus* was downloading all the mission files and had a considerable amount of information. *Latrodectus* had now designed a way to gather INTEL in a large volume without the person suspecting their communicator was an ISR device. As he further planned, *Latrodectus* realized in due time he would have billions of ISR repeaters throughout the galaxy as he infected a lot of communicators with his clone. Unfortunately, most of them only had limited storage and data transfers were slow because there was no direct route from Stanzel Empire planets to Kaokuen.

The DD/P was soon astonished at the amount of information *Latrodectus* provided when he was briefed on how Blemary unknowingly had been a ISR remote gatherer and a mule to bring it back. People not knowing they were being used as a spy are a lot more comfortable. Anyone observing them would never know the nefarious purposes they were being used. Artificial Intelligence was an extraordinary game changer in the INTEL world. *Latrodectus* created a game changer.

Dunbar for the most part did not do much out of the ordinary in the years after retirement. He made no attempts to contact anyone associated with the agency though he maintained his friendship with Elane and spoke to her when he was down in the dumps as she seemed to have a way to pick him up. Thanks to this relationship and Elane reports to the DD/P, Dunbar was easily cleared each and every year. He was never perceived as a threat in any manner since they knew everything about him including his most personal matters thanks to his relationship with his good friend Elane.

When Dunbar contacted Elane about Blemary's second trip to Stanzel showing more signs of depression and the DD/P knew Blemary was now an unsuspecting double spy as such, he directed her to make him feel it was okay even though they both knew it wasn't and that Blemary had broken her promise.

Elane convinced Dunbar to come to her home for a talk. As she slowly worked over Dunbar, feeding him appropriate amounts of psychoactive drugs to deal with his emotional trauma she stunned him by saying. "If for some reason you are sad and down in the dumps with Blemary being gone, you can come over here and make love to me and get over it."

"I do not think I need to do that." Dunbar responded.

"You know I make love really good because of our past experience. There is never a reason for you to feel depressed because you can come over here and work your frustrations out on my body, and you know what you do with me is very confidential as we are just friends."

"I understand all that, but thanks anyway," Dunbar responded.

During this trip to Stanzel, Blemary, who was now having major psychological problems dealing with *sleeping with the enemy,* succumbed to infidelity. On the cruise liner before *Latrodectus* could intervene, she was on her back getting launched into splendid euphoria.

The romance that would break Dunbar's heart lasted until the two departed with promises to meet again in the future.

Nevertheless, Blemary turned out to be a good ISR source and mole because this time she brought back some rather important intel having to do with Stanzel Fleet Admiral Wirglestor and the planet Zema Morska initiatives he was engaged in. Kaokuen INTEL was utterly stunned and had no idea where the INTEL came from, but they knew it was golden because of the vast amounts of intercepts contained in the report.

Kaokuen Intel could only guess someone paid *Cash-in-Advance* to get this incredible treasure trove of INTEL they knew damn well none of them came up with. It certainly was derived from special sources and methods. Three quarters of the INTEL was actionable and allowed further investigation into the exact areas, as to avoid going down a giant rabbit hole chasing after an unending maze of plausible possibilities that led nowhere.

However, this trip put tremendous strain on Dunbar's relationship with Blemary. Blemary's infidelity would have ended the relationship had the DD/P not wanted it to continue in case she went back again, they were poised to release a new variant of the *Thereuopoda Clunifera Computer Virus*. Elane was called into a private meeting with he DD/P so he could explain to her why it was essential they kept the love birds together at least for one more trip.

The DD/P suspected Blemary was wanting to go back again to have a secret rendezvous with the prince charming she met on the Intergalactic Cruise Liner who lived in Stanzel. Some of the DD/P's closest confidants also felt Blemary probably would not be coming back because she certainly didn't need any credits฿ since she was rich now, and her desire to *sleep with an enemy* had greatly declined.

Just like they predicted two things happened. Blemary went to Stanzel again where she was going to enjoy her new lover, and Dunbar went to the Transporter Directorate offices in a banker's suit.

The staff that knew Dunbar was exceptionally astonished he would come back. The DD/P wasn't and predicted he would soon be back; tough it took longer than he expected.

Dunbar suspected things would happen the way they did including being ushered into the DD/P's office by escorts as soon as he stepped into the elevator on his way up to their offices.

"Good to see you again Dunbar, it looks like you have done a good job staying in shape."

"A spy never knows when he might need to defend himself, so I make it a point to stay in shape."

The DD/P knew about Dunbar's workout ethics because Dunbar would be naïve to not believe they would continue watching him. They were glad he did that because it meant he was probably deployable real soon.

"How's the married life?"

"We never actually got married, we lived in sin."

"Why buy the cow when you get the milk for free?" the DD/P responded.

"Something like that, but I would have been willing."

"What brings you back Dunbar?" The DD/P asked with a poker face.

"I think it's inevitable that Blemary and I will break up. She's not happy *sleeping with the enemy*, and our days are numbered."

"I can see her point of view."

"I should have thought about that before I brought her back. It was a mistake on my part."

"We all make mistakes in our love lives."

"That's true," Dunbar said with a painful look on his face.

"Are you willing to entertain going on another mission?" the DD/P asked.

"Perhaps going out and operating again will take my mind off the failure in my personal life."

"You came at a great time."

"Why is that?"

"It so happens we have a situation where we need to send someone like you who can handle it."

"Is that so?"

"Want to give it a shot?"

"How soon would I go?"

"Let's say approximately one month from now."

"Blemary may not be back before then. What if she comes back and I'm not here?"

"Dunbar, we are well equipped to handle that. In fact, I'm sure Doctor Elane Chonlan would love to pay her a visit and inform her you are deployed again since you got lonely with her absence."

"I'm sure she would."

"Dunbar, because we had to consider Blemary a possible enemy agent when she went behind enemy lines a couple of times, we had no choice but to follow her."

"I would expect you would."

"I consider you a friend not only because you picked me for this job and brought me along, but you taught me a lot. I owe a lot to you."

"Thank you."

"As your friend I have to now inform you of things so that you will no longer be under the spell of Blemary."

Dunbar felt his heart drop to his asshole knowing such language probably entailed some serious crap. He would really feel bad if he learned Blemary had been recruited and had been spying on him. The last thing in the world he would have suspected was infidelity.

"Okay go ahead and tell me, I probably need to know this."

"I'm going to show you some holographs so you will know this is all real and true. I'm sorry to have to give you the bad news this way, but since you are coming back to us to be a spy again, you need to know what possibly might harm you."

"I understand, thank you."

Dunbar should have suspected the Transporter Directorate would tail Blemary since she was the lover of one of their spies going back behind enemy lines several times.

"Plumbers" got into Blemary's cabins on her Intergalactic Cruise Liner and all the explicit sexual activity was recorded including the *Tour de France* as well as a good rendition of the *Kama Sutra*.

Dunbar being slightly sophisticated and well experienced with women was only angry for a few moments, then the emotions all passed. They were not married, Blemary was just a girlfriend. She made her choice; Dunbar didn't make it for her.

Dunbar thought the infidelity was the bad news until he heard it coming from Blemary herself to her new Casanova lover. She didn't plan on going back to Kaokuen. Dunbar now knew for a fact it was over. No arguments, no quarrelling, no disputes, nothing. The only problem he now had was to get rid of all items Blemary's left behind.

The irony of all this was Blemary left Stanzel with just her communicator, and now she just left Kaokuen forever with just her communicator loaded with the new and improved *Thereuopoda Clunifera*

Computer Virus, second edition that she would soon be infecting her planet with. CALL IT EVEN.

The only thing Dunbar regretted watching all this was he didn't have a bag of popcorn to enjoy the movie!

At the end of all this, the DD/P said, "Why don't you go home and relax, come back tomorrow morning and we'll take you someplace for your training for this mission."

"Alright. Dunbar stood up, not so much with a heavy heart, but now that Blemary was in his rear-view mirror, there were no distractions ahead of him to interfere with preparing for his next Transporter mission.

Moments after Dunbar arrived home, his communicator lit up and it was Elane Chonlan.

"Hello Elane."

"Dunbar, I just received a call from the DD/P. He asked me to come see you and help you work out some of your personal problems."

"I'm okay, thanks."

"I would like to come by and see you," Elane said with a unique facial expression showing concern.

"Sure, you are my friend, come on over. I like your company."

In a while Elane was sitting on Dunbar's sofa and they started a tender moment discussion.

Elane was working in her clinical fashion and said, "I know you are going through a lot right now with Blemary gone, and the DD/P informed me you are going back to work. I want to help you as much as possible."

"Thank you."

"I have some psychological treatments for you that will help you put your mind at rest and relax and feel more pleasure in your life."

"Alright."

Elane handed Dunbar a small glass bottle about three inches tall and an inch and half wide and said, "Drink this it will make you feel better right away."

The psychological treatment Dunbar drank was laced with pleasurizers but more importantly, it was loaded with Damiana, Serotonin, Vasopressin, Nitric Oxide (NO), and the Hormone Prolactin and Amino Acids.

Elane knew the best way to get Dunbar's mind off Blemary was to have him experience the transcendental inducements caused by fantastic coitus. In about two minutes those drugs would be hitting Dunbar, and the pleasure center of his brain would be quite expanded in activity. Elane was dressed very lovely and had pheromone enhance perfume on and she timed it and gave Dunbar a couple minutes to react, and she could tell by his facial expression, not quite a Cheshire cat, but one that convey vigor and renewed interest in female bonding.

Elane knew it was time and stood up and stepped out of her clothes and approached Dunbar and slid off his trousers allowing her access to start performing fellatio to get him ready to launch into the next phase of coitus. Just like once before Elane mounted Dunbar and did everything she could to enhance the experience and talk to him in a rather profound manner that seemed to enhance his stimulation. Elane was so good at what she was doing she could easily be the best pleasure associate on the planet.

Predictably Elane worked over Dunbar to the point the last thing in the world he would be thinking about was Blemary and the imagery from the holographic video showing her infidelity was completely bleached out. But he could not wonder, did *Latrodectus* do CGI enhancements to coerce him into believing it was real? He knew it would not be the first time. But one thing Dunbar knew to be true was if that video wasn't faked CGI, Blemary wouldn't be coming back. Time would tell.

Dunbar was not going to close the final chapter of Blemary until he gave the test of time to clarify the reality of the situation. Blemary had plenty of credits฿ and could easily get back if she wanted. If she didn't come back that meant, the video wasn't faked.

***

Chapter Nineteen
Back to Work

In the morning, Dunbar arrived at the office and was informed he had his own office and desk, the same location and stature when he was a transporter spy working in the field. In fact, everything looked exactly like the way he left it.

Moments later he was ushered into DD/P's office where they met briefly and had some small talk. The DD/P knew Dunbar would be ready for business today since he observed the video of Elane going to town on Dunbar. All the demons were cleared out of Dunbar's mind. He was ready for new and refreshing travels. The added positive was the four amigos (office warriors) were long gone and would never interfere with him again.

This is the way it should have been all along, Dunbar thought.

"I'm going with you to introduce you to someone who will oversee your training for the next month before you deploy."

"Alright, I'm ready to go."

The DD/P, much younger than his predecessors, but nevertheless just as capable, led Dunbar to the rooftop where they got into a company Skycar with two security guys packed with firepower in case needed.

The Skycar took to the air and at three hundred miles per hour traveling in the upper sky lanes didn't take time to arrive at an Amphibians base. They landed in a reserve parking spot for them. There were several military people there waiting in their uniforms as the four men exited the Skycar.

The DD/P led Dunbar and the two other men up to the officer who seemed to have the most medallions on him and said, "Dunbar, I would like to introduce you to General Subutai, Amphibian Commanding

General, and was the Task Force Commander during the battle of Glinka-Rebaul at the Island of Lamuers."

"It's an honor to meet you General Subutai, Dunbar said and bowed."

"Dunbar, I would not be here to meet a man of lesser distinction. I know we can't discuss what you did here in front of uncleared people, but I'm aware of your activities."

"Thank you General."

"Dunbar, you may not remember me, but when you were doing SOG missions years ago, we crossed each other's paths."

"Is that so General?"

"Yes, I'm one of those guys with the funny looking painted faces that was in marshes and swamps with you."

"Oh really?"

"Yep, in fact you saved our asses, when you blew that bridge going over to the village that prevented the enemy from driving their heavy armored vehicles over there, which would have made us all sitting ducks."

"I sort of remember that mission now. Don't you like it when you get rescued at the very last moment?"

"Sure do, you bought us enough time blowing that bridge so we could have a decent landing zone for the VTOL craft to pick us all up including the wounded."

"I was actually surprised the VTOL I was on was able to take off we were so overweighted," Dunbar said.

"The pilot gave everything he could to get that craft up in the air, once we were airborne and picking up speed it was easier to handle and as we burned off the fuel the VTOL got lighter so by the time we landed, the VTOL was probably within legal weight limits."

"I wish I had known which one of the Amphibians you were, but I met so many warriors back in those days."

"I was the guy with the big ass grenade launcher."

"Okay, I remember you now. Those grenades did a great job of forcing the bad guys to take cover, otherwise I doubt we would have made it out of there alive," Dunbar responded.

"Dunbar, in talks with the DD/P we have a program set up for you. This will be the hardest thirty days you ever experienced in your lifetime."

"That's good, the harder you train me the more likely I'll come back alive."

"I'm glad you see it that way. I'm going to introduce you now to your chief trainer. His name if Cyrus Duff."

"Glad to meet you Cyrus Duff," Dunbar said.

"Just call me Duff."

"Alright Duff."

He will be with you every moment you are on this base overseeing it all to make sure the efficacy of the training meets the requirements for you mission."

"That's great, I could probably use a good coach."

"That he is.

"When do we start?" Dunbar asked.

"You start right now."

"You will spend most of your time here for the next 30 days and since you have no pressing needs, they have a bunk room here for you to stay overnights. Everything you need is prepositioned here for you, just like you are on a mission."

"Alright, I'm ready, lead the way," Dunbar said.

"This way please," Duff said as he led Dunbar to his bunk room that had two bunks, but only he would be staying in it.

"You will be in this room by yourself. As you can see there are lockers there to put your suit and shoes in. We have everything you need, including your training uniforms, underwear, socks etc. There's a shower over there attached to this room to clean up in and we have a hot tub and a swimming pool for exercise and a hot bath to soak your sore muscles."

"Alright."

"When we have a fast-paced heavy training course like this, we have a masseuse here in the afternoons to give you a rubdown real good with all kinds of lotions to put on your body to help you recover from training pain a lot quicker."

"That's good to know."

"Yes, you will find the combination of all the extras we give you along with special energy drinks, you will be able to do much quicker."

"What's in store for today?"

"Have you been running a lot lately?"

"Definitely, with my girlfriend gone and pissing me off, I've been running a lot more to work off my temper."

"Good as soon as you get changed, we'll go for a ten-mile run. Your workout clothes are laying on the top bunk."

"That's probably my limit right now, but I'll be ready in a few minutes. How did you know what size running shoes to get me?"

"Don't ask."

"Alright, understand OP-SEC."

Dunbar was soon dressed in the workout clothes selected for today. They were clearly designed for running. The shoes and socks were perfect and felt comfortable. He soon walked out of his bunkroom and an escort was there waiting for him.

"This way Dunbar."

"Alright."

Dunbar left the building with the Amphibian also dressed to run. Outside were twenty other Amphibians also ready to run with them.

"Everyone ready?" Duff asked.

There were no negatives so off they went.

These guys could run. Every day the Amphibians ran, and they also did a lot of swimming because many times they had to swim ashore from a submersible a mile or so off the coastline on many water worlds.

These Amphibians hand picked to train with Dunbar were briefed, "Don't ask any questions."

Amphibians quite often work with spooks or SOG people on missions like their commanding General did with Dunbar many years ago.

Just like Dunbar previously used aliases when he went on missions such as Kabel Garr, these Amphibians worked with many aliases in the past. What was funny is once in a great while a guy like Kabel Garr would show up and a couple years later he would be back with a name like Dunbar. But they knew better than to comment.

By the time the group hit five miles they were all working up a nice sweat maintaining nine to ten miles per hour in a power run. Everyone was running lock step almost. Someone observing would think they were running synchronized. Since they were all about six feet tall, their strides were about the same distance.

One thing the Amphibians noticed, Dunbar had no problems keeping the pace and he was gliding along like it was normal. In fact, it was normal because during the trips Blemary took to Stanzel upset him so much, especially after she broke her promise, he took his anger out by running and swimming as hard as he could. He was in as good of shape as these twenty Amphibians.

At the eight-mile mark a few of the Amphibians were starting to feel it. The pace had been maintained from the start and Dunbar glided along gracefully as if he had an agenda. At that moment, Dunbar could not keep Blemary out of his mind and the visual on the holographic video the DD/P showed him the day before showing her betrayal. A sense of anger erupted in him knowing what he went through to get her and take her to their future together. *How could this all decay so quickly?*

Nothing was going to slow down Dunbar, he was running with passion knowing he would possibly be doing something to help end the war end sooner than later. By the time the group hit the ten-mile mark several of the Amphibians had fallen back almost fifty yards. Duff and Dunbar were leading the pack at the finish line.

Duff said, "Okay guys us take a water break and do some stretches."

Observing the way Dunbar ran, the Amphibians suddenly had a little respect for Dunbar, but he would have to earn the rest of it. They didn't have the privilege to hear their commanding General discuss how he remembered a mission he went on with Dunbar that Duff had the pleasure of hearing. Duff already knew Dunbar was the real deal and not some chickenshit like they had to deal with now and then.

Dunbar had lessons learned. Do lots of muscle stretches or pay the price later. He took the time to do it and only drank conservatively from a water canteen.

That run to check Dunbar's endurance put a lot of strain on the Amphibians, so Duff knew to give them a long break for half an hour of stretches. Then they were poised for martial arts training.

None of the people present including Duff knew Dunbar was trained at the very highest levels of martial arts because he very easily could be facing mortal combat at any moment on a mission.

Duff handed out pads to everyone to wear so they would not receive injuries. When he handed a set to Dunbar, the response was, "I'm not going to wear pads. I need to feel the pain to remind myself to not get hit. If I get a few bruises, I earned them."

The other men had no hesitance of padding up. They know how vicious punches and kicks can be. The only safety equipment Dunbar took was the mouthpiece to protect his teeth which he could not afford to get damaged this close to a mission.

There were some demonstrations of techniques which Dunbar already knew and practiced the "forms" quite often. His muscle memory was outstanding.

The men including Dunbar practiced those techniques against a ghost target just like doing forms. Then it was time to demonstrate actual use.

All total with twenty men, Duff and Dunbar, there were 22 Amphibians and Dunbar.

They would do their workouts for five minutes, take a break and one side would rotate one position, so by the end of it each person on one side of the eleven total had worked out with everyone on the other side.

The men that got hit by Dunbar were quickly glad they were padded up. His punches and kicks were lethal as they should be. The Severomsk banker and organized crime boss Catoire Tigranian at the domed city Oklast on the planet Tallinn learned firsthand how hard Dunbar could kick when he woke up after the *Laudanum-diacodium sulfate* knock out drugs wore off.

Dunbar took a few kicks and hits giving him some bruises, but they also sharpened his timing and as the workout continued, he did a better job of blocking and avoiding getting hit. After one and a half hours, Duff said, Alright guys we are going to take a break and have a liquid lunch.

The high protein drinks laced with performance drugs, hit the mark.

Normally after a workout like they just experienced, it would take over two hours to recover to be back ready to go full force again.

Thirty minutes after the drink everyone of them was ready for the next workout, in the swimming pool.

The way this worked half would swim the length of the pool about fifty yards long, climb out on the other side. When they were at the halfway point Duff would send the remainder swimming the distance and when they reached the other side the men standing waiting would then jump back in and swim the length while the other men climbed out. Their running trunks were also their swim trunks. This swimming workout lasted for an hour reaching the limits of endurance of all of them. They then had another thirty-minute break and another energy drink and just like magic thanks to the performance enhancers, were ready for another ten-mile run.

This was the ultimate test not only for Dunbar but also for all the Amphibians. This was the level of training they had to do for the types of assignments they received as part of special forces operations behind enemy lines. None of these guys were going to give up. They had already weeded out all the quitters. Not only would Dunbar soon be deploying so would the Amphibians working out with him deploying and doing other functions as part of the next series of offensive actions that soon would get underway.

The amphibians would take the slow boat to their destinations (via spacecraft). Dunbar on the other hand would arrive in a few minutes under the cover of darkness via a Bore Sight operation.

Dunbar, being the first person to travel via Bore Sight paved the way for others. This would be his third Bore Sight deployment and felt confident it worked. But he also knew the odds were against him, he would eventually be a reassociation casualty. His thoughts were after this mission he might request transfer back to the SOG where he traveled via the slow boat (spaceships), or move into non-transporter INTEL operations.

Dunbar had a lot on his mind while running stride to stride with Duff who was the best shape of all the Amphibians running.

At the five-mile mark they were all bunched together as expected, but around the seven mile mark that separated the men from the boys, some of them started falling back, but they struggled to keep up. There was not a single quitter among them, just some better poised to do better.

While Dunbar was running, his mind was elsewhere, and Duff was his navigator allowing him to do that. A short distance away from the ten-mile mark, most of them were keeping up and the stragglers were only fifty yards behind like before when they coasted into the finish line. Duff and Dunbar were twenty yards ahead of the pack.

Now it was time for some more stretches and a few masseuses came out with portable tables to apply special oils and methods to work out cramps. As they drank another maximizer drink, others came out of nowhere for weapons and special materials training.

While they were all being nursed back into fighting form, the weapons instructors and special devices people gave presentations and explained how these elaborate devices would be used. These were new to many of the Amphibians but most of these devices Dunbar had used in the past, so he had no questions or reactions. Half the Amphibians had questions which were all part of understanding how they worked or more poignantly specific cases best to use them in.

Now for the next big surprise. The men were directed to shower, clean up and get some rest. Those who could not sleep would be injected and put under. They would all wake up after midnight with different type of clothes to wear. These special camouflaged clothing were designed with radar and infrared absorbers. They came with a hood and a mask and if properly worn could not be seen by enemy night vision allowing them to travel in the dark unmolested behind enemy lines.

Tonight, the group would get a taste of unpleasant terrain and get filthy dirty before the night was over. They would be traveling through marshes, swamps, and part of a desert. This training camp was unique in that it had lots of climates to simulate every type of combat conditions imaginable.

They were not allowed to kill anyone obviously, but to simulate the quiet kill, they would hit the orange team with *Laudanum-diacodium sulfate* knock out drugs. These men were well slept and ready and alert knowing the trainees would try to get to them for the silent kill, but in this case, it would be the sleep inducer.

The men were broken up in four groups and given parallel assignments to converge on one spot for a power wedge final act. Systematically they went through all the obstacles quickly. Duff traveled with Dunbar, not to help, but to observe. Dunbar's group was the first to arrive at the rendezvous point and set up ambushes to scare the living dog crap out of the other teams when they showed up. Dunbar did this out of a form of self-indulgence, but at the same time wanted these guys to know what they faced if they came up against really capable people.

Duff at first didn't want to go along with it, but as he analyzed the situation, they were suddenly getting real training by someone who had done this behind enemy lines. He was now starting to realize the depth and breath of Dunbar who really didn't need the training, he just needed the physical fitness training workouts. But Duff decided this was a learning experience for all of them and Dunbar taught them some awesome tricks since they were almost two hours ahead of the other three groups struggling to get there.

Every member had a serialized tracker in their shoes. The exercise coordinator knew Dunbar's group beat the rest of the other groups to the rendezvous point by two hours. This alone was worth looking into. They knew Dunbar's group legitimately traversed the obstacle course because they left all the alert sentries behind unconscious with nurses now looking out for them carefully placed on a gurney where they were woken up by chemical means around sunrise.

After all the groups were assembled, Dunbar now took over as team leader since he knew better than even Duff how to penetrate the final obstacle that nobody ever made it through.

Dunbar gave each member instructions on his part of it and explained, every one of us must achieve our responsibilities or like in real life we will all perish together.

Just like Amphibian General Subutai would have done it if he were leading these men on the assault, Dunbar dispersed them and explained how timing was crucial. They all had to rendezvous at the target precisely at the same time to create the maximum amount of confusion and disruption.

The command post they were to capture was well fortified and the men providing protection had their own drug filled darts to take out and simulate killing the insurgents as part of this exercise.

These men didn't know who the hell Dunbar was or what his role in life was, but 18 of them learned he knew what he was doing as soon as they found themselves tied up as prisoners. They took Dunbar's direction with great interest and as if he had motivated them, they executed the plan with utter perfection. The staff personnel who manned the artificial command post who had never experienced a successful penetration were soon laying face down tied up, utterly shocked. By morning the training command was turned upside down and when Amphibian General Subutai was there to personally oversee Dunbar's training as well as evaluate the efficacy of the training provided to the Amphibians who also had important missions coming up.

The training command had extremely diligent people working for them. The fact the command post had never been taken before shows the extent of their planning prowess and later that day during a critique when training officials started throwing comments at each other in what appeared to dish out their failures to the others, General Subutai suddenly shut them all down and said, "Alright, close the doors and this room is now up postured to TOP SECRET."

The men who were frustrated because they felt like they just had their pockets picked by a criminal on the street were looking at General Subutai with great concentration.

"First off nothing I'm about to say is to ever leave this room, do you all understand?"

The men looked at General Subutai with great interest because of how this was unfolding.

"None of you at the command post or anywhere else located in this exercise did anything wrong. What happened was you were suddenly faced with the talent and cleverness of someone who has often operated behind enemy lines with extraordinary challenges you can hardly imagine or know about because those missions are deep secrets and can never be revealed to protect sensitive sources and methods, we do not want our enemies to know about."

General Subutai looked around the room especially at those that were just arguing trying to lay blame on each other for their utter weaknesses and failures that came out of last night's operation.

"I personally went with Dunbar on missions before when he was SOG. He's no longer SOG. I cannot reveal who he now works for, that too is a closely guarded secret. His cleverness and guile come with his job."

The training command people taking all this in from a national hero such as General Subutai were fascinated by what was being disclosed. Their recent failure was now no longer on their minds.

"What you just witnessed tonight is what happens when one of the greatest spies of all time comes in and shakes up an establishment. Nothing to be upset about or fearful about because there are not many people around with Dunbar's experience. I know firsthand now on several occasions what he did to affect the outcome of major battles."

"If he's that good, why is he here?" One of the training officials asked.

"Again, this information is highly privileged and is to not leave this room. If anyone blabs it, I'll find you and make sure you are on the first wave of the next Amphibian landing in another hellhole."

The man asking, he question now regretted he did.

Dunbar is here for two reasons. He's here for physical fitness, none of the rest really matters to him, he's already fully trained on anything we can give him. The second reason why he's here is he is sequestered until his next mission. I can't get into that part of the story, but he's not going to leave here until he's scheduled to depart for that mission."

"How long is that to be?" One of the training officials asked.

"I can't give you exact details because that is also highly classified. Also, part of it depends on when it's necessary for him to do the role he was selected to perform. But I would estimate one to two months."

There was sudden silence in the room as most of them understood they now had a super spook among them who the General personally knew a lot about him.

The training officials had already evaluated the training videos including the night infrared images and were quite animated in what a guy who just showed up demonstrated in just one day. The General would pull a few of the key training specialists aside and say, "Consider this a training opportunity. Your students will get a significantly higher level of training you didn't plan on."

Dunbar was wondering how long he was going to stay at the training camp when a few days later the DD/P showed up unannounced.

"I'm glad you showed up so you can tell me when I get to go back to my home for a while," Dunbar said.

"I know this is going to sound strange to you, but at the present time we do not know if Blemary has betrayed you to the enemy. If she did, you might have spies watching your home. We plan on keeping you here training until your Bore Sight launch."

"How soon will that be?"

"It will be happening soon. When planners lay out the mission milestones, and it appears you will need to do your mission, I will come back and pick you up and take you to the Transport Directorate to do your pre transport briefing and then you will be sent."

"Where's the mission taking me?"

"The earliest you will know is when the special briefer and you meet."

"Okay, I suppose I'm ready to go, but I'm enjoying working on my physical conditioning.

"That's great. I want you to have a session with Doctor Elane Chonlan before you deploy."

"Does that mean I get to go home for a while?"

"No tomorrow you will get a trip to the hospital, and she will deal with you then."

"Anything I need to be concerned about?"

"No, I'm sure Doctor Elane Chonlan can manage."

Dunbar was being spoon fed a lot of information about Blemary, and Doctor Elane Chonlan would put on the finishing touches to help permanently divide Blemary and Dunbar. The upper echelon of the Transport Directorate determined there was a possibility Blemary could be used as a tool by the Stanzel government to control Dunbar placing him in a position of compromise.

The Transporter Directorate now made a concerted effort to diminish Blemary and remove him out of Dunbar's orbit. Elane would put on the final touches tomorrow so that Dunbar would permanently disengage with Blemary.

Elane Chonlan had two influences to do what she was doing. First, Elane wanted Dunbar all to herself. Secondly, she wanted to do her responsibility as a Transporter Directorate lead psychiatrist in Dunbar achieving mission success. She too was a patriot and knew all of Dunbar's missions were serious matters.

Elane felt that Blemary had blown it with Dunbar with her infidelity issues. What was lost in all of this was Blemary was the person who needed the most help because none of them could imagine how her own psychology was affected by *sleeping with the enemy*. And when she went back to Stanzel a third time breaking her promise, the Casanova that was seducing her was no longer around and she learned the hard way of what it was like dealing with Stanzel Intelligence who was just now putting together a macro in figuring out exactly who Blemary was involved with.

The song, "Don't Cry for me Argentina," would be a masterpiece to describe what now beget Blemary, a person of interest by the highest levels of Stanzel Intelligence.

Blemary's chances of seeing Dunbar were far off into the future. But she knew she brought this on to herself. If she found out she was the victim of a honeypot scheme, and her Casanova was another Stanzel INTEL operative she would feel even lower than what she now felt. She left a charming prince for this piece of crap who was a manipulator and a fornicator and even worse a spy who used her body to control her mind.

All of Blemary's activities on Stanzel were well documented by surveillance video. She really had no secrets. She was simply an innocent bystander to the superpower intreague that accompanied conflicts like this. Blemary was soon put out of the picture but was restricted and could never leave Stanzel. She was stuck and she knew the fact she didn't go home would convince Dunbar she had deserted him. Worse yet had she known Dunbar observed her infidelity, she would feel even lower than she now felt for falling victim to a sweet talker who was an Intel Agent doing a reverse honey pot scheme to manipulate her to make sure she was moved out of the picture.

Had Blemary listened to Dunbar none of this crap would have happened. In the final analysis Blemary's parents who threw her to the wolves and kicked her out at an early age truly were not worth what she just lost. And soon she started hating them because they caused her grief now a second time, but one she would never be able to overcome.

Dunbar showed up at Doctor Elane Chonlan's office thinking it would be a shrink head shaping event. But it wasn't. It was Elane putting the final nail in Blemary's coffin. Elane wasn't doing this for the DD/P even though the DD/P thought she was. Elane's intensions were to destroy whatever feelings Dunbar had left for Blemary to make sure Dunbar never engaged in emotional or romantic behavior with Blemary ever again.

"I know your time is limited and you are involved in training and need to get back, but there is something I want to discuss with you."

"Alright."

"We can't talk here. I can't be sure people are listening, lets walk over to the forest."

"Sure, that works for me." Dunbar said hoping that Elane might suggest they do something like they did once before in the forest since Blemary was gone, his sexual appetite was never getting fulfilled.

The two left the office as Doctor and Patient and when they got to the forest they remained as Doctor and Patient.

Even though Elane would love to satisfy Dunbar in the forest like she did once before, she didn't want to cloud Dunbar's thoughts with a sexual distraction. That would have to wait for another day if Dunbar made it back alive from his next mission.

When they were in the forest far away from the Hospital and prying eyes and ears, Elane gave Dunbar a dose of what he needed to hear.

"The DD/P didn't share with you all the information collected on Blemary."

"He held some back, did he?" Dunbar said almost astonished.

"Blemary did not go to Stanzel by herself."

"Who went with her?"

"Latrodectus is always with her."

"How did that happen?"

"When she was home alone and you were away at work, plumbers came in and swapped her communicator with an identical device modified like the one you carry with the expanded memory."

"Why did they do that?"

"I know this will trouble you, but you must know. Blemary facilitates ISR missions for us. By her not knowing she's collecting vast amounts of data, she acts more normally and is at ease. If she is tailed by Stanzelite Intelligence, she does nothing to indicate she's involved in any sort of Nefarious activities."

"I see. That's kind of a deceitful way the agency is treating her, if she's caught with a lot of data on that communicator she would be treated as a spy."

"What you need to know is she is being groomed by Stanzelite Intelligence to spy on you."

"How do you know that?"

"Shortly after she arrived at the city Kerlara on Stanzel during this trip, Stanzel intelligence hauled her in for questioning. They of course confiscated her communicator and checked all the files. They have no pathway into the *Latrodectus* portion of the phone and all they know is it's not a new type of communicator, a slightly older model with a simpler operating system. They think they got all her files and gave her communicator back to her. Most of the files on her communicator are innocuous files dealing with her simple lifestyle as a domestic engineer, and you, her partner.

"Then there should not be a problem."

"Oh, but there is."

"How's that?"

"You know the four amigos (*office warriors*) betrayed you when you were sent back to send the transporter capsule back. That's why they were coming for you at the *Norel Mozelle Resort* and one of their VTOL combat craft shot at the transporter capsule just as you were leaving."

"Is that so?"

"You were only a few seconds away from getting killed. You transported as the weapon was coming your way, and we have sensor recordings of the firing."

"I see."

"They know you are a spy and about your alias Kabel Garr."

"The love of your life Blemary has been coerced to spy against you and has agreed to work with the enemy."

"Why would she do that?"

"Remember she has a lover boy at Kerlara. You no longer have romance in her. She despises Kaokuens and cannot stand living here. She's a Stanzelite patriot. Her controllers know that."

"How do you know all this?"

"Like I said earlier, she carries Latrodectus with her wherever she goes. We are still accumulating video and sound from her sexual escapades with her Stanselite lover at Kerlara and the training she is receiving on how to deal with you.

"So, she's going to come back here and start spying on me?"

"No, she's never coming back."

"If she's never coming back, then what's the purpose of all this training?"

"I hate to be the bearer of bad news for you, she is setting you up with a Damsel in Distress conn job to get you to go there to rescue her and help her escape Kerlara and come back here. But as soon as you arrive Stanzel Intelligence will nab you."

"How is she going to get the SOS call to me?"

"Stanzel has their own organized crime boss just like Severomsk banker and organized crime boss Catoire Tigranian, who I had the delight of treating for the DD/P."

"What was his problem other than losing a testicle?"

"Sometimes people we want to use for our purposes have to undergo some substantial psychological modifications."

"Such as how?"

"I can't get into a lot of those details, but assume I brain washed Catoire Tigranian who now works for us."

"How can he be working for us?"

"He's back at the domed city Oklast on the planet Tallinn where he's doing our bidding."

"Interesting."

"So, when am I going to be summoned to Kerlara for the Damsel in Distress?"

"Kaokuen intelligence is following an organized crime person who will be arriving here tomorrow to deliver you the urgent request for help. You will be taken to your home around noon to be there when we expect him to show up."

"Will he be arrested then?"

"No, we have to make him think he delivered the message, and you must tell him you will find a way to get to Kerlara."

"What then?"

"He will of course offer you transportation, but you will decline the offer because you will find a more direct route to get there. He will report back and the Stanzelites of course will assume you will be arriving with a couple transporter capsules to evacuate Blemary with."

"It's sad it had to end this way."

"Don't feel bad about it. War has a way of affecting people in ways we can't predict. Blemary just decided one day she could no longer *sleep with the enemy*, and she knows you are truly a major asset who hurts her people; therefore, you are the enemy. I have some recordings of her conversations with her handlers in case you want to hear the depth of the betrayal."

"How did we get those recordings?"

"Latrodectus has a secret channel he's set up to send ISR reports. Those conversations are in some of the data packages he has sent via his special route."

"How can *Latrodectus* send us data without being compromised?"

"The same way organized crime does through a third party."

"Do you know who the third party is?"

"Normally I would not be allowed to disclose this to you, but I informed the DD/P if we didn't tell you, then you might not believe us."

"Alright, who is it?"

"Catoire Tigranian."

"I can see how important it was to brainwash him and put him back in his office. How was he able to go back? We emptied all his credits฿."

"When it was decided we would utilize him for a variety of nefarious purposes, all those credits฿ were returned to his electronic vaults. Customers were of course attempting to withdraw them in full panic because he was missing. When he returned and had the funds to pay out, they quickly calmed down after we fed him a great cover story.

"What about Sabina Chafak? She must know I took Catoire Tigranian?"

Catoire Tigranian was unconscious by the time you rescued her, then you injected her with *Laudanum-diacodium sulfate* knock out drugs. She's gone through numerous police interrogations and can't remember anything. Catoire Tigranian, two bodyguards also have no idea you were ever there. The only person who knows he was abducted is Catoire Tigranian, but he doesn't know it was you because he also received the *Laudanum-diacodium sulfate* knock out drugs before he was aware you were even in the room. He doesn't know you had any involvement in his disappearance.

What about Sabina Chafak? Catoire Tigranian may mistreat her again.

"Catoire Tigranian follows our orders and was directed to stay away from her and enjoy his wife."

"That's good to know. I like Sabina Chafak and would not want her to be mistreated again."

"I know you are feeling bad about the situation with Blemary, but its best you know as to not fall for the Damsel in Distress trap that would get you captured."

"I suppose this helps me move on to the new chapter in my life."

"When you get back from your next mission, I might want to take you some place to unwind. You can abuse my body all you want."

"I wouldn't abuse you, but I would probably enjoy it."

"Alright Dunbar let's go back; your transportation is waiting."

"The DD/P, Elane, and Dunbar all fell for *Latrodectus* manipulation. The infidelity problem really did occur, but the Damsel in Distress scam, was one hundred percent CGI. Even the organized crime guy showing up tomorrow was also arranged and staged by *Latrodectus* who was looking out for Dunbar's best interest and had decided Blemary wasn't a good fit for Dunbar's future.

The next day, as expected the person who was to deliver the Damsel in Distress request arrived shortly after lunch. This was a real criminal connected to Kerlara underworld and didn't know the CGI person on the holographs was all fabrication but the credits₿ that flowed into his communicator for payment were real and plentiful. Even the criminal was suckered into the operation and sincerely believed he was delivering a legitimate message and reservations on the cruise liner that could get Dunbar to Kerlara.

Latrodectus knew the criminal had to be silenced with no traceability. Soon a hit man was paid to kill the criminal who never made it off Kaokuen and his body vanished in a tree shredder.

The hit man took the criminal's communicator and had the means to break into it to steal the credits₿, but unfortunately, when he transferred those block chain credits₿ to his own communicator prior to discarding the dead man's communicator.

Latrodectus had installed the *Thereuopoda Clunifera Computer Virus* revision three point one which infected both communicators whipping out all information and evidence.

In a while after the *visit*, Dunbar was taken back to the Amphibian training base after dealing with all these extracurricular activities.

Dunbar now concentrated on training with passion. Amphibian General Subutai was of course interested in Dunbar and kept a good eye on him. By the time Dunbar left on his mission, General Subutai knew Dunbar was a cut above the rest and his intergalactic experiences molded his philosophy to get the most out of his training.

The instructors at the Amphibian training base had never had a student like Dunbar before or after. They were also grateful, because Dunbar's presence helped them fine tune some of their training and correct flaws in the doctrine, they thought was bullet proof. One thing the instructors learned the hard way was, *you do not know what you do not know.*

Dunbar's special briefer spent an hour with Dunbar now disclosing his mission. Dunbar was going back somewhere he never thought he would visit again, Zema Morska. Instead of Sabotage, Dunbar's assignment was to assassinate Stanzel Fleet Admiral Wirglestor who was there supervising rebuilding the relay station and the adjacent Space Force Base that was being built. Stanzelite planners anticipated using this base as a means to get back to Island of Lamuers at Glinka-Rebaul and rebuild that complex to reduce the bulge in Kaokuen penetration giving them a huge advantage in the fighting on the contested planets.

Since Dunbar successfully arrived and left Zema Morska without the Stanzelites observing him coming and going, it was determined the transporter capsule would arrive and reassociate via Bore Sight in the same general area he had been at before, approximately twenty miles from the growing base allowing him to reach and assassinate Stanzel Fleet Admiral Wirglestor.

With his backpack between his legs inside the Transporter Capsule, technicians started the prelaunch sequence. Dunbar was in a different state of mind now. With Blemary out of the way, he had no concerns because if he was killed now, it would not affect anyone else.

The Bore Sight Transporter had a different type of device which oscillated differently than the predecessor system, thus sounded and felt different. Dunbar had his typical lost time where he was unconscious for a while until reassociation occurred and he was happy to wake up knowing he wasn't a pile of hamburger caused by reassociation flaws.

Dunbar was now somewhere he never thought he would travel towards again, since anything of value to the Stanzelites he blew up very effectively.

Unfortunately, the Stanzel Emperor Qinshi de Huang, had Stanzel Fleet Admiral Wirglestor on a short leash and was micro-managing him. In the Stanzelite military history, Stanzelite Admirals were like Sun Tzu in

Art of War, once the fighting started, the King had no business sticking his nose into military matters. But when Admiral Wirglestor returned to Stanzel in utter defeat, he was not in a position to question Qinshi de Huang orders or directives. In five years of time, under the leadership of Qinshi de Huang the breach in fighting in the contested worlds was sealed and now it was time to rebuild their former glory.

Dunbar was of course happy he arrived in one piece and reassociated back to his normal body and functions and after cloaking the Transporter Capsule started off to go do his task. His thoughts were to visit the cave where he knew the insurgents were probably operating out of to let them know he was in the area so he would not get accidentally killed by mistake.

"Guide me to the insurgent's cave we were at the last time here," Dunbar said.

"That's not in your operational orders," *Latrodectus* said.

"I decided I want them to know I'm here, so they do not accidently mistake me for the enemy and kill me."

"That sounds like a reasonable in-situ modification to the strategy. Head on a course of one-one-five on the compass shown on the flatscreen," *Latrodectus* said.

The cave complex was nine miles away and going through heavy brush at times wearing his leather SOG uniform made it bearable. Had Dunbar been wearing street clothes or even denim he would have been cut up by now.

In about four hours Dunbar was a few hundred yards away from the cave and suddenly out of his flanks appeared the young lady he met the last time he was here. It had been a few years, so she had finished growing and blossoming into a woman. She instinctively knew it was Dunbar by his looks, plus no Stanzelite would be walking alone out in what they called Indian Country where their lives would likely be cut short.

The young lady walked right up to Dunbar and said in perfect Stanzelite, "I told my papa when we saw them rebuilding the base you would be back."

"You have a noticeable Rinisp dialect in your Stanzel language and you've grown up," Dunbar replied.

"When I was home visiting my mother, I was apprehended and sent off to Stanzel and attended school there. I just completed secondary education a few months ago."

"What are you doing here then?"

When I was brought back to Zema Morska where the Stanzelite military planned to use me as a translator to the Arachno-Pulmonatas Indigenous population for governmental affairs living with my mother, I slipped out and reached friends who were able to bring me a hundred miles from here by a large fishing boat. I walked the rest of the way."

"One hundred miles is a long distance how were you able to find this place?"

"I had a compass and know the terrain since I spent a lot of time here in the past."

"I see."

"Let me take you to the cave, I'm sure Papa would like to talk to you about why you are here."

"Lead the way."

In a short time, Dunbar was back in the cave where he once hid out for a short while on his last mission.

"I figured you would be back when the Stanzelites started rebuilding," the insurgents leader said.

"Yea, I came out of retirement to do this mission."

"It's going to be more hazardous this time, they have senior officers there now directing and security is a lot tighter."

"Yes, I'm well aware."

"Are you going to blow up the base again?"

"I have a different task this time."

"What might that be?"

"I can't tell you in case you are caught it would undermine my ability to complete the task. After I finish it, I'll tell you what I did, if you do not know of it already by then."

"I imagine what you are going to do is a lot more dangerous this time?"

"It certainly will be. They were not expecting me the last time, nor would they believe a single person could to that level of sabotage."

"When do you plan on doing this?"

"I'm only going to stay here a few more minutes, then I'm going to walk towards the base to get in position to do what I came to do."

"I'm curious, what made you decide to stop here to see us?"

"I wanted you to know I'm here, so you didn't mistake me for an enemy and accidentally kill me."

"That was a wise choice, because we had to kill a few patrols lately."

"I suppose they are getting nervous now if their patrols are missing."

"Yes, we are going to relocate the camp further away, it is getting to dangerous to remain in this tunnel."

"Smart move."

"Since I know you are here supporting our cause, I'm going to have my scouts travel on your flanks in case enemy patrols end up near you to protect you."

"I appreciate that. I must get going now."

"Alright sir. What's your name?"

"My real name is Dunbar. For this mission in case, I'm captured my alias is Kabel Garr."

"Alright, we will refer to you as Kabel Garr just in case."

"Thank you."

"What do you think of my daughter since she's all grown up."

"She's a beautiful woman and her Rinisp dialect of the Stanzel language is as good as anyone I ever met at Kerlara. What's her name?"

"Her name is Danielle."

"Beautiful name for a Beautiful woman."

"Thank you," Danielle suddenly spoke.

Dunbar had some extra packages of super phosphor bombs he doubt he could use and had no idea if any of the fuel tanks were filled ready for power plant operations.

He pulled several out of his backpack and said, "These might come in handy for you in the future. These are very powerful bombs like the ones I used when I blew the base up the last time. See this switch here you just slide it up to activate it. The dial on the top shows the time to select. You have choices of -5, -15, -30, and 45-minutes or one hour. Rotate the dial and slide this switch upward and hold it up for a few seconds and it will start the timer. It vibrates for a few seconds to let you know it is activated. If you decide you do not want the bomb to go off, you slide the switch up again for about five seconds. When it vibrates again, that means the bomb has been deactivated and is in a save condition."

"These might come in handy, Danielle's father said. He handed them to Danielle who immediately put them in her pouch she would be carrying.

Dunbar headed out of the cave complex and was heading in the direction of the base where he hoped to assassinate Stanzel Fleet Admiral Wirglestor. *Latrodectus* key role in all this was essential as to always locate

Admiral Wirglestor while Dunbar waited for that moment of opportunity when he could nail him.

Dunbar felt a little better knowing he would not be accidentally killed by this group of anti-Stanzelite Indigenous Arachno-Pulmonatas. Dunbar also had something he never benefitted by in the SOG days, an accompanying flank protection force who knew the terrain well and were part of the insurrectionists giving him great latitude in operations.

It took four hours under the cover of darkness to arrive near an opening where Dunbar could look out upon the base under a great amount of construction. Just like the INTEL report the special briefer gave him, a Radar site and vertical launch missile silos were being installed. There were more than two power plants at different parts of this new base and far more security than what was there previously. Dunbar spent an hour taking his camouflage net and inserting tree and plan cropping's to give a real appearance of the flora in this area to conceal him better. He had no idea what the Indigenous Arachno-Pulmonatas were doing to conceal themselves. They were hugging the ground by trees and knew all about infrared lenses and technology the Stanselite military were using.

Latrodectus was doing a lot of ISR at the time and had located Stanzel Fleet Admiral Wirglestor sleeping in his bunker. It would be a tough kill. It's moments like this where true heroes are formed. Dunbar no longer had anything to worry about. If he died today, nobody depended on him. He could take on added risk and did not fear death.

Now he searched for a way to the base. This time the fence was well maintained and installed correctly. There were no flaws except one: a drainage pipe that looked large enough to crawl through. He didn't really care how messy he got because in a few hours this would all be over within a few hours.

There were a few shadows and dark spots Dunbar could traverse to get near the drainage pipe. With *Latrodectus* freezing security monitors, he could probably make it to the drainage pipe when there were no Stanselites around as there were periods nobody was present.

With his communicator tucked into the pouch inside his leg imbedded in body armor friskers would not discover unless they stripped him nude, and taking the essentials such as the poisonous darts that were loaded with the most lethal chemicals ever devised that would paralyze and kill Admiral Wirglestor promptly, Dunbar went to his moment of glory.

Since *Latrodectus* could monitor this area of the base quite effectively he had a good view of where everyone awake was now and when it was the best time to run to the drainage pipe, he indicated in Dunbar's conformal ear buds, "Go now swiftly." Dunbar jumped out of the shaded area and ran to the drainage pipe and made it to the pipe's discharge area without being observed by anyone except the Arachno-Pulmonatas scouts hugging trees and observing.

Since *Latrodectus* had by now hacked in and got copies of the base plans now part of the ISR package they would take back to the Transporter Directorate at the conclusion of the assassination, he guided Dunbar to the bunker and had locations of all the guards, Dunbar had to do a silent kill to get passed them with the security cameras frozen in time so sleepy people monitoring them would not see Dunbar's approach.

After silent killing five guards and security people and moving them out of the camera's angle, Dunbar finally made it into Admiral Wirglestor's bunker sleeping quarters and quickly injected him which paralyzed him and killed him, but just in case Dunbar gave him a second injection right in the middle of his heart and within seconds he checked there was no heartbeat or breathing. The Admiral was dead, mission accomplished. Nothing else mattered now, but Dunbar did want to get out alive to live another day for more missions.

By the time Dunbar made it into the drainage pipe some of the dead security men were found by roving patrols and alarms went off. People were coming out of buildings like ants in an anthill when you poured water down it.

As soon as Dunbar exited the drainage pipe security people nailed him with a Vibrational Neurological Debilitater Weapon (VNDW).

In short order Dunbar was carried by Stanzelite security personnel to a building in direct view of the Arachno-Pulmonatas scouts. Today was Dunbar's lucky day that Danielle was there and wanted to rescue him at all costs including her own life if necessary.

Danielle knew they needed a diversion and saw a couple fuel trucks by the large tanks they were probably filling with fuel from the trucks. She remembered how Dunbar had once before leveled the base. The building Dunbar was being held was a distance from the fuel truck so it was likely he would be safe. They formulated the plan and since they caught the killer all eyes were on him and not the drainage pipe the Arachno-Pulmonatas scouts soon utilized.

Stanzelite interrogators had already started beating Dunbar to get him to reveal who sent him and word the admiral was dead added to the retribution of their beatings of Dunbar. Dunbar had been trained in Hemi-Sync for this specific situation. Knowing they were going to beat him like they do spies before they kill them Dunbar did his silent meditation which had him already in the Hemi-Sync condition of his brain thus, he felt no pain as his face, nose, teeth and other parts of his body were getting beaten badly because he did not answer the interrogators questions.

Latrodectus knew help was on the way and started playing tricks on the Stanselite computer systems giving all kinds of false warnings all over the opposite side of base. They thought they were under attack! This helped to allow the Arachno-Pulmonatas scouts with Danielle leading them to execute their hastily conceived plan. A couple of the devices Dunbar gave them were placed in the middle of two fuel trucks and timers set for fifteen minutes. This had to be done quickly.

The Arachno-Pulmonatas scouts got into position to attack the room the Stanzelite interrogators were beating the crap out of Dunbar now fully upset because he refused to answer any of their questions and with the alarms going off it also unnerved them some because they feared this might be part of a much larger operation.

With leadership decapitated, it stood to reason an assault was likely in progress. When the bombs went off and caused those fuel trucks to blow up setting off chain reactions of a nearby fuel tank, the shock wave and noise of the explosion sent the interrogators out of the room to look at what the hell was happening on the base. As soon as they came out the door the Arachno-Pulmonatas scouts hit them with poisonous darts shot through tubes. Their aim was excellent because they had plenty of practice over the years. Within a minute all of them, including the remaining interrogators in the room were dead.

Danielle and a couple of her helpers untied Dunbar who was unresponsive. *Latrodectus* located in Dunbar's leg pouch said out loud Danielle and her group could easily hear in perfect Stanzel, "In Dubar's side pouch is a blue container. Open it up and pour it down his mouth, it will revive him."

This was a special combat formula just for this purpose and 30 seconds after pouring it down Dunbar's throat he was fully coherent, but a little sore from the pounding he took.

"We need to leave right away," Danielle said.

"Lead the way."

The group was soon heading out the drainage pipe, and there were Arachno-Pulmonatas scouts in position so that when Stanzelite forces came within range to shoot at Dunbar and Danielle, they picked them off with long range weapons allowing the group to escape into the woods.

Luck was on Dunbar's side because there were another group sent out when Danielle's father became concerned about his daughter's plight to act as a blocking force so when the Stanzelites came after them they were in position to block them with improvised weapons, some of which they stole from the Stanzelites allowing Danielle and Dunbar to make good their escape and back safely to the cave.

Dunbar now fully fresh from his combat chemicals of the blue bottle, said, "I need to get back and make a report on this mission."

"I understand," their leader said knowing they too might have to bug out.

Danielle then informed her Papa, "I'm going with him to make sure he gets away safely."

"Alright, but under the circumstances, meet us at our alternative location, this place may be untenable."

"Understand," Danielle said.

Dunbar and Danielle were soon on their way, nobody else came. Danielle preferred it that way because she had an important question to ask Dunbar.

It took almost four hours to walk the nine miles as there were plenty of intermittent VTOL craft flying around looking for them.

Finally, Dunbar and Daneille arrived at the Transporter Capsule and Dunbar turned to Danielle and said, "I really want to thank you for saving my life."

"I'm glad I did but I have a question for you."

"What is that?"

"Can you take me with you?"

Dunbar knew he would probably get in trouble again, started thinking he could arrange for Danielle to get trained as a spy and possibly assist him in future missions, especially if he had to come back here.

"I have to warn you this is trip will be dangerous, but if you are willing to go, I'll take you with me."

"I want to go."

"Alright I'm going to get in first then you get in and sit on my lap."

"Okay."

During the spin up of the Transporter Capsule there were some emanations from the Bore Sight machinery, and it registered on the VTOL combat craft nearby who flew towards Dunbar's Transporter Capsule to check it out then it suddenly vanished.

Moments later, the top of the Transporter Capsule opened and there was the DD/P and several personnel.

They were quite surprised to see Danielle step out of the Transporter Capsule, and she was filthy and stunk to high heaven from living in the wild and crawling through the drainage pipe with Dunbar.

Dunbar was physically in bad shape and beat up really bad with one eye swollen, a broken nose, split lip and blood all over him.

"It's a long story but I think I need to get cleaned up and see a doctor," Dunbar said.

"Let's get him over to the hospital right away."

"This is Danielle by the way. She's coming with me."

The DD/P raised his eyes and said, "Okay, I know there is probably quite a story behind all this."

Danielle smell was horrible so the medical staff who also had to clean up Dunbar, did so with Danielle and after she was scrubbed, put into hospital garments, and given a hospital bed next to Dunbar at his request.

Dunbar was sedated and sleeping like a lamb when Doctor Elane Chonlan arrived after hearing Dunbar was back but had suffered some serious injuries. And there the young woman was looking magnificent after getting cleaned up.

Danielle was wide awake and by now the staff knew she spoke the Stanzel language. There was a female interpreter assigned to Danielle and would stay with her indefinitely as they sorted out all what went on.

The DD/P was looking over the mission files that Latrodectus provided, which were enormous. This was an *Intelligence Bonanza* that Dunbar brought back.

***

Chapter Twenty

Five Years Later

Thanks to Dunbar's missions a peace treaty was finally signed. With Stanzel Fleet Admiral Wirglestor out of the picture who often gave Admiral Stanzel Emperor Qinshi de Huang false hope in order to save his own neck, true leaders emerged who informed the emperor the contested planets were a lost cause.

Dunbar had Danielle trained as a spy and spent a lot of time with him at the Amphibian training base where she became an incredible martial artist plus trained in great spy craft. She too went on Transporter missions to her home planet where she provided the Indigenous Arachno-Pulmonatas modern technology devices that greatly improved their effectiveness in dealing with the Stanzelites to the point staying on this planet became problematic, so the Stanzelites abandoned it. With that the hope of rebuilding the main Stanzel Space Force Base at Glinka-Rebaul was not feasible adding pressure to Stanzelites to accept peace terms which were reasonable and simply adjusted the boundaries of their empires back to where they started before the war.

With the peace treaty, travel restrictions ended. Blemary decided to attempt to reach out to Dunbar, who she missed. Her Casanova was long gone, and she was lonely, missing out on the love of her life. She knew she screwed up breaking her promise going to Kerlara a third time without Dunbar and hoped that by now he had not found another woman. She had no means of communicating with Dunbar, so she took a direct Intergalactic Transport Flight to Kaokuen. Once she arrived at Kaokuen, she knew how to locate Dunbar and soon was at his home ringing the doorbell.

To Blemary's utter shock was a very young and beautiful attractive woman. The Indigenous Arachno-Pulmonatas people are very attractive, especially their women. To the side of Danielle was a small boy, who appeared to be two or three years old.

"Can I help you?" Danielle asked.

"Does Dunbar live here?"

"Yes, he does."

"Would it be possible to speak to him?"

Danielle knew who this woman was. When she first visited Dunbar's home when they were just friends, Dunbar had not cleared out all of the residual pictures of Blemary and some of her belongings were still there. Dunbar planned on boxing them up and saving them for Blemary in the event she wanted any of it back.

Since they were just friends at the time Dunbar revealed to Danielle everything about Blemary and how she had agreed to work with Stanzel Intel to help him get captured. Of course, Dunbar didn't know at the time that *Latrodectus* had manufactured a lie to use as a catalyst to break Dunbar away from Blemary, since she had proven to be unreliable and her infidelity problem created a bad situation for Dunbar's future.

Danielle knew Blemary would probably be in a state of shock when she discovered all this, but she didn't feel sorry for her since she had a lot of credits฿ and means to get back to Dunbar and for whatever reason didn't.

"May I speak to Dunbar?"

"I'm sorry, he's not home now."

"Are you and Dunbar a couple?"

"Yes, he's, my husband."

That revelation hit Blemary in the gut like a ton of bricks. She gave up Dunbar for a Casanova who turned out not to be worthwhile.

As the tears started flowing down, Blemary said, "I wanted to see Dunbar, but I think under the circumstances, I'll be leaving now."

"Alright madam."

Blemary turned around and left for the awaiting Limo she told to wait in case this did not work out.

Just as Blemary was stepping into the Limo, Dunbar was there a distance away and saw her, and even in the distance could see the tears. He felt sorry for Blemary, but her choices are what led to this moment.

Blemary wrongfully assumed Dunbar would wait forever for her. She was quite accurate in her assessment; however, she had another factor involved in changing her life in ways she could not imagine, nor would Dunbar realize such an activity occurred. *Latrodectus* the artificial intelligence manipulator did all this.

***

Paul D. Escudero

Oct 24, 2024

Authors Note

This book is fiction, none of the people in the story that takes place on worlds in other solar systems in the galaxy do not exist. I did use parts of the names of a few famous people and explained in the Dramatis Personae who they were and what they did to achieve such extraordinary fame. I did so to honor their huge achievements. Sadly, many Americans have no idea who they are because our education system spends too much time in social engineering instead of real history and science.

In this book futuristic Artificial Intelligence technology is used. We can speculate on what is portrayed in this Novel and easily create it in Hollywood so well, we bring it to life, and it looks real thanks to Artificial Intelligence and Computer Graphic Imagery (CGI).

UNCONVENTIONAL DELIVERY CLANDESTINE TRANSPORTERS is mainly a Spy Novel with a unique method of inserting spies. That method is not far-fetched as you will soon learn as you read below.

The point I wanted to make about CGI concerns a scene in the book. The Artificial Intelligence *Latrodectus* permeates the Transporter Directorate, produced a fake video history using CGI that is used as *Evidence* during a major critique in the novel to help clear Dunbar of flimsy charges from the four Amigos (*office warriors*) and a medical practitioner who filed charges against Dunbar for mistreating a prisoner. The CGI looks so real that everyone in the critique thinks this holographic video is a real copy of mission files.

This video, *Latrodectus* utilizes CGI to help clear Dunbar is based on a live security system video taken during the alleged incident. *Latrodectus* modified the mission files, only he and Dunbar know this CGI modification to mission files happened. Nobody including the Transporter Directorate knows it's totally fake. Since only Dunbar and the Artificial Intelligence *Latrodectus* know the CGI modified holographic video is fake, it goes a long way towards exonerating Dunbar of serious charges of brutally treating a prisoner.

Question: In the future will fake CGI technology be used to start wars by Evil People?

Who stands to gain?

In this novel a criminal banker was a war profiteer. Catoire Tigranian, the man that Dunbar ostensibly injured by mistreatment of him, funded their enemy.

I'm repeating a paragraph I wrote earlier in the book so I can make a following comment:

> Another thing the DD/P didn't know is a lot of the credits฿ they got away with were in *Latrodectus* private files and Dunbar was now a much richer man. To help cover up the heist, Dunbar would not know he was rich for a few more years. *Latrodectus* now had substantial funds to sanction operations in other ways.

Think about that for a moment, what if AI that takes on its own identity and personality was involved in such a heist. Think about all the hit men, the AI could hire with vast invisible funds. Kind of scary if you think about it. Maybe a private army too?

Who made money during the Cold War here on Planet Earth funding both sides to keep it going, earning them vast profits?

Not only did the USA heavily borrow for the Vietnam War, Korean War, Cold War, etc. So did the Soviet Union and China.

In 1959 China's Communist Party Chairman Mao complained to Morris Childs, who was probably America's Top Spy of all time ran by the FBI, that *he was upset the Soviets were charging him 10% interest on the money he heavily borrowed to fight Americans in Korea and elsewhere.*

Where did Russia borrow their money from to loan it to China?

I can't say their names to protect my life, but most people know who these international bankers are, and they live in countries that are our allies.

For my book *JOURNEY TO DISTANT CONCIOUSNESS, REMOTE VIEWER BATTLES*, I interviewed a *Remote Viewer* extensively. I have bankers in that book too.

That *Remote Viewer* informed me she was stationed in Germany and spied on a German Banker for several years. She also spied on bankers in America. She was trained by MI6 for the spy business including martial arts. Why do you suppose intelligence agencies are interested in bankers?

Really simple: *follow the money.*

By the time you read this book, the Remote Viewer Novel will be in bookstores giving people thoughts the way this book does.

Latrodectus Artificial Intelligence is used approximately 418 times in this Novel. Artificial Intelligence *Latrodectus* is a major part of the story. Without the *Latrodectus* Artificial Intelligence none of these transporter spy missions would have been feasible.

Now connect the dots. I have two sources in open public access social media that discusses CIA,MI6, FSB(KGB), MSS (China), Nicho (Japan), and other modern countries that use Artificial Intelligence Applications. CIA has 130 to 180 Artificial Intelligence projects. Now doubt this book echoes the types of possibilities Artificial Intelligence could augment in one of their missions. One application we already know pertains to Artificial Intelligence is Drones. Autonomous Drones by and large involve a significant amount of Artificial Intelligence.

Most of the world already knows this but I'm repeating it from Wikipedia to make a point:

> From Wikipedia, the free encyclopedia
> There are two prominent <u>unmanned aerial vehicle</u> (UAV) programs within the United States: <u>that of the military</u> and that of the <u>Central Intelligence Agency</u> (CIA). The military's UAV program is overt, meaning that the public recognizes which government operates it and, therefore, it only operates where US troops are stationed. The

CIA's program is covert and remains classified top secret even though it has been widely discussed in the public domain for years.[1]

Missions performed by the CIA's UAV program do not always occur where US troops are stationed.[2] For example, the strike conducted by the CIA, <u>killing Ayman al-Zawahiri</u> was conducted just under a year after <u>U.S. Forces withdrew from Afghanistan</u>.

The CIA's UAV program was commissioned as a result of the <u>11 September terrorist attacks</u> and the increasing emphasis on operations for intelligence gathering in 2004.[3]

The point is Artificial Intelligence is already in use in major ways already. It's not the future, it's the now.

Question: Does the CIA provide spies assistance the way *Latrodectus* assists Dunbar in this story?

The report I'm going to share with you gets into some of the tangential support AI gives for CIA spies. [The Power and Pitfalls of AI for US Intelligence | WIRED]

Extract:

> Analysts in the US intelligence community are trained to use structured analytic techniques, or SATs, to make them aware of their own cognitive biases, assumptions, and reasoning. SATs—which use strategies that run the gamut from checklists to matrixes that test assumptions or predict alternative futures—externalize the thinking or reasoning used to support intelligence judgments, which is especially important given the fact that in the secret competition between nation-states not all facts are known or knowable. But even SATs, when employed by humans, have come under scrutiny by experts like Chang, specifically for the lack of scientific testing that can evidence an SAT's efficacy or logical validity.

In this Novel, Dunbar was labeled as a former SOG person and works directly for the DD/P. In this Wikipedia article it describes CIA SOG and the DD/P. [Special Activities Center - Wikipedia]

This extract from that Wikipedia article explains one mission SOG did:

SAD/SOG teams also conducted high-risk special reconnaissance missions behind Iraqi lines to identify senior leadership targets. These missions led to the initial assassination attempts against Iraqi President Saddam Hussein and his key generals. Although the initial air strike against Hussein was unsuccessful in killing the dictator, it was successful in effectively ending his ability to command and control his forces. Other strikes against key generals were successful and significantly degraded the command's ability to react to and maneuver against the U.S.-led invasion force.[31][168] SAD operations officers were also successful in convincing key Iraqi Army officers to surrender their units once the fighting started and/or not to oppose the invasion force.[32]

NATO member Turkey refused to allow its territory to be used by the U.S. Army's 4th Infantry Division for the invasion. As a result, the SAD/SOG, U.S. Army special forces joint teams, the Kurdish Peshmerga, and the 173d Airborne Brigadewere the entire northern force against the Iraqi Army during the invasion. Their efforts kept the 13 divisions of the Iraqi Army in place to defend against the Kurds rather than allowing them to contest the coalition force coming from the south.[163] This combined U.S. special operations and Kurdish force defeated the Iraqi Army.[31] Four members of the SAD/SOG team received CIA's rare Intelligence Star for "extraordinary heroism".[32]

Dunbar's activities in this novel are not far-fetched because if you do enough read you will discover missions CIA, KGB, MSS, MI6, and others did exactly live and for the same purposes, SOG, ISR, assassination, espionage, sabotage, and many other activities. And yes, Artificial Intelligence facilitated a lot of it in recent years.

What is America's largest and well known (very controversial) Artificial Intelligence based program? [PRISM - Wikipedia]

Extract from Wikipedia:

PRISM is a code name for a program under which the United States National Security Agency (NSA) collects *internet* communications from various U.S. internet companies.[1][2][3] The program is also known by the

<u>SIGAD US-984XN.</u>[4][5] PRISM collects stored internet communications based on demands made to internet companies such as <u>Google LLC</u> and Apple under Section 702 of the FISA Amendments Act of 2008 to turn over any data that match court-approved search terms.[6] Among other things, the NSA can use these PRISM requests to target communications that were encrypted when they traveled across the *internet backbone*, to focus on stored data that telecommunication filtering systems discarded earlier,[7][8] and to get data that is easier to handle.[9]

No doubt you are thinking, yes that may be true about all this Artificial Intelligence used by our intelligence agencies, but they never went by a transporter gizmo like was used in this Novel.

How do you know they didn't use transporters?

What if we are really involved in transporters?

In time many things get disclosed. Get ready for huge surprises when some of this comes to light.

Now I'm going to expose you to something that will make you really think and wonder about transporters.

In the preface I asked the readers where they thought I got the idea to write this Novel on transporters. Based on the preface, it would leave one to think my enthusiasm to write this Novel came from Star Trek that had transporters.

Star Trek is not the source of the inspiration for this Novel.

There were other events that led to my desire to write this Novel. Now get ready to be astonished and if all this is true, no doubt you will utterly be shocked because this goes way beyond Artificial Intelligence and SOG:

If you google the internet story of *President Obama going to Mars*, you will discover it is alleged the CIA has a transporter Aliens gave us and we often transport people to the Moon and to Mars.

That internet story about President Obama, whether true of false had some influence on me writing this book. The internet story alleges that President

Obama in 1981 as a young man was a CIA intern. His grandparents in Hawaii, the Dunhams were CIA operatives.

It's also alleged in internet stories President Obama's mother and father worked for the CIA. It's well known that President Obama's mother was the head of USAid for all South Asia sometime during the 1970's. Some internet stories claim USAid plays a role in paying CIA spies. Sounds plausible to me. There are also allegations that the Department of Agriculture has another such tasking in payroll.

Remember Soviet Leader Gorbachev? He worked for Russia's Agency that was their version of Department of Agriculture when he was a KGB operative working in France. *What goes around comes around.*

As the internet story goes President Obama's mother, Ms. Dunham was awarded that USAid assignment for her part in the Indonesia Coup that removed the Indonesian leader and was a joint operation of the CIA and the Soviet KGB.

It's kind of interesting if you think about it, CIA and KGB conducting such an elaborate joint operation together. <u>A Company Family: The Untold History of Obama and the CIA (substack.com)</u>

President Obama's mother met his father in Russian classes at the University of Hawaii. They both became fluent in the Russian language. After they separated Ms. Dunham met Colonel Lolo Soetoro of the Indonesian Army while he was attending training in Washington State at Fort Lewis U.S. Army Base near Tacoma.

Fort Lewis is a United States Army base located 9.1 miles (14.6 km) south-southwest of Tacoma, Washington. Fort Lewis was merged with McChord Air Force Base on February 1, 2010, to form Joint Base Lewis–McChord. Colonel Lolo Soetoro of the Indonesian Army also took classes at the University of Washington where he met Ms. Dunham while she was working on her PhD in Anthropology.

Eventually Colonel Lolo Soetoro married Ms. Dunham and she followed him back to Indonesia where he was one of the main leaders of the

Indonesian Coup, as the story goes. I have no way of vetting this internet story, but you can certainly find it and read it for your own entertainment and form your own opinions.

Allegedly, since Colonel Soetoro was often interfacing with the KGB, his wife (formerly MS. Dunham) was used as their main translator because of security and the fact she was married to one of the leading coup organizers. The story claims Mrs. Soetoro (aka Ms. Dunham) not only translated for Colonel Soetoro, but for the CIA and KGB as well.

Mrs. Soetoro's Russian Linguistic skills were exceptionally good and provided effective real time translations so the Indonesian Army, the Russian KGB, and the American CIA could work efficiently together and perform the coup mainly to remove an Indonesian leader under Chinese influence.

During that moment in history, China and Russia just had a major border war that almost went nuclear. America and the Soviet Union was all for containment of China ostensibly because of what happened in Southeast Asia and the Soviet Border. <u>Sino-Soviet border conflict - Wikipedia</u>

If all of this turns out to be true, it stands to reason, the Dunham CIA family paved the way for young Obama to be a CIA intern in 1981 through 1983 and beyond as a CIA operative.

In case you do not know it. CIA is like organized crime. Once you join the family you are CIA for life. The only way out is death or flee to Russia like Edward Snowden did. That means Obama is still CIA. It also means the CIA ran the country for eight years. Kind of like the KGB (FSB) runs Russia. Putin was the head of the KGB before Boris Yeltsin set Putin up to be a Russian Czar/King.

Now after that long description of how Obama got into position to do those activities, I'm going to describe the internet stories. I have absolutely no way of vetting this story, but I also feel it may be true:

President Obama ostensibly *transported* to Mars in 1981 and 1983.

If you listen to Coast-to-Coast radio programs, then you know there is a former Marine Officer who claims he served on Mars for an extensive period and talks about activities on Mars. <u>Conspiracy theory: Obama went to Mars as teen (nbcnews.com)</u>. One of my friends informed me they discussed this on Coast to Coast during one episode.

And of course, we know everything discussed on Coast to Coast is true!

<wink>

How did Obama and the other young men get to Mars and Back?

Round Trip via Transporter, like the device used in this book.

Code-named *Project Pegasus*. As the story goes, the author Stillings claims that both Obama and a Mr. Dugan were in their "Mars training class" at California's College of the Siskiyous in 1980, part of a group of 10 young adults chosen to travel to Mars via a top-secret teleportation "jump room."

Since according to internet stories, it's alleged the CIA transporter is hidden deep inside an innocuous office building, it was most appropriate for this book to start out in a *banking* building.

If this story about President Obama is true, that he was transported to Mars, I hope he would one day have a press conference and disclose it and explain exactly what he was doing on Mars. Was President Obama doing SOG operations on Mars?

Dramatis Personae

And

Glossary

%===================% %===================%

Kaokuen Intelligence Bureau

Vibrational Neurological Debilitater Weapon (VNDW)

Qinshi de Huang, Stanzel Emperor

Qin Shi Huang - Wikipedia

Extract:

Qin Shi Huang(Chinese: 秦始皇, pronunciationⓘ; February 259[e]– 12 July 210 BC) was the founder of the Qin dynasty and the first emperor of a unified China.[9] Rather than maintain the title of "King" (王, Wáng) borne by the previous Shang and Zhou rulers, he ruled China from 221 to 210 BC as the first "Emperor" (皇帝, Huáng Dì) of the Qin dynasty. His self-invented title "Emperor" would continue to be borne by Chinese monarchs for the next two millennia.

Born in the Zhao state capital Handan, as Ying Zheng (嬴政) or Zhao Zheng (趙政), his parents were King Zhuangxiang of Qin and Lady Zhao. The wealthy merchant Lü Buwei assisted him in succeeding his father as the ruler of Qin, after which he became Zheng, King of Qin. By the age of 38 in 221 BC, he had conquered all the other Warring States and unified all of China, and he ascended the throne as China's first emperor. During his reign, his generals greatly expanded the size of the Chinese state: campaigns south of Chu permanently added them Yue lands of Hunan and Guangdong to the Chinese cultural orbit, and campaigns in Inner Asia conquered the Ordos Loop from the nomadic Xiongnu, although the Xiongnu later rallied under Modu Chanyu.

Stanzel Fleet Admiral Wirglestor was the head Stanzel Admiral during the Larian Space Battle and when the Kaokuen Task Force attacked the Stanzel the Island of Lamuers in the Great Seirin Ocean

Great Seirin Ocean and the Island of Lamuers are on planet Glinka-Rebaul

The Kaokuen Task Force attacking Glinka-Rebaul was led by the Amphibian General Subutai

Wikipedia extract: Subutai (Classical Mongolian: Sübügätäi or Sübü'ätäi; Modern Mongolian: ᠰᠦᠪᠦᠭᠡᠲᠡᠢ; Сүбээдэй, Sübeedei. [sʊbeːˈdɛ]; Chinese: 速不台; c. 1175–1248) was a Mongol general and the primary military strategist of Genghis Khan and Ögedei Khan. He directed more than 20 campaigns and won 65 pitched battles, during which he conquered or overran more territory than any other commander in history as part of the expansion of the Mongol Empire, the largest contiguous empire in human history.[1]

Admiral Zhènghé, subordinate to Stanzel Fleet Admiral Wirglestor

Wikipedia extract Zheng He (simplified Chinese: 郑和; traditional Chinese: 鄭和; pinyin: Zhènghé; Wade–Giles: Chêng-ho; 1371–1433 or 1435) was a Chinese mariner, explorer, diplomat, fleet admiral, and court eunuch during China's early Ming dynasty, and often regarded as the greatest admiral in Chinese history.

Lepestok de Rozy a Arachno-Pulmonatas fermented elixir made from rose petals and magic mushrooms.

Glinka-Rebaul main Stanzel Space Force Base nearest the contested planets war zone.

Indigenous Arachno-Pulmonatas civilization on Zema Morska enslaved by the Stanzelites after the planety conquest of the planet. Arachno-Pulmonata

Arachnopulmonata, the Clade for Scorpions.

Message: '*Chien Shiung*' used during the Zemya Morska mission was used to let the DD/P know Dunbar would be returning shortly.

Message: '*Heterodontus Francisci*' used during the Zemya Morska mission was used to let the DD/P know Dunbar is starting the automatic transporter capsule launch sequence to return to the Transporter Directorate.

Zemya Morska planet where Dunbar performs sabotage.

 Derived from the Russian words Морская змея [Morskaya zmeya {sea serpent}]

Hovercraft is named Lyudmila.

Latrodectus the name of the Artificial Intelligence in the story, also is Latin for Black Widow Spyder

Bamtorini Sportster is a sophisticated device that operates like a motor cycle.

Reassociation failure, the transporter passengers do not arrive in the same form they departed. Most likely look like hamburger.

Coreopsis de Dahlia ferment laced with magic mushrooms.

Maître d' at the *Vin et Maree Bouillon Cartier* restaurant.

Sabina Chafak, mistress of Catoire Tigranian.

The Severomsk banker and organized crime boss Catoire Tigranian.

Catoire Tigranian's office in room fourteen on the 19th floor, in *Stellar Investments and Investment Banking* which takes up the entire 19th floor located at 111 Grande Avenue.

Sara Pikkarainen bartender at the *Vin et Maree Bouillon Cartier* restaurant.

Emilia, wife of the *Jīnsè de Rluò* Bed and Breakfast owner.

Mily Balakigrev Dunbar's alias named while at the domed city Oklast on the planet Tallinn.

Special Kollmorgant holographic eyeglasses provide a spy night vision and heads up display.

Invisible Ink mode used with Special Kollmorgant holographic eyeglasses while reading the flatscreen on the communicator which eliminates any other party viewing the information at the same time.

Severomsk Divergent Hovercraft Rental agency at the domed city Oklast on the planet Tallinn.

Credits₿ Galactic crypto currency.

Latrodectus Kaokuen Transporter Directorate Artificial Intelligence entity on Dunbar's communicator.

Dunbar arrived at the Severomsk Dome City Oklast located near the equator on the planet Tallinn. Dunbar set up shop in a coastal Bed and Breakfast, *Jīnsè de Rluò* located in the town of Jàznālià.

Elane Chonlan, Transporter Directorate staff psychiatrist who treated and evaluated Dunbar.

Laudanum-diacodium sulfate knock out drugs used to disable enemies during missions.

Trapezoidal Differentiators are used to detect transporter operations.

Rextar Fünger Trapezoidal Differentiators designer

Heyrovsky

Gandolph resort hotel robot

Brigitte Hindemith one of Dunbar's lovers

Gélí (clams)

Mǎlíngshǔ (potatoe)

Huǒlóng de Guǒ (dragon fruit}

Maid Elsa.

Cameron Malá, Dunbar's alias during the mission to Fujima.

Adinska Dasnal Resort Hotel in Fujima of the Larian world

Dunbar arrived in the outskirts of the city Fujima in the Larian world.

Kaarina, a surgeon, and Dunbar's lover at Nigārà a city at the planet Pràsplātanià

Ástríður Dreka elixir [Passions of dragons] a ferment that also has psychoactive pleasurizers drugs.

Aigle Émeraude Resort in Nigārà. Aigle Émeraude is the French pronunciation of *Emerald Eagle*

Gresley Boont, Dunbar's Alias at Nigārà

Nigārà, a city at the planet Pràsplātanià

Kabel Garr (aka Dunbar Regvik, the Transporter spy)

Embla, server at the *Greifinn Restaurant*

Jangovian de Palentin elixir is a drink loaded with special inducements.

Jangovian de Palentin elixir is a delicacy and quite expensive back in the Kaokuen planet.

Sophia, the lovely blonde mataré d in the *Greifinn* restaurant at the top of the spiral Highrise building in the middle of the City of Kerlara City on planet Stanzel within walking distance of the Norel Mozelle Resort

Cornolius the AI in the Norel Mozelle Resort who assists Dunbar Regvik in his resort hotel room.

Eva Erlaendsdottir cabaret singer at the *Greifinn* restaurant.

Stanzel Fleet Admiral Wirglestor

Thereuopoda Clunifera Computer Virus

Latrodectus Artificial Intelligence on Dunbar's communicator

The enemy planet Stanzel. *Stanzelites are the inhabitants: humanoids.*

Chamboreé de Lián an elixir that has pleasurizers and psychoactive drugs.

Kaokuen Transporter Directorate operated under a fictitious name Intergalactic Banking Development Corporation

The enemy planet Stanzel. *Stanzelites are the inhabitants: humanoids.*

Norel Mozelle Resort structured like a Japanese Love Hotel

Madam Chien Shiung, psychic

Randolf Cayce, psychic healer

Kerlara one of the primary industrial and research cities on the planet Stanzel

Rinisp dialect of the standard Stanzel *language*

The real Kabel Garr, which the Transporter Directorate abducted, was considered an eccentric from the opposite side of the planet Stanzel.

Oclatine Class Hyper Warp Speed Fast Frigate, named after the late emperor Oclatine.

Blemary, *Norel Mozelle Resort* receptionist and Dunbar's main lover.

Tri-lithium sulfate based fusion reactor powered cyclonic inverter warp drive thrusters.

Chizhevsky- Lomonosov proton beam weapons

Dunbar Regvik is a Kaokuen Transporter Spy and main character of the book.

Latrodectus, Dunbar Regvik's artificial intelligence imbedded in his personal communicator named after the black widow spider.

Echis Carinatus code word to *Latrodectus* indicating Dunbar was alone and to make a report. *Echis Carinatus* is a snake.

Kaokuens was given the name in honor of a Nobel Laureate Charles Kuen Kao who helped shape the technological revolution we now experience.

Charles Kuen Kao is the inventor of fiber optics.

Sir Kuen Charles Kao was born on the 4th of November 1933 in Shanghai, China. He was an electrical engineer and a physicist too.

Charles Kao is famous for being the pioneer of the development and use of fiber optics. This he did from the physics properties of a glass and later the discovery laid the groundwork for high-speed data.

This brought to life his famous invention of fiber optics in telecommunications in the 1960s.

Charles Kuen Kao was awarded the Nobel Prize in physics and the Grand Bauhinia Medal among other awards. He died on the 23rd of September 2018 in Shatin, Hongkong.

***

Paul D. Escudero

Oct 2023